What the Experts say about Frank Hopkins

"Hopkins should have been awarded the World's Greatest Liar award." *Dr. Vine Deloria, Jr., leading Native American scholar, retired professor emeritus of history at the University of Colorado and author of many acclaimed books.*

"The only endurance Hopkins ever did was with his pencil." *James Davidson, Vermont Historical Society*

"I would judge the evidence as overwhelming that Frank T. Hopkins was a fraud." *Professor David Dary, emeritus professor and former head of the Gaylord College of Journalism at the University of Oklahoma.*

"Did this man Hopkins say anything true?" *Dr. John Gable, Executive Director, Theodore Roosevelt Association.*

"What Hopkins claims to have done on horseback is all very interesting, but where is the evidence?" *Jeremy James, Expert on equestrian travel, Fellow of the Royal Geographical Society, Long Rider and author of "Saddletramp."*

"Hopkins is a phony! He was obviously just repeating stories he had read. We don't know of any contemporary sources that even mention him." *Leo Remiger, expert on the history of 19th century buffalo hunting and co-author of the "Encyclopedia of Buffalo Hunters & Skinners."*

"It is so obvious that Hopkins is a fraud – I cannot see how he could have fooled people for so many years." *Gregory Michno, author of "Lakota Noon" and "The Encyclopedia of Indian Wars"*

"I find Frank Hopkins suspiciously absent from any authentic historical events." *Dr. Juti Winchester, Curator of the Buffalo Bill Museum.*

"I have determined Hopkins to be a narcissist with sociopathic tendencies.... Hopkins seems to have an underlying anger about his life and this would also be a contributing factor in his lies." *Dale Yeager, criminal psychologist and President of Seraph Security.*

"Our heroes need to be real!" *Susan Gibson, publisher of Trail Blazer magazine.*

Hidalgo

And Other Stories

by

Frank T. Hopkins

The complete works of Frank T. Hopkins, with a comprehensive study by an international team of experts.

Edited by Basha and CuChullaine O'Reilly

Foreword by Professor David Dary

The Long Riders' Guild Press

Cover illustration, which originally
appeared on an 1895 poster for
Buffalo Bill's Wild West show, used
here by kind permission from the
Library of Congress. With special
thanks to Dean Tolliver for digital
enhancement of the image.

Dedicated to
Dr. Donald E. Worcester,
Long Rider and Scholar,
who had the courage to admit,
"I was fooled by Frank Hopkins."

Table of Contents

Chapters 3 to 18 were originally published in the *Vermont Horse & Trail Bulletin*.

Illustrations

Foreword

By Professor David Dary

The real Wild West had faded into memory and history books by the start of the twentieth century, but it lived on in the minds of many Americans thanks to the embellished stories produced in dime novels, pulp westerns, traveling wild west shows, and early Hollywood motion pictures. These things made men like Buffalo Bill, Kit Carson, Gen. George Custer and others bigger than life. They became legendary figures, and helped to make the settlement of the American West romantic and colorful. It was then that many old-timers began setting down on paper what they remembered, or thought they remembered, about helping to settle the West. They wanted their share of the glory. Many books of old-timer tales were published even though many of the works were poorly written and garbled. Many people, even a few scholars, believed the accounts. After all, the writer said he had been there. What other proof was needed? Why should they not accept what a man had to say about his own life and times and believe the stories about what he did and the people he said he knew. Some suspected the accounts were not true but refused to correct them and repeated them because they had been accepted as authentic by the masses for many years.

By the middle twentieth century a new generation of scholars were becoming interested in the history of the West. They began to check the old-timers' accounts and it soon became evident that many such accounts were not accurate, that the writers' minds were hazy. They had not checked the facts, and their fading memories remembered only rumors or conjecture and not the truth. Scholars began to write books containing the truth. When the real lives of many legendary characters were compared to the true facts, their real lives were hardly recognizable.

While scholars excused the errors made by old-timers because of their ages and a lack of scholarly training, they were more critical of another type of old-timer who told outright lies in writing about the old west. This type of old-timer deliberately made up stories apparently to elevate their stature in history. Many such men had really led dull lives which they regretted in old age. Certainly it is not uncommon for people who have led dull lives to dream of being associated with prominent persons and events. There is nothing wrong with such dreaming, but when one put his dreams into words on paper and publishes them as the truth, it is wrong. Claiming to have been associated with well-known historic or notorious persons and events is simply fraud. Such people apparently counted upon the reader's ignorance to believe instead of challenging what is written. Such liars include Fred Sutton, Frank Tarbeaux, Frank Harris and others.

In Fred Sutton's case, this old-timer recounted stories to a Kansas City, Missouri, newspaper reporter who published them during the 1920s. The reporter, A. B. MacDonald, never checked the facts and got Sutton's stories published by a New York publisher in a 1927 book titled *Hands Up! Stories of the six-gun fighters of the Old West.* Sutton claimed to have been personally acquainted with all of the outlaws in the Old West, but because Sutton died in 1927, such acquaintances would have been impossible. His claims were bunk.

Another old-timer similar to Sutton was Frank Tarbeaux, who told his story to Donald Henderson Clarke. It was published as a book titled *The Autobiography of Frank Tarbeaux* by a New York publisher. Like Sutton, Tarbeaux claimed he was a close friend of Wild Bill Hickok, Jesse and Frank James, and many other western outlaws. He even claimed to have shot Bob Ford, the man who killed Jesse James, through the lungs in a southern Colorado fight. Clarke never checked the facts of Tarbeaux's story which was filled with half-truths and outright lies.

Frank Harris was a somewhat different case as is suggested in the title of Vincent Broome's biography titled *Frank Harris, the Life and Loves of a Scoundrel.* Harris, a native of Wales, came to America as a young man and attended the University of Kansas for a year or two and then spent the rest of his life in Europe and the eastern United States working as an editor, novelist, playwright, biographer, fighter against injustice, liar, and lover. When his career failed because of his poor character, he wrote *My Reminiscences as a Cowboy* which was published in 1930. The book contains what he claimed were his recollections as a cowboy only in his imagination. In fact, it was an embellished version of stories that originally appeared in his book *My Life and Loves.* Harris's cowboy reminiscences is full of inaccuracies, wild imagination, and is historically worthless. The late Texas author, J. Frank Dobie, called Harris's book "a blatant farrago of lies and of supreme worthlessness." Biographer Broome observed that Harris's sheer poverty drove him to write and sponsor exaggerated books some of which he later regretted. The late George Bernard Shaw perhaps summed up Harris by writing that he "is neither first rate, nor second rate, nor tenth rate. He is just his horrible unique self."

Any educated person might believe that in the twenty-first century all such phony writers dealing with the old west would be a thing of the past, but now come the alleged true recollections of Frank T. Hopkins, who with his wife created tales that made Hopkins bigger than life. Hopkins and his wife, the subject of this book, sought to make their stories plausible by linking Hopkins to well-known old west personalities and events. Like the other writers mentioned above, Hopkins and his wife knew that if you wish to strengthen a lie, mix a little truth in with it. That is exactly what they did. But unlike the other writers mentioned, Hopkins and his wife died before their tales received wide circulation in the published world. The Hollywood screen writer who found Hopkins' yarns failed to check their claims against historical facts, believed them to be true, and sold a story to a major motion picture company which invested millions of dollars in turning the story into a film. They also failed to check the facts. It is a good story, but it is not true. But in typical Hollywood fashion after being told the story was fiction, the producers failed to acknowledge the falsehoods in the Hopkins' story and promoted their motion picture as true. In so doing they lost credibility.

Herbert Agar, the late Pulitzer Prize winning *Louisville Courier-Journal* columnist, once wrote, "The truth that makes men free is for the most part the truth which men prefer not to hear." This book examines the <u>truth</u> of the Hopkins' story.

David Dary, emeritus professor and former head of what is now the Gaylord College of Journalism at the University of Oklahoma, is the recipient of many awards including the Wrangler Award from the National Cowboy & Western Heritage Museum, two Spur awards from the Western Writers of America, and Best Book Award from Westerners International. He is the author of more than a dozen published books on the West including *The Buffalo Book* (1974), *Cowboy Culture* (1981) *Red Blood and Black Ink: Journalism in the Old West* (1998), and *The Santa Fe Trail* (2000).

Acknowledgements

The Long Riders' Guild would like to extend its special thanks to the following members of the Research Team, without whose uninterrupted support and encouragement this massive project would not have been possible. They freely gave their time and expertise in this international search for the truth about Frank Hopkins.

Professor David Dary	Author and expert on the Old West
Peter Harrigan	Investigative Journalist
Gregory Lalire	Editor of *Wild West* magazine
Gregory Michno	Author and expert on the Indian wars
Katherine Pennavaria	Research Librarian
Dr. Juti Winchester	Curator, Buffalo Bill Museum

Research Team

The Long Riders' Guild would like to thank the men and women listed here for the invaluable part they played in this unique international scholastic effort. These academics, researchers, librarians, genealogists, authors, and experts graciously donated their time, energy, support and resources to help The Guild discover the truth about the life and legends of Frank Hopkins.

We would also like to extend a special "thank you" to Robert Easton, now deceased, whose academic principles shone like a light through the fog of Frank Hopkins' mythology.

Magdy Abdul Aziz: Vice President of the Egyptian Endurance Riders Association (EERA)

Dr. Awad Al-Badi: Director of Research, King Faisal Center for Research and Islamic Studies

Ghalib Al-Quaiti: Was the last ruling Sultan of the Quaiti State in what is now Yemen and is an informed source on the equestrian history of his country.

Dr. Mohammed Talal Al-Rasheed: Scholar in Arabic and English literature and history

Janis Ashley: Administrator, William S. Hart Museum

Jeffrey Bridgers: Reference Specialist, Prints & Photographs Division, Library of Congress

Marcelle Brothers: Co-founder of the Billy the Kid Historic Preservation Society

William Buckner: Manager, Genealogy Division, Waco-McLennan County Library

Paul Carnahan: Librarian, Vermont Historical Society

Frances Clymer: Librarian, McCracken Library, Buffalo Hill Historical Center

Nancy Coleman: Genealogist

Paula Covington: Research Librarian, Vanderbilt University Library

Charles Craver: Arabian Horse Expert

Sharon Cunningham: Buffalo hunting expert and co-author of *Encyclopedia of Buffalo Hunters & Skinners*.

Fred Dahlinger: Research Librarian, Circus World Museum

Professor David Dary: Emeritus professor and former head of what is now the Gaylord College of Journalism at the University of Oklahoma, is the recipient of many awards including the Wrangler Award from the National Cowboy & Western Heritage Museum, two Spur awards from the Western Writers of America, and Best Book Award from Westerners International. He is the author of more than a dozen published books on the West including *The Buffalo Book* (1974), *Cowboy Culture* (1981) *Red Blood and Black Ink: Journalism in the Old West* (1998), and *The Santa Fe Trail* (2000).

James Davidson: Historian at the Rutland, Vermont Historical Society

Steve Davis: Assistant Curator, Southwestern Writers Collection, Southwestern University, Georgetown.

Dr. Vine Deloria Jr.: a leading Native American scholar, whose research, writings, and teaching have encompassed history, law, religious studies, and political science. He is a retired professor emeritus of history at the University of Colorado and the author of many acclaimed books, including *God is Red* and *Red Earth, White Lies*. Dr. Deloria, a Standing Rock Sioux, has been hailed as "one of the 11 great religious thinkers of the twentieth century" by Time magazine. His first work, *Custer Died for Your Sins* (1969) was one of the most influential books written on Indian affairs and helped launch the field of Native American studies.

Anne Marie Donoghue: Associate Registrar, Buffalo Bill Historical Center

Chris Doran: British Horse Society

Janis P. Duffy: Reference Supervisor, Massachusetts State Archives

Jim Dullenty: Author of *Harry Tracy, The Last Desperado* (1989), *A Place called Earp: the town named for Wyatt Earp* (2001) and *The Butch Cassidy Collection* (1987)

Rick Ewig: Associate Director of the American Heritage Center of the University of Wyoming

Elly Foote: Long Rider and author of *Riding into the Wind*

Dr. John Gable: Executive Director, Theodore Roosevelt Association

Professor Henry Giroux: Waterbury Chair Professor of Education at Penn State University and author of dozens of books including *The Mouse that Roared – Disney and the End of Innocence*, in which he explores the many ways in which Disney strives to dominate global media and influence the future of children.

Green Mountain Horse Association: Vermont Riding and Equestrian experts

Casey Edward Greene: Head of Special Collections, Rosenberg Library, Galveston Historical Museum

Mark Greene: Director of the American Heritage Center of the University of Wyoming

Peter Harrigan: Investigative Journalist

Kathleen Henkel: Executive Director of American Endurance Ride Conference

Joy Holland: Research Librarian, Brooklyn Public Library

Lynn Hows: Curatorial Assistant at the Buffalo Bill Museum, Buffalo Bill Historical Center

John Hudson: Chairman of Endurance GB

Ann Hyland: British expert on the history of endurance racing and author of many books, including *The Endurance Horse - a World Survey* (1988), *Riding Long Distance* (1993), *Endurance Riding* (1976) and *Beginner's Guide to Endurance Riding* (1974)
John Irwin: Research Librarian, Denver Public Library
Jeremy James: Founder Member of The Long Riders' Guild and Fellow of the Royal Geographical Society
Judith Johnson: Genealogist, Connecticut Historical Society
Jim Kroll: Research Librarian, Denver Public Library
Gregory Lalire: Editor, Wild West magazine and Senior Editor, American History magazine.
James Lewis: Reference Librarian, New Jersey Historical Society
Katherine Maher: Curator of the Barnum Museum
Dale Manning: Research Librarian, Vanderbilt University Library
Miles Matthews: Research Intern, McCracken Library, Buffalo Hill Historical Center
Linda Merims: Endurance Rider and researcher
Gregory Michno: Author of *Lakota Noon: the Indian narrative of Custer's Defeat* (1997) and *The Mystery of E Troop: Custer's Gray Horse Company at the Little Bighorn (1994) and Encyclopedia of Indian wars: western battles and skirmishes, 1850-1890*
Tom Mueller: Reference Librarian, Citrus County Library, Florida
Carol Mulder: Arabian horse expert and biographer of Albert W. Harris
Marcy W. Murray: Curatorial Assistant, Ringling Circus Museum & Archives
Gordon Naysmith: Fellow of the Royal Geographical Society and Long Rider
Barbara Oakleaf: Fremont County Library Manager
Professor Edward T. O'Donnell: Department of History, Holy Cross College, author of *Ship Ablaze - The Story of the General Slocum Disaster*
Melissa Paul: Curator, W. K. Kellogg Arabian Horse Library
Wendy Peckham: British Horse Society
Katherine Pennavaria: Research Librarian, Western Kentucky University
Gregory Plunges: Archivist, New York Federal Archives
Professor Ione Quigley: Chair of Lakota Studies, Sinte Gleska University
Bonnie Rand: Business Manager, Ohio University Press and informed source on the history of the Swallow Press
Leo Remiger: Buffalo hunting expert and co-author of *Encyclopedia of Buffalo Hunters & Skinners.*
John Rigsby: Library Supervisor, Newspapers & Microfilm Center, Free Library of Philadelphia
Eric Robinson: Reference Assistant; New York Historical Society Library
Louise Samson: Curator of the Fort Laramie National Historic Site

Arthur Saxon: Circus expert and author of *Enter Foot and Horse - A History of Hippodrama in England and France*

Brian Shovers: Research Librarian, Montana Historical Society

Jonathan Simons: Lakota Studies, Sinte Gleska University

Dr. Donald Smith: Professor of Canadian History at the University of Calgary, an expert on Indian Imposters, and author of *From the Land of Shadows – the Making of Grey Owl* and *Chief Buffalo Child Long Lance – the Glorious Imposter*

Waddell W. Stillman: President, Historic Hudson Valley, New York

Jacquelyn Sundstrand: Manuscripts & Archives Librarian, Special Collections Department, University of Nevada

Mariam Touba: Reference Librarian, New York Historical Society

Timothy Weidner: Director, Chapman Historical Museum

Tara Wenger: Research Librarian, Harry Ransom Humanities Research Center, University of Texas, Austin.

Dr. Joe Wheeler: Founder and Executive Director, Zane Grey's West Society

Dr. Juti Winchester: Curator of the Buffalo Bill Museum at the Buffalo Bill Historical Center

Mary Witkowski: Head of Collections, Bridgeport Public Library, Connecticut

Dr. Donald Worcester: Past President of Western Writers of America, the Western History Association, and Westerners International. Recipient of the 'Saddleman' Award and distinguished Emeritus at Texas Christian University

Dale Yeager: President, Seraph Security, with extensive training in criminal profiling and forensic psychology.

Introduction

The Trail of Deceit

Frank T. Hopkins claimed to have an extremely impressive résumé.

According to Hopkins his father was the only white survivor of Custer's Last Stand, his mother was a Sioux Indian princess, and he was born at Fort Laramie, Wyoming, in 1865. During the 1930s and 40s the self-proclaimed legend told a naïve American public that he became a dispatch rider for the US government on his twelfth birthday, then went on to work as a buffalo hunter, Indian fighter, endurance racer, trick rider, bounty hunter, Rough Rider, big game guide, secret agent and star of the Wild West show. In his spare time Hopkins said he taught frontier lore to Billy the Kid, was the inspiration for Zane Grey's novels and "rode knee to knee with Teddy Roosevelt."

Do you believe Hopkins' amazing tales?

If so, then you join a long list of respected American authors, magazine editors and media moguls who have been duped by the biggest Old West hoax in American history.

As Gregory Michno, noted author of *Lakota Noon: the Indian narrative of Custer's Defeat* (1997) wrote, "It is so obvious that Hopkins is a fraud, I cannot see how he could have fooled people for so many years."

In search of the answer to that question, 77 academic experts in five countries decided to take a closer look at the emperor's clothes!

Hoofprints through History

Though Frank Hopkins claimed to have done everything and to have known everyone in the Old West, it is his endurance racing pretensions that have propelled him into twenty-first century notoriety.

This counterfeit cowboy said he won an 1800 mile race from Galveston, Texas, to Rutland, Vermont, in 1886.

Not according to Casey Greene, Head of Special Collections at the Rosenberg Library in Galveston, Texas.

"We've referenced every newspaper between 1880 and 1890 but there is absolutely no mention of Frank Hopkins or a race from Galveston to Vermont. I think we better start a new file called 'Galveston Bogus Claims'," Greene said.

Further north, James Davidson of the Rutland Historical Society was equally scathing.

"The only endurance Hopkins ever did was with his pencil," chuckled Davidson.

According to Hopkins, it was because of his stunning imaginary victory in this non-existent race that he was hired by Buffalo Bill Cody to star in the Wild West show.

That's not what Dr. Juti Winchester, the Curator of the Buffalo Bill Museum at the Buffalo Bill Historical Center, says.

"We are unable to find **any** Frank T. Hopkins in our database of known cast members, acquaintances, employees, or friends of Colonel Cody. We find that after Cody's death in 1917, some people made pretty spectacular claims about their relationship with him, what they did in the Wild West Show, and so on."

Dr. Winchester went on to denounce Hopkins as one of "a legion of early twentieth century pretenders that used Cody's name and reputation to bolster their own."

But Cody was in his grave by the 1930s when Hopkins began circulating the greatest equestrian forgery of all time.

Having invented his endurance racing credentials and faked his friendship with Cody, Hopkins next claimed that the Wild West show paid for him and his mustang stallion Hidalgo to journey to Arabia in 1890.

According to the Hopkins mythology, the American was invited to take part in a 3,000 mile race across the burning sands of Arabia. This race had been run, Hopkins said, every year for a thousand years, and until then only the finest Arab horses had been allowed to participate. Hopkins and his mustang stallion, Hidalgo, supposedly won the race with 33 hours to spare.

If such a race had really taken place every year for a thousand years, then surely it would have been enshrined in Arabian history?

Experts in both Saudi Arabia, and Yemen where the race allegedly started, ridiculed the very idea of such an elaborate equestrian contest.

Dr. Mohammed Talal Al-Rasheed, a scholar in Arabic and English literature and history, laughed at the very notion of Hopkins' race. "The idea of such a race in Arabia is a non-starter and can be debunked simply from an intellectual point of view without even getting into the ludicrous logistics of it. It is a shabby fantasy."

Meanwhile, Dr. Awad Al-Badi, Director of Research at the King Faisal Center and an authority on western travelers to Arabia over the centuries, said "There is absolutely no record or reference to Hopkins with or without his mustang ever having set foot on Arabian soil."

If anyone had information about this thousand-year-old race, then surely it would be the ruler of the country in which it was supposed to have taken place. Yet the last ruling Sultan of the Quaiti State in what is now Yemen, Ghalib Al-Quaiti, was equally dismissive.

"There is absolutely no record of any horse race in the past staged from Aden!" said the former Sultan, who has studied history at both Oxford and Cambridge universities and written extensively on his ancestral homeland.

So how is it that so many people, from magazine writers in the 1930s to screenplay-writers in the 21st century, have been fooled into believing Frank Hopkins?

Who helped turn his twisted daydream into a cinematic event?

Passionate Promoter

Frank's fantasy might have been lost to history if one of America's slickest salesmen had not pedaled it to a gullible public.

Americans have recently been reintroduced to the heart-warming 1930s tale of Seabiscuit, the heroic little horse that refused to be beaten. Seabiscuit was the ultimate underdog who triumphed against the mighty and previously-unbeaten thoroughbred, War Admiral. Charles Howard, Seabiscuit's owner, understood that everyone wants David to beat Goliath.

Nobody needed to explain that ancient concept to Charles B. Roth.

Roth had made a career out of championing the underdog. He was a Denver-based author whose income was generated by books written for salesmen of his day. Two of Roth's titles, *How to use your imagination to make money* and *How to remake your personality to get more out of your life,* could have been written with Frank Hopkins specifically in mind.

While Seabiscuit was racing around the track, setting records and melting American hearts, Charles B. Roth, who dabbled in American history, was selling stories of overlooked underdogs around the country. These included promoting Fred Kimble, an American who claimed to have invented the choke-bore shot-gun, Frank Mayer, a forgotten buffalo-hunter, and Gama, an Indian wrestler.

Roth's disregard for facts was recently illustrated by Graham Noble, a historian who has studied the famous wrestler. Noble wrote about the "error-filled article of 1947 by Charles Roth," and went on to dismiss Roth's scholar-ship as "simply a fantasy."

What evidence did Roth have to support Hopkins and his claims to Arabian racing fame?

None!

In a letter dated August 1966, Roth admitted to a fellow magazine writer, "I do not have any documentary proof of Mr. Hopkins' race in Arabia."

Proof or no proof, over the course of the 1930s Charles B. Roth relentlessly publicized Frank Hopkins' mythology, especially Hopkins' claims to have won the non-existent race in Arabia.

"A modest man," Roth wrote in a 1936 article in *Horse* magazine, "Mr. Hopkins does not list himself in the great riders, but in my opinion he not only belongs in the list – he belongs at the head of it. Look at his record: in over 400 long distance races, he was beaten but once, and then by foul; he finished first but was disqualified. These races varied in length from 50 to 3,000 miles.

Three times he won the title of 'World's Greatest Horseman,' in competition with picked riders from the cavalry of the world. Other horsemanship prizes too numerous to mention he also won. So I place him first in the list of greats."

It was this and similar articles which laid the foundation stone for the Hopkins myth.

Roth, who died in 1973, was not an impartial observer, but a visitor to the Hopkins' Long Island home. Frank Hopkins also visited Roth in Colorado.

What did Roth feel about the Old West liars of the time?

In an article, *The biggest blow since Galveston*, published in *The Denver Westerners Monthly Roundup* in January 1956, Roth reveals his sympathy with the braggarts.

"When we deal with the West, we deal with a myth. It is a lusty myth, as strong, as beguiling, as immortal as any that came out of Rome and Greece. If you ask me, the myth of the West is about ten times as interesting besides," Roth wrote. "Maybe what they contributed is even more valuable than truth, which is usually dull and stodgy."

Roth concluded the article with an astonishing admission.

"I hope I can always be an Angel towards the blowhards of the Old West. It's nicer that way."

While Seabiscuit was making documented history, Roth was busy elevating Hopkins' chicanery into the next level of public awareness. The Denver salesman did this by helping Hopkins to deceive one of America's most respected equestrian historians.

Eager accomplices or naïve victims?

Albert Harris knew horses and endurance riding. He admired and bred the hardy mustang as well as the pure-bred Arab. Harris raised and raced mustang-Arabian crosses in the early 1920s, with a notable lack of success.

On the other hand, Harris had won a 300 mile endurance ride in 1919, mounted on a pure-bred Arabian mare, Ramla.

When not in the saddle, the wealthy Harris was running the Chicago bank that his father founded.

The general opinion, then and now, was that Albert Harris was an honorable gentleman.

But he had a weakness – he wanted to believe.

The Chicago banker and author had a pet theory. The mustang, he thought, was a direct descendant of Arabian war horses brought to the American continent by Spanish Conquistadors.

Imagine the Arabian breeder's excitement when he read Roth's article, *Great Riders*, which seemed to validate Harris' hypothesis that mustangs and Arabians were historically linked. In Roth's story, Hopkins was quoted as saying that after he won the Arabian race he left his mustang stallion, Hidalgo, behind so the American stallion could be bred to Arabian mares.

Harris was overjoyed.

He contacted Roth.

The Denver salesman put him in direct touch with Hopkins.

The Long Island cowboy realized he had an unexpected opportunity to maneuver his far-fetched stories into respectable circles and wasted no time in repeating them to the trusting banker.

"My dear Mr. Harris," Hopkins wrote on February 18, 1940, "Mr. Charles B. Roth, whom I esteem very highly, has asked me to answer your questions in your letter to him."

That letter details the imaginary Galveston to Rutland race.

In a second letter about the Arabian race, dated March 9, 1940, Hopkins said what Harris longed to hear.

"My Hidalgo began passing other horses on the fourteenth day of the ride and gradually moved up toward the front every day. Hidalgo reached the finish stone thirty-three hours of actual travel ahead of the second horse. I was sixty-eight days in all on that ride of over 3,000 miles...I left him [Hidalgo] in that land of fine horses where he belonged."

Harris reverently copied Hopkins' accounts of the make-believe races, word for word, into his privately printed book, *Blood of the Arab,* published in 1941.

"The account he [Hopkins] gives us must surely leave the reader with the impression that the blood of the Mustangs, or Spanish Barbs, they rode had not deteriorated and that they were as much Arab war horses by heritage and performance as when they left Arabia in 647," concluded Harris triumphantly.

What evidence did the author receive that verified this tale?

Hopkins sent Harris a photograph of a wooden carving which he said resembled the fictional Hidalgo!

Unbelievably, Harris fell for it.

"The statuette of Hidalgo and Indian is characteristic of the Indian war horse. Mr. Hopkins says it is a good likeness of the horse, including his tail carriage," wrote the trusting Harris.

The banker should have listened to his father instead of Hopkins!

"No one's judgment is any good unless it is based on facts," the elder Harris had frequently warned his son.

Carol Mulder, a published expert on Arabian horses, has recently completed a biography of Albert Harris, published in *Imported Foundation Stock of North American Arabian Horses* (Volume 3).

Mulder is sure the renowned horseman would be mortified to learn the truth about Hopkins.

"I firmly believe Harris was a very honest man and that now, today, when Frank Hopkins has been exposed as a fraud, Harris would be appalled and try to do something to rectify his mistake in believing Hopkins."

But the damage was done.

Once the Hopkins tale had been printed in *Blood of the Arab,* later authors had no hesitation in recirculating the lies.

The first to fall victim was famous Old West author, J. Frank Dobie, who wrote about the non-existent Galveston to Rutland race in later editions of his book, *The Mustangs.*

Where did Dobie get his information?

From Harris!

"The Arabian Horse Club Registry of America, Chicago, has granted me permission to use the letters of Frank T. Hopkins, as quoted in the book by Harris," wrote Dobie in 1952.

Professor David Dary, who headed the School of Journalism at the University of Oklahoma, is not impressed with Dobie's sloppy research.

"It was typical of Dobie to quote from other books," said Dary, the recipient of the Cowboy Hall of Fame Wrangler Award and author of more than a dozen books on the American West, including *Red Blood and Black Ink: Journalism in the Old West* (1998).

"I am convinced that Dobie dropped Hopkins and his claims after quoting from Harris's *The Blood of the Arab* in *The Mustangs.* Someone probably informed Dobie that Hopkins' stories were fiction. If not, Dobie would have reused the Hopkins material in later writing, which was his habit," Professor Dary said.

Wishful thinking and a lack of research had fooled Charles Roth, Albert Harris and J. Frank Dobie into believing the tall tales told by Frank Hopkins.

When Hopkins died in 1951, he must have been pleased with the way his equestrian fantasies had progressed from insignificant magazines into reputable books by respected authors.

This Pecos Bill of Long Island could not have foreseen that he would become the center of a 21st Century international controversy.

Was he the greatest endurance rider that ever lived, as Hollywood would try to depict him?

Or would he go down in history as the biggest equestrian liar of all time?

Would Frank's falsehoods pass away with him?

Not if his widow, Gertrude, could help it!

Instead of remaining silent, the Lady Macbeth of this story took the helm of the Hopkins Ship of Charades. Gertrude spent the rest of her life trying to hoodwink the world into believing that her late husband was the hero he pretended to be – and the first person she fooled was the author of *Shane* and *Monte Walsh.*

Long on Credulity, Short on Suspicion

Jack Schaefer was the author of two best-selling books about the demise of the Old West, both of which were made into movies. The classic *Shane* was released in 1952. Starring Alan Ladd, it told the bittersweet story of a gunfighter trying to come to terms with a changing world.

Monte Walsh, Schaefer's book about the life and times of a turn-of-the-century cowboy, was turned into a movie in 1970 and starred Lee Marvin. More recently, America was treated to a television version of *Monte Walsh*, this time starring Tom Selleck.

Though trained as a journalist in Connecticut, Schaefer spent his spare time absorbing the history and memoirs of the men who had lived in the Old West. After the success of his first book, *Shane*, Schaefer moved to New Mexico and wrote about the west full time.

One of his lesser-known works was a delightful little book, *The Great Endurance Race – 600 Miles on a Single Mount, 1908, from Evanston, Wyoming, to Denver*, published in 1963. This book tells the story of a documented race. It also makes brief mention of the imaginary Galveston to Rutland endurance ride which Frank Hopkins claimed to have won in 1886.

Where did Schaefer get that information?

From Gertrude Hopkins!

"Jack Schaefer wrote me a while ago," Gertrude said in a letter to a friend. The widow Hopkins went on to explain that the famous author was, "seeking information regarding the Galveston-Rutland ride and I did my best to be helpful."

By "helpful," Gertrude meant she tried to mislead Schaefer into believing the race actually happened.

In a letter dated June 1962, Gertrude apologized to Schaefer for not replying sooner to his request for confirmation of the Galveston ride. "My delay in replying to your letter is due to my trying in vain to find something that might lead to a clue in finding a record of the Galveston to Rutland race."

Schaefer, who was known for his impeccable research, had been seeking independent proof of Hopkins' alleged equestrian achievements.

He couldn't find any!

We do not know if he believed Gertrude's version of events.

We do know, however, that the scales tipped for Schaefer when he found what he thought was proof in another book. Unfortunately, the author of that book was Albert Harris, who had himself been duped by Frank Hopkins in the 1940s!

In a letter dated June, 1962, Schaefer writes, "Very interesting, and somewhat consoling, to learn that someone else has been plagued with negative results in regard to Frank Hopkins and his races. In the last few days, however, I have begun to get a few positive results. There is some data about Hopkins and the Galveston-Rutland race and his activities in Arabia in Albert Harris's book *The Blood of the Arab,* 1941…."

Schaefer was hooked.

With the publication of his own small book, *The Great Endurance Race,* Schaefer became the next victim of the Hopkins Hoax.

And who was Schaefer discussing Frank Hopkins with?

Anthony Amaral, the magazine writer who did more to kick Hopkins' tales onto the international stage than anybody else.

A Make-Believe Map

In July 1962 *Horse Lover's Magazine* published a story entitled *Hidalgo and Frank Hopkins.*

This article describes how Frank Hopkins, an overlooked underdog of the American West, and his forgotten pal, Hidalgo, triumph over great hardships and beat Arab horsemen on their own ground.

Sounds like the premise for a great movie.

"Hidalgo will never have a bronze monument erected in his memory to grace a green turf as have Man O' War and Citation," lamented the story's author, Anthony Amaral. "And for some reason his name and pluckiness escape the pages in the books that list the 'Who's Who' of the equine world."

Could the reason possibly be that there are photographs and documents proving the existence of Man O' War and those other equine heroes?

Strangely, there was no map of this 1,000-year-old race, so Anthony Amaral invented one to illustrate his story.

The American author made no secret of his admiration for the man he described as "slender and dauntless" – even though he had never met Hopkins. So what evidence did the enthusiastic Amaral have to promote the tainted story of Hidalgo and the Arabian race?

A single letter from the merry widow, Gertrude.

"Dear Mr. Amaral, I am sorry I do not seem to have any records of the [Arabian] ride you referred to in your letter to me of June 27th, 1962, although some mention must have been made of it at the time since the Congress of Rough Riders of the World backed it. The late Theodore Roosevelt (later our President) was the most interested."

The unsuspecting Amaral had no way of knowing that it would later be proved that Frank Hopkins never went to Arabia and almost certainly never met Roosevelt.

Gertrude elaborated on the lie by hinting that the *New York Times* or the *Herald Tribune* may have reported on it.

In order to strengthen her argument, she wheeled in a long-time Hopkins ally, Charles B. Roth, the Denver salesman turned magazine writer.

"Perhaps Charles B. Roth in Denver knows where this [Arabian] ride was written up as he was a friend of Mr. Hopkins and knows of his rides."

What proof did Roth, who wrote extensively about Hopkins during the 1930s, offer Amaral as evidence that Hopkins had won a 3,000 mile race in Arabia?

"I do not have any documentary proof of Mr. Hopkins' race in Arabia. I am sorry, I have never seen a picture of Hidalgo," Roth told Amaral.

Like Schaefer, Amaral was still looking for independent proof of Hopkins' claimed feats.

Four years after contacting Gertrude, Amaral finally followed her suggestion regarding possible newspaper reports on the 1,000-year-old Arabian race. He wrote to the Library of Congress, asking if they had "anything that might indicate authenticity." The prestigious National Library replied three weeks later.

"An examination of the 1888 and 1889 editions of the Index to the New York Daily Tribune and other sources has failed to reveal a reference to the 'annual endurance event' described in your letter."

Amaral was stymied.

He could find no evidence.

What did he do?

He decided to publish the increasingly suspect Hopkins story again!

Only now his luck was changing.

Bob Gray, the editor and publisher of *Horseman* magazine, wasn't buying it.

After being offered another version of the Hopkins tale, Gray raised a red flag of caution.

In a letter dated February 10, 1967, the editor wrote to Amaral asking for some documentation to prove the Arab race ever happened.

"Frankly, a lot of Arabian breeders simply won't believe that tale. Not unless you've got some sources and some reliable authority to back it up. So can you come up with some sort of written award, newspaper clippings, letters from somebody other than Hopkins to pin down the authenticity of that ride?" Gray asked Amaral.

The wary publisher then expressed strong reservations about the story Amaral was trying to sell him.

"You can readily understand that our magazine would be accused of irresponsible reporting if we printed a story such as this without knowing the basis of the background facts."

Heedless of Gray's warning, and ignoring the lack of any independent proof to substantiate Hopkins' Arabian race claims, Amaral sold the story elsewhere.

Who bought it?

America's most widely-read equestrian magazine!

Amaral's article, *Frank Hopkins… best of endurance riders?* was published in *Western Horseman* in December, 1969.

It was thanks to the *Western Horseman* article that the Hopkins tales multiplied beyond the boundaries of the United States and entered the English-speaking world at large.

When *Western Horseman* was contacted on 4 June 2003 by The Long Riders' Guild and warned that Hopkins' credibility had been destroyed by more than seventy academics, neither the editor nor the publisher responded. Follow-up emails and telephone calls also went unheeded.

What did *Western Horseman* do?

In the July 2003 issue of *Western Horseman* there was a short article about the forthcoming film in the "Horses and People" section.

"*Hidalgo* is based on a true story about the annual race in which entries typically were restricted to top Arabian horses. However, in 1890 a sheik invited Frank T. Hopkins, cowboy and U.S. Cavalry dispatch rider, to compete against the Bedouin horses and riders, and thereby hangs the tale," wrote *Western Horseman* reporter, Fran Devereux Smith.

Having sold the unsubstantiated Arabian race story to *Western Horseman* in 1969, Anthony Amaral apparently had second thoughts about Frank Hopkins, though Amaral never went public with his new reservations.

Curiously Amaral's book, *Mustang*, published in the late 1970s, does not mention either the much-vaunted Hidalgo or Frank Hopkins.

Had Amaral finally seen the light?

Too late – the damage was done.

Amaral died in the 1980s, but his original *Western Horseman* article reaped enormous publicity for Hopkins and became a legend in its own right.

Now there was only one step between Hopkins and Hollywood.

In 1976, the prestigious University of Oklahoma Press published a book entitled *The American Paint Horse*. In it, author Glynn Haynes swallowed the Hopkins legend hook, line and sinker.

Why?

Because Hidalgo, the mythical mustang, was said to be a pinto-colored horse.

And where did Haynes get this information?

"*In the words of Anthony Amaral,*" Haynes wrote, and then went on to re-circulate Hopkins' lies as they had been passed on from one lazy writer to another for forty years.

Starting with Charles B. Roth in the 1930s, the Frank Hopkins fantasies had been quietly making their way up the media food chain.

After generations of slapdash research, the myth reached its zenith when it was embraced by Hollywood.

The Key to the Magic Kingdom

Frank Hopkins needed a friend in Hollywood and he found one in John Fusco.

An award-winning screenwriter, John Fusco has a string of films to his credit including *Crossroads, Thunderheart* and *Spirit – Stallion of the Cimarron.*

"I really believe in research," Fusco told *Screenwriter* magazine in April 1993, and went on to talk about how he became "deeply immersed" in his subject-matter.

Yet Fusco resembled Charles Roth, the self-proclaimed "Angel towards the blowhards of the Old West." Like Roth, who first wrote about Hopkins in the 1930s, Fusco has shown sympathy for dubious characters of the Old West. Consider Fusco's decision to go against the historical trend and present Brushy Bill Roberts as the real Billy the Kid. Though most academics are convinced Roberts was a fraud, Fusco depicted Brushy Bill as the famous outlaw in his film *Young Guns.*

Hopkins was out of the same stable as Brushy Bill Roberts.

And Fusco found him equally intriguing.

He decided to write a screenplay that immortalized the counterfeit cowboy!

What Fusco could not have foreseen was that, like Harris, Dobie, Schaefer and Amaral, he was about to be led astray by Hopkins.

"I never took native history at face value, I always looked deeper into it," John Fusco told *Cowboys and Indians* magazine in April 2003.

Yet in the screenplay for the movie *Hidalgo*, Fusco included a scene in which Hopkins is supposedly present at the Battle of Wounded Knee.

What did Hopkins himself have to say about this infamous massacre?

In his unpublished manuscript, *My Years in the Saddle*, Frank wrote, "I saw Black Elk riding toward me. He was wild-eyed. I yelled at him to stop; there was a tepee that the women had left there and meat was still boiling on the fire. Black Elk and I went in there and ate the stew. While we were eating, some soldiers rode by and fired into the tepee and the shot went through the pot of stew, but we kept on talking just the same."

What inspired Hopkins to write this story?

He plagiarized it out of the 1932 first edition of *Black Elk Speaks*!

Famous Lakota mystic Black Elk really was at the massacre of Wounded Knee.

This is how he remembered it:

"We rode into the camp, and it was all empty. We were very hungry because we had not eaten anything since early morning, so we peeped into the tepees until we saw where there was a pot with papa (dried meat) cooked in it. We sat down in there and began to eat. While we were doing this, the soldiers shot at the tepee, and a bullet struck right between Red Crow and me. It threw dust in the soup, but we kept right on eating until we had our fill," Black Elk said.

There is no mention of Frank Hopkins in *Black Elk Speaks,* or indeed any other document linking him to the Lakota people.

That is one reason that famed Native American academic, Dr. Vine Deloria Jr., who is himself a Lakota, has denounced Hopkins as "the World's Greatest Liar."

Viggo Mortensen, of Lord of the Rings fame, has been cast to play Frank Hopkins in *Hidalgo.*

"This should be a Western like no other," Mortensen told *Cowboys and Indians* magazine in April 2003.

Truer words were never spoken.

Like Fusco, Mortensen too has been beguiled by Hopkins' stories, especially the episode at Wounded Knee.

"*Hidalgo* corrects historical misinformation, particularly with regard to the Lakota people," Mortensen told *Cowboys and Indians* magazine in April 2003. "The highlight of the shoot has been the painstaking recreation of the tragic massacre at Wounded Knee."

When doubts were raised about the credibility of Frank Hopkins' so-called "true story," John Fusco went on the attack.

In an interview with *The Hollywood Reporter* in March 2003, Fusco said, "I've been researching Hopkins' life for more than 12 years now and compiled research from more than 15 well-respected historians that verify this story."

The screenwriter went on belittle those who questioned Hopkins' version of events.

"Their comments sound like saloon tales to me," Fusco said.

Yet Fusco has never publicly announced the names of his "well-respected historians," nor revealed the sources of his "12 years of research."

Nevertheless, the Walt Disney Studio believed the story to be true.

Why?

Disney's Dilemma

According to various film-buff websites Disney was looking for a script which could compete with the Universal Pictures juggernaut, *Seabiscuit.*

Disney wanted a true story.

In rode Frank Hopkins.

The stage was set.

As the sun rose on the year 2003, Hidalgo, the mythical mustang, was lined up against Seabiscuit, a documented equine hero, in a cinematic horse-race.

A skillfully orchestrated publicity campaign began when the Walt Disney Studios trumpeted their forthcoming film *Hidalgo* as a $90 million epic action-adventure film about "the ultimate underdog who became a legend."

Sound like Seabiscuit?

The screenplay delivered by John Fusco was allegedly "based on the true story of the greatest long-distance horse race in history. Pony Express rider Frank T. Hopkins (Viggo Mortensen), becomes the first American ever to enter the Ocean of Fire – a 3,000 mile survival race across the Arabian Desert and the greatest endurance horse race ever run."

So what justification did Disney have for claiming its film was historically accurate?

None!

Gregory Michno, noted author of many books about the Old West, said, "Coincidentally I am currently working on a book that discusses Hollywood versus history in western movies. These are some of the very points that will be examined, such as whether or not it is Hollywood's duty to tell accurate history, or simply entertain us with a good story. The latter may be the case, but it should not give us falsehoods under the guise of truth."

Nina Heyn, Disney's Executive Director of International Publicity, dismissed concerns about Hopkins' authenticity out of hand.

"No one here really cares about the historical aspects. Once a movie has been shot people move on to the others. We are like a factory. It's like making dolls, once the latest baby is out we go on to the next one. If it transpires that the historical aspects are in question, I don't think people would care that much. Hidalgo is a family film. It has little to do with reality," Heyn told the international press.

Professor David Dary, a recipient of the Cowboy Hall of Fame Wrangler Award and author of more than a dozen books on the American West, took exception to Heyn's stance.

"Yes, the Hopkins story is exciting," Dary agreed. "It has all of the ingredients that make a good story and in turn a good motion picture. But to misrepresent to the motion picture viewing public that the upcoming film is a 'true story' is not only misleading but it raises a serious question about the credibility of the Disney organization. Disney should simply tell the public Frank Hopkins' story is just a story and not the truth."

Due to the unprecedented international controversy swirling around *Hidalgo*, Disney delayed release of the movie from October 2003 to March 2004.

To add to the confusion, although the trailer for *Hidalgo* still maintains the movie is "based on a true story," a synopsis of the film which appears on the Disney website now claims it is "based on the autobiography of Frank Hopkins."

This is disingenuous.

Firstly, an "autobiography" is assumed to be a true tale of somebody's life.

Frank Hopkins' claims to have raced across Arabia on Hidalgo are untrue!

Secondly, the so-called "autobiographical manuscript" written by Frank Hopkins in the 1930s was discovered by the international research team headed by The Long Riders' Guild, <u>after</u> filming had been completed.

With pressure building from the press, Disney circled their wagons and are now maintaining a wall of silence regarding the historical fantasies upon which their movie is based.

Emails to their publicity department have gone unanswered.

A letter to Michael Eisner, CEO of Walt Disney, has never been acknowledged.

Professor Dary thinks he knows why.

"The problem seems to be that they [Disney] made no attempt in the beginning to confirm John Fusco's claim that the Hopkins story was true. They are now trying to ignore the truth and brush off questions about Hopkins' credibility in hopes the issue will go away," Dary said.

Hidalgo-gate

Thanks both to the Disney movie and the Internet, Frank Hopkins' lies are spreading at an alarming rate. Even today magazine writers, authors, webmasters, screenplay writers, and Hollywood moguls are eagerly embracing this exciting, though implausible, tale.

The September 2003 issue of *Cowboys and Indians* magazine published a story entitled "Hollywood Horses," which stated, "To be released later this year is the Disney period epic, Hidalgo, the true story of Pony Express rider Frank T. Hopkins and his paint horse Hidalgo, who take on the challenge of the 3,000 mile 'Oceans of Fire' race across the Arabian Desert."

Insight Magazine recently reprinted a syndicated *New York Times* newspaper article from July 2003 which quoted Anthony Amaral's 1969 *Western Horseman* magazine article and stated the movie *Hidalgo* is "being billed as an 'epic action-adventure' based on a true story."

The internet site of the American Paint Horse Association boasts, "*Hidalgo*, an epic action adventure from Walt Disney Pictures, based on the true story of the greatest long-distance horse race in history, started production recently and will feature a registered American Paint horse in the starring role. In all, five American Paint horses are being used at various times to play the role of Hidalgo, the colorful equine star of the film."

Hopkins' lies are being circulated as fact in dozens of languages on websites around the world.

But the most alarming development came when extracts from the unpublished Hopkins material, which had been discovered by The Long Riders' Guild in University archives, were published out of context on the Internet in such a way as to imply that Frank Hopkins was a genuine equestrian and Old West hero.

But if the Internet has been used to promote the Hopkins Hoax, it was also thanks to this 21st Century tool that the team of academics in five countries was able to uncover the paper trail which unmasked Hopkins as a fraud.

Intelligent use of the World Wide Web means the public is no longer forced to bow to the Disneyfication of history.

The famous Hollywood studio should follow the example of noted American scholar Dr. Donald Worcester.

Though 88 years old, Worcester had the courage to admit Hopkins fooled him.

The Distinguished Emeritus at Texas Christian University briefly mentioned Hopkins in his book, *The Spanish Mustang*, and acknowledged he used passages from J. Frank Dobie's book and Amaral's articles instead of researching Hopkins himself.

But when presented with copies of Hopkins' unpublished manuscripts and articles, Dr. Worcester realized the man who claimed to be the world's greatest horseman was a complete fraud.

When asked if Hopkins should be credited with having created the largest Old West hoax of all time, Worcester laughed.

"I wouldn't say Frank Hopkins should be 'credited' with these stories but rather 'discredited' by them. I certainly can't think of a bigger hoax!"

The retired academic believes it is important for historians and researchers to come clean if they discover they have been duped.

"If the Walt Disney studio does not announce that the movie *Hidalgo* is fiction, then years from now people will be misled into believing it is a true story." said Worcester. "If these people don't admit they were misled, then I wouldn't trust them on anything else!"

Dr. Worcester and the research team have demonstrated that Frank Hopkins wears the dubious double crown of the greatest equestrian hoax and the biggest Old West fraud of all time.

Here then are all the known writings of the man known as Frank T. Hopkins. Chapters 1 and 2 have never been published before. The remaining chapters were printed in an obscure Vermont magazine during the early 1940s.

They are published here, in their entirety, in chronological order, for the first time in history so that you, the reader, can make up your own mind about the man and his myth.

Although Frank Hopkins (above) claimed to have won more endurance races than anybody else in history, there is no documented photograph of him in the saddle. This photograph of Hopkins on a stool is believed to have been taken in the early 1940s and was the one most often used to illustrate his articles. Like the date and location, the photographer is unknown.

Chapter 1

The Last of the Buffalo Hunters
As told to Jahkwah[*]

After many years' absence, I return again to the Big Horn country, where long ago "nobody lived and the dogs barked at strangers". At the CH Ranch[1] corral, I pick out a likely-looking cow pony to carry me over the sagebrush and cactus and through the rough canyons where I spent my childhood. How natural it seems to breathe again the familiar alkali-dust of the rolling plains and hear the clinking of my spurs, as I ride along!

Drawing rein, I halt my pony on top of a rolling hill, wave my old sombrero and look down on the slow-flowing river beside which once stood the old Fort in which I was born[2] – a fort destined to become famous in history for the part it played during the Indian troubles. All that remains of old Fort Laramie to-day, are the few posts visible above the ground and the trees that I remember planting when I was a boy. What was once the old Bozeman Trail is now cut up into roads leading into the Town called Laramie.

---

[*] **Editors' note**: "Jahkwah" is allegedly the Lakota name Hopkins bestowed upon his wife, Gertrude. We have been unable to locate a Native American authority who can identify the name "Jahkwah" in any Native American language.

[1] **Editors' note:** Hopkins claimed the "CH Ranch" was owned by his father, Charles Hopkins. But **Rick Ewig**, *Associate Director of the American Heritage Center of the University of Wyoming,* was unable to find any trace of a CH Ranch, or of a CH brand, in Wyoming.

[2] **Louise Samson,** *Curator of the Fort Laramie National Historic Site:* "We don't know in which fort Hopkins was born but it wasn't Fort Laramie as he claims. His physical description of Fort Laramie, as it existed any time after abandonment in 1890, is perhaps the most outlandish of all – "a few posts visible above the ground and the trees that I remember planting as boy." The remains of Fort Laramie consist of 44 building remnants, including thirteen intact structures. Though extensive restoration and rehabilitation has occurred since the National Park Service acquired the site in 1938 there has been no new construction.

First, the geographically challenged Hopkins places Fort Laramie somewhere in the vicinity of the Big Horn Mountain region, when in fact, Fort Laramie is some 200 miles from present day Sheridan, Wyoming, which is situated at the base of the mountains. He has the Bozeman Trail running west into Laramie, when it ran north through Wyoming and northwest into Montana."

In the early days, when trouble was expected with warring Indian tribes, the whites who lived in the surrounding country, were notified and they and their families, together with the peaceful Indians, were rounded up and sheltered in the nearest Forts. It was at such a time, known as the "bloody year on the plains", that I was born in the isolated army garrison, the scene of many treaties. Trouble started over a treaty under which our government gave the Sioux and Cheyenne Indian tribes some ground from the Platte River to the Missouri and from the Dakota Black Hills, to be used by them for their hunting ground for antelope, buffalo, deer and wild ponies.

Now this land yielded to the red man not only his food supply, but also the needful materials for clothing, shelter, weapons, etc. He used every part of the buffalo. Small wonder, then, when this army of white settlers rushed in, apparently to rob him of his very livelihood and what he considered rightly his under the terms of the treaty he had signed with the white man's government, the Indian bitterly resented this intrusion. The Indian's word is good, and it is part of his religious belief that his word should never be broken. He had given his word to the white man's government and had faithfully lived up to his part of the treaty and could therefore not understand the attitude of this government whom he thought had violated the treaty in this manner. This led the Indian to lose faith in the white man's promises and the treaties of his government and the outcome was disaster – bloodshed, terror and massacre. I believe the 7th Iowa cavalry was stationed at the fort at this time.

As I gazed at the spot where this old fort once stood, I see again in memory my rides in the early days with men of the plains – real men they were too, who braved all kinds of danger and suffered untold hardships to make the West what it is to-day. Although memories are still clear of those brave heroes of the frontier, many friends of bygone days have passed beyond the Great Divide: those I rode with on the buffalo trails, the horse hunters, brave men of the cavalry, the scouts – real plainsmen, all of them; I make no distinction between the white man and the red, the outlaw or the peaceful citizen – all played their parts in those days. Yet, though it seems but yesterday, I must acknowledge that more than half a century has elapsed and now, in the evening of my active life, I find I am alone – the last of the buffalo hunters[3].

My first recollection of the days I spent in the Fort is rather dim, but I remember the log cabin my father built when he was not riding the trails for the

---

[3] **Editors' note**: Sharon Cunningham, one of the co-authors of *Encyclopedia of Buffalo Hunters and Skinners,* was quick to point out that there is no documented evidence linking Frank Hopkins to nineteenth century buffalo hunting. Cunningham and her fellow authors, Leo Remiger and Miles Gilbert, have spent years compiling what is believed to be the largest private collection of buffalo-hunting knowledge in history. Despite Hopkins' claims to have been a famed mounted buffalo hunter, Cunningham dismissed Hopkins out of hand, saying, "We have never heard of him."

government. He drove out of the Fort with a mule team to draw the logs. In building the cabin, the logs were notched and keyed together on the corners, and on the inside, the bark was carefully shaved and then polished. There was a big stone fireplace with baking oven at the side, and there was a stone hearth. I have seen many log cabins, but never one built so neatly as the one built by my father. It still stands to-day, as a landmark, about twenty-two miles from what is now the town of Laramie[4]. In times of peace, I spent in it many happy hours with my dear mother, and at rare intervals, when father was off duty, he shared these happy times with us.

GENERAL GEORGE CROOK

Most historians consider General Crook to be one of the US Army's best Indian fighters. He respected the native Americans as brave adversaries, and considered they should be well treated when they were defeated.

Born in 1828, Crook graduated from West Point Academy in 1852. Very early in his career he witnessed for himself how the Indians were betrayed when the US Senate threw out eighteen negotiated treaties, and left the Indians with no rights at all.

Although he led successful campaigns against several tribes in Washington, Oregon and California, Crook said afterwards, "When they were pushed beyond endurance and would go on the warpath, we had to fight when our sympathies were with the Indians."

After the Civil War, in which he served, he was put in charge of Arizona Territory by President Ulysses Grant.

By the autumn of 1872, Crook had brought peace to the Arizona Territory and President Grant promoted Crook to brigadier general. Crook stayed in Arizona until 1874, and continued to champion humane treatment of the Indian tribes.

In the winter of 1875, Crook was sent to the northern Plains where he defeated the Cheyenne chief Dull Knife. He then recruited men from a number of other tribes to fight against the Sioux. When Crazy Horse surrendered in 1877, the last battle was over.

He went back to Arizona Territory and for four years tried to force Geronimo to surrender, but without success. It was General Miles who finally exiled Geronimo to Florida.

For the rest of his life; Crook carried on his lifelong crusade in support of his former enemies, condemning broken treaties, unfair treatment and white encroachment.

My father took a very active part in the history of those days. He was engaged, along with other scouts, to scout for General George Crook in Crook's campaign against the Apaches in Arizona. The work was hazardous, great hardships were endured, and mention is made of this by a Major John Bourke in his experiences on the Border with Crook, in which these scouts were commended most highly and my father's name mentioned among them. I first

---

[4]**Louise Samson,** *Curator of the Fort Laramie National Historic Site:* "In his rendition of the log cabin birth place, he seems not to have remembered his own stories. He places it in two different locations, south of the parade ground (Fort Laramie) and 22 miles from the town of Laramie. The town of Laramie is 100 miles west of Fort Laramie. He refers to the cabin as a landmark. Where?"

saw General Crook (old scrub whiskers they called him) when I was but a boy – about the time of the Yellowstone Expedition – and I never dreamed then that I was later to bear important dispatches for him that helped to make the history of the West.

One summer, I was about ten – father had to go down to Old Fort Oray Bull, Wyoming, to get his orders to report to Flagstaff, Arizona, and his first duty was to guide a wagon train. I pleaded with mother that I might go on the trails with him, and when he got back to Laramie, I asked to go along. At first, he hesitated to take me, giving as his reason, that there was liable to be too much trouble with the Apache, but I teased so hard, that when mother said, "take him", he finally agreed, and I prepared for my first long-distance ride. I shall never forget it. They got me a small "Squaw pony". It was very busy on the trails on account of its size – it could run about as fast as you could kick a barrel uphill, but once it was with the pack-train, it was led most of the time behind the wagons. I had great confidence in my father – therefore no fear of anything with him along.

We boarded a train – I don't just recall where – it was the first train I ever saw or rode on, and where we got off I don't recall,[5] but the wagon-train was made up near the town of Buckskin, Arizona.

Now we'd been out on the trail about two days; the second day, my father who rode some distance ahead (in the manner customary with scouts) picking the trail, suddenly drew rein, and shading his eyes with his hand to the rim of his hat, seemed to fix his attention on the slopes beyond. With us were Yellowstone Kelly – a famous scout and one of the best I ever met, and "Red" Wilson, noted in the army as an expert pack-train man, the drivers of the bull teams, the mule skinners, about twenty-eight men in all. This was a mixed train – partly wagons drawn by bulls, and mules packed with ammunition and army supplies for the army camp, and saddle mules for the drivers and packers.

After searching the slopes and horizon, father turned his horse around slowly and rode back to us. He stood for a few moments, talking with Wilson who was riding just behind him, and then they both jogged their horses back to the wagon train. Father then ordered the drivers to draw their wagons round in a circle and unyoke their cattle, and told the men in charge of the pack mules to unpack them and to stack the big boxes between the wheels of the wagon. This was done. He then told all men to look to their guns and to break open one of the boxes of ammunition and distribute it amongst the men. This done, he spoke to them calmly, "Well boys, there's nothing to do now but wait."

---

[5] **Dale Yeager**, *Criminal Psychologist:* "It is interesting that Hopkins stories eliminate important details related to dates but add excessive details in other parts of his tomes. The use of excessive details in minor parts of a conversation or story points to deception.

YELLOWSTONE KELLY

Luther (Yellowstone) Kelly was born in New York in 1849. He acquired his nickname by scouting for the US Army on Yellowstone River during the 1870s and 1880s. After serving in the Civil War, Kelly ended up out west where he spent many years hunting and guiding government expeditions through the area.

From 1876 to 1878 he was Nelson Miles' chief scout at the Wolf Mountain and Tongue River battles.

Yellowstone Kelly later guided two expeditions into Alaska, then accepted a post as agent of the San Carlos Indian Reservation.

Nelson Miles once said of the man, "Yellowstone Kelly was of a good family, well educated and fond of good books, as quiet and gentle as he was brave, as kind and generous as he was forceful, a great hunter and an expert rifleman; he explored that extensive northwest country years before serious hostilities occurred and acquired a knowledge of its topography, climate and resources that was extremely valuable."

It might have been an hour or more before anything happened – suddenly, a spotted war pony leapt out from behind a small jack-pine on the slopes just above us. As this pony came loping towards us, a number of other ponies followed behind it. Their riders were Apaches who bore down on our little group, and when they got close enough, they fired and then rode away, taking their positions behind the jack pines on the slopes. This was repeated with twice as many horses and men. The second time they swooped down, four Indian ponies loped away across the sand without their riders. They charged on our little group in this manner until nightfall.

Knowing the Apache so well, father said it was a sure thing that the Indians would not fight after dark, but that they would be on our trail with reinforcements at sun-up the following morning. So, after it got dark, he gave orders to pack the mules and to hitch the bulls to the wagons and to urge them on in an effort to reach a water hole before morning. The drivers lashed the bulls; you could hear them urging them on, and their cries of "Gee auf, haw to" and "abroad away" and as I laid in one of the wagons I could hear the cracking of their whips all night. The poor animals were played out – they lolled (tongues hung out) from the heat of the sand.

Next morning, about daybreak, we pulled up to a large water-hole. The wagons were placed in a circle, one lapping by the other, the packing boxes between the wheels and under the wagons serving as a barricade. At sun-up, we heard the wild ki-yi-yi-yi of the Apaches yelping on our trail. Our men waited until the Indians drew within shooting distance then they opened fire on the Apaches.

This continued all day, and along about four o'clock in the afternoon, when Red Wilson raised himself to get a good shot at a disappearing Apache, he (Red) was hit by a bullet from an Indian's rifle, striking him in his middle. He crumpled up like a green leaf on a camp fire and lay prostrate on the sand. We were under heavy fire by that time from the Indians, so nobody paid much attention to "Red" till after the Apaches rode away to reload their rifles. Then father told Kelly to look after Red, and after examining him, Kelly pronounced him dead. Somewhat later, when things were a little quieter, Father took his buckskin coat and handed it to Yellowstone Kelly who placed it over Wilson's face, then he dug a shallow hole in the loose sand with his hands and placed Red's body in it; he then took his own coat and covered the body and says, "Well, boys, Red's left us this time for good." Then he covered him lightly with some sand.

By now, darkness had fallen and the Apaches retreated for the night. Father told the men they had better break up some of the packing boxes and build a fire so they could make coffee. While we were sitting by the light of the fire, drinking coffee from tin cups, surrounded by dead mules and oxen, the sand where we had laid Wilson suddenly parted; with his hands braced behind him, he gradually and with some difficulty raised himself to a sitting position in his shallow grave.

Looking straight at Father, he muttered painfully, "See here, Black Horse, what the H---- kind of fellers are you to bury a man before he thinks of dying"? That was the only time I ever saw my father look surprised. He did not answer, but handed "Red" the cup of coffee he was about to drink himself. Then Kelly says, "I was sure that you wuz dead." "To H---- I am, but I'm sure stiff and sore – give us a chew of tobacco". Father examined Red in good shape and found that the bullet had nearly paralyzed him. Well, they made a bed of heavy army blankets in one of the bull-carts, and laid poor Red in it. He was powerless by now in the hips and legs.

Next morning the fight continued and it looked mighty like we were going to lose. Wilson pleaded for his gun and ammunition and from his bed in the bull cart he did the best he could under such trying circumstances. Shortly after midday, a detachment of cavalry came tearing up the slopes. They passed our little band behind our packing boxes and bull wagons, but instead of stopping at the water hole and losing time, they went right by in pursuit of the Apaches. They had heard the noise and went after the Indians – I think they were Gatewood's men. They returned along about sundown. Most of our bulls had been killed and only 9 pack mules remained alive out of 128. Father, in his calm way, told the officers that we had better stay where we were till mules or cattle could be sent to draw the wagons. So, the cavalry was split into two divisions – one stayed with us for protection, the other went back to their camp.

A few days later they brought in enough mules – some of them harness mules – to draw the wagons; others were pack mules, and we started on again. We made the trip into the army camps which laid in the 'siwash' where the supplies were to be delivered, without further trouble. In camp, Red Wilson was taken care of and I didn't see him again for some years after. He never did fully recover after that. He was a hardy man, and as I remember him, his hair was as red as a fox's tail and the back of his bull neck was wrinkled into squares that looked like a checkerboard.

He lived to guide many wagon trains after this experience, though, and finally was killed down on Indian Territory, in a two-handed knife fight with an Indian, an old enemy of Red's who bore him a grievance which he held against Red for years. I suppose I shall never forget that ride, but though I was only a boy, my confidence in my father was so great that I had no fear nor did I suffer from the experience. I did not meet Yellowstone Kelly again until I was man grown.

After our return from Arizona, I did not see my father again until late in the Winter. He was ordered to go to Fort Bufford and was under orders from General Alfred H. Terry, who commanded the troops at that time. This was the winter previous to the Custer massacre. There was a band of Lakota Indians, a family of the Sioux nation, who had their winter camp about twelve miles from Fort Laramie and they were friendly; some of them visited the Fort often and boys of my age came there daily throughout the winter to play with me, among them one boy who as known to be very devout. No matter how interested he was in play, his religion and prayers were always first with him. He probably grew up to be what is known amongst the Indian tribes as a holy man, and it was through him that I became acquainted with most all of the Lakota tribe.

When the new grass (spring) came, the Indians were going up to Warbonnet Creek to catch up their ponies. They always turned their ponies out in the wintertime as they do not keep any saddle ponies, but turn them out on suitable pasture. The holy boy asked if I might go along. Even at that age I was a good rider so I was no trouble to those people on the trails, though the ride was long. Chief Crazy Horse said I could go with them.

We moved along slowly and when we got to Warbonnet Creek we saw many ponies there belonging to the Sioux nation – there were so many they could not be easily counted. They had shed their winter coats and looked sleek and fat. Although it was early, there were some baby colts running beside the herd. As far as the naked eye could see were tepees pitched by the different families belonging to the Sioux nation; these tribes had come in from every direction to round up their horses for summer use. Hunters had been sent into the upper prairies to bring in buffalo meat. When they returned with buffalo on their drags, we had feasts of fresh liver and buffalo hump and hams. The women got out their drying poles and jerked a lot of meat from the hind quarters, cured it and hung it over the poles to dry, while some of them cured the hides.

Everyone seemed happy, the chiefs addressed their people and there was no talk of war and I am sure there was no feeling of war in the hearts of these people. This time one of the holy days was being celebrated; it made no difference what anyone did, no one resented it or became cross. Small boys took advantage of this by playing pranks like taking small bows and arrows, the kind used for hunting birds, and when the women came along with containers full of water, we shot the small arrows through the containers, which not only wasted the water but destroyed the containers which were made mostly from the casing of buffalo hearts. The women did not resent this or say anything to us because everything was supposed to be taken in good humor at that time.

CRAZY HORSE (Tashunca-uitco)

Celebrated for his ferocity in battle, Crazy Horse was recognized among his own people as a visionary leader committed to preserving the traditions and values of the Lakota way of life.

Even as a young man, Crazy Horse was a legendary warrior. He stole horses from the Crow Indians before he was thirteen, and led his first war party before turning twenty. Crazy Horse fought in the 1865-68 war led by Red Cloud against American settlers in Wyoming, and played a key role in destroying William J. Fetterman's brigade at Fort Phil Kearny in 1867.

Crazy Horse earned his reputation among the Lakota not only by his skill and daring in battle but also by his fierce determination to preserve his people's traditional way of life. And he tried to prevent American encroachment on Lakota lands, helping to attack a surveying party sent into the Black Hills by General George Armstrong Custer in 1873.

When the War Department ordered all Lakota bands onto their reservations in 1876, Crazy Horse became a leader of the resistance. Closely allied to the Cheyenne through his first marriage to a Cheyenne woman, he gathered a force of 1,200 Oglala and Cheyenne at his village and turned back General George Crook on June 17, 1876, as Crook tried to advance toward Sitting Bull's encampment on the Little Bighorn. After this victory, Crazy Horse joined forces with Sitting Bull and on June 25 led his band in the counterattack that destroyed Custer's Seventh Cavalry.

General Nelson Miles pursued the Lakota and their allies relentlessly throughout the winter of 1876-77. This constant military harassment and the decline of the buffalo population eventually forced Crazy Horse to surrender on May 6, 1877.

Even in defeat, Crazy Horse remained an independent spirit, and in September 1877, when he left the reservation to take his sick wife to her parents, General George Crook ordered him arrested, fearing that he was plotting a return to battle. Crazy Horse did not resist arrest at first, but when he realized that he was being led to a guardhouse, he began to struggle, and while his arms were held by one of the arresting officers, a soldier ran him through with a bayonet.

Some of the boys tied buckskin string around the legs of warriors by sliding in between them on their bellies and some succeeded in tying two men together in this manner, while others were tied to a tepee pole, and some had their legs tied to a dog; anything might be done on this day in fun but no resentment nor anger may be shown by the victims of these pranks.

I played the games of the Indian boys, from early morn till dark at night, one of the favorites being "throw him off the horse". It is played with twenty-four players twelve on each side, the players are lined up on their horses about 500 feet apart, facing one another; then, at a given signal, they ride at full speed towards each other and each player tries to throw his opponent off his horse. They clinch and drag at each other and more often both of them go on the ground in a crash; the side that succeeds in throwing the biggest number is the winning side. If both go to the ground together, that does not count, but the boy who throws his opponent, and still remains on his own horse is the victor for that point. Although I was smaller than most of them, I entered this game.

We played another game called "pick up the stick" Every boy has a coup stick with his special mark on it. He lays his stick in the pile and tried to remember exactly where it is laid; the sticks must be laid in criss-cross fashion; then the boys stand in line about twenty-five feet from the pile of sticks and a master coups man calls one of the boys to pick out his stick. He must come as fast as he can run, grab his stock and make the goal, but at the same time there are six coups men with stick in hand and as he goes to grab his stick from the pile the coups men strike at his hand to keep him from picking it up; if he is lucky enough to get his stick, he can safely make the goal, but he is quite sure to have a well bruised hand if he is not on the alert. This game is taught with a view to training the boys to be quick thinkers, while the game of "throw him off the horse," an ancient one in that tribe, is meant to teach the boys to be good riders and to know how to handle themselves on horseback when they become warriors.

As I remember, young Black Elk, who afterward became Chief Black Eagle 3rd, was the greatest player of both of these games. It looked almost impossible for anyone to hit his hand as he grabbed his coup stick; many years later, he rode in the Buffalo Bill Wild West show with us, and now he is at Standing Rock Reservation, a pitiful, hopeless old man who has lately become stone blind.

BLACK ELK

Black Elk was a holy Lakota Medicine Man who was forced to live through the destruction of his culture and the darkest days of his people. He was a visionary who had his first revelation when he was about eight years old. When he grew up he was healing the sick and trying to keep the old "sacred ways" alive. He was said to have the power to change the weather, experience of the healing power of herbs, and great wisdom.

Black Elk was 13 years old when he fought in the Battle of the Rosebud and the Battle of Little Big Horn in 1876. In 1887 he really did travel to London and meet Queen Victoria.

Black Elk told his story to John Neihardt, and the book "Black Elk Speaks" was published in 1932.

Then we played the game which would seem to most onlookers a dangerous one; it was catching rattlesnakes alive. A set of boys would be chosen – maybe 6 or 8 at a time, to go out on the prairie where it was likely there were rattlesnakes. There were always two old men to accompany the boys, and these old men were called the "snake whip men". The whip is made from a cluster of eagle feathers fastened to a buckskin string about four feet long, the other end of the string being tied to a pole or young tree about twelve feet long. The boys scattered out to search for the snakes, and when a rattler was found by a boy, the boy called the whip men who stood within the length of his twelve foot pole from the snake and by gently swinging the pole, the feathers at the end of the buckskin string would brush over the snake.

This continued until the snake stopped striking and appeared to be subdued; then, the snake uncoiled himself and started crawling away, the fight apparently taken out of him. Then the whip man would tell the boy to go get his snake. The boy would make a rush and with one hand grab the snake just back of the head. He must not under any circumstances let go, or kill the snake, but he was permitted to leave at once for the Village with his snake to the Chief (of any rating) who was to be the judge. If a boy refused to catch his snake after he had been told to do so by the "whip man" he was considered a coward, not only by the other boys, but also by the chiefs and warriors, and told that he would never make a good warrior. I never knew a boy to be bitten by a rattlesnake after a snake whip had been used in this manner, but a boy was never permitted to use such a whip – only an old man well versed in the game.[6]

We boys had lots of fun, and it looked as though the whole Sioux nation was camped there for the season, till one day Rain in the Face, a young chief, beautiful of body, an athlete and the pride of his people, came in. He had not been living with his tribe since he was made a prisoner two years before by Captain Tom Custer, taken into Fort and handcuffed or chained to another prisoner, a white man, and kept like this for months without being allowed a hearing. It seems there had been a veterinary and a fourteen year old boy who ventured outside the Fort for a ride at that time, who were shot, and Captain Tom Custer with a few cavalrymen, rode out to the Reservation and seized Rain-in-the-Face. The soldiers warned the other Indians that if they made any trouble it would cost the lives of many. As I understood and spoke the Sioux language fluently, it was very plain that all the tribes of the Sioux nation were intensely bitter against this treatment of young Rain-in-the-Face, although he had escaped from the Fort, and their hatred towards the Custer family, who were officers in the 7th Cavalry, increased.

---

[6] **Editors' note**: Despite Hopkins' early success at avoiding rattlesnakes, his luck later ran out. He claims to have been bitten three times during the course of his Old West career, the most famous incident being related to Robert Easton by Gertrude Hopkins.

"After selling some horses in Sioux City, Frank went home to Wyoming. He stopped somewhere to rest along the way; was very tired – when he went to pick up the reins he did not look down, and was bitten (right over the pulse) by a six-foot diamond-back rattler. He treated himself thus. Pulled off the fang from his wrist, shot the snake, cut out a large piece of the still-warm flesh, and clamped it on the bitten wrist tightly, then walked. The horse knew and acted accordingly. When he neared home his father saw him in the distance and said, 'Valley, the boy's been bit – he's walking,' and came to meet him. They warmed some milk and father walked him around the corral for hours at a time to keep him from getting sleepy. When Frank got drowsy, father had to slap him with the back of his hand. Finally, the poison went into the flesh of the snake and Frank's teeth, which had all gotten loose, were back to normal. He carried the white fang mark all the rest of his days."

As soon as it was know that Chief Rain-in-the-Face had come to the village, Crazy Horse, a Hunkpapa Chief, at once called a council of all the chiefs of the nation. Although the council lasted until well up into the night, Rain-in-the-Face had left earlier. I learned the reason for this was that he was afraid of being captured again by the troops. This little move of Captain Tom Custer's probably was the beginning of the end of the entire Custer family.

We stayed at Warbonnet Creek until the ponies were all caught up. One morning, Chief Crazy Horse ordered the criers of the camp to go around telling the people that we were to move to Plum Creek. It used to amuse me to hear the criers as they walked through the tepees yelling what translated might mean "pull it down" (meaning the tepee) "let your ponies be saddled, your drags fastened tight" (drags: an arrangement of poles fastened to the ponies neck with other poles laid cross-wise and they are used for drawing materials, and the old and helpless people and little children) and, "let your moccasins be good for our travel is long, the weather is good and our hearts are strong." These criers went around singing this like a chant while the tepees were being taken down. I could not understand then why they should want to move from this beautiful site as it seemed to me ideal and they all seemed to be enjoying themselves and happy there.

RAIN IN THE FACE

Chief Rain in the Face was born in 1835. He started building a reputation as a strong warrior while he was still a boy, frequently winning childhood games. He himself admitted that he loved to fight.

He acquired his name after a fight in 1845 – when he was about ten. He and some friends encountered a band of Cheyenne boys. Although they were friendly, they started a mock fight. Rain in the Face was pitted against a much older Cheyenne boy, who hit him in the face several times. Rain in the Face won in the end, but his face was spattered with blood and streaked where the war-paint had been washed away.

In 1868 he attacked Fort Phil Kearny in Wyoming – known later as the Fetterman battle. Almost every tribe of the Sioux nation was represented, and nobody inside the fort survived.

When the white men came after the gold of the Black Hills, Rain in the Face took the warpath against the white man for the last time.

He was captured after being betrayed by some of the reservation Indians and taken to the Fort near Bismarck, North Dakota. The Indian scouts who worked for Custer warned Rain in the Face that they were going to hang him. He was saved by an old soldier who was supposed to be feed and guard him; this old fellow unfastened Rain in the Face's shackles and spoke to him in sign language, "Go, friend! take this chain and ball with you. I shall shoot, but the voice of the gun will lie."

Rain in the Face ran for his life and returned to the Powder River. The following spring he joined the largest gathering of Sioux tribes in history.

Rain in the Face participated in the Battle of Little Big Horn, or Custer's Last Stand, and is said to have killed Tom Custer.

He died in 1905.

But I learned the following night, when we camped with the Ogallalas, that they were expecting war. An old chief of the Ogallalas, spoke to his people and said there would be much fighting from then on. The following morning, Chief Crazy Horse spoke to me and said he was sorry, for he knew I was happy with them, but it was better for me to go into the soldier's town because there was liable to be trouble. Later, I learned that the trouble was over making Rain-in-the-Face a prisoner. The whole Sioux nation had declared war on the Custer family, and the Sioux were only waiting at this spot for the troops to pursue them. Their own Indian scouts were scattered throughout the country, watching every move of the cavalry. The U.S. troops had no reason for pursuing them – these people were in their own country, interfering with no one.

Chief Crazy Horse sent twelve of his braves with me for my protection and we went into the nearest soldier's town. There I saw a number of Sioux Indians called "the hang-around the town" by the other Indians. Although they were fed at the fort, and in fact were dependent on the army for their living, they were never scouts for the U.S. government, nor were they friendly with their own tribes. Probably they could be called traitors to both sides.

After staying in the soldier's town about a week, I was transferred with the troops to my home in Fort Laramie. This was late in the month of Fatted Calves (May). There I learned that my father had moved up the Yellowstone River that Spring with Major Reno and General George A. Custer (the 7th Cavalry). On about the 6th day of July, 1876, the Kansas "Hays City Star" newspaper was the first to publish the news of the Custer fight in the Little Big Horn Valley about forty miles from the Big Horn mountain, that General Custer's troops had been surprised by four thousand Sioux Indians on June 25th and his entire command of five companies had been killed (including the entire Custer family). I still have this newspaper clipping.

Letters were sometimes four months in reaching my mother; they had to travel with the army and often they'd get sidetracked. Mother was much worried and was sure that father had gone down with Custer as he was a scout and naturally would lead and ride in advance of troops. About a month later, however, she received news from Major Reno and Captain Benteen that my father was not with the troops, but further information they could not give her, nor did they know his whereabouts.

One day, about the latter part of October, I think, I was playing outside the fort with a pet lamb someone had given me. I noticed a lone rider loping along from the direction of the Bozeman trail. As he drew nearer, I could tell by the way he set his saddle, that it was Father. He came into the fort and did not at the time give any explanation of his experience or absence. Although he was a hardy man, his face showed what he had evidently endured. He looked worn and haggard. Silent, as usual, he would not talk about that terrible tragedy.

It was not until many years later, when sitting with a few intimate friends at the ranch, who during the conversation mentioned Charley Reynolds, Custer's favorite scout, that father chimed in and said "Charlie was a brave man" and praised him highly. Reynolds was quiet and modest looking and the only scout I ever knew who wore his hair short. Father said Charlie was a good scout, but when he got into the Big Horn country he appeared to be lost. Two days before the Custer massacre, General Custer sent the Indian scouts on ahead, and Reynolds was guiding Custer. The Indian scouts returned with father and advised Custer to go no farther. Custer was not satisfied, believing that the scouts were betraying him.

On the morning of the battle, while they were camped on the banks of the Powder River, Reynolds appeared nervous; he told Custer that he was not familiar with that country and knew nothing about the river which they soon found had a treacherous bottom. Yet possibly a year before, Reynolds had brought a valuable message to Fort Laramie, coming through that country alone and riding mostly by night and under great difficulties and danger.

It seemed to father that Reynolds for some reason did not want to lead the troops. Custer asked father if he knew the country, and he answered, "Yes, as well as any man." The General then ordered father to find a crossing place for the troops as they had to ford the river. Father said he would find the place, but objected to leading the troops across the river into the Little Big Horn Valley, and his objection to this angered Custer and they had words over it, Custer accusing father of being over friendly with Indian tribes as well as Indian scouts which Custer had sent ahead and who had returned on the twenty-second, advising Custer not to advance. Then father said, "General, you are disobeying orders. I heard General Terry tell you to take forty-eight hours on this March to the Powder River and offer no attack on the Indians – this is only a scouting expedition – and General Terry said he would come up and meet you here, but now you are here in twenty-four hours and want to cross."

General Custer was furious; he threatened to have father court-martialed and ordered him to do as he was told. Finally, father said he would find the crossing for him. Reynolds hung back, and father returned shortly, telling Custer that he found the hard spot in the River sufficient for the troops to cross. Tom Custer made two trips through, to be sure the bottom was solid, while father waited. Father then led them north of the Big Horn mountains. They saw the Indian village through the glass, but no signs of an Indian; blankets were thrown about and the tepees all standing.

Father warned Custer to turn back, but the General refused, saying that the Indians had seen the troops coming and were so scared they fled their camp leaving everything behind them. Father, turning to the General, said "You don't know Indians – they don't leave their things around like that – it's only a decoy to get you to ride in there – you'd better turn back." Custer was angry at this and accused father of scouting for the Indians and then ordered him to lead, at which father said, "All right then, I'LL come back – you won't." Father rode quite a distance ahead, picking the trail, and as they drew near the site of the battlefield, father was lost to view of the troops and Custer saw him no more.

What happened was this: as father was riding some distance in the lead of the cavalry he rode out of sight, while turning a bend by a clump of bushes, he was suddenly ordered to "halt." Chief Gall himself with several other warriors, rode out from behind the bushes, seized father and took him prisoner. His horse and gun were taken from him and he was taken to a nearby hillside with some of the older Indians who were to guard him.

CHIEF GALL

Chief Gall was a Hunkpapa who was an important chief in the long war waged by the Lakotas against the US. He was a warrior in Red Cloud's campaigns, but later allied himself with Sitting Bull, eventually becoming Sitting Bull's military chief. He led the Hunkpapas in the battle of Little Big Horn.

It was said that Gall gained his unusual name when, as a starving child, he ate the gall of some animal.

After the battle of Little Big Horn, Gall and Sitting Bull fled to Canada, but they quarrelled and Gall recrossed the border in 1880.

He finally surrendered in January 1881, and spent the rest of his life trying to encourage his people to accept their fate on the reservations.

He died in December, 1894, at his home in South Dakota.

Chief Gall asked father if Miles Kellogg was with the troops. Miles was a reporter for a paper called the Bismarck Times. He often traveled with the troops to get news, and at this particular time he was riding a mule and carried his brief case at his side. Father said, "Yes, Miles is with the troops" and the Chief said he was sorry to hear this as the Indians would not like to have Miles Kellogg killed as they liked him. Chief Gall was commanding the Sioux for Sitting Bull. From the hillside, father saw the battle, which he said lasted just 55 minutes, and he saw Charlie Reynolds fall first.

Afterwards, in order that father could be prevented from making a report, he was taken, still a prisoner, to the Canadian northwest, where Sitting Bull, who was supposed at this time to be suffering from an attack of pneumonia, was with the women and children. Chief Gall, like other commanding chiefs of different tribes, was friendly towards father, although they knew he never neglected to do his duty towards the U.S. government as scout.

Many years later, I heard some Indians say how father was a good friend to the Indians yet loyal to the white man's government.

Father did not like Sitting Bull; he thought he was a coward who never came out to fight for his people but laid around in the tepees with the women and children and old men.[7]

SITTING BULL

Sitting Bull, whose Indian name was Tatanka Iyotake, was born in the Grand River region of what is now South Dakota in about 1831. He was a member of the Sioux tribe, and was hunting buffalo when he was ten years old. He joined his first war party against the Crow when he was 14.   Sitting Bull soon became known and admired for his fearlessness in battle, as well as his generosity and wisdom.

The U.S. army continually invaded the Sioux hunting territory, which caused problems with the native economy. From 1863 to 1868, the Sioux fought off the army. Finally peace was made with the U.S. government, and the Fort Laramie treaty promised the Sioux would keep the Black Hills forever.

Unfortunately gold was discovered there in the mid-1870s, which brought many prospectors. The government told the Sioux to go to the reservation, but the Sioux ignored the demand.

On 25 June, Lieutenant Colonel George Custer led his soldiers along the Little Big Horn river, and by the end of the day he and his entire army of more than 200 were dead.

Sitting Bull was held as a prisoner of war for two years before being sent to the Standing Rock Agency in North Dakota. In 1885 he joined Buffalo Bill's Wild West show.

When he returned to the reservation in 1889, many natives had joined a new religion called the Ghost Dance, so as a precaution, Indian police went to arrest Sitting Bull on 15th December 1890. When his warriors tried to rescue him, he was killed.

I once read where father was supposed to have gone down with General Custer, but it is a fact that my father lived years after that to serve the government as scout, and he died at the age of ninety-seven, not far from the town of Cody, Wyo. in the year 1914.

It is the general belief that General Custer was betrayed by his scouts; one reason for this talk might have been that the scouts Custer sent ahead two days before, returned and pleaded with him not to advance; another may have been the action of scouts such as Reynolds, for instance, who told Custer that he, Reynolds, knew nothing about the country that they were in, yet it is known that Reynolds had been through this very part of the country with an important message less than a year before.

There were three divisions, all on the banks of the river Custer was going to cross, and the men remaining separated in two divisions but did not go into the Big Horn Valley. Some of them may have heard the bitter argument that arose between Custer and the scouts that did lead him across; there was no way to learn this except through the men who were really there that morning.   There were only four companies of the 7th Cavalry who actually went into this battle

---

[7] **Professor Ione Quigley,** *Chair of Lakota Studies, Sinte Gleska University:* "The remark made about Sitting Bull would never be made by a Lakota (I speak only for the Lakota) as we view our medicine men with honor and deep respect."

with Custer; the rest were divided under different commands; I believe some were under Captain Benton, the others under Major Reno.

Some of those men lived to give their explanation of what happened that morning regarding the scout's and Custer's takeoff into the Big Horn Valley, but when it came to the actual fighting, they were so far away that they could not give accurate accounts. I have often been abused through this misunderstanding of my father's actions but never by the survivors of the 7th Cavalry. In reading, from time to time, newspaper accounts of the deaths of different survivors of the Custer massacre, every individual claimed to be the only survivor, and all told, I think there are now about forty-two only survivors to date. This might arise in the minds of people who did not know that those men were actually with the 7th Cavalry but not with Custer at the time of the battle.

It has long been thought that an Indian called "Curley" was the only survivor, but he was not, nor was he within 50 miles of the battlefield at the time of the fight. He said so himself a short time before he died, in 1931. What really happened was that he had gotten into a jam with some of the warring Indians and made his way up the River on foot and some of the troops found him wandering alone. As he spoke no English, they had no way of explaining his presence there, so it was believed that he had escaped from the battlefield as he was a government scout.

Some years ago, I became acquainted with men who were under Major Reno at the time of the battle and they were positive that my father, Charles A. Hopkins, led Custer into the Big Horn Valley. I know I am sure that he came back, although he never spoke much about that tragedy; he did admit that he was not in the fight but was taken a prisoner by the Indians and witnessed the battle.[8]

---

[8] **Gregory Michno,** *Author of Lakota Noon: the Indian narrative of Custer's Defeat (1997) and The Mystery of E Troop: Custer's Gray Horse Company at the Little Bighorn (1994) and Encyclopedia of Indian wars : western battles and skirmishes, 1850-1890:* "I sat down in my den with all my western books, armed with pen and paper, and was prepared to hunt up what I assumed would be many fine points that bordered on the truth. It only took a minute to see that I had no need of my books.... These items are so atrociously phony that they are actually amusing. Hopkins's sense of geography and time are horrid. The sequences are so befuddled and anachronistic as to be nearly impossible to sort out into the real historical order.

Rain in the Face was not young, he was over 40, he was not a chief, and he was rather flabby. The veterinarian and other person (not a boy) who were said to be killed outside the fort did not die there, at that time, or under those circumstances. Crazy Horse was an Oglala, not a Hunkpapa. Crazy Horse would have nothing to do with any white man before he surrendered in 1877, and he certainly would not be on any English speaking terms with a white scout (or a young boy as this seems to indicate that this is the younger Hopkins). Again, the 7th was never based at Laramie as Hopkins claims. Terry never told Custer to take 48 hours on a march to the Powder and attack no Indians. The final battle sequence is nonsense. Gall did not capture any white man. Mark (not Miles) Kellogg had

The winter after the massacre, many new soldiers came into the fort, all young men – some appeared to be only boys – officers West Point graduates. There was not much trouble on the plains, and all these young officers talked about was killing Indians. There were no Indians in the fort except a few government scouts. It was a long, hard winter for me as there were no Indian boys for me to play with; my father was at the fort most of the time and as there were no schools there, he taught me himself. Early that spring, he helped me to get some trees down at the river. We drew up several loads with the mules and planted the trees around the fort. There was rain that spring so most of the trees lived and as there had not been a tree or shrub of any kind there before, it was a good improvement.

Sometime early in the Summer, some of the Indian scouts came into the fort and told us that "Three Stars" was on his way coming to the fort with more soldiers. The Indians called General Crook "Three Stars." He had not been in the fort but a short time when my father and most of the soldiers including General Crook went up to the Smoky Earth (White) River. From time to time we learned at the Fort that they fought small battles; in the month of August, my father came into the Fort; I well remember this for it was my birthday and I was twelve years old then. He told us that Chief Red Cloud and Chief Spotted Tail had stopped fighting and that they had moved their people to camp near one of the soldier's towns. It must have been in Dakota. He also said that these two chiefs wanted to sell the Black Hill country to the government and that they were both cheap men and traitors to their people; the Black Hills country was valuable to the whole of the Sioux nation, and without it they could not live in peace.

After a short time at the fort, my father started out with a party of Crow scouts, and as it was fine weather I went along. I think our first camp was on Goose Creek. One morning, some of the scouts came in and told father that the soldiers were coming. We went to the lookout and saw a long line of them winding through the valley, and from the south we saw many Indian tepees; in the afternoon we heard shots fired. The soldiers must have been fighting on the other side of the hill the day before and had located the camp where the Indians had retreated.

From the lookout, we could see what looked like a big dust that seemed to be rolling in our direction. They must have fought till dark and the band of Indians moved past our camp through the night. Father saw their tepees the next morning and he went over to see them; there were only women, old men and

---

never before ridden with the 7th. Charley Reynolds was not the first one killed. Sitting Bull showed at many times in the past that he was a brave man--at the Little Big Horn, however, he was a spiritual leader and did not fight. Five companies went with Custer, not four. Curley was at the battle. General (Hugh) Scott did not recruit the 7th. He was only commissioned a lieutenant on the day after the Battle of the Little Big Horn.

This is probably enough. Hopkins is obviously a fraud."

children in the camp, the warriors being careful to stay away from there as they figured that if they left only the women, old men and children there the soldiers would not attack the camp. But the soldiers charged on the camp.

SPOTTED TAIL

Spotted Tail was a Sioux who was raised by his grandparents. From a young age he studied the white people and their habits.

Spotted Tail was the first to voice concern at permitting the white man so much freedom, and for many years he led the Brules in raids against the white men along the Oregon Trail.

When General Harney protested at these attacks on the travelers, Spotted Tail immediately announced that he was going to give himself up. In so doing, he obtained the admiration of his own people and also the trust of the U.S. Army. He was an exemplary prisoner, and took full advantage of this opportunity to study the white man's ways, and when he was returned to his tribe they made him Conquering Bear's successor.

Spotted Tail was the only Sioux who foresaw that the white man would ultimately conquer them.

When the peace treaty was signed, Spotted Tail urged his people to submit, and General Cook rewarded him by making him chief of the Sioux, thereby humiliating Red Cloud.

Perhaps not surprisingly, Spotted Tail had made enemies among his own people, and just before he was due to go to Washington for negotiations with the government, Crow Dog, Conquering Bear's nephew, shot him.

It was a pitiful sight to see the helpless, frightened children huddled up against a small knoll as the soldiers rode up and fired directly in amongst them. Some children scattered and ran for their lives – there were women and small children lying dead all along the trails. About sundown the braves returned and licked General Crook's men and drove them away – they did not fire a single shot at our camp, but they kicked up such a dust we could hardly see and we heard them hollering' hoka hoka hoka-hey (come on) as they rode after the soldiers. Sometimes an Indian voice came out of the dust "Be brave," "courage," "think of the helpless ones – they are our people – it is a good day to die".

The next morning we learned that this was Crazy Horse.[9] I do not clearly recall whether it was that year or the following, but I know that they had sent for him to come into a soldiers' town to make some agreement with him, and when he rode into the soldiers town, they told him they would take him to the General. They took him into a building instead, where they locked up prisoners and tried to lock him in; he protested that he came there to see the General, and at this, a young soldier without any warning, thrust a bayonet through Crazy Horse's body.

---

[9] **Editors' note:** Biographer Robert Easton contacted colleagues at the University of Wyoming in 1970 to share his concerns about Hopkins' manuscript, *The Last of the Buffalo Hunters*. "It indicates that Frank T. Hopkins was a great 'identifier with the great – but what else was he?'"

The following evening, after the soldier had killed Crazy Horse, I saw his father and mother taking his body away in a box placed on a pony drag; they took it down to where there was a heavy growth of timber – I do not remember the exact spot – and it is likely they buried him there. That soldier killed a great warrior who loved his people and won many battles for them; he was only a young man in his early 30s. If he had been an officer in our army, his name would have gone down in history and he would have been honored as a hero.

Most of his people died the following winter from exposure as there was much snow and very cold and they were being steadily pursued by the soldiers.

Young Black Elk and many of the Indian boys lived near Fort Laramie the following spring, and there was no fighting that summer except for a little trouble in Nebraska; Father was wounded up there and returned to Fort Laramie, but was there only a short time when he was sent out to lead a wagon train. I had been with him many times since I was ten years old, and was therefore familiar with the trails; I asked to go with him this time and we rode to the Pryor Mountains in Montana, named for Jim Pryor who died while I was still a boy.

It is said that in his early years, Pryor discovered these mountains and later had a fur-trapping line at the foot of them; he had been a scout for General Carson. This was the location of the Crow Indian Reservation. When we had pitched camp, father took his saddle horse and told the men that he would be back in a few hours. We saw him ride out from camp in a large circle as he rode over the high spots. With us were two Indians, a number of teamsters and pack mule men. I was sitting by the campfire after finishing a meal, when father returned and said, "This is just the place for the Crows." He then asked the men how well they knew the trails in the Big Horn country.

Apparently he was not satisfied with their answers, for he walked over to me and spoke in the Indian language; "A message must go back to the Shoshone Valley; I haven't a man to send – you have ridden the trails with me and know them well – I am going to send you back with it." There had been some trouble over hunting grounds between the Crows and the Sioux; the land really belonged to the Crows and the government was protecting the Crows and holding them in the valley until they could be brought to the Reservation.

Father gave me a sealed message, instructing me to deliver it to the General commanding the troops on the Shoshone River at the choke in the valley, and then return with the troops and the Indians, and that he would pick me up on his return. The camp site was at the foot of the Pryor Mountains, Montana – one hundred and sixty miles from the Crow camp where I was to go. My father gave me plenty of ammunition, but little to eat, for he knew I would get there. Although I was but a boy, I made the ride in less time than I was expected to and safely delivered the message.

I went with the officer to the council tent of the Indians; all the chiefs and head men were called into the council – they talked long. Finally, the head chief, an old man, asked me to sit in the middle of the council ring; I was questioned very carefully in the Indian language in regard to the country, and with a stick I drew a rough outline of the country on the dirt floor of the tepee. I showed them where there was rich grass to graze their stock – small streams where a pony could always drink – the prairie chickens that flew out from under the ponies' feet, and the many antelope on the slopes and the high bluffs at the north of this site; Then I told them of the scattered families of wild horses.

They wondered, and then the old chief knocked the ashes from his council pipe as a signal that council was over. He said to me "We have listened to you for you speak the word of your father – we know his word and medicine to be good and I have long known him as a friend to my people; you have rode to bring this word and the Crow will not forget; tomorrow we ride with you to see this country of which you speak."

Next day, when the sun was directly overhead (midday) camp was broken, and Indians and soldiers started on my back trail; riding a little in advance in scout style as I had seen my father do, I guided them to what is now the reservation and the tribe is there to this day. They certainly were homesick for higher ground. I was quite proud of that ride – my first duty for the government.

I returned to the fort and from then on, until the Indian troubles were over, I bore dispatches and often acted as scout; but when times were quiet on the plains I hunted wild horses or shot buffalo in the fur season for some of the big hunters.

William Madison and William Hitner, both from the state of Kansas, were old buffalo hunters who had made big profits in years gone by when the herds were large and buffalo could be shot on stands (stands: where men stood, protected by nature – buttes, etc. from the sight of the buffalo as they passed by). Now, the herds had thinned out, and it required horsemen to ride with the herds in order to shoot the buffalo from horseback as the animals moved swiftly.[10] These expe-

---

[10] **Editors' note**: Nineteenth-century buffalo hunter, Frank Mayer, disagrees with Hopkins' method of hunting. In an article entitled *The Rifles of Buffalo Days – Part 2*, published in "American Rifleman," October 1934, pp. 13-14, Mayer wrote: "There were two methods of hunting the buff. One, the stalk-and-stand method, was the professionals' way, while the other, the horse-running method, was the show-off's way. The professional meant business. He was efficient; direct. There was nothing spectacular in the way he went about things. He hunted till he had located the game, concealed himself 300 yards or more away, then cut down his buffalo: one, two three.
The show-off method was spectacular. Also it was wasteful. It consisted of finding the game, pursuing it on horseback, and firing into the herds while alongside. It was never used by professional hunters. It was too uneconomic. It was hard on horses, in the first place, and horses trained to the work were scarce and very expensive. It wasted time, in the second place, because you chased your game all over creation, and spread your kill over two or three miles of plains, so that your skinning outfit had to traipse after you. What was the sense, when you could down a hundred buffalo from a stand and keep them

rienced men, Madison and Hitner, knew that it took someone light in weight in order for the horse to keep side of the herd any length of time, so they decided to get boys who were good riders for this work.

They had heard of me being a hard rider and a good shot and I was light in weight – not much for a horse to carry, so I could ride beside the herd and carry my horse under me all day, and the Month of the Falling Leaves (October) I shot on the buffalo trails for them, on the Texas border in Indian Territory – now the state of Oklahoma. Most of the shooting was done on Cherokee Strip.

They had hired another boy to shoot – I do not remember his name – but for some reason or other he only stayed a short time. There were six skinners in the outfit, and after the other boy stopped working I tried my best to keep these six skinners going. It was only a short time before I learned more about the buffalo and then I kept all the skinners busy; this pleased the two old buffalo hunters I was working for and we got along fine.

I had a string of ten ponies for my own use – all short, chunky horses, close to the ground. Most of them had been Indian buffalo hunting horses and were pretty fast and had wonderful endurance. No one horse in the string was used more than one day a week – for it was very hard work on the little fellers. Although I was but fourteen years of age, I had a reputation with these experienced hunters of being the fastest "dropper" on the buffalo trails, riding in severe weather and standing quite a bit of hardship both on the trails and in our makeshift camps as we followed up the herd.

The choice hides for making robes and coats were taken only from the spikehorn buffalo – that is, a young buffalo, eighteen months to two or two and a half years of age; his horns at this time come straight out of his head like a spike; when he gets to his third year, the horns start to curve; that is how we were able to tell them while riding the herd – by their horns. The older buffaloes' hair might be as thick and warm, but their skins were too thick to make up for fur and the old hides would not bring as much money. Things such as this were what counted with the hide hunters. I soon learned to please them and the word spread amongst the other hide hunters that I was an expert "dropper."

I shot for these men until the buffaloes' fur started to loosen – that was in the Month of the Blinding Snow (March) and then the hunt was over for that season. They both told me that they surely would want me another season and when the buffalo hides were sold at the railroad, they paid me off with more money than I expected to get, but I did not shoot for that outfit again and I do not recall that they did any more hunting after that.

---

within an area of fifty yards? Very few buff in comparison were killed by the horse-running method – probably not more than ten per cent of the total kill," Mayer stated.

It was while shooting for Madison and Hitner that I met William F. Cody,[11] a fine looking man in the saddle; he had been a scout, and at this time was driving the wagon which hauled the buffalo hides, and whenever they had a contract to furnish buffalo meat, he also hauled the humps and hams. I have heard long since, that he was supposed to be a great buffalo hunter; he might have shot some buffalo – he did shoot a few when there was nothing to do for the team which he was driving for Hitner, when we started the herd in the morning, but after they got headed into the wind and got under full speed Cody could no longer keep up with the herd, for even in those days when he was young, he was a large man, and it would be impossible for a man of his weight to ride beside a lumbering herd and keep up with it for any length of time without wearing down his horse.

After I left the buffalo hunters, I returned to Fort Laramie.[12] General Nelson A. Miles was in command there. There didn't seem to be any trouble with the Indians, although a number of scouts were sent out from the fort from time to time. My father had orders to go with his Crow scouts up to Wood Louse Creek and I went with him. We camped at this creek a short while, and after his scouts that he had sent out in different directions came into camp, we moved up to the Greasy Grass. There was some ice in the creek and it was hard to get our horses through on account of the ice and thick mud underneath; after we had camped in the Bad Lands, Father told me that we were going up to the big reservation which I had not yet seen although I had been through that country many times before. The work of building up the reservation had been going on for some time.

We came up on the west side of the Rosebud River and we saw a valley full of tepees; there were few ponies but many people, and from the fewness of the ponies it was plain that the Sioux nation had been broken. The people represented many families of the Sioux nation. There were Blackfeet with their chiefs, Hunkpapas and their Chiefs – Gall, Sitting Bull, Crow King and Black Moon; Big Road, Chief of the Ogallalas and his people; Brules and their great men; Minneconjous and their Chiefs Fast Bull and Young Hump; Ice Bear, Dull Knife with their Shyelas; Spotted Eagle of the Sans Arcs with his people; the Yanktonais and Santees with Inkpaduta and many Blue Clouds, Sitting Bull and Gall had recently returned from Grandmother's Land (Canada).

Father spent several days talking with these people; their great men had taken off their war bonnets and untied their horses tails – a sign that they were done

---

[11] **Editors' note:** Compare the above statement with the article by Hopkins entitled "The Truth about Buffalo Bill," in which he declares that "Cody bounced me on his knee when I was a small boy."

[12] **Louise Samson**, *Curator of the Fort Laramie National Historic Site:* "There is not only no documentation, written or oral, to substantiate Hopkins' claims, the overwhelming evidence leaves no doubt that he was not born at, lived anywhere near, or ever returned to Fort Laramie.

fighting. The soldiers had taken most of their ponies from them. It looked as though there would be no more trouble with the Sioux – most of them appeared to be spirit broken, for their hunting paradise – the Black Hills – was gone and they could not live nor roam there any more.   Instead of the white man's government paying them for it as Red Cloud and Spotted Tail said it would, it just took it from them. Father sent his scouts off in small squads, giving them orders to meet him in Pine Ridge where they were building a big reservation for a part of the Sioux.

After we got to Pine Ridge, we pitched a camp at what is now known as the Town of Manderson, at the edge of the Reservation. East of what is now Manderson, lay Pepper Creek, where I remember – I am not sure whether it was two or three years before – seeing the father and mother of Crazy Horse taking his body up this Creek on a pony drag towards the heavy timber. I clearly recall that it was sundown and all of us felt badly that he had been killed. The old man rode a bay horse with white hind legs and the pony drawing the drag was a buckskin, while the old lady rode a brown mare with a baby colt running at her side.

Where they buried their son's body nobody knows, for it is a custom with Indians not to follow the old people when they bury their dead; I have heard people speak of Crazy Horse being buried over in the Bad Lands, but it is most likely that he is buried near Pepper Creek although both his parents are now dead and they never told. I do know though, that they returned shortly after dark that night with the empty drag. However, it makes little difference where his body lies – I believe his spirit lives on.[13]

The day after we camped at Manderson, my father went across the Reservation to see General Crook; that afternoon, one of his scouts came for me. I rode back to the General's headquarters; they talked inside quite a while – father and several others – finally, General Crook came out with my father and asked me to carry a message for him over to the Tongue River. It was a long ride and I knew most of the country although I had never been that far before. I got to the River and had days of hard riding to locate the group of cavalry I was to deliver

---

[13] **Editors' note:** In one of his most blatant acts of plagiary, Hopkins took the above description straight from the 1932 first edition of *Black Elk Speaks*. Compare Hopkins' version with Black Elk's: *"When it was day, Crazy Horse's father and mother brought him over to our camp in a wagon…. They fastened the box on a pony drag and went away toward the east and north. I saw the two old people going away alone with their son's body. Nobody followed them. They went all alone, and I can see them going yet. The horse that pulled the pony drag was a buckskin. Crazy Horse's father had a white-faced bay with white hind legs. His mother had a brown mare with a bay colt. …. It does not matter where his body lies, for it is grass; but where his spirit is, it will be good to be."*

the message to; they had been sent out to bring in Chief Standing Bear and his people.

I found places where they had camped and I could distinguish the camps of the cavalry from the Indians' on account of horses tracks – the cavalry horses had shoes on their feet – sometimes the tracks were mixed with the barefoot tracks of the Indian ponies which somewhat bewildered me, but I finally got the trails straightened out and followed them for some days, till one morning I rode to a high butte to look over the country and saw soldiers coming with the Indians on their back trail some miles away.

I pushed on and delivered the message about midday; my horse was wore out from many days of hard riding. They wanted me to make time ahead of them as they had to come with the Indians; I changed horses and make the trip back to bring the word that they were on their way. I bore dispatches continually that summer between General Miles and General Crook and carried a few messages for General Terry who was an old man then and his hair was very white; I remembered this General when I was a small boy, but did not see him again after that summer.

GENERAL NELSON MILES

Nelson Miles was born in 1839 in Massachusetts. After the Civil War was over, he played an important role in the army's campaign against the Plains Indians.

In 1876-77, after Custer's death, he led the campaign to force the Lakota onto reservations.

In the winter of 1877 he captured the Nez Percé Chief Joseph. This led to a life-long disagreement with General Oliver Howard, who had been pursuing Chief Joseph for 1500 miles and who considered he should have got the credit for Joseph's capture.

Miles then took over from General George Crook as commander of the Geronimo campaign in Arizona. Miles used Apache scouts to negotiate Geronimo's surrender, then exiled them, with Geronimo, to Florida. Crook never forgave Miles for betraying the troops that had served both men so loyally.

It was Miles who reacted to the "Ghost Dance" situation on the Lakota reservation by directing his troops in a way which panicked the Indians. This led both to the death of Sitting Bull and the massacre at Wounded Knee.

Miles believed that the only way to cope with the Lakota was to disarm them and put them under military control.

Miles commanded the army during the Spanish-American War, and retired in 1903. Theodore Roosevelt called him a "brave peacock," considering him vain and pompous.

Some of these rides took me into Nebraska, and as there were some of the Indians who had not come in, it was quite dangerous with them at large. Other times I went up into northern Montana, and I remember two of these rides that took me up to the line of the Canadian northwest, and that summer I also carried notes over the state of Wyoming, and both of the Dakotas.

On all of these rides I had the company of a large eagle who always soared above me in circles, and at daybreak I often heard his scream; I cannot say whether or not it was the same eagle, but whether I rode in the north or the southwest, the eagle was always there way above me, and this happened when I made my first ride from the Pryor Mountains to the Shoshone and I don't remember a long ride after that without the eagle circling above me. Even officers I carried messages for and who knew me well used to search the sky for the eagle cutting his circles when they thought it was about time for me to arrive, and it was well known in different camps and forts.

I once told my father about it and he mentioned it to an aged, toothless, Crow Chief, and one day, when I was near to where he was, the old chief called me into his tepee and explained to me in his simple way that the eagle was sent by the Great Spirit to protect me wherever I rode and that I would be guarded and never be killed while performing my duties. This might have been an Indian superstition, but once or twice I was afraid the old man was wrong, as although the eagle still accompanied me, I was very near the shadow of death on two occasions.

That fall, the government had run in a lot of range horses to the fort, to be broken for cavalry purposes. I was taking a hand in breaking them; one day, Charles J. (Buffalo) Jones, later known as the "preserver of the American Bison," came to the Fort and inquired for me. I had never seen this tall, brawny, man before; he was bronzed, square jawed, and had the keen eyes of the plainsman. A soldier brought him down to the horse corral where we were breaking some broncs, and when he got there I was sitting in the middle of a pony who was doing his level best to shake me out of the saddle. I heard Mr. Jones say, "I've never seen him, but I reckon that's him."

When I'd bucked the pony out and left the saddle, Mr. Jones strolled over and said "Well, son, you sure can take a shaking. Are you the boy they call the 'Lone Rider' who shot for Madison?" After I'd gotten my wind, I admitted I was. "Well, I'm Buffalo Jones – I hear you are well acquainted with the buffs, and I'd like to hire you to shoot for me – and I want to catch some calves, to start a herd of my own. The only buffalo at large in the southwest are at Cherokee Strip, and some are on the plains of Texas." There were two herds in the Northwest, but the species he wanted were in the southwest. "How'd you like to go with me, son?" I said I would like to talk with my mother about it. Three days later I was on my way with Buffalo Jones to what is now the state of Oklahoma; we shot buffalo for about six weeks.

One day while I was riding a distance away from the skinners (there were very few buffalo in the herd) I saw two horsemen coming towards me, one a captain of the Texas Rangers whom I'd met before. He signaled for me to stop, and I rode in his direction. He asked if I was shooting for Jones and when I told him yes, he took from his pocket a slip of paper and asked me to listen and understand him right, so long as I was doing the shooting. He said to tell Mr. Jones that the law prohibiting the shooting of buffalo in that territory and the state of Texas, would go into effect at sunrise the following morning, and from then on, I could not shoot any more buffalo. (N.B.[14] This law was lifted the following year.) After leaving the ranger, I shot just one more buffalo and then went back to the skinners.

Then Jones decided to catch some calves as the law said nothing about taking them alive. He planned to get the calves from a small band of buffalo which was in staked plains – Texas. The weather was very cold. Jones had some Mormons with him – they seemed a sullen lot of men – whom I had always thought were great plainsmen, but these were not. We had been following up old signs of buffalo for about three weeks. We had a light wagon which was drawn by four mules; our saddle horses were led behind the wagon most of the time to save them for the big chase when we came in contact with the buffalo.

The Mormons got tired of the long ride and cold weather and threatened to turn back, although Jones said they had agreed to stay with him. But they argued that they did not know he wanted to catch buffalo alive. At night, by the campfire, after a hard day's ride in rough country, he asked me how I felt about it. "Are you with me, son"? I agreed to go with him until he was ready to turn back. This seemed to please him. He said, "Well, son, in the morning you and I'll take our saddle horses and cover some of this country looking for buffalo signs." Along about noon, next day, we returned to camp with only evidence of old signs – some of them probably two months old.

As we munched dry biscuits, I gazed off into the distance and was quite sure I saw a lake. Jones, looking through his glasses, laughed at me. "No, son," he said wearily, "that is just mirage – just the lure of the plains". Although I had been taught to respect my elders and was rather shy at saying anything more, yet I couldn't help but say, "Mirages cannot fool wild fowl like duck and geese descending from the sky to that spot where I see the 'mirage'." "As sure as you're born," says he, "there are wild fowl in that direction."

I walked over to my saddle pony, mounted him and rode him back to the wagon while Jones talked with the Mormons. I said I would just ride out a ways, but if it fell dark before I returned, to keep the fire burning so I could easily locate the camp. I rode till after sunset, but as night fell I came to the lake and dismounted to let my pony drink; while I stood there in the fast gathering darkness, I heard a sound familiar to me; it was the grunt of an old bull buffalo on the far side of the small lake. I flattened my body to the ground and looked; I saw the form of a bison going up the bank on the opposite side. I had suspected if there were buffalo in that vicinity they would be around the lake.

I rode back to the camp in the cutting wind and found the old buffalo hunter patiently waiting for me beside the big camp fire. I was chilled and stiff from the cold wind and snuggled beside him near the fire, and boyishly whispered,

---

[14] **Editors' note:** "N.B." stands for the Latin, *nota bene*, which means "take note."

"How'd you like to see the buffs you've been looking for, Mr. Jones, for the last three weeks?" His big hand fell on my shoulder – "You don't mean to tell me you've found any fresh signs, do you?" "I haven't seen signs, Mr. Jones, I've seen the animal that makes them!" The old plainsman's eyes lit up – "You haven't seen buffalo!" "Yessir, and a full grown bowback."

He sat silently by the fire a while and finally spoke. "That small herd is all there is in the southwest and I must try to get some of those calves to prevent the extermination of these great animals – the monarchs of the plains. For thirty years I've tried to keep them in captivity without success. Now, my only hope is to catch young calves and trust that they will take kindly to captivity. All the grown ones I tried to keep have died from being kept inside a fence. This is my last chance. If you'll stick with me, we'll surely get some of those calves." Then we crawled into our blankets and were soon asleep.

Next morning, we faced a strong wind and moved towards the little lake. Late afternoon brought us to the water. While the Mormons pitched camp, the old buffalo hunter and I took our saddle horses and rode to the farther bank which rose about eight feet from the water level. There, in the distance, standing on the level plain, about half a mile away, we saw the buffalo clustered together, chewing their cuds, and with their heads towards the wind as I had so often seen them before. I never saw a man look so pleased as Mr. Jones when he saw them. He called my attention to the little buffs straying close under their mothers' shaggy sides, and said, "Well, they are the ones I must have." We turned our horses back down over the bank, so as not to disturb the buffalo.

Next morning, we were out at daybreak, ready for the chase. Jones gave the Mormons orders to follow us up with the wagon and to come a'humming. I rode an Indian pony – a smoky buckskin, who seemed tireless. Jones rode a Kentucky bay which he had been sparing for this chase. We had brought some soft cotton ropes for hog-tying and we had two lassos apiece hanging on our saddles. Jones had already tried me out at throwing the rope, which he was satisfied I could do better than himself.

We jogged along until we attracted the buffaloes' attention. They headed up into the wind with a swinging gait which we knew they could keep up all day. So we rolled the spurs down the ponies' sides and in half an hour's time we were riding close to the herd. About two hour's ride and the calves began to lag behind. "Now's our time," says Jones, as he whipped his lasso from the horn of his saddle. He started to beat the lasso against his leg to take out the kinks. Both of us threw the rope at the same time but at different calves.

The little heifer that Jones threw at jumped right through his loop and Jones coiled his rope again just as I leapt from my saddle to hogtie the little wooly one I'd roped around the two hind legs. Before I had done tying him, Jones yelled at me and I looked up to see a little calf tugging at the end of Jones' lasso and a vicious cow-buffalo charging straight at his horse. I gained my saddle and rode to where Jones was circling his horse to keep away from the cow and still hold his prize. I pulled the old forty-five from my belt and stopped the argument between buffalo-hunter and the vicious cow. That was the only battle we had that day with grown buffalo. When the sun set, we had nine little buffs in the long wagon.

Jones' horse had played out early in the afternoon, but I still rode on. Our horses were a sorry looking lot that evening, and Jones and I did not look as though we had been taking life easy either. Both of us got into the blankets without even eating supper. Next day, we started for the railroad with our nine calves. Jones took them to his place in Montana where he was very successful in raising them, and I believe he started quite a herd from these nine. It was through this he was called "the preserver of the American bison." He afterwards moved his herd to Arizona, where I often visited him and hunted with him along the walls of the Grand Canyon in his last years.[15]

I shot buffalo for Jones a number seasons after that in the northwest. During this first trip in the southwest, I learned a lot about buffalo and their habits. The American bison, or buffalo, is nothing more or less than the American Indians' cattle. It is hard to tell the difference in the taste of the buffalo meat and that of common beef cattle; buffaloes are hardy animals – practically immune from diseases. I have seen a few that showed symptoms of mange. When running at large, they seem to be quite timid, but when brought to bay they will put up a vicious fight. Although they look to be clumsy and sluggish, they are very quick when aroused.

There are many stories afloat about the habits of these animals. But some of these tales have no foundation. I've heard old plainsmen and Indians tell how buffalo cows bury their young calves in the sand on the edge of wallows, continuing to do this until the calves are strong enough to travel with the herd, and that the mothers go a distance of five or six miles away to graze leaving their calves buried in the sand with just enough of their noses sticking out, for air.

I have never found this to be so, for a buffalo cow is a great mother and her calf is never away from her side, and at night one of the bulls in the herd will walk all night in a circle around a cow and her small calf, the reason probably being to keep away the wolves who always follow a herd. In the calving season these circles may be seen worn deep into the ground, all over the place where the buffaloes grazed. Men who traveled the plains called them "fairy circles". The path was about a foot wide and a circle about twenty-five feet across; a single bull would wear one of these circles down to a depth of two inches in a single night. I don't know of any animal that protects its female and young more carefully than the buffalo.

---

[15] **Editors' note:** We are unable to find mention of Frank Hopkins in any of the biographies of Buffalo Jones.

The buff does not dig for food in snow and ice with his feet as is generally supposed, but roots the snow and sleet with his nose, somewhat after the fashion of a hog, and I have known buffalo to break ice in waterholes with their heads, so that they could drink. They roll, in the manner of a horse – the hump on the back doesn't seem to hinder them. When they lie down to rest, they lie with their feet down hill and nose to the windward (or up against the wind) so they can scent any danger.

The buffalo has three gaits – trotting, loping, and when he is forced to run for a long time and becomes tired, he will swing into a true pace, much like a pacing horse. In wintertime, when they have come into one massive herd, they seem quiet towards each other – even the bulls do not fight – but in the spring, after they have separated off in families, the bulls fight all the time when they are not resting or eating.

When attacked by wolves, the cows and calves form in a circle – the bulls standing shoulder to shoulder in a circle, with heads pointing out, ready for battle. I have known of wolves often attacking a herd of buffalo, but when riding to the scene of battle I have sometimes found buffalo wool lying on the ground, but never a dead or disabled buffalo – although on several occasions, I have found dead wolves.

The young calves run with their mothers until the mother has another calf. A buffalo can be very easily tamed if taken when small, and made a playful and affectionate pet. When weaned, and feeding him milk is stopped, he commences to grow shy and no matter how much of a pet he has been, never trust him after he is four or five months old, for the minute you turn your back to him, he is liable to charge. I have tamed calves since my boyhood and even had them work under a yoke like oxen, but they could not be depended on. For instance, if you have a tame buffalo and you notice him standing stock still looking at you, you had better start backing away slowly, and after you are some distance away, make a beeline for safety, as he surely is going to charge. Without any reason whatever, I have seen them do it.

Buffalo do not bellow like steer or cattle, but give short, guttural grunts, almost like pigs. When a cow moves along grazing and wants her calf to move along with her, she calls it with a low, short, heavy purr. I have heard of bellowing buffalo, but when I've seen them excited and furious in fights, I've heard them whistle through the nose like a maddened horse. On one occasion, when a bulldog held on to a buffalo bull's nose, the buffalo grunted sharp grunts which ended in a screech.

I have also heard of a single buffalo being a great leader of his herd. This may be so, but in all my days of riding with large herds, I have noticed that any buffalo running ahead of the herd is leader and they change often – one being ahead now and sometime later another is ahead, and it just appears to me that any buffalo who happens to be running ahead of the herd is the leader.

Plainsmen sometimes talk of herds migrating south; it is true that they do move on when it becomes cold weather, but when they come to suitable pasture that is between hills and bluffs to break off the severe winds and storms, they will remain there until Spring if they are not disturbed. I have also heard that the buffalo was a roaming animal – here to-day and there to-morrow, but I have not found him so. Rather, I believe he is a home-loving creature. The only reason I know why buffalo traveled in long distances, was for feed in droughts, or when they were disturbed by hunters, wolves, mountain lions, etc. If not molested by enemies, a buffalo might be born and live all his life in one valley.

The milk of the cows is similar to that of common cattle, only perhaps a little richer, and my mother often made butter from the cream of a buffalo cow that we had tamed, and this butter was delicious. The period of gestation for a cow buffalo is the same as for common cattle, and they have been successfully crossed with different breeds of cattle, the female of these cows are fertile, but the bull calves generally die at birth. This cross is known as catalo and makes delicious beef.

After I returned from hunting with Buffalo Jones, I met General Scott. The Sioux and the Cheyennes were quiet and General Scott had recruited the 7th Cavalry which was commanded by General Custer before the massacre. General Scott was to take charge down at Indian Territory, now the state of Oklahoma. He was a fine man. What was left of the 7th was a mere handful of spirit-broken men; nevertheless, he built this command up and used it to patrol the Indian territory. My first duty with this General was to guide his troops to the Territory. This was a long ride. Most of the new men were not saddle-wise and couldn't ride so many miles in one day, nor did they seem to know how to care for themselves in the open. After a few days on the march they were a sorry-looking lot and couldn't be compared with some of the women who traveled with the troops at times, in order to be near their husbands and families. The men got hip-locked, and about everything that could, seemed to happen; but I felt sorry for these side-walk raised lads and was often called upon to help.

The troops halted at the Kansas Outpost to rest, and although they were in better shape at the start again, many of them sickened when they were out on the march again. While waiting at Kansas, I stayed away from the camp most of the time – the damn men made me sick.

One morning I rode out to Haze to call on a friend of mine. As I rode, some-where on the road a white bulldog showed up and ran beside my pony; after he had run a considerable distance, I knew he intended to follow me and when I paid attention to him he looked up as if to say "I'm your dog." When we got to the Camp he immediately started in to show the other dogs that he meant to be "boss" and he licked every scrapper in that camp. He stuck close to me and I learned to like him, although he was despised by some others because he fought all the time when he was not sleeping. I called him 'King.' There were some other dogs with the outfit and every day, King made his rounds to lick any dog that showed fight. Finally, orders were given to get rid of all dogs at the next town.

Most of the way we rode in single file. I was riding a distance ahead to pick the best going, and as my pony came up a sharp grade, onto a level plain, I saw two large bull buffalo. I was surprised because there hadn't any buffalo been seen in that part of the country for some years. I rode close to them without them seeing me, and as I advanced there seemed now before me every buffalo at large in the southwest. It is quite likely they had moved down from the north being chased by hunters a year before; there might have been fifty in the herd.

I stopped my pony and gave a signal to halt the troops as I knew the old bow-backs and just what they would do. The men were in the cut – the gorge in the slope; the buffalo were headed to come down through the cut to a lower plain to water. AND BUFFALO DO NOT TURN BACK! If the animals charged, the troops had no chance of getting away as they were all in this narrow pass. As I watched the two bulls, one began to paw the ground and let out a string of grunts; the sound I knew only too well – he was the leader and was getting ready to charge. If I shot at him there would surely be a stampede.

As he lowered his shaggy head, the herd came close behind him and stood as close together as they could, ready for battle. The old leader moved slowly, with fire in his eyes. I thought for a moment that he might charge at me and that I would swing to one side and pass the herd so as to save the men who would surely be trapped if the buffalo charged into the cut. Here I was at the mouth of this cut which was about fourteen feet wide and the sides about as high, with the buffalo facing me. As he stood there, with his head lowered, I wondered would he charge if I swung past the herd or would he go straight ahead as he had evidently intended before I came in sight. I rolled the spur down my pony's shoulder in an attempt to pass the leader when he suddenly charged.

My pony did some fine side-stepping, when out from under his feet shot a white streak and the big bull came to a stand, the little bulldog locked tight to his nose. The bison, in trying to shake him clear, dropped to his knees and rubbed his great shaggy head on the ground, his horns lifted the grass sod in large chunks. He grunted with rage and the steam shot out of his nose like two snorting steam pipes, but he could not shake off King.

That little dog put up one of the gamest battles I ever witnessed. At last he jerked at the bull's nose and down fell the bull with the dog still tugging away. The big bull grunted and blowed with pain, but it was useless – he could not gain his feet. Meanwhile the troops had ridden back to level going and I knew that they were safe and that I also had a running chance, for it was sure that the herd would not move a foot while their leader did not charge.

I rode close with another look toward the troops to see if they had all left the pass and then I reached for my rifle. I had looked over this gun in many buffalo in days gone by. I must hit that buff in the right spot so that he would rise no more. The little dog did his work well by holding on and soon the buffalo was straightened out. Then King let go and came over to my pony, with his tongue hanging out and looked up at me as if to say, "Well, that job's done." When I was sure their leader was dead, I eased my pony to the rear of the herd as the animals were all headed in the direction of the pass or cut. It would be easy to stampede them past their dead leader, but to turn them, meant instant death to me and my horse.

As my pony closed in on them, I fired a few shots over them and they ran straight into the pass as I knew they had intended. When they came to level ground again they raised a cloud of yellow dust. The troops watched them until they could no longer be seen – only the dust they made. A few days later, the troops were camped near Bliss, Indian Territory, now Oklahoma. Here the General modified his orders regarding dogs and I was permitted to keep King. That little dog sure earned his reward and he had the run of the camp till he died of old age at Fort Sill.

When I was at Indian Territory, General Scott spent much of his time riding with me. When the weather was bad, he sometimes sent for me and I would stay in his quarters sharing the comforts provided for him. There was no trouble, so I had very little to do. The General had caught the hounds belonging to General Custer's pack, who had run master-less about the fort before he left north, and they were cared for and in good shape. They were fine old Virginia hounds and of good blood lines. I asked him to allow me to try them on bear and wolf; he laughed – "You can't learn an old dog new tricks – those dogs were broken on deer and fox." But he consented to let me try them.

I was pleased that he permitted me to use that pack of fine hounds. For some time the General paid little attention to either the hounds or me, so far as hunting was concerned. But one day, late in the summer, I brought a large black bearskin in off the range. The General looked it over and said "That's a fine pelt, but did you get him with the hounds? "Yes, sir, and they are as good bear dogs as anyone wants to ride after," I answered, feeling quite proud of the first bear that was taken with them. After the hounds had trailed the bear and he was shot, they learned to know what I wanted them to hunt, and in a surprisingly short time they were true on bear and wolf.

The General loved to ride the range with these hounds, not for killing, but for the sport of following them and watching them work. When they would give tongue on the trail of a bear, their oo--ooo-oo would so excite him that he would ride away from me and I would not see him for hours at a time. Many times he asked me how I taught them to hunt bear; they were broken to hunt only deer and they wouldn't look at a deer now if one jumped in front of them. I merely answered, "General, they're **bear** dogs now, aren't they?" That was all he learned about their training. I will admit that I spent many tedious hours with them though, before they got their first bear.

As I rode out often with the General, I learned to like him. He was pleasant, of good disposition and laid his commands to one side when we were together and he was just one good pal. Often, he asked me to tell him of my many rides in the northwest. Once, he said, "But you never told me a complete story of one of those long rides." I never did because I never told anyone. I was sorry when I was again sent for by government orders and I think this General was too. As I rode out of the garrison he waved and waved until I was out so far I could no longer see him. He was sent to Washington a few years after that and I believe he holds some kind of office there.

Then I went to join my father with the scouts in New Mexico and was sent to various posts with dispatches. There was some trouble amongst the Apaches at this time. While on a long ride over into Arizona, I met a notorious outlaw.

I was riding through forbidden country with a dispatch – it was very dangerous and day riding was out of the question. One morning, when I stopped to hobble my horse out for the day, I saw the freshly made tracks of a shod horse – and at a glance I knew it was not an Indian riding ahead. It occurred to me that it might be a scout though, or someone connected with the army, and I spurred my horse on. In a short while I came up to the rider ahead.

He turned on me with gun in hand, but I kept riding up to him just the same.

"Gad," he said, "I near shot at you. You're the lad they call 'the lone rider,' I reckon, ain't you?"

"Well, I'm the man who rides with you now," I smilingly answered.

"Well, I've heard a lot of you, although I never met you before, so I know you well enough. I'm Billy the Kid. The army men run me out here and it looks kinda bad in this Apache country. How'd you get by all these years 'n not get killed?"

I laughed – "Just watch my bronco's ears!"

"There's something in that", he chuckled.

"Now, Billy, if you want to hang out with me, we'll have to get under cover pronto – here's the sun and we're riding in dangerous country alright – a little too much for the cavalry man to follow you."

"Well, I've heard you're on the square," said Billy. "Now, are you to be trusted if I camp with you?"

His eyes searched mine as I questioned, "Never heard of me turning coward, did you? You're as well armed as I am – besides, it would mean death probably for both of us if only one of us fired a shot in this country, with Apache scouts lurking around; I ain't got anything against you, Billy, and I guess you don't want to kill me for this nag or anything else I've got with me."

"Let's have your hand then – you're all that I've heard of you and we'll fight together if it comes to the Apache running after us," says Billy.

"I'm with you, Billy."

After a while, Billy laughed, and said, "So you can shoot like Hell and ride a dead horse in front of a prairie fire, I've been told." I barely listened – my eyes were riveted on something in the distance.

Billy asked, "What's that?"

"Indian smoke signs – they've seen something and are warning the main camp. Come along, Billy, we must hide for the day."

I led the way into the roughest spot in sight, where nobody would be likely to ride – a good ways from any trails and well protected by heavy shrubbery.

"Now, Billy, here's where the horses get hobbled to graze." (Horses are hobbled with straps around each ankle and a swivel chain between, so that they cannot travel far, yet they can graze and rest – a horse that has been ridden hard will not try to travel off good pasture.) "You and I will go a distance away; if anyone notices the horses, he will look for riders nearby. One of us can watch while the other rests."

Billy was the most wanted man in the west and had a price on his head, but in him I found a friend, the same as I did in other outlaws I'd met this way. He said, "You look pretty haggard and worn out, feller. Lay down and rest yourself first, and I'll stay on the lookout for the first trick." There was no doubt in my mind of him. The last words I recall him saying were, "You know these red folks, all right – camping away from the horses is clean stuff." I said, "Call me in an hour or so, Pard" and then my eyes closed, heavy with sleep.

But the sun had already set when I awoke. "Billy, why did you let me sleep so long and you got none?" All he said was, "You look fine now – it was rest you needed bad. I wouldn't wake you – there was no danger."

We went over to our horses and soon had them loping along in the direction of Arizona. Being familiar with the country, I knew there was only one place where we could find water on this trail, so I told Billy, "There is only one drink on the trail from here to the army camp, and if the horses don't drink, neither of us had better touch it."

"Why?"

"Indians passing this way, would poison the water."

"I learned something from you, Pard, in a short time," says Billy. "Can a horse know the water is poisoned, but a man come along and drink and die of poison? That's queer. How does the horse know it?"

"The only reason I can give, Billy, is the horse's sense of smell, but he knows."

"H'm, now I see why all plains men think so much of their horses."

No need to tell me he was not a native of the hills and rolling plains – he knew little – almost nothing in the way of caring for himself in the open. As we rode in the night toward the water hole, our ponies just jogging along and he talked freely; he said he was born in New York City and come to the southwest when only a kid and they still call him "kid." I said, "Those gambling shacks in the towns of this country here spoiled many a young man," and he answered, "You guessed right, I got in bad through them and I'm in too deep now to get out."

My horse showed signs of more speed and I drew rein. "We're near a water hole; see how the horses have brightened up? – They smell water." "That's it," came Billy's voice through the darkness from the rear. Soon my horse came to a stand – the water hole at his feet. I slid to the ground and gave him free rein. He shoved his head into the water up to his eyes.

"Water's all right, Billy – get down, this is the only drink on the ride." I dipped water from the hole with my hat and threw it over my dusty bronco and also washed myself. Billy remarked how fresh he felt after splashing water over his face. We filled our saddle bottles (canteens) with nice cool water, and left, both men and horses refreshed and ready to go on again.

After a while the sky before us showed long streaks of the first sign of the day before us. We rode on in silence as the trail was rough and single file was our safest way to ride. When we came to the parting of the trail, the sun had climbed the California peaks that looked near but were miles away. The army camp lay some twenty miles to the east. I drew rein.

"Now, Billy, you take this trail; it will take you to not many miles from the Mexican Line and they don't know you there." I gave him the dried meat and the solid army biscuits that were left in my saddle bags (biscuits I often used to knock down mules with!) "Tell no one you met me, and I'll do the same about you. Take care of yourself."

I watched him out of sight and that was the last I heard of him for some time. I never did learn his real name and never expected to see him again, but I'll have more to say of him later.[16]

I delivered the message in Arizona and carried back the return message to New Mexico; after that, most of the scouts had been discharged in New Mexico and very few soldiers remained in the army camp, so there was nothing left for me to do. I returned with some of the troops to Fort Lincoln, Nebraska; then I spent a short time with a wild horse hunter, running horses into a horse trap, while waiting until the bison season opened.

When it did, I joined Dick Rock's outfit. The buffalo runs lay up at Timber Creek, northern Montana. Although the buffalo had been growing scarce, this

---

[16]**Marcelle Brothers,** *Member of the Billy the Kid Historic Preservation Society and the Western Outlaw and Lawman Association:* "There is no truth to Mr. Hopkins' statement about meeting Billy the Kid. Hopkins isn't the only person to falsely tie himself to Billy the Kid. Due to Billy's fame and popularity I think everyone who was a person of interest, whether that be another outlaw, lawman, politician, cowboy, long distance rider, etc, said he met, rode with or had dinner with Billy the Kid. Some even went one step further and said they <u>were</u> Billy the Kid."

www.horsetravelbooks.com

was a large herd – most of them probably had come down from the Canadian Northwest; it didn't appear as though this herd had been hunted before, because the very sight of a man on horseback stampeded them. When riding up close to them, the bulls would turn and charge.

I rode with this herd about three weeks before I could head them up to the wind; they would form in a large circle for battle, but when a few shots were fired amongst them, they'd stampede and it was hard to drop many of them for skinners for the first two or three hours in the morning; at the time, I was discouraged, but the men I was shooting for had many years' experience and they knew the herd wouldn't keep this up for long. Every evening when I came in off the run they encouraged me to go on, that I was doing well under such circumstances.

There were times when going near the herd meant being charged on; a number of hunters followed this same herd and the following spring I learned many of them quit on account of the herd being so wild. Not only were the bulls vicious, but the cows would charge at a pony at any time when you were riding side of the herd.

I recall one morning in particular, I rode out to start the herd that had been standing chewing their cud. As I drew near the herd, the buffs charged at me and I was obliged to jump my pony across a wash; in doing this, the pony lost his footing and went down on the opposite side of the bank with the herd stampeding close behind us. When the pony struck the ground, I rolled out of the saddle into the wash which might have been about six foot deep. I crawled up under the roots of some scrub pine on the side of the wash and watched the flying feet as they leapt across the span and felt I was very lucky that the bank didn't cave in from the heft of those heavy animals. It might have, but for the roots of the scrub pines acting as a reinforcing in the ground.

After I was sure the herd passed, I crawled out onto level ground, saw the herd loping away with my brave little saddle horse leading them – he was trying to work to the outside, so they would pass him. Then I heard shots fired down near the head of the herd; the skinners had come out to follow up and they were trapped in front of the herd between two large washes which were impossible for their horses to jump.

Although I was fortunate in escaping injury, four of the skinners meeting the herd head on were killed, their bodies so mutilated by the hoofs that they could not be properly identified. Those skinners who did escape, jumped their horses down into the deep washes, killing the horses from the jump and the men were seriously injured; there were plenty of broken limbs and ribs. Dick Rock and Zeth Smith somehow had not left the camp.

There was no buffalo hunting that day and none for several days thereafter. We had to take out bodies and injured men; we cared for the injured the best we could at the camp, till out our three hide wagons came in; they had been sent out a few days before to deliver hides. Then it was necessary for Rock to hire a new outfit of skinners and that was not an easy job because skinning was a trade by itself and good skinners were scarce, especially when you had to travel so far away to find them. I think Dick Rock and Zeth Smith got most of these men from Nebraska.

Meanwhile, I was left at the camp alone to care for the string of saddle horses in the corral. It was mighty lonely for me as they were gone away many days and the weather was bitter cold; I hugged the camp fire at night while the coyotes sung and yelped all night.

When the men returned, Rock brought me two new rifles, the latest models at that time of Springfield make – somewhat heavier than the guns I'd always used. I practiced with them by shooting at targets on a tree to get used to them and found that I could operate them and shoot faster than I could with the old single cartridge rifle that I'd been using[17].

We then moved camp, up here where the herd was. As the country was rough, it took a few days of travel. With this herd causing us so much trouble, it was surmised by the other hunters in camp that I had declared war on them. The first morning I rode out to start them I had made up my mind to shoot any old bull who turned to look at me whether his hide was worth a nickel or not. By the language used in camp by the skinners when I returned that night, I knew I dropped more old bulls with thick hides than I did buffalo with skins of commercial value. Rock told his skinners. however, that this would not continue as I was really a first-class dropper, but I had to shoot my way into that herd through this ring of old bulls who had been standing me off for over a month; he said this herd was the toughest bunch that he'd seen. Although I couldn't see the difference, he explained to the skinners that these were timber buffalo. The men skinned by piecework – that is, they got so much pay for every buffalo they skinned.

A few days of shooting off the vicious old bulls and I was able to keep the skinners busy taking the hides from spikehorns. The price of the thick hides from the old bulls at that time was only bringing about a dollar and a quarter, while the prime hides of the spike horns had been jumped up to sixteen dollars a pelt. In a few days the tired skinners came into camp at night smiling and appeared to be good-natured. I often heard Rock say, "Didn't I tell you boys that you had the best dropper ahead of you that ever shot on a buffalo trail?" They agreed with him.

We took a heavy toll from this herd and there were few other hunting parties left in the northern Montana except ours – the vicious herd split in different divisions and ran the hunters out of the country. Our outfit was not the only one

---

[17] **Editors' note**: Hopkins was wrong. At that time Springfield only made single-shot rifles.

that had lost men – there was an outfit about twenty miles from our camp when we started to hunt that season. We learned, when we came in, in the spring, that it had been wiped out to the last man, and that a large number of Indians who had come up there to take skins and meat from this herd had been trodden to death by the vicious brutes that winter.

By spring, we had wiped out the herd with the exception of the strays who had left the herd from time to time, and the report came in the middle of summer that there were only about a hundred and fifty buffalo left in that great herd. They surely were the most vicious herd I've ever shot over, but their hides were the best I'd ever seen. After we broke camp and our hides were loaded on the railroad, all of us went into Cody, Wyo. to spend a few days there.[18] Then we bid one another goodbye, separating in different directions after we had all agreed to meet on some good buffalo pasture the following season.

After this bison hunt, I went home, glad of the chance to be with my folks, as I had seen very little of them since I was thirteen years old.

My father was off the trails and had started to raise horses on the range from a herd of wild stock that he had been accumulating for two or three years. He had bought some well-bred Kentucky stallions and turned them out with the wild mares, and in this way the tame stallions would keep the wild mares from roaming too far off the range that they had been turned out on. Father and I spent a few weeks riding to keep away the wolves and mountain lions during the foaling season. As the baby colt cannot see for twelve days after it is born,[19] it is easy prey for those prowlers of the plains, who are more apt to attack at night. When the young colts were strong and old enough to travel and outrun their mothers, there was nothing more for us to do.

There was no more trouble with the Indians in that part of Wyoming and there were a few friendly Indians who lived without being molested by the army – most of these Indians knew my father – some of them had been in his scouting party in years gone by – and when they saw the horses ranging out too far they often turned them back.

My father had visited the Lakota Indians who lived in the high range, and told them that these horses were his herd, so that the Indians would protect them. There was danger of the white horse thieves running off with these horses, but the Indians would never run off horses unless they needed them for saddle horses in battle. Before leaving the Indians' main camp, we talked with their aged chief, who asked my father into his council tent; this chief, thinking father could not

---

[18] **Dr. Juti Winchester**, *Curator of the Buffalo Bill Museum at the Buffalo Bill Historical Center*: "It is not possible that Hopkins and his friends could have visited Cody, Wyoming in 1879, because there was no Euro-American settlement here until the town was founded in 1896."

[19] **Editors' note:** As all horsemen know, horses can see perfectly well from the moment they are born.

speak the Indian language, said, "My people watchem hoss day, watchem night; white man stealem hoss, Injun run em white man with gun." This old chief was surprised to hear my father answer him in his own language; then it was thoroughly understood that the Chief intended to have his people care for the horses and not permit anyone to disturb or take them.

The horses taken care of, I went with my father up to Fort Custer, where he reported for scout duty. He went over to the Rosebud Reservation for a while and then he was sent down to the Mexican border. He wasn't there very long before he sent a letter to Fort Lincoln, Nebraska, saying that they might need me on the border and that I'd better come down as soon as possible. I went down there and was soon carrying messages again.

Here I was amongst strange people and I soon found that the Apaches were totally unlike the tribes of Sioux, Cheyennes, Crow, Blackfoot and Cherokee that I had come in contact with in the Northwest. Although I had been down here before, I could speak very little Apache and all the time I was amongst them I could not find a name for all these people and I don't know if they had a tribal name; there were families of Tonto, Mohave, Chiricahua, Warm Springs, White Mountain, Navaho, but the name APACHE as they were called by the Mexicans is not an Indian name and not the name of their people. These Indians felt insulted when they were called "Apache" and resented it – as near as I could come to it, the word means "bone smasher" and was given to them by Mexicans.

There were families of these people under different chiefs; I have heard them called Yumas. The men were of small stature, most of them, and especially the women. Treachery and thievery were practiced by these people, and some of them were traitors to their own families. I never knew of any thieves amongst the Northern Indians, but the "Apache" did not think anything of raiding a Mexican range and killing the people on it for the sake of robbing them. After such a raid, they would move across the line into the United States, Arizona or New Mexico.

Sometimes they would be at war in one town in Old Mexico and friendly in another. After they had returned to the United States and lived around the reservations for a while, they would raid American ranges, kill the people and ride far into the mountains of Old Mexico. In fairness to them it might be said that they were not known to steal anything while they were around the reservations, and there were comparatively few instances where they were not loyal to the U.S. army when they were employed as scouts. The scouts used by the army in the southwest during the troubles were Apaches, except the leaders, who were white men.

I was once told that a band of these scouts under an officer of the U.S. army, went into the mountains of Old Mexico to route out a hostile band, and they all turned on this officer and deliberately killed him.

One instance where such a scout turned on his own family is that of a short, squat, scout known as "Dutchy" because of his features; he had been loyal to the army until the end of the Apache troubles and was thought a great deal of by his superior officers; He was once called into the army camp and told that if his father who had committed a crime of some kind did not surrender to the soldiers, it would mean trouble for the whole band of their people.

Immediately after talking with the officer, "Dutchy" left the camp; three days later he returned with a bag hanging over his shoulder and when he dumped the bag, out fell the head of his own father. I did not get this story second hand. It was told to me by an officer of the 6th Cavalry who saw Dutchy dump the head out of the bag.

Their treachery was shown in the killing of Captain Hentig and his men in August, 1881. This captain attempted to arrest an Apache medicine man named Noch-a-del-klinne. He and his men were killed by the Apaches, and the hostiles then turned on the scouts who were with Lieutenant Cruse, and killed most of these scouts who were their own blood relations!

Just a month from that day, the Chief of Police Sterlen at Camp Goodwin, a sub-agency, was killed in attempting to arrest an Indian. Immediately, three hundred Apache left the Agency and made their way into the mountains of Old Mexico. These Indians were under the leadership of Juh and Geronimo. These are the only instances that I recall where the Apache did not remain loyal when acting as scouts or when they were on the reservation.

Although I learned from early childhood to speak the language of the Indians, and could speak it as clearly as they could themselves, yet I could not seem to understand nor speak the Apache, which as so different. The people were not like the Indians of the northwest either. They seemed tricky and a filthy lot and of a very cruel nature. But in spite of these traits I noticed some good points about them and some whose confidence I gained remained lasting friends. I do not believe this race of people belonged to the plains Indians as they resembled Esquimos more than Plains Indians. Through what I could learn, they claimed that hundreds of years ago they came down from the north into Arizona and Old Mexico (even at this late day the true Apache dog resembles the sled dog of the far north).

But the army was helpless without the aid of these scouts who knew the habits and haunts of their people and seemed ever ready to betray them to the white man's government. I spoke about this once to an old White Mountain chief, and he told me the reason for this was his people had been at war for many, many years with the Mexicans and also with the American soldiers, and his people had become tired of warfare and wanted peace, but some of their chiefs still urged their people on to fight and carry on raids as they had done before, and those who had become scouts for the U.S. army were the ones who were tired of this warfare and would therefore do anything to break the spirit of those who still held out. This probably explains why they were so treacherous toward each other.

Most of the army officers down there were young men and strangers to me, and following this trouble at Camp Goodwin they were very bitter. Not knowing that I was the son of the secret service scout who had been sent into the mountains of Old Mexico amongst the hostile tribes who had left the United States, I was probably looked upon by them as just another treacherous Apache hanging around the army camps to be fed by the government. It is true that I was of Indian blood, but far from being related to any Apache.

One morning, I went to the horse corrals to saddle up my pony. I had come into the camp through the night; a young officer at the corral told me to let the horses alone and ordered me out of the corral. I told him that this pony belonged to me and that I had put him into the corral the night before and proceeded to saddle my horse. The officer walked over and pushed me away from the horse and talked roughly to me in English, referring to me being only another hang-around the camp, etc. and as I started to lead my horse out, this young officer struck at me; immediately the horse corral became a fighting ring.

I didn't take time to explain to this officer that I had been trained to box by the soldiers at Fort Laramie who put the gloves on me when I was only eight years old and stood me on a large bench so that I would be tall enough for my lessons which they continued daily until I was well able to defend myself. I had boxed in the army camps where I bore dispatches in the north. I was now over 16 years old and as lithe and wiry as the bronco that I rode.

Although this officer was much older and larger it did not take him long to decide he had undertaken something that he could not finish. One of his eyes was closed and he was severely cut about the face. Of course for this act I was made a prisoner. When I was locked up, some of the officers, hearing me speak English, became suspicious, and I told them I carried dispatches from the scouting parties to army camps and had stopped here to feed my horse and rest for the night and that I also had a dispatch on my person to deliver to Captain Emmet Crawford who was some seventy odd miles north of this camp.

I refused to show it to them, however, and they must have informed General Miles, for in a short while he came to see me. They were surprised to hear him address me familiarly as "little general," a nickname I'd gotten in the Fort where I was raised and made much of as I was at that time the only child there and well liked by the soldiers. The General asked the injured officer who had fought with me what the charge was against me. This officer surely bore the evidence. I had nothing to say and the General said that it was impossible to hold me as I was a bearer of dispatch and had carried many notes for him in the northwest and I was permitted to take my horse and continue my ride. From that day on, to the end of the Apache troubles in 1886, I was well-known amongst the officers, and not as the "little general" but as the "lone rider."

Some of my long rides took me into the Senora Mountains of Old Mexico and others into Arizona. On one of these rides, in territory that is now the State of New Mexico, I was riding with a division of the 6th Cavalry, for the purpose of carrying messages back from the moving troops to the commanding officer.

On one of these rides back, I stopped to rest for the night and hobbled my weary bronco. While looking for a place for myself to rest, I happened to step out into an open spot where there was no sagebrush, only Arizona sand brightly lighted by a full moon, and crossing the middle of that patch of moonlight, I met a fast traveling piece of lead which smashed into my left hip; down I went, not daring to move an eyelash. Soon a large shadow came from the 'skeet brush, and in less than a second there passed through my brain the thought of my mother way up in Wyoming, my father somewhere in the hills of this big West riding for the government, and I wondered whether I ought to take a chance and kill the man who held the rifle that wounded me.

Evidently, the big warrior was sure he had killed his man and shortly would have the scalp of the "lone rider" to show his Chief; crouching low, he came on like a soft-footed panther. My finger stiffened on the trigger of the old gun that once belonged to that well-known gunman, Bill Hickok, who gave it to me when I was but a lad. Once again, the old side-action spoke, and on the sand, in the silvery moonlight, lay silent one of my mother's race – a brave man. I recognized him as Sun Cloud, the pride of his tribe as a scout for many years in the northwest, who, on account of his work, was wanted by the white man's government there. So he had gone down and joined some of the Apache tribes and probably was acting as scout for them.

Although I was in great pain and the blood was flowing freely, and I kept getting weak, I was sorry I had killed him. To get to my horse was my only hope. After several rather painful efforts, I finally managed to get into the saddle. The army camp lay off to the south; about thirty miles of rough going. It was some time before my bronco brought his unconscious rider into view of the General's command. When I came out of the stupor as the men worked over me, the first thing I asked was, "Did the General get the note?" "What note are you speaking of?" asked a doctor. I demanded my riding shirt – it was brought to me, and the dispatch was in it.

I was in much pain at the time, but I insisted upon seeing the General as I must place it in his hand. He came, and it was General Miles. "What can I do for you Frank?"

"Nothing, General – here is your answer from General Lawton." I don't remember any more, but I know my stay with the General was extended for a long time. The government did not give its men a bit of gun metal to pin on their chests for doing their duty in those days; you were expected to do it – that was what it had you there for. After I came in from one of those long rides there was no story told of the trip, nor could I be enticed to talk of previous ones; I do not care to praise myself by writing some of the facts that happened in my days on the frontier – they will go with me when I have joined those I rode with and who know them.

One morning, while I was lying around the camp in the sun, crippled from being shot by Sun Cloud, I noticed four men coming in on horseback. As they lit to the ground, one of them asked for me, and I called out, "Over here, Pard." As they came toward me, I recognized the man who asked for me, but I dared not call him by name for he was one of the most hunted men in the southwest, and in this garrison, he could be made a prisoner at the bat of an eye.

He was none other than Billy the Kid, whom I had left at the parting of the trail down in the Siwash country after riding and camping on the trails the year before. He said, "I heard you were in bad, so I made my way into the barrens (Barren lands) with a drive of beeves." I talked with him for a while and then cautioned him to get going and keep going, for there were pictures of him about and some of the officers might look at him a little too sharp.

That was the last I saw of him – but I did hear that he was shot and killed – maybe a year or so later, by someone who did it for the reward money. I have known many of these so-called "bad" men. In them I have often found more loyalty than I can say for many so-called first-class citizens who are called "gentlemen" for whom I have another name when they put one over on you in a crooked way; and then excuse themselves by calling it a "business deal" and say, "Oh, well, that's business."

Now, there were still two large herds of buffalo in the northwest – one split herd grazing on both sides of the Yellowstone, and one herd on the Cannon Ball and Moreau River, Dakota. The following winter I shot with Dick Rock from Henry's Lake, Idaho, (who was afterwards killed by a pet buffalo that he had on his range there) Zeth Smith and King Stanley. Jones did not come out on the range that winter: he just looked after the hides at the railroad. Dick Rock was the hardest worker I had met on the Bison trails – he could skin a "buff" as quick as two men. In camp he was never idle – a fine man in every way. He had been at the bison game for years and knew the animals, he thought, as well as anyone could, yet he was killed by a tame bison that he had reared from the time it was born.

Hides at this time had risen in value and there were many hide hunters on the winter pasture grounds that year. That season, our run was alongside the Yellowstone and there were about ten thousand in this herd. The cold weather, high winds and snow up to their briskets, helped make the bison cross. By fighting and swerving my pony, I managed to keep the skinners busy. The country along here being very rough for hard riding, there was always the danger of your horse taking a tumble while riding side of a bison run, and when your horse took such a tumble, you might as well think of the old folks at home, close your eyes and drift off to whatever heaven is waiting for bison hunters.

At such a time a good horse is appreciated. For this work, I always kept a string of ponies born and raised in the roughest country so they learned to be sure-footed. I don't believe there is a horse living who can compare with the American Indian pony and I have rode every known breed of horse from the high-strung Arab to the little wild horse of Asia. The "cow-pony" bears the blood of the Indian pony, or as we call him "mustang" (supposed to be Indian word for horse, but in reality it is not – there is no such word as horse in the Indian language. When an Indian refers to a horse he says "mush-or-au-tank" – meaning the power of many dogs.)

I have ridden these ponies all my life and have had a cow-pony that would handle a steer three times his weight at the end of a lasso. He is a sure-footed little animal and has wonderful endurance. He can be taught in fifteen minutes more than a well-bred horse would learn in his whole life. Right here I recall one little buckskin in particular. I got him wild, when he was about three years old, and he was the hardest pony to break that I ever met, but I treated him kindly and broke him and he surely was a one man's horse. He wouldn't allow a stranger to pick up his rein if I left him standing somewhere. He never did get right tame.

This little feller weighed about seven hundred pounds and I could ride him three days a week on the buffalo runs – pretty severe work on a horse that you had to keep on a steady lope all day. I once rode him ninety miles from sunrise to sunset in the month of September, and I also rode him from Galveston, Texas,[20] to Rutland, Vermont,[21] in a cross country race and we came in fourteen days, four hours ahead of the other riders, and that little feller was heavier when we got to Rutland, Vt., than when we started. I pensioned him off on the CH Ranch, Wyoming, and I honestly believe that he was the greatest piece of horse-flesh that ever lived.

This same winter that I shot on the Yellowstone, I saw a freak-color buffalo; he was a dark red roan and I had never seen one before. He was a spikehorn, about a year and a half old, and I was riding along keeping my eye on him so that when the time came I could drop him. The buffalo herd had split the day before, part going around a big hill on to a level plain, while those that I rode side of kept straight down about two miles from the river.

While I was watching this roan buffalo, I did not take notice when the other part of the herd that cut away from us the day before were closing in on me,

---

[20] **Casey Greene,** *Head of Special Collections, Rosenberg Library, Galveston, Texas:* "We've referenced every newspaper between 1880 and 1890 but there is absolutely no mention of Frank Hopkins or a race from Galveston to Vermont."

[21] **James Davidson,** *Vermont Historical Society:* "There is nothing in the local news-papers around that time about a race ending here in Rutland. At that time everything was reported on, even somebody going to New York for the weekend, so it is inconceivable that such an interesting event would have gone unnoticed. The only endurance Hopkins ever did was with his pencil."

although I did notice something strange about my pony – most likely he had seen them. So the first thing I knew I was in the middle of the large herd as they had come together from behind. There seemed no way for me to escape, my only chance seemed to ride the pony and try to keep ahead.

My pony had been on a lope six hours then, and was no longer fresh, and the buffalo soon closed in on me. As they tightened up, one of them must have struck my pony with his shoulder and the little feller (pony) fell. But before he struck the ground I grabbed both hands full of shaggy wool on a buffalo's shoulder and landed high up on his hump, and by hanging on to the wool on the buffalo's shoulders I managed to stay with him.

I rode many a wild horse in my time but that surely was the wildest ride that I ever expect to take, and I stayed on that buffalo it seemed for an hour as the herd stampeded on for miles. As they came into very rough country the buffalo scattered on account of the hard going and the one who carried me on his back worked to the outside of the herd. Maybe it was the fright of my being on his back that wore him down, for he slowed down to a walk and as I saw no other buffalo was within quite a distance from me, I slid to the ground and made my way to the edge of the river.[22]

Late that night I made my way into camp. The skinners came up to the last buffalo that I had dropped and not finding any more down, were sure something had happened to me. They all spread out on horseback to cover the buffalo trail, but when they came to my little saddle horse trampled to death, they became alarmed and searched the plains until dark, when, not finding any trace of me, they decided to wait till daylight. They were sure that I had fared the same as the pony, but could not understand why they did not find my body. When I oozed into camp they were the most surprised looking lot of men I ever saw. This was one time when I came in off the buffalo run without any of the skinners calling me down about how I had dropped buffalo that day, and I will admit that was once in my long experience that I was surely scared.

A few days later, the skinners came into camp one night and reported that the hair had started to loosen on the buffaloes' hides and the hunt was called off for that season. I returned home, and was not there very long before I was hired by a horse hunter who was catching wild horses to ship to dealers in the East. There

---

[22] **Editors' note:** Riding buffalo appears to have been a popular pastime in the Old West! Buffalo Bill Cody's publicist, Major John Burke, told a New York Times reporter in 1897 that when his horse broke a leg, the resourceful major jumped onto a passing buffalo to escape a prairie fire. Then in 1928 an Indian imposter known as "Chief Buffalo Child Long Lance," took up the buffalo riding story, claiming he witnessed his childhood Indian friend race away from the hunting grounds on a bull buffalo. It hardly seems surprising, therefore, that Frank Hopkins incorporated this thrilling tale into his own personal mythology a few years later.

seemed to be a large demand for small horses; we went up to the Red Desert, Wyoming and built a large horse trap.

This trap was the first one I had seen built out of wire. He had hired a number of first-class cowboys for this work and it took all of us very near a month to complete the trap as it was a large one – more than a mile across the mouth. Then we split up into different squads and covered the country searching the wild herds.

Our party jumped a herd about ten miles from the trap. They were headed in the opposite direction from which we wanted them to go. A few days of hard riding and we turned them towards the trap. Some of the other boys had noticed us coming and took their stands so as to help us as we came along. By this time the wild horses were getting tired as we didn't give them much chance to rest. We got most of that herd in the trap with the exception of a few old mares who had been hunted before.

It gave me a sick feeling in the pit of my stomach to see those beautiful young animals run against the barbed wire of the trap. They never were in an enclosure before and knew nothing about a fence; some of them would run up against it and break their necks and others were badly cut up. After we had the first herd, the others were not so wild.

I always admired the gameness of the leaders of these wild herds. They showed such intelligence in trying to free their herds. I recall particularly one such leader or "King" horse; he was an old horse, and evidently he must have led his herd for years. We had moved about sixty miles north of our main horse trap, following up signs of this large herd, and finally we located it and also the spring where they came to drink. We pitched camp and sent a rider back to our boss. Mr. Conklin, to tell him we had located the large herd – there were between five and seven thousand horses.

A week later, when he moved up with the teams, a lot of us cowboys protested violently about using barbed wire and Conklin explained that we wouldn't lose many horses through catching them that way. The next day he gave orders to string out the fence. I argued with him about using the wire with barbs and told him if he used straight wire without the barbs it might be all right and some of us tried to make him change his mind about it. When he saw that we were serious about this method of tearing up horses (I went so far as to tell him I'd ride out to the nearest town and send a telegraph message to Cheyenne reporting him for this crude use of barbed wire for this purpose) he decided he'd do differently. We started by fencing off the canyon with small trees above the spring where the herd went to drink. Of course, that left the entrance to the canyon without any fence so that the horses would run in there.

When we had the fence completed, our whole outfit spread out over the country, keeping a good distance away from the horses – maybe five miles or so, to keep off our scent. Some men were sent out behind the herd to start them towards the canyon; as the horses came along the men on either side closed in to tighten up the herd. This old lead horse that I speak of, noticed the men closing in on both sides, tried his best several times to crash through the line of riders. Finally, he gave this up and headed straight for the canyon as he knew a few miles beyond the spring the canyon opened out on a level plain and he was sure of leading his herd to freedom.

After the herd had all passed into the canyon, we started building the fence to close them in. When this leader passed their watering hole and found a strong fence ten feet high confronting him, he turned and came back. Some of the boys were dragging small trees with their ponies by hitching the lasso to the butt of the tree and the other end hitched to the saddle horn. Some of them were cutting down trees a distance away from where we were building the fence – the boss and remainder of the men were building the fence. The old king horse saw he was trapped; he showed no fear of the men but came at sudden and full speed and fought his way through. Beside him ran a lovely buckskin mare; we all jumped on our ponies shouting at the tops of our voices and managed to stop the herd from coming through.

It would have been sure death for any rider had he tried to halt the leader. As he came on through the group of men, he stood on his hind legs and struck out with his forward feet and no one was prepared at the time. Of course he could have been lassoed had any of us had our lariats free to do that with, but it was so sudden a turn that we were not prepared for it. I noticed as he passed by that his neck and shoulders were covered with healed up scars and both his ears looked like the cauliflower ears of a prize fighter; this looked like evidence of hard battles he must have had with other horses. We turned the herd back in to the canyon and completed the fence.

That night, in camp, we heard this game old lead horse calling to his herd. It is quite likely he tried to break down the fence, for the next morning there were tracks around it. The following day we saw him standing high up on a cliff, looking down into the canyon, the buckskin mare beside him. To me it was a beautiful picture as he stood guard above his herd, the wind blowing his long, thick, wavy mane and tail. He did not give up the battle in trying to get his herd. For more than a week, he stood guard on the cliff at day and at night tested the fence with his hoofs and we heard him many times throughout the night calling to them. Finally, the boss took a notion to try and catch this king horse.

Some of the men were left on horseback, riding amongst the wild horses inside the enclosure. This was done so that the horses would get used to men on horseback and so that it would be easier to drive the horses out to where they were to be shipped. The boss selected some of the best riders to catch the leader, and saw that they were mounted on the strongest saddle horses that we had in the outfit. I hoped to be one of the chosen men.

When we gave him chase, he started across the level country to where the ground slanted toward the foothills. There were a number of deep washes or gulleys in the ground that slanted from the hills. He appeared to jump most of these washes with ease, the buckskin mare always at his side. Finally, he came to one that he cleared, but the mare missed the bank on the farther side, going down into the wash about fifteen feet.

By this time the cowboys were closing in on him from all sides, trying to force him straight up the hill. A half mile above us, was a growth of pine timber. As the king horse drew near this timber, he stopped racing then turned around and looked at us. He squealed and prance back and forth as though he saw something among the trees. We might have been quarter of a mile away from him then. We knew none of our men could have gotten into the timber land, for they were riding on both sides to crowd him up the hill. As we spurred our horses on to form a circle round him, I saw him lie down, and when we got up to where he lay, the man nearest jumped out of his saddle and saw that the horse was dead. As he was an old horse, the exertion of jumping over the washes might have been too much for him. He died a game horse rather than be captured.

Riding back to camp, I felt very sorry for this brave animal I had seen the day before, standing high on the rocks gazing down on his herd in the canyon below. Then I had seen him race across the plains as we headed him towards the slopes. How bravely he cleared those deep washes. His body was strong, but his heart was old. I really felt as though I'd committed a great crime. I do not think I was the only one among those riders who felt that way.

We trapped and brought out many horses that season. That was not the only king horse who died fighting for his freedom. We came across a small band of horses – maybe twenty – in the latter part of August. Probably this herd had been robbed by other horse hunters and these twenty were all that were left of the herd. They were good size, although they were wild horses and averaged about nine hundred pounds a piece. They were grazing near the rim wall of a canyon. The boss thought that we might round them up by forming a circle and forcing them to the edge of the canyon, which was about three hundred feet deep. As there were only a few, he suggested that we might lasso all of them.

The king horse of this herd was seal brown with a silver tail and mane, a rare color for a horse even amongst the wild herds. So the day following that on which they had been spotted, our whole outfit formed a half circle and moved up to the herd and crowded them close to the rim wall. As we tightened up on them from three sides, the king horse started up between the rocks. He looked down into the canyon then turned and came back to his herd which we were tightening up on all the time. He let out a squeal and made a dash straight for the riders in an effort to pass through. Some of the boys wanted to rope him, but the boss yelled out "Beat him off boys – beat him off and turn him back."

If they had roped him, not having the herd squeezed up tight, we probably would have lost the whole herd. One fighting horse at the end of a lasso would surely have opened a large space between the riders, and the boss wanted to get the horses clustered tight together before we roped any so that every man would have a chance to pick out a horse. The riders succeeded in beating him off with their lassos and turned him back; he made straight for the edge of the canyon again.

Then, seeing he had no chance of escape he looked back towards his small family and called, and then deliberately leaped off into the canyon. We heard the thud of his body as it struck on the ragged rocks below. This was a little too much for me to bear. I spoke to the boss who was riding beside me and told him that was the last "king" horse that I would ever try to catch; I didn't mind trying to catch a herd, or any horse in it, but from then on, if I was closing up on a herd and the leader came my way, I was sure going to open up and give him plenty of room to escape, and up to this day I kept my word.

I have helped to catch thousands of horses in my day, but the king horses always went free, if it was at all possible for me to liberate them. It is just as well, I think, for if one is caught, nobody can do anything with him – he either will die fighting at the end of the lasso or under the saddle. I have never known one to be subdued. It is a strange thing that all horse hunters will go to great expense at a risk of lives to capture a king horse and very seldom do they bring one out alive.

When I returned to the buffalo pasture in September, I learned that General George Crook had taken charge of the District of Arizona and that they had searched all the forts in the northwest for me; even my father could not tell where I was. I had gone out with the horse hunters without telling anyone. I expected there would be a lot of trouble in Arizona that summer and I had already had two summers of hard riding in that country, and as I was not enlisted in the U.S. army, I did not care to go.

I hunted buffalo that winter on the Yellowstone with the Dick Rock outfit. There were buffalo still on both sides of the Yellowstone and the country was swarmed with buffalo hunters from the southwest. Along about New Years, the hides jumped up in price; prime hides would bring about twenty dollars. When we had made camp near the grazing ground, Dick Rock and Zeth Smith came up. They both told me when I started out on the range, to shoot any buffalo – bull, cow, calf, or spikehorn; of course the spikehorns were more valuable – but not to pass up any.

This sounded like it would be easy for me to keep the skinners going, but when I saw all the rifles that they unloaded out of the wagons, I knew that there was going to be someone else shooting buffalo besides me. When I started a herd in the morning, the skinners all took a rifle with them and as I fell in behind the herd to get them started, the skinners rode ahead on each side of the herd.

When they got under way, the skinners blazed into them and dropped all they could. Then the other hunters closed in – some of them came head on to the herd; they came from all directions. That made the herds split into small groups. This kind of buffalo hunting was entirely new to me and a rider was in as much danger as the buffalo. It was impossible to keep the herd together, but when they stopped racing them at night, the animals would cluster together again.

I have heard many stories told by old hunters, of a large herd of buffalo crossing the Yellowstone that winter; they say there were about forty to sixty thousand in the herd and they believe they went into the Canadian northwest and never returned; but I doubt if there were that many buffalo in the whole United States at that time. Some of these old hunters stick to it that they saw them cross the Yellowstone. If so, I do not know where they came from. There were about three thousand head of buffalo on the side of the river we were shooting on when we commenced hunting that season, and probably the same amount on the other side. On account of so many hunters swarming around this herd every morning, they worried the buffalo so badly that one morning although there was thin ice in the river when we started them, the hunters came head on to the herd and on the sides they were shooting in every direction.

Those buffalo who remained made a mad rush for the river just above Fort Keogh and were jammed so tightly that when the hunters shot into them some of the animals ran down the banks of the river in small groups. I started to ride after one of these stray groups and a bullet from one of the hunters' rifles struck me below the knee in the "lumber yard" (shin) splintering a piece of bone off my shin about three inches long, and it (the bullet) went on into my horse, killing him instantly. There were four other men belonging to different outfits wounded that morning.

I was taken out to the Northern Pacific R.R. in one of the hide wagons and I laid around my father's ranch till late in the summer before I recovered from that shot, and was able to ride again, but some of the buffalo hunters told me when they came out in the spring, that the herd on the Yellowstone was completely wiped out. Some of the cattle men told me that summer that they had seen stray buffaloes moving over towards Dakota who at times stopped and grazed with the cattle. These were probably the remains of that great herd making their way into North Dakota.

Dick Rock came up to the ranch to see me and to make sure that I would shoot with him the following season up on the Cannon Ball and Moreau River. He had been up there with a party of men and said there were probably fifteen thousand buffalo up there and some joining the herd all the time. I agreed to shoot for him the next October. I did a little riding for General Miles the latter part of that summer in the Northwest – nothing special, as there was hardly any trouble with the Indians – mostly rounding up those who left the reservation from time to time.

The days passed swiftly and the first of October the big buffalo hunt was on. Hides had jumped up to twenty-five and thirty dollars a hide in the beginning of the season and by the first of the year they had gone to fifty dollars for prime hides. This herd of more than fifteen thousand buffalo was completely wiped out before the last of February. I have heard it mentioned that Chief Sitting Bull was the cause of the extermination of this great herd, but I shot the first buffalo in that herd and milled around in this herd until they were wiped out; I did not see Sitting Bull or any of the Sioux tribe shooting buffalo that year.

As a matter of fact, it was the hide hunters who cleaned out this herd. It didn't make any difference what kind of a buffalo was shot, the hides all brought a good price. There was a small herd that had taken refuge in the Yellowstone National Park, and several small families of buffalo scattered all over the northwest; I daresay there were not three hundred buffalo left at large on the plains after that Spring of 1883.

There were many noted buffalo hunters and crack shots in our outfit at the Cannon Ball that winter; among them a noted gunman from Kansas by the name of Bat Masterson, who some years later became a U.S. Deputy Marshal in New York, and a Dr. Carver[23] who was probably the greatest shot in the world.[24]

The editors believe this manuscript was written in the 1930s.

---

[23] **Editors' note**: William Frank Carver was widely known in the American Old West as "Doc" Carver. A champion marksman, Wild West showman and big game hunter, Doc Carver was a legendary, and documented, hero of the American West. Despite Frank Hopkins' claims of friendship with Carver, we have been unable to locate any reference to Hopkins in Carver's autobiography, *Spirit Gun of the West, the Story of Doc W. F. Carver,* or in any other Carver-related manuscript. Hopkins' claims to have hunted buffalo for their hides with Carver fly in the face of Carver's contempt for hide-hunters. Though he himself often hunted buffalo on horseback for sport and meat, Carver is on the record as saying that he "hated hide-hunters more than he did Indians."

[24] **Professor David Dary,** *who headed the School of Journalism at the University of Oklahoma, is the recipient of many awards including the Cowboy Hall of Fame Wrangler Award, the Western Writers of America's Spur Award, and has authored more than a dozen books on the American West* "Anyone who claims to have had the experiences that Frank T. Hopkins had would certainly have attracted attention of newspapers from the late 19th into the early 20th century. The fact that his name has failed to turn up in any substantial way strongly suggests to me that he did not experience the events he writes about nor was he involved with all of the personalities mentioned to the extent he claims.... It is obvious that the Hopkins manuscripts were not just embellished old-timer recollections but a deliberate attempt to make Frank T. Hopkins a bigger than life figure in the Old West. I have tried to logically determine WHY the Hopkins did what they did, and what they hoped to gain. If it was financial gain, they failed. If it was an attempt to leave Frank's footprint on history for future generations, they succeeded but not in the way they planned. At this writing I would judge the evidence as overwhelming that Frank T. Hopkins was a fraud."

www.horsetravelbooks.com

Frank Hopkins maintained two contradictory equestrian biographies of his mythical mustang, Hidalgo. In the better-known story, he rode Hidalgo in the Wild West Show, won a 3,000 mile endurance race across Arabia on his pinto pal, and then left the mustang in Arabia to breed with Arab mares. In a lesser-known version of Hidalgo's life, Hopkins claimed the pinto was a performing horse in the circus for 32 years. Either way, there is no evidence to indicate that the horse ever existed. When pressed in the early 1940s by the equestrian writer, Albert Harris, to produce a personal photograph, a Wild West show poster or any visual evidence proving Hidalgo existed, the only thing Hopkins could come up with was this photograph. Hopkins told Harris the wooden statuette "is a good likeness of the horse, including his tail carriage."

Chapter 2

My Years in The Saddle

I was born in a small log house south of the Parade Grounds, at Fort Laramie, Wyoming, many years before that district was admitted to the Union as a State. My father carried out that old tradition of the plainsmen in those days, by laying his new born son in the seat of his saddle. I have often heard the story told of how Father led his horse to the house and laid me gently in the saddle, although that act hasn't a thing to do with making a great rider.[25]

I grew up in that Fort among real horsemen and riders of the plains; at the age of seven, most of my time was spent in those old McClellan saddles, and I still have a liking for that seat. When I was ten years old, I graduated from my small squaw pony; he was getting old and braced his forward feet out as he traveled: Father came home from a long scouting trip in Nebraska – he noticed little Ned was stiff and he said "Son, I got you a good horse – that pony has done his work and you mustn't ride him any more."

I liked the new horse, a fine war pony, but he could never take little Ned's place in my heart even after all these years. That little horse Ned wandered about the Fort as he pleased and when he died the troops mourned as if that pony were one of their rank. I've long since covered most of this Globe in pursuit of horsemanship and fine horseflesh, handled the finest horses raised in Arabia; also the good blood of most every strain known in the world, but still in my memory the first horse of my childhood, little Ned, was the greatest of them all. He was given a good burial and his remains lie deep beneath the soil at Fort Laramie.

As I grew older, I often rode the trails with the scouts. I clearly recall the first message I carried for the army, on the 11th day of August, (1877) and also my birthday. Father was guiding a large pack train; he had called a halt to feed the mules and rest at the foot of the Pryor mountains, Montana. After we had our noonday meal, father rode out in a large circle looking the country over. When he returned, he asked the packers if there was any of them who could ride down to the Shoshone Valley; they claimed none of them knew the lay of the land nor were they familiar with the trails; father walked over to where I was sitting on a blanket.

---

[25] **Dale Yeager,** *Criminal Psychologist:* "My opinion is that Hopkins had serious childhood trauma and in his formative years he began to lie to create a happier life for himself. However by his teens he had changed the focus of his lies towards others to manipulate them."

"Sonny, I'm going to send you to that army Camp in the Shoshone Valley. These troops are guarding a band of the Crow Indians and these people are disliked by other tribes on account of their loyalty to the army. Many of them are scouts; this land is the place for those people."

After Father wrote the note which I was to carry, he saw that I had food and a few rounds of cartridges, then he warned me not to push my horse too fast. Also to stop often so the horse might graze. Then told me of the trails and where I should cut them to gain another. As I rode away, father waved till a butt shut off his view.

I was a happy boy; this was my first duty for our government. I slept in the blankets that night, while the horse grazed. Next day I made better time, for I was riding level country and swimming streams. The third night, I came to the tepees beside a crooked creek; there was a large band of ponies with herders watching over them. Beyond, were the small army tents which showed in the gathering darkness. I greeted the Indians with a stretched out hand as I rode through their village.

When I had handed the message to the commanding officer of the troops, he asked me to accompany him to the council tent. Soon, all the advisers and head men of the Indians sat in a circle on the ground; the head chief lit his long stemmed pipe and passed it around, each man taking one puff. The interpreter talked long into the night while the rest sat and listened.

Finally, the old chief knocked the ashes from his pipe as a signal that the council had ended; he arose to his feet and spoke to me: "Winneque, (boy) you have rode far to bring this word – it is the word of your father; the Crows have long known him as their friend, many of my braves have scouted with him." Then the chief questioned his people and found his answers in their eyes.

Turning to the officers, he spoke, "My people accept this land; we ride with your troops tomorrow;" camp was broke the following day. Both the troops and the Indians moved slowly for there were many children and old folks who had to ride in pony drags. I stayed with them at the foot of the Pryor mountains until father returned – what a time I had, racing ponies and playing the war game of "throw him off the horse." It was beautiful country up there; I did not like to leave.

From then, until 1886, I was a dispatch rider, riding from one fort to another to outpost army camps and often to distant stations where those messages were telegraphed to the War Department at Washington. My trails led across the north and south west, far down into the Sonora Mountains of old Mexico and up into the Canadian Northwest. I rode many endurance races with the troops. With the Sioux and the soldiers I rode 181 races in two years. I won 112 ponies besides other articles (including money). I always had a race in view, either with the cavalry or the Indians.

In the Spring of 1878, I was sent over to Pine Ridge, across the Snake and Powder Rivers. As I came to the Powder, the banks were full; when more than half way across, my horse stopped swimming and tried to sound the bottom – the mad, rushing current caught his hips as he lowered to sound and turned him over backward; as his shoulders raised above the water I left the saddle, only to be shoved down beneath the horse as he turned over.

I was under so long I came up partly filled with water; I could swim fairly well but there seemed to be something holding to my left foot. The horse was close behind me; I fought hard to swim to one side to escape from those hoofs, but try as I did, I could not. Finally, both of us swung to one side as there was a sharp bend in the stream which brought us close to the shore. The horse stood on the bottom. Then I found that the rein had caught around my boot above the spur. I used an army bridle and a buckle at the end of the reins – from that day until the present, I have never tied or buckled the reins. If I used a bridle with a buckle at the end of the reins, I cut the buckle off. This is a simple-looking thing, but never fasten the end of your reins.

At Pine Ridge, I rode in 9 endurance races with the different companies; at the Red Cloud Agency, I rode 17 none of them less than 50 miles. I must say those rides were harder to win than many I have ridden since then.

The following winter things were quiet on the plains – not a fight to get into or a message to carry, so I hired out with that great old plainsman, Buffalo Jones. He gave me the job of dropping bison for the skinners. I had a nice string of ponies, all gun broke; they were the toughest bunch I ever expect to find – none of them weighed over 850 pounds, and they'd rather let you walk than ride. Jones told me one cold evening when I had come into camp, "Boy, those nags you ride are wilder than a wild cat and you are wilder than the nags." They were all Indian ponies, of as many colors as there is in a crazy quilt.

That spring, I rode 7 races against the cattlemen down Kansas way – Jones backed me; he often said he could never lose a dollar when I had a pony between my knees. But the racing was brought to a halt as General Terry (Alfred Terry) sent for me. I rode up to the White Clay Creek. (This is across the line into Canada.) Many of the bands of Sioux had gone there for they were tired of warfare and of being starved on the reservations. This was a long ride and it did no good – the Canadian government would not order those people to go back into the States, so those were the few words I brought back.

After my return from Canada, I rode for General George Crook: I had delivered a message to one of the outpost camps. On my return to the Red Cloud Agency, I had to swim the Grand River – there wasn't any living thing in sight when I put the horse into the water, but as I neared the other bank something struck me in the hip with such force I swung over in the saddle. The hip burnt like fire. Then, I saw four Rees on pony-back ride out of the alders. I levelled my rifle at the one in the lead – when the smoke cleared he lay on the ground. I aimed steady at the next rider – he slid back over the horse's hips; the third one pitched forward to the ground.

C. J. "BUFFALO" JONES

(From text written on the base of the bronze statue of C. J. "Buffalo" Jones, located on the grounds of the Finney County Courthouse, Garden City, Kansas)

Charles Jesse "Buffalo" Jones, immortalized by author Zane Gray in his book "The Last of the Plainsmen", is listed in the national archives as one of the "preservers of the American bison" and his colorful many-faceted career spanned several continents. Born January 31, 1844 in Illinois, Jones became fascinated as a youth with the capture of wild animals. He came to Kansas in 1866, where he developed into a skilled plainsman. With his knowledge and love of outdoor life, he made a good living for his wife, two sons and two daughters, hunting buffalo and capturing wild horses.

Fearing the extinction of the buffalo, Jones made numerous adventure-filled treks into the Oklahoma and Texas panhandles where he captured 57 buffalo calves, returning them to his ranch here. Offspring from this basic herd spread throughout the world, thereby saving this race of noble prairie animals.

Zane Grey visited the ranch, and his book "Roping Lions in the Grand Canyon", tells of their adventures. Grey, a little known dentist from New York, became enchanted by Jones and the west. He went on to become a great western story writer. By his own admission, Grey based the character of his hero on some facet of the character of Buffalo Jones. Other books about Jones are "Lord of Beasts" by Easton and Brown; "Forty Years of Adventure on the Plains" by Colonel Inman; and "Buffalo Jones" written by Ralph Kersey, a local pioneer.

Frank Hopkins is not mentioned in any of them.

Then, I head that familiar yelp "Hy kee ho" and from the alder brush rode a number of Rees. They rode to a small knoll and fired at me. I tried to make my pony go over there and had to roll the spurs along his sides as the little feller reared and plunged at the sound of the shots. He was willing to go the other way and I have often thought that that was good. Had that horse gone over there where I wanted him to I would never have lived to write about it. I was wounded and in great pain and I wanted to wipe them out; they rode after me but my horse was too fast so they gave it up. I was getting weak, soon the trail got dark; I dropped my arms down each side of the pony's shoulders. For over twenty miles that pony carried me. The next thing I remember was voices and then looking into the face of General Terry as he bent over me. I had been shot through both hips. In a short time I was polishing saddles again.

In the Fall, I shot bison for Mr. William Matheson and William Hitner. They had a large outfit. Col. W.F. Cody was with us a short time and he told me about his show which at that time was very small.

After the bison run was wiped out and the hides sold, I got mixed up with some cattle men; they got money together for a race from Kansas City to North Platte. How these men bet when they were before the bar! They had more money than I ever saw. Well, I went over the road and got the bag of gold at the end of the rainbow. Then I was sent for to ride down through the Apache uprising in Arizona, for General Crook. Now that country was strange to me; I could not speak the language of the Apache. But I got plenty of riding – in fact I spent three of the hardest months of my life in those sand deserts. Finally, the Apaches settled down to farming at Turkey Creek, but it was a feeble attempt.

COLONEL WILLIAM "BUFFALO BILL" CODY

Young Bill Cody was orphaned at nine. A few years later he was carrying dispatches through dangerous territory. At the age of thirteen he was attacked on one such assignment but killed his assailant. He next became one of the most daring riders of the Pony Express and was forced to make a round trip ride of three hundred and twenty-four miles without stopping. After that he became a scout for the army. Next he became a buffalo hunter for the Union Pacific railroad and provided fresh meat for their laborers by shooting more than 6,000 buffalo in one hunting season. His hunting horse, "Brigham," was so adept that his rider often chased buffalo without using a saddle or bridle. His fame as a plainsman was so great that he was promoted by the US army to the rank of "Chief of Scouts." During the battle of War Bonnet Creek, he fought and killed the famous Cheyenne chief, "Yellow Hand," in hand to hand combat.

After that he became a legendary showman. Because of his previous military experience he had already met every famous American general of the time, including Sheridan, Custer, Terry, Miles, Crook and Carr. Now he became friends with Europe's royalty and aristocracy, including the Earl of Dunraven and the Prince of Wales in England. An even greater honour was conferred upon him when he met Queen Victoria.

His deeds were recorded in annals of the US War Department, press dispatches from around the world, General Sheridan's autobiography, General Dodge's "Thirty Years among the Indians," and a myriad other books and publications all bearing evidence from eye-witnesses and participants in the story of those times. It would require a public gallery to hold all the photographic evidence of his many accomplishments and friends.

I had bought a good spotted stallion from the White Mountain band and this pony was just what I wanted – a tough-souled hoss. I used him on long rides and knew he was worth taking home. I would breed him with my little albino mare "Whitey." This mare I bought from the army and I rode her ninety miles from sunrise to sunset and knew she had all the staying qualities that could go with any horse. This mare was also an Indian pony. I really was homesick to be with my people and ponies.

Soon the soldiers were going away in small bands and finally, most of the cavalry was transferred to the northwest. I was to go with them. Some of the young officers talked of an endurance race and I was asked to take part in this. Every rider must put up one hundred dollars in cash and pay his own expenses. There were three prizes. First man to ride into Fort Russell got two-thirds of the money; the other third was to be split between the second and third riders. This was one of the hardest rides I rode in, for my pony was dopey most of the way on account of the change of weather and the climate.

I managed to win only by an hour and a few minutes, but that stallion afterwards was the daddy of some of the best endurance horses I ever expect to see or hear of. As I had been wounded twice while in Arizona, I did not feel so good after that ride; I stayed at home with my people. One day, Dick Rock came to see me – he was a great bison hunter. He told me that Jones (Buffalo

Jones) and Zeth Smith were to be with him that season and he wanted me to do the dropping for them. I agreed to go on the runs.

During the three months' wait, I went out horse hunting. There were many wild horses in all parts of the northwest at that time. There were Indian ponies and army horses mixed together. You could sell anything in the shape of a horse that had four legs. I had run wild horses with old time hunters, so it was not new to me. I found where a large band grazed and came for water; I built my trap in the shape of a V. At the narrow end I fenced off about 18 feet and here I put Andy, a stallion that had been caught when a young colt.

For three weeks I fed him grain and hay in this enclosure. The wild horses smelt him; at first they did not come near, but as time passed they got bolder; they went into the trap and around the fence. Each morning I went to see the tracks.

At sundown one evening, I let Andy out; he wandered down to the grazing ground. I had made a place where I could stay near the entrance of the trap without being seen – this was not strange to the horses for they had seen it every night; so I hid in this dugout. I heard the horses calling as they came out to feed. As morning grew near, Andy started for the trap to get his oats; the others followed him. When they were at the lower end I hung pieces of old clothes on the posts across the entrance; these posts were about eighteen feet apart; this held the horses while I put up the fence. They were afraid of these rags flying in the wind; all of them huddled in the far end of the trap. I had all of the rails lying flat on the ground, so it was easy spiking them at the posts. I had thirty ponies and nine army horses. I notified the army and returned those horses.

The ponies I gentled in the trap and took them out with Andy as a lead horse. The gentling was easy; every day I went in the coral and moved around slowly, not paying any attention to the horses. Soon they came around to me and some of them got real friendly. When I started out with them I saw that they had plenty to eat before we started. I led Andy on a long rope and every one of them followed.

This was a one man's job from start to finish. I have been with other horse hunters who tried to run horses into their traps with a large force of riders; they got some horses but the best ones they don't get. I caught a number of horses with honest old Andy; he never failed to bring them in, and he didn't care much about fighting. When he was twenty-two years old, I got the last family of ponies with him and Andy died shortly after.

That fall, when I rode for the bison hunter, I found another great endurance horse. Jones had bought a string of horses and there was a small buckskin in the lot; this horse was wild and had never been handled. Jones said he had bought the lot and this one was throwed into the bargain.

"If you can break him in your spare time, he's yours," says Jones. He continued, "I don't think that mustang will amount to anything, he is too small."

I roped the pony and took him away from the bunch. Every evening I worked on him, but the pony did not get friendly. Finally, I got the saddle on him; he fought hard and threw himself. All of the men told me there was no use fooling with that pony, that he was the worst kind of an outlaw and it was not worth while getting hurt for the horse was small and good for nothing. But all this did not discourage me. Every day after I rode off the runs, I went to the small corral and spent an hour or so with the little yellow plug. Finally, I got him to lead fairly well; still, he would fight the saddle. Every evening I put the saddle on him. It was quite a job, but I put it on just the same. After a month of fighting this horse seemed to get no better.

I began to lose courage. I fed him, but for a week I did not bother to saddle or do anything with him. The men noticed this and began to make fun of me. They'd say, "How's that buckskin coming along? Mighty fine gait he's got under the saddle," and such things to work me up. This put me to thinking that I must try that pony again. One evening I rode into camp ahead of the skinners – I went to the pony and he seemed friendly. I got the saddle and this time he did not mind when I placed it on his back. Then I led him around the corral and he did not fight. Then I stepped up there with the intention of staying.

The pony did not know what to think of me being up there – still, he didn't buck. When the skinners rode in, I was riding that yellow colt around the camp and from then on, that horse and I were the best of friends. I named him "Joe." It would take me a long time to write the whole story of that pony.

Soon, I used him on the bison runs; when he got hardened to the work, what a bison horse he was! He could stick to it all day and then go out the next day and do it all over again. That spring, I rode him against other riders, from Laramie to Denver. During that summer, I rode him in three fifty mile races, all of them I rode in the Dakotas with the army boys. I went to Arizona to ride for General Miles.

On my return, I was told there was a race in the making. This was to be a real race across the states; then I heard it was to be run from Galveston, Texas[26] to Rutland, Vermont.[27] I saw Buffalo Jones at Fort Russell and he was eager for me to get into that race. I told him I had put all my money into brood mares and that I could not afford to spend the time training. Then he said, "You don't need money – I will back you" and it was there at Fort Russell that I signed on.

Jones laid down one hundred and fifty dollars; the next day I began training Joe. Two months later, I rode away from the ferry slip from Galveston and

---

[26] **Casey Greene,** *Head of Special Collections, Rosenberg Library, Galveston, Texas:* "We've referenced every newspaper between 1880 and 1890 but there is absolutely no mention of Frank Hopkins or a race from Galveston to Vermont."

[27] **James Davidson,** *Vermont Historical Society:* "There is nothing in the local news-papers around that time about a race ending here in Rutland. The only endurance Hopkins ever did was with his pencil."

continued to Rutland, Vermont; that little buckskin stallion carried me there in thirty days.

I got three thousand dollars for that ride and a job that lasted thirty one seasons, for Col. W.F. Cody hired me to ride in his Wild West show.[28] I went with him to New York and played in Madison Square Garden that winter.

The next Spring, we went to England on the steamship Nebraska and we played at Earl's Court Expedition where the show stayed for a year. I soon got tired of riding in a circle; my spirit began to lag and I was tired of it all and longed to be in my own free country of the mountains and plains. One day, while I sat brooding, on a bale of hay, Cody came to me and said, "You are not yourself, boy, what is the trouble?" I answered that if there was any way to ride across that ocean or around it, I would start right away.

Then Cody asked me if I realized what my riding and horsemanship meant to those people who came to the show. True, they shouted and applauded when I came into the ring, but that annoyed me and I didn't care about that. He said if those people didn't like my performance they wouldn't show it when I was in the ring, but I didn't like the noise they made.

I met many great people. There the Queen came to the Crystal Palace often and many times she talked with me; she, (Queen Victoria) was a motherly sort of little woman.

Cody put on many special things to amuse the people. He had Charlie Miller ride against the champion bicycle rider of the world. Charlie changed horses and in a three hundred mile race all in a circle, round and round, Charlie beat the man on that high wheel.

Then came the endurance race[29] from Earl's Court to Land's End which is in South Wales.[30] I had one of Whitey's colts with the show and I rode him in that race. This horse finished those two hundred miles and was twelve hours ahead of the next rider and that colt was only four years old at the time. When I returned to the show, on my first performance the crowd left their seats and crowded into

---

[28] **Dr. Juti Winchester,** *Curator of the Buffalo Bill Museum at the Buffalo Bill Historical Center*: "We are unable to find any Frank T. Hopkins in our database of known cast members, acquaintances, employees, or friends of Colonel Cody. We find that after Cody's death, some people made pretty spectacular claims about their relationship with him, what they did in the Wild West show, and so on. Frank and Gertrude Hopkins are only two of a legion of early twentieth century pretenders that used Cody's name and reputation to bolster their own. I hope researchers will no longer continue to allow the Hopkins' work to muddy the historical waters any more than has already been done."

[29] **Ann Hyland**, British expert on the history of endurance racing and author of many books, including *The Endurance Horse - a World Survey (1988), Riding Long Distance (1993),* and *Endurance Riding (1976)*, said, "I have never heard of that [Earl's Court to Land's End] race, nor of Frank Hopkins!"

[30] **Editors' note**: Land's End is in Cornwall, not Wales.

the ring and delayed the performance, for it took more than an hour to straighten things out; I could not step out on the street without being mobbed. I got orders to cut down on my trick riding for it excited the audience and held up the show.

I came home again, a tired, worn out boy, but after looking over my herd of horses and colts I was happy. There were Whitey's colts – one most three years old, whom I named Pardner. Then, there was Hidalgo, Whitey's grandson, who was two years old, a nice put together colt and spotted all over. I looked him over very closely; although I had spent most of my few years in the saddle and rode many horses, I longed for the day when I could ride that spotted colt.

I broke Pardner and when I returned to Europe the following Spring, Pardner went with me.

After looking over my horses, I went to Fort Custer to visit my father; there was trouble with the Blue Clouds, and I was back at the old job carrying messages. I had left my horse Jigger at the fort; I carried many messages, all the time getting farther away; soon I found myself in Montana. I had spent the night at Grantrice Pillars.

My horse was an army charger who appeared to be very tired from the day before, so I led him, thinking he might limber up after a mile or so, but in less than that mile the horse was riddled with bullets and his carcass served as a barricade to save me from that hot lead. However, I did not miss all of those shots and I do not think any man ever used a Springfield rifle any faster than I used that one. I will never know how many Ree Indians shot at me that morning for they were in heavy brush and I was passing on a beaten trail. For over four hours I lay there and returned shot for shot. Finally, some Blackfoot Indians heard the shooting; they rode a long time before they got to me and I know for sure that they did not get there any too soon. Now, the Ree was enemy to the Blackfoot. The Blackfeet cared for me as well as did the Sioux and they also sent out a runner to make known my whereabouts and my condition.

The news reached Fort Custer. King Stanley was there and when the news came he went out to the corral, saddled my horse and rode from Fort Custer to Grantrice Pillars in Montana in Seven days![31] The horse was well fed and cared for most of the way. Even so, I think both man and horse should be called the greatest endurance team of all time. That little spotted stallion was the same horse that I brought up from Arizona and the founder of that family of endurance horses which I refer to as the Whitey family.

---

[31] **Brian Shovers,** *Research Librarian, Montana Historical Society:* "We have absolutely nothing concerning this Frank T. Hopkins. As for Grantrice Pillars, I find nothing. Perhaps it is confused with Pompey's Pillars, which is located on the Yellowstone River near Fort Custer, and was named by William Clark of Louis and Clark fame. Who are the 15 'historical experts' that have fashioned this hoax for Disney Pictures?"

KING STANLEY

His name is now largely forgotten but in the late nineteenth and early twentieth centuries, King Stanley was a household name. Thrown on his own resources at fourteen, the youth made a living being a wagon master across the Rocky Mountains and a United States Marshal in the Badlands of North Dakota. Stanley was a close personal friend of Teddy Roosevelt and was one of the pall bearers at the funeral of Buffalo Bill Cody.

His knowledge of Indians and his skill in dealing with them were a great service to the Federal government and promoted friendly relations between the two races. Stanley joined the Arapahoe tribe and was made a medicine man.

In June, 1929, The New York Times wrote in Stanley's obituary, "Cut off from the rest of his party at the battle of Wounded Knee Creek, Stanley shot his way out to safety and won the sobriquet of 'Dead Shot.' For years American school boys gazed with awe upon the picture of "King Stanley - Indian Scout" in the old McGuffey Fifth Reader,[32] and read below it the tale of his heroism."

When Stanley died at the age of 73, the gnarled Frontiersman's body bore the scars of 62 knife and bullet wounds received in the old days !

I crossed the ocean with a number of horses for the show, including that intelligent colt of mine called Pardner. The show played in many towns of England and Scotland, then on, to Spain and there Cody put on a race of one hundred miles; this was free for all. Riders from Spain or anywhere could enter in the contest. I rode my Pardner and won. Then, there was a fifty mile race arranged by the crack riders of the Spanish Cavalry. I was asked to enter this race and won it in seven hours and eighteen minutes, a little over half an hour ahead of the next rider.

Then the show came back home to the States. At Aristeena Staten Island, we played and we also made it our headquarters. There was a large dock built there for the chartered ship the Persian Monarch to land. The latter part of the summer the show played at the Richmond Virginia Fair, and here Cody placed fifteen hundred dollars to the man who would cover one hundred fifty miles ahead of fifty one riders. These riders were invited to contest without paying any entry fee. I came in and collected the money and finished eating my supper before any of the other riders showed in sight.

In 1889 the show recrossed the ocean to Havre, France and we camped on grounds secured from the government, on the military grounds of Paris, outside of the wall in Nueilly, Pres la Porte de Terne.[33] Here the show created such a

---

[32] **Editors' note:** First published in 1836, the McGuffey Readers were the standard school books in thirty-seven states for three-quarters of a century.

[33] **Editors' note:** Compare with the text from Frank Hopkins' own copy of the **Wild West Show Program - "Buffalo Bill Bids You Goodbye" – 1910:** "In 1889 recrossed the ocean to Havre, France, and camped in elegantly prepared grounds secured from the government on the Military Zone of Paris just outside the wall, in Nueilley, Pres la Porte de Terne."

fury that the Assembly discussed the matter of closing out one performance a day.

Then Cody put on a world horsemanship contest which included riders of all nations of the world, and this took place at Marseilles, France. The contest was started off with the long ride to Bordeaux, which I won. Then each man in his turn, contested two hours every day. This took most of a year in order to give all of the riders a fair chance. This contest included everything that could be done on horseback. There were many judges of all nations. I had little hope of winning that contest, but when it was all over I was judged the best rider. Besides this contest, I rode through performances of the Wild West show.

At Marseilles, I met that great Arabian gentleman Ras Yankin who had journeyed from his native Arabia with a number of the finest horses his country could produce. This man was deeply interested in my work. He had already asked me to visit his country but the show was to go to Rome, Italy, and then on to Germany, besides other countries. At that time I was under contract with a heavy bond and so I could not then accept Ras Yankin's invitation at that time.

There was an epidemic of glanders in France at the time, so our horses could not be shipped out of the country. I regret to recall that some of my good endurance horses went under the hammer. But not Pardner. Rather than see him go to another owner and perhaps mistreated, I bid him a fond farewell and then shot him with my own gun and when the auctioneer called for him there was no answer, (many disappointed bidders). I left Pardner buried in French soil and the show went to Italy.

Naples was our first set-up; then to the Jubilee in Rome where the World Contest was put on and the same riders from all over the World took part; it was more thrilling than the previous contest in France and there were more people who came to look on – some strange looking folks from all four corners of the earth. After the contest there was a three hundred mile race over the roughest country I have ever rode; this race was more of a challenge than anything else and I also won it with my hardy horse Hidalgo.[34]. Then there were seventy-five miles with the mountain climbing Italian troops. At Genoa I rode one hundred and twenty-five miles against mixed cavalries and then on to Austria and Germany.[35]

When the show was in Berlin I was told that there was a request and a challenge for me to take part in a two hundred and fifty mile race near the Austrian Border (in Germany) The riders were of the German, Austrian and Italian Cavalry. I won this race with a horse that I called Snuffbox, a full brother

---

[34] **Editors' note:** If there was an epidemic of glanders, how did Hopkins get Hidalgo out of France?

[35] **Editors' note:** It seems improbable that the Europeans, who calculate distances in kilometers, would be putting on races measured in miles.

of Hidalgo. On my return to Berlin, I was requested to ride at the head of a cavalry revue. At this time I learned that the Congress of Riders of the World was to pay my expenses if I wished to go to Arabia, that I was to take my own horses and to contest in three rides as well as other feats of horsemanship. I came home to the States for the winter and a much needed rest.

I learned there was some good horse play going on down in Indian Territory; that there was a boom as the Territory was open for white settlers. So I took my buckskin Joe and three other horses of the Whitey family, and started for what is now the State of Oklahoma. The first race was two hundred miles; the prize was to be a homestead. I rode Joe in this race – a horse mighty hard to beat. When about nine miles from the finishing line, one of the riders made a desperate attempt to pass my horse on a sharp turn in the road; as the horse passed he leaned over to make the turn and the horse's hip brushed against Joe's shoulder; both horse and rider rolled down a fifty foot dirt embankment, neither of them seriously hurt, but that was the end of that ride for them.

I rode in on Joe quite some time ahead, but learned I was disqualified on account of that incident. This was my first defeat and the last and only race in which I failed to capture the prize. I lost to the second rider that crossed the line – I have often thought that that ride was supposed to be won by him before the race started. He was an agent and educator on the Pawnee Reservation and afterward was a partner of Cody's in the Wild West show; I made light of my defeat for I could not lose to a better man.

The other two races I won – one seventy-five miles, the other ninety miles. They claimed there were one hundred miles of road, but there were only ninety.

When I returned from Oklahoma, I went to see my old friends of the army at Pine Ridge, and I got there just in time for the last stand of the Sioux, the battle of Wounded Knee. General Miles (Nelson A. Miles) was pleased to see me; he said I could be of great help as I was acquainted with the Indians. At once I was riding the trails of my beloved West.

The first ride was to the Grand River, and there Sitting Bull was camped. Shortly after I had gained the old warrior's camp, a number of Indian police came riding in. There was nothing evil in the hearts of those people – they had merely gone over to the Grand River to hunt and dance and enjoy themselves, but Miles would have it that they were planning to go on the warpath.[36] Sitting Bull

---

[36] **Gregory Michno**, *Author of many books including Encyclopedia of Indian wars : western battles and skirmishes, 1850-1890:* "General Miles wasn't at Pine Ridge. He set up headquarters in Rapid City, South Dakota. Sitting Bull wasn't camped on Grand River, although he was near it. And it could hardly have been called a "camp." Sitting Bull and many of his followers lived in wood cabins at this time. It was Indian Agent James McLaughlin who ordered the arrest, not Miles. Sitting Bull only appeared in Bill's troupe for four months in 1885. The man who shot Sitting Bull was not Crow Nose. There were about thirty Indian police that came to arrest Sitting Bull. They knocked on

had been with the Buffalo Bill Wild West show for two years and was happy to be back with his old friends.

I had left my horse in the pole corral (made out of poles) that was roughly put together, to rest. As I returned, Sitting Bull came out of his teepee to speak to me and just as he stepped down a small bank, one of the police fired a shot which passed me and struck Sitting Bull low in the breast. The old man crumpled up like a green leaf on a camp fire, then he slowly straightened out and breathed no more. I have often heard that the police who shot him was his own cousin, but that is all talk, for I was the only one there except the Indians. The Reservation police were also Sioux – the man who shot him was Crow Nose and a Lakota Indian.

All the men in that camp ran out into the brush and disappeared, leaving their horses. They made their way into the Bad Lands and joined Chief Big Foot and his band which was mostly women and children who had gone up there to pick the Indian nuts which are liked so well by those people. The police reported there was trouble and the soldiers came as far out as Porcupine Butte; there they met the Big Foot band coming with me and those old men who were with Sitting Bull.

I told the officers there was no trouble with these people. Old Big Foot was in a pony-drag, very ill with pneumonia, and the children were suffering with the cold that had come on so soon; there was an old man walking in the road who carried a rifle – a young officer slid down off his horse and tried to twist the rifle out of the old man's hands – in the struggle, the gun went off and killed the officer. There were only four other old guns amongst the Indians, but the soldiers were like crazed men – they shot into the groups of frightened children and women. One of the soldiers shot Big Foot as he lay ill in the pony drag.

If I hadn't gotten over blushing long ago, I would probably blush for this, and I would blush with shame in recalling the unfairness and brutality of the soldiers. My own horse, Fiddler, was shot that day; he was one of the best endurance horses I think any one could find. I caught one of the army horses and rode to the Reservation.[37]

---

his door and went in to talk. They came outside and some of Sitting Bull's followers gathered around. There were harsh words exchanged. The first shot was fired by Catch-the-Bear, who shot the Indian policeman Bull Head. Bull Head shot Sitting Bull, then shots erupted and Sitting Bull was hit again. Several Indians on both sides were killed."

[37] **Gregory Michno:** "Bigfoot rode in a wagon, not a pony-drag. The Indians had camped in the valley with the soldiers for the night. Bigfoot was given a large tent by the Army for his own use. They had all agreed to surrender, but they were to be disarmed first. In the morning, when the soldiers gathered everyone together to take their weapons, the Indians said they had no weapons, when the Army had seen many weapons just the day before. The soldiers had to dig out the guns, which were hidden everywhere, even up some of the women's skirts. On the first round, they got 38 rifles – not many for 350

BIG FOOT

Big Foot was the leader of the Miniconjou band massacred at Wounded Knee Creek in December 1890, and so he haunts the history of the American West.

Big Foot and his people lived in what is now South Dakota and were among the most fervent believers in the Ghost Dance ceremony when it arrived among the Lakota in early 1890, believing as they did that it would reinstate their traditional lifestyle. The hunger and deprivation following the break-up of their reservation in 1889 made the Lakota even more receptive to the Ghost Dance message, and the movement swept swiftly through their encampments, much to the alarm of the local Indian Agents.

After Sitting Bull was killed, many of his band fled south to Big Foot's encampments.

Big Foot decided to head south toward the reservation at Pine Ridge, hoping to find safety there. Increasingly ill with pneumonia, he had no intention of fighting and was flying a white flag when soldiers patrolling for roving bands caught up with him on December 28, 1890 at Wounded Knee Creek.

Big Foot himself was one of the first to be killed. His frozen corpse lay untouched for three days until it was dumped into a mass grave.

I could not find anyone to report to – they were all crazed; one Indian rode past me and cried, "They are butchering the people over there" None of the officers would listen – they were crazy mad. I was very hungry for I hadn't eaten since the fight started at Porcupine the day before. I saw Black Elk riding toward me – he was wild-eyed. I yelled at him to stop; there was a tepee that the women had left there and meat was still boiling on the fire. Black Elk and I went in there and ate the stew. While we were eating, some soldiers rode by and fired into the tepee and the shot went through the pot of stew, but we kept on talking just the same.

Then both of us rode out to the south. There were cannons going off over there. All the people were gone from the Reservation; now there was shooting near that dry, crooked creek. I rode over there; the women and frightened children were huddled in groups against the small scrub pines in the dry creek bottom. The soldiers turned the mule cannons on them – it was a pitiful sight.

I saw a small baby crawling among the dead down the creek. The soldiers were still shooting at the group when I slid down the bank and got the baby. Black Elk brought a baby in that night too. I found a woman who had milk (she had a small baby of her own) and she nursed and cared for the two children. I

Indians. When they tried to search the men individually, an Indian named Black Coyote pulled out his rifle and fired. That started the chaos. At the end, about 125 Indians were killed, but the 7th Cavalry lost 25 killed and 35 wounded – more losses than in any other battle they participated in except for the Little Big Horn. The Indians were obviously armed and able to fight."

thought she was a great woman in a time of trouble like that for she was so kind and shared her own baby's food with another.[38]

The Creek was covered with dead women and children; late in the afternoon the soldiers rode away; the sun was shining and the sky was clear, but when even came there was a strong wind blowing up. The next day I rode out to the Creek. My heart was saddened and I thought it was the work of the Great Father who sent a merciful snowfall that night, for it covered completely those mothers and their little ones so cruelly slaughtered. I had known General Miles for many years, but after that I could not think of him the same as I had heretofore. He seemed like a fine man, but I know he was always for taking praise for himself, no matter what the cost and I think that was a horrible way to get it.

After that, I took Hidalgo and two of his brothers, and sailed to Aden, a port on the Gulf of Aden, Arabia.[39] That was a long way to ship a horse; the horses were sick most of the time; I did not leave their care to any one but cared for them myself. As soon as the ship was tied up to the dolphins (a bunch of piles) a funny looking sort of dock – my Arab friend Ras Yankin came on board.

Two of my horses were in very good shape, outside of being a little sluggish, but Hidalgo was weak and shaky. He was in the habit of having shipping fits on the trains and on the ship; he had them often, and this weakened him badly. I used to hold a piece of maple board out to him when he got a fit on the circus train[40] and he would seize it in his teeth and hang on to it for an hour at a time, but on shipboard he would not bite the board. A horse with shipping fits[41] is surely vicious and dangerous to go near, but once Hidalgo stepped on the ground he was himself again and in a few days I was riding him.

---

[38] **Gregory Michno**, *Author of many books including Encyclopedia of Indian Wars : Western battles and Skirmishes, 1850-1890:* "Black Elk told his story to John Neihardt in the 1930s and it was in the book 'Black Elk Speaks.' Some of this is taken right from Black Elk's book, but it was Red Crow who was with Black Elk, not Hopkins. It is so obvious that Hopkins is a fraud – I cannot see how he could have fooled people for so many years. Coincidentally, I am currently working on a book that discusses Hollywood versus history in western movies. These are some of the very points that will be examined, such as whether or not it is Hollywood's duty to tell accurate history, or simply entertain us with a good story. The latter may be the case, but it should not give us falsehoods under the guise of truth."

[39] **Ghalib Al-Quaiti**, *the last ruling Sultan of the Quaiti State in what is now Yemen:* "There is absolutely no record of any horse race in the past staged from Aden!"

[40] **Editors' note:** Why would Hopkins talk about being on a Circus train, instead of the Wild West show train? Presumably because in real life he was employed as a horse-handler for Ringling Brothers Circus in 1914 and 1915.

[41] **Editors' note:** A qualified veterinarian wrote, "I have never heard of 'shipping fits.' It sounds like Hopkins' idea of an epileptic fit translated from humans. Horses do not fit like that."

Of course, neither of my horses was in shape for work. Slowly they were hardened to the training. I had been in the company of Ras Yankin in France, Germany, also Rome, but I did not get to know the real man until I had seen him in his native land. He was a gentleman in every respect and a great horseman as well as a leader of his people. He said he was educated in England and he surely spoke the English language well.

He told me of that three thousand mile race which had been held each year for many years[42] by the Arabs; it had been run since the horse was brought from Africa across the Gulf into Arabia. I asked how many years, and he said, "About two thousand B.C."[43] The course was from Aden along the waters of the Gulf to Syria, and up the border. There were a large number of Turks in Arabia and they are also great horsemen; there were many in the big race. I rode Hidalgo as I thought he might stand the long road best. He stood the hard training I had given him and he was older than the other horses. I will say of those people they were fair in every way – no trickery amongst the judges nor the riders.

Hidalgo got the gold twenty-two hours ahead of the next horse.[44] I don't think there ever lived a horse who got so much petting and kisses from men and women equally as did that spotted stallion. It did not end with the race – for more than four months it continued. The ladies did not want this horse to leave the country; as the time came for him to leave, I promised Ras Yankin's daughter that Hidalgo would always stay in that country. She was ten years old at the time and she raced through the neighborhood screaming to every one she met that Hidalgo would always stay there. I rode in two races which were five

---

[42] **Editors' note:** Despite Hopkins' claims that a 3,000 mile endurance race had been held in Arabia for a thousand years, none of the major Arabic texts dealing with the Arabian horse mention this race at all. The famous ninth-century author and equestrian historian, Hisam Ibn Al-Kalbi, for example, makes no reference to such an event. Nor is the race mentioned by any European who travelled in Arabia in the ensuing centuries.

[43] **Dr. Awad Al-Badi,** *Director of Research, King Faisal Center for Research and Islamic Studies*: "There is absolutely no record or reference to Hopkins with or without his mustangs ever having set foot on Arabian soil. The idea of a historic long distance Arab horse race is pure nonsense and flies against all reason. Such an event in Arabia any time in the past is impossible simply from a technical, logistical, cultural and geopolitical point of view. This race has never been part of our rich traditions and equestrian heritage."

[44] **Editors' note:** All three of Hopkins' major endurance race fantasies have one thing in common. The Galveston to Rutland race, the London to Land's End race, and the Arabian race all share the fact that Hopkins could never decide how long it took him to reach his inevitable victory! In the account above, for example, he reached Aden "twenty-two hours ahead of the next horse." Yet in the article "Mustangs," Hopkins wrote, "I was in Aden thirty-six hours before the next horse came in."

hundred miles each, using the other two horses; they both showed the stuff they were made of.

Cody wrote me, saying the Columbus Fair at Chicago would not be ready to open early in 1892, so I could stay longer if I wished, so I went across the Gulf into Africa in the company of Yankin who told me he would show me the last of the wild horses that roamed in Africa; these horses are the true blood of which the Arab horse sprang from. He then surprised me by saying that there is no horse that is a native of Arabia – they should be called Libyan for it was the Libyans who first domesticated the horse in Africa and they were shipped across the Gulf and sold to the Arabs. He went on, "In fact there are no Arab horses – these horses in my country have been called Arabs so long now that it is too late to correct the fact that they are all Libyans."

I spent three months with my Arabian friends over there in Africa. I roped a number of the wild horses; they were the same type of horse our Indians had on the Western Plains, only they did not fight so hard when caught. I had heard that the Zebra was the only species of horse left in Africa. I also caught three zebras; they are a dumb sort of animal.

The Arabs are smart horsemen; I've seen many horses in the States which were shipped from Arabia and very few of them were true Arabs; these people are wise, knowing that their horses have a good reputation throughout the world, and also that most buyers of Europe want a fairly large horse, so the Arabs get horses from other countries, breed them and sell them for Arab horses, although many of those horses really haven't a drop of Arab blood in their veins.

The true Arab horse is a small horse – mostly white or gray. There are other colors among them – some spotted. In all the time I was there, I did not see one real Arab horse that was clear bay in color. I might mention my horse averaged fifty-eight and a quarter miles during the three thousand miles; this was sand country I was riding.

I gave that horse to Yanken's young daughter. They used him as a stud for years after and he produced many great offsprings. He breathed his last after the age of 28 years.[45] I often got letters from Yankin – he too, passed on in 1928.

I brought out of that country an Albino stallion whose name was Arap. He was a true Arab weighing about 900 pounds when in good flesh; he was supposed to be one of the best. I had seen him at three Worlds Fairs in Europe and he was the prettiest horse I ever laid eyes on. Now I have told the whole

---

[45] **Editors' note**: According to an unpublished Hopkins transcript, Hidalgo was not left in Arabia. In that version Hopkins claimed that Hidalgo became one of the greatest circus horses of all time. "Hidalgo really liked to perform, and I shall long remember the spring of 1889 when I performed with him in Madison Square Gardens and Hidalgo made his first bow to the world as a great show horse. There are people living who clearly recall his acts. I have spent thirty-two seasons in the show ring riding Hidalgo, and he was the greatest show horse that ever acted under the Big Top."

story of that horse for he was not worth a punched nickel – only to look at.   He was very nervous and could not stand any hardship and I did not try to raise any colts from him.   He was highly intelligent though and I learned him many tricks which he would do without coaxing.   I bought him for the sole reason that I liked him, he died at the age of twenty-two.

It took me over two months to come from Arabia and Cody met me at the dock in New York.   Nathan Salisbury was pleased with the horse I brought with me; they were getting ready for the Fair at Chicago.   Cody said, "There is a race waiting for you from Casper, Wyoming to Chicago – 1100 miles riding.[46]   I want you to sharpen up one of your horses for that ride."   I had some colts out of good endurance stock back home, but I didn't know what they were good for.   Then, there was old Joe, fourteen years old.   Would he do?   I took a train to Wyoming.   Joe looked good to me – the boys had used him culling stock; the horse was in good shape; none of my colts were broken.   I said, "Well, I'll try to get Joe into shape for that ride."

He stood the training very well at the start although I was careful not to overdo it; soon, I saw that the old yellow nag was just as game and tough as he always had been.   I sent word to Cody that I was ready to take on any rider or riders anywhere.   Then came a stroke of bad luck – all the riders shipped their horses to Casper; we were met by a real Western sheriff whom I had known for years and he said very sternly, "If you riders try to start this ride in this here state, all of you will get locked up, and I have the law behind me.[47]"

---

[46] **Editors' note**: There is no historical evidence to support Frank's fantasy race from Wyoming, or Kansas City, to Chicago. Hopkins has in fact incorporated elements of the two most famous documented "cowboy races" of the turn of the century. A 1,000 mile race from Chadron, Nebraska to Chicago, Illinois, did occur in 1893. The Finish Line was at the "1000 Mile Tree" located next to Buffalo Bill's Wild West show. Cody himself presented a prize to the winner. Later, in 1908, a 600-mile race was run from Evanston, Wyoming, to Denver, Colorado. Hopkins claimed to have won 452 endurance races in more than a dozen countries, including 289 in the United States alone. Yet the man who said, "I've ridden enough miles to girdle the globe," was nowhere to be seen in either the Chadron or the Denver endurance races.

[47] **Editors' note**: Throughout the course of their deceptive literary careers, both Frank and Gertrude Hopkins maintained the illusion that the reason nobody had ever heard of Frank's many endurance racing victories was due to the fact that the Society for the Prevention of Cruelty to Animals (SPCA) frowned on these nineteenth century events.

In an undated letter to biographer Robert Easton, Gertrude Hopkins wrote, "I think these rides were not published, probably because the Society for the Prevention of Cruelty to Animals was opposed to the rides. They were constantly 'on the trail' of such rides and didn't permit them if they could stop them."

It is indeed true that the National Humane Society did send an agent, W.W. Tatro, to observe the Chadron to Chicago endurance race of 1893. Yet, at the end of the race he wrote, *"It started in foolishness and was foolish business all through, but it has been an*

I got in touch with Cody – in a few days he sent word that all of us should ship our horses to Kansas City, and there we rode a little to keep our horses in shape, and not riding in one bunch. The road was laid out at last and we rode up the river as far as Sioux Falls, then tacked back to Rock Island, then straight into Chicago. This route was laid out so we would cover the eleven hundred miles that the riders had signed up to ride. Old Joe came in hours ahead of the rest; the game old pony rolled his eye as I stepped down out of the saddle, as much as to say, "Boy, that last mile was tough!" Joe never looked at me like that again, for he never wore a saddle again; although he had the best of care, he did not live a year.

In 1894, the show spent the summer at Ambrose Park, South Brooklyn, N.Y. There I got acquainted with a veterinary from New Hampshire. He was interested in endurance races and asked me to look on. This race was from Westmoreland to Hillsborough Bridge, New Hampshire. I rode in it. The horse was four years old, also of the Whitey family. When I unloaded, the doctor told me I didn't have a chance.

"Why?" I asked.

"Because that horse is too small and he is spotted and a spotted horse has no endurance."

"Well, Doc," said I, "I have no other horse so I will have to use this spotted colt, and I wish he was older."

The Doc looked him over and remarked that he looked sure like a nice put together pony, but said, "Well, boy, you will never run that stallion against those strong horses that are entered in this race."

Three days later, I had four hundred dollars of the Doc's money in my pocket besides the prize money from the race, and the doctor was the most surprised man in all New Hampshire. He wanted to buy that horse Turk, but I had not sold a single horse of the Whitey strain and it was too late to ask me now. Turk was good on mountain roads – a great horse in muddy going.

The doctor was not to be discouraged easily; three months later, he sent me word there would be a good race on and would I like to sign on for that ride? I made a train that got me into Hancock, New Hampshire the next day. Everything looked alright to me so I signed on and laid down the required money. This ride was from Hancock to Hollis, New Hampshire, said to be one hundred and twenty-five miles, but I have always doubted if it was that far, for Turk carried me to Hollis in nineteen hours, forty-six minutes of actual riding. There were six

---

educator of the people, showing them that the so-called cowboys are not a set of horned animals, all wild brutal men, and the Humane Society discovered it was wrong in supposing that the riders would treat their horses badly. We consider the race a big success in every way." Nor was there any official Humane Society opposition to the Wyoming to Denver race in 1908, further eroding the Hopkins' claim that Frank's endurance record was kept secret for this reason.

Morgans in this race – they were in their own country, but they failed to show their ability as mountain climbers.

At the start of this race, I was some distance behind when a large man drove up beside me in a buggy and commanded me to halt.

"Where are you going?" he asked in a gruff voice.

"Well, I'm riding this horse over to Greenfield."

He pointed to a short red post driven in the ground at the side of the road – "What's that"?

I answered, "I don't know – maybe its an engineer's mark or something," but he came back with the question "Are you sure it is not a marker for a long distance race?"

"What sort of a race is that?" said I.

"Well," he answered, "they are horse-killing races and there is one on now and if I am not mistaken, you are riding in it."

"Well, mister, does this horse look like a race horse, or was he traveling as though I was trying to win a race? This horse is to stand as a stud for one month in Greenfield."

Then he showed me his badge – "Well, I'm sheriff of this county and I'm sorry I hailed you in such a manner; I can see you're alright"! He rode along the road with me for a mile or so. Finally, I saw a sign which read, "Wines and Liquor" I asked the Sheriff if he would have a drink. "Sure I will." I slid to the ground and tied Turk to a large elm tree. The sheriff was acquainted with the man behind the bar.

After buying my friend some few drinks of whisky and myself some of the worst cigars I ever had to smoke, I started to send Turk along. There were the Temple mountains before me – a long ride of over eight miles of steady climbing. Turk never slacked his fast walk. At the summit I set him into a swinging lope; now I could see the other riders. Between three and four o'clock that afternoon, I passed them all and did not see any of them again until they came in at the finish, late the following evening. This was not at all bad for a four year old colt.

On my way home, I stopped in Boston, as there was a great horseman giving exhibitions there in the Mechanics Building. This man was Professor Gleason, also a good friend of mine. There was a vicious horse brought to him which he was to subdue in the ring. I sat at the ringside; the horse was brought out with four men holding him; when he was turned loose, he started straight for Gleason – the Professor slipped and fell; the horse struck with both forward feet while Gleason rolled to get away.

I saw he was in grave danger and I jumped down into the ring and seized the horse by the mane and sprang onto his back, then I reached for his nose shutting off his wind, and the Professor got to his feet unharmed. "Alright, Frank, let him go now, I'll handle him," commanded the Professor. That was one of the best shows of breaking a bad horse I ever saw. The best of it was that the audience thought that my part went with the performance.[48]

In the Professor's company, I met Albert Knowles. This man was the agent of the Arapahoe Agency; he told me of the many fine ponies his Indians had at the Agency and that they indulged in much horseplay. Knowles asked me to visit the Agency. I was in need of a good stallion and this horse must be a straight Indian pony; so I went out to Washington that winter.

I found the Arapahos very friendly – they were good horsemen – they asked me to ride in three different races. Now, I didn't have a horse with me, but they insisted that I ride their horses. I had spotted a nice stallion which I wanted to buy. First, I must find out what this horse was good for, so I agreed to ride that horse. Sure enough. He was just what I thought he might be and I won all three of the races with him. My winnings were – nine good ponies. I bought the stallion and gave the nine ponies back to the Indians.

Early in April, the snow began to melt away. Some of the Indians came to me with the story of five white men who had come on this Agency to gamble and they said these men had won many of their ponies from them and also that these white men had cheated at cards which they had taught the Indians to play. I listened to the stories, then asked where these men camped. They told me these men lived in a board shanty at the far end of the Agency, so with some of the Indians as guides, I went to meet the five gamblers. When I rode to the shack, a rough looking man greeted me with a surly halloo. I said, "That's a nice band of ponies you have there." Most of them were mares, heavily laden with colt, and I

---

[48] **Editors' note**: Professor Oscar R. Gleason was the most famous horse-trainer of the late 19th century. Gleason was proud of the fact that he overcame the most vicious horses without the use of any cruelty. He based his success on two principles: treating the horse with kindness, and appealing properly to the horse's sense of understanding. Arriving in a city, he would issue an invitation to horse-owners to bring in their worst charges. Horses would arrive that had a host of problems, including animals that kicked, bit, balked etc., all of which Gleason would overcome in the arena without the use of tricks or savage equipment. The Professor's performances were the talk of America and he put on equestrian exhibits in major cities. When he booked Madison Square Garden, New York, in 1887, he drew the largest crowd ever assembled there. 5,000 people had to be turned away from the door. His fame became so great that Gleason was commended in a special Bill to the U.S. Congress. Yet Gleason's most famous 'duel' with a man-killing equine occurred on April 19th, 1886, in New York. At the Cosmopolitan Hall Gleason met the most savage horse of his career, the four-time man-killer known as Rysdyk. He overcame the animal's fear, placed a bit in his mouth, hitched the previously wild horse to a buggy and drove him around the arena – all within the space of ten minutes. Gleason was the author of five books on horse training and opened a famous school of equestrian science. There is no mention in any of the books by or about Gleason of the incident which Frank Hopkins described above.

knew what a loss the Indians would suffer in the next four years if those ponies were taken away."

Next, I asked the man if the ponies weren't the Indians' and he snarled, "They're mine now." I noticed that this man was heavily armed and also that none of the others came out of the shack. I pointed out to this man that it was not right to fleece the Indians out of their stock, then I mounted and rode down to speak to Knowles about it. Knowles said the ponies belonged to the Indians and if they gambled them away, that was their lookout and he would not interfere.

I then asked him, "Are white men allowed to come and live on this Agency?" "Well," said he, "there is a lot of room here;" also, that he got along well with his Indians and if those men got along he would not order them off the Agency. But I had already fully made up my mind that those ponies were going to stay on the Agency.

The next day, those men broke camp and drove the ponies North; by that time there were over three hundred ponies in the herd. I got a few Indians to go with me; at sundown I came up to the band of ponies. The men scattered among the large boulders as I came upon them and one of them asked what I wanted.

"Those horses."

"Well, you can have them, if you are man enough to take them," he replied. At this, the Indians scattered for cover. the man laid two forty-fives on the boulder – then he said, "I am Harry Tracy, who are you?"

"I'm the man who came to herd those ponies back to the Agency." Then I rolled the spur along the pony's flank, sending him into an open spot. Shots came from all sides, but I kept the pony moving in a zigzag movement till I got out of the range; but my pony was hit in the hip and I got a slug just below the knee joint. When I looked the pony over, I knew he was not hurt badly, and I charged back, firing with both my guns.

Soon, soldiers came on at full speed, and by this time it was getting dark; however, I rode around the ponies and drove them back; the next day the soldiers found three men badly wounded. Tracy was wounded, but he sneaked off up the mountain side in the dark, leaving his pards to die.[49] This man Tracy was one of the worst outlaws this country ever fought; he had been sentenced to

---

[49] **Jim Dullenty,** *Author of Harry Tracy, The Last Desperado (1989), A Place called Earp: the town named for Wyatt Earp (2001) and The Butch Cassidy Collection (1987):* "While it is possible that Hopkins had some involvement in an episode involving Harry Tracy it is not likely. Tracy, his real name Harry Severns, ... was arrested in Portland with a cohort in 1898 and put in the Oregon prison from which he and the cohort escaped in 1902 and after a long chase, was surrounded by two posses in August 1902 about 50 miles west of Spokane and killed himself. No one named Frank Hopkins had any role in any of these events. The name is unknown to me and I am about as familiar with the Tracy story as anyone can be. So add this to Hopkins' list of hoaxes."

death and broke jail and his record shows he had killed many officers of the law besides other men.

When I left the Arapahos, I bought three horses – the stallion and two mares, which I shipped to Wyoming. The time was near for me to ride in a circle again with the show. We played in towns and cities of our own country and Canada, and continued to do so until the Spring of 1903.

In Canada, there was talk of a long race; that was the fall of 1895. Cody wanted to boost the show, so he offered one thousand dollars to the rider who would ride one hundred miles and come in first. I asked him if I could ride in that race; he told me to stay out of it for the people might think the race was fixed for me to win, so I let it go at that.

After the race, there was much talk about me being afraid I might lose in that race as there were riders from the Mounted Police who took part in it. Then that made Cody sore and he challenged the winner, who was a Royal Mounted Police. Cody even went so far then as to say I must ride one hundred and twenty-five miles against the Police who wouldn't ride more than one hundred miles. I didn't like the idea at first, but when the Colonel dared me to ride against those odds I told him I would ride against any rider.

Then I stopped riding in the show and began sharpening up Turk for that hard ride. Turk was then five years old and weighed a little over nine hundred and fifty pounds, a real blocky horse with a lot of fight in him when it came to long roads. In the two previous races I rode him, he covered the ground without wearying and they were hard rides. I don't mean to say Turk was not tired at the end of each day, for he <u>was</u> tired and hung his head down as did most every horse I had ridden in long races, but there was no trembling of the muscles nor swelling of tendons when he was only a colt of four years. Now he had one more year to his age and that was a lot to an endurance horse. The training did not seem to affect him – only to harden his flesh.

Then the big day came. There was nothing to fear – the people up there did not object to the race; there were only two of us – the Mounted Police and I. The officer rode in his uniform; his horse a fine looking animal of a good size. I noticed the horse was high strung and full of "style." As I watched that horse move about I made up my mind right there that rider and horse were beaten before they started and I thought so loud that Colonel Cody heard me. But he said, "Boy, you've got something on your hands now that you never had before."

"Yes, Colonel, and I'm sitting on something that these Police never saw before. And now, Bill Cody, I'll bet you one hundred dollars that I will finish one hour or more ahead of the Mounted Police." The money was placed in the hands of Jonny Baker, and both of us rode to the starting line.

That big horse reared and plunged away as though he was crazed with fright. After a few miles, I came up behind and there I rode for over twenty miles; the big horse worried and I noticed he was wet with sweat; he did not like my horse tagging on behind. I thought I'd worried the big brainless fool long enough to make him lose the race and I picked up Turk to make a bid to pass the big horse.

Not so easy though – the big fool wanted to race, so I dropped back. Again I tried to pass and I did that many times till the big horse was worn out completely. Turk was still cool and fresh. Then I rode along, and when my day was done, Turk was in good shape.

The next day I rode until four o'clock and the finish. I had come to the line five hours and twenty-eight minutes ahead of the police. I must admit that it was the only time in all my years in the saddle though, that I ever tried to worry the horse of another rider, or tried a mean trick to win a race and I really was ashamed for doing it this time when I began to think about it.

That Fall, I went home to see my people and horses. Father was on the ranch as the scouting was ended. I rode with him to look over the many horses on the range. There was Josey, an albino mare, four years old; this colt was a picture of her grand dam little Whitey, only she was over nine hundred pounds in weight while Whitey weighed 700. The boys had broken this mare. Father thought she was as tough as a burro and fast as any cowpony on the ranch; I tried her out on many long rides and thought she would do for a brood mare. I mated her with the horse from the Arapahoe Agency and also bred several of my best mares to that horse; this breeding brought my ponies up to 950 lbs or a little more.

That fall I rode three races – one from Fort Bridger to Fort Kehoe – one from the Great Basin Montana to Laramie City, the third was with the Crows (Indians) from the Pitch Fork range to the Wind River, each ride over one hundred miles.

Cody wrote me he wanted me to look after the schooling of the riders before the show went to Madison Square Garden as there were many new acts. So I left the west shortly after the New Year; then I purchased a number of work horses for the show.

That summer was spent visiting the many towns and cities of the States, just riding with the Bill show. That Fall, the band played home sweet home down at Tampa, Florida. Cody told me I was to work on the stage with Arap, as I had trained him to dive into a tank which I had made at the winter quarters. I got the albino stallion to dive fifty feet, so when I got to New York it was arranged that I was to appear at the Hippodrome twice daily. I was not to start for three months as there was a company already performing there and their time did not expire until then.

I was invited to ride in a six hundred mile race at Fort Ethan Allan, Vermont. But after learning about the rules, I would not book on, but I did make the statement that I would ride against the winner of that race and that I would put down one thousand dollars if anyone wished to cover it. I waited until the race was over; then there were a lot of those soldiers who were willing to place their money on the winner, but the officers who had conducted the race would not submit to my conditions – they argued that it would be against the humane law, therefore they would see to it that such a race would not be run.

Then some of the troops got together and asked me if I still wanted to back up my offer. Sure I would, but the race could not be run over the same ground, and it was arranged that we would start from a small town in New Hampshire, the town of Peterboro. Our route led out of the State into Massachusetts. Passing the outskirts of Nashoway this ride was to cover six hundred miles.

After I had ridden to Peperat, a distance of two hundred and sixty-one miles according to men who laid out the route, I stopped at Pepperal to feed at noonday. Two men stepped into the stable and informed me I should not ride any farther, for the other rider's horse had "gone to pieces." The horse could not go any farther and who could compete against such a pace as I was going? They said the horse I was riding against had won the six hundred mile race three different years and he was considered to be the best endurance horse in this country; he was a full-blooded Morgan.

I told them their horse surely was a wonder – when he was ridden under army rules – but when he got out on the road against a real endurance horse where the first horse to finish was the winner, their great horse could not stand up to the work.

I have often been asked if my horses got tired. Sure they do – good and tired and they show it every night after a hard day, but after a good night's rest, they are ready for the road the next day. They must be in good shape; that is, they must be trained and conditioned for that work, or they can't do it. I rode my horse Turk in that race; at the time he was just in his prime, going on his seventh year. What a tough horse he was, then, but I am sorry to say that the following summer he was killed in a railroad collision down in Kentucky. I won over two thousand dollars on that race, and I sure would have liked to go the full six hundred miles, for I knew Turk could have done it.

I then returned to New York with Arap and I got soaked twice each day for three months when I dove into the tank with him. I did not care much about this act because there was always a large audience and they would make a lot of noise and this fretted Arap for he was exceedingly nervous. Sometimes I had considerable difficulty with this horse as he got so scared of the noise. The crowd thought I was a woman (because of my long hair) and I was always glad when the time was up to leave.

When the show started in the spring, there were many new riders, amongst them three Mexicans. One of these Mexicans was the best rope thrower I ever saw. He told me of the many long races in New Mexico and along the border and how he had taken part in many of them, so, when it was all over that Fall, I went with him. I brought three of my endurance horses along – they had been rode all summer as cow ponies, and they were in good shape. I rode in nine fifty-mile races. Over in Old Mexico, I rode two more – one a hundred and twenty-five miles and one of one hundred miles. At this time I had a number of horses and colts of the Whitey family, although they were not all endurance horses. Although out of the same family, there were some of them not good for much but they looked to be.

The next year something happened – the Spanish American War. Cody shipped horses and men. But it was ordered his service was not needed. But that did not mean that his men were not wanted. I rode with Teddy Roosevelt and Woods. Soon after landing at Santiago, I was used as a scout. Roosevelt loved to box and did so nearly every evening with some of the officers. I happened to go into the tent one evening and he spied me; at once he asked me to put the gloves on with him. He should have been a prize fighter for he loved to box and he could hit hard, and quick. I liked the sport myself and I visited his quarters often. One night I watched him box with a young officer; they were punching hard and fast: the young officer landed a hard left to Teddy's eye and Teddy backed away saying "Hold on there is something wrong with my eye." That punch had blinded him in one eye, and although very few people knew it, he was blind in it afterward[50].

I was wounded in the right leg the morning of the San Juan scrap. A splinter of bone shot off my shin; I got off lucky for there were only four others of my company alive after that scrap. I will speak this for those boys of the Rough Riders. There never was a braver body of men who rode into battle. Three weeks later I was sent home on account of being disabled. Teddy said he did not like to see me go, but it would be better for me in the States on account of the climate where there was fever and other diseases. It is not my aim to speak of that battle or of the mix-ups on the western plains that I came into contact with – only to speak of different places where I have spent my life in the saddle. However, when the troops returned, I rode with the Rough Riders up Fifth Avenue, New York. Teddy Roosevelt got a great welcome – the people cheered and swarmed every inch of the streets as we rode behind that great man Teddy Roosevelt.[51]

---

[50]**John A. Gable, Ph.D.,** *Executive Director, Theodore Roosevelt Association:* "There is no listing of a Frank T. Hopkins in the Rough Rider roster in Virgil Carrington Jones' *Roosevelt's Rough Riders.* The boxing incident took place with a naval officer when Teddy Roosevelt was President, not in Cuba. There is no listing of a F. T. Hopkins in the index of the Theodore Roosevelt Papers in the Library of Congress - Roosevelt's correspondence files - and virtually everyone who knew Roosevelt is represented by letters in this collection. Did this man Hopkins say anything true?"

[51] **Editors' note:** Ironically, though Frank Hopkins was nowhere to be seen in the Roosevelt parade, there really were two famous, albeit tiny, American Long Riders riding down Fifth Avenue in a place of honor behind Roosevelt's carriage. Bud and Temple Abernathy, aged ten and six, had just ridden 2,000 miles, without adult supervision, from

---

THEODORE ROOSEVELT

Theodore ("Teddy") Roosevelt is of course well-known for being one of the Presidents of the United States – the twenty-sixth – and was at that time (1901 to 1909) the youngest man to hold this high office.

He was also noted as an historian and a naturalist, and led two long and arduous scientific expeditions into South America and Africa.

Among his multitude of achievements, Roosevelt began the Panama Canal, negotiated an end to the Russo-Japanese War, which won him the Nobel Peace Prize, reduced the national debt, and passed laws to protect consumers.

When Spain declared war on the US in 1898 Roosevelt, a keen advocate of the liberation of Cuba from Spain, asked the Department of War for permission to raise a regiment.

Roosevelt himself had no experience of war, so Leonard Wood – President McKinley's physician – was made colonel of the new regiment. It was officially called the First U.S. Volunteer Cavalry, but it soon became known as the "Rough Riders." The regiment consisted of more than a thousand men – cowboys, Indians, various Wild West types and, more surprisingly, Ivy Leaguers and aristocrats.

This disparate group, whose only common element was that they could ride and shoot, was shipped out to Cuba. On 1 July, Roosevelt led the Rough Riders and elements of two other regiments up Kettle Hill, and captured it. He then led a second charge up the San Juan Heights above Santiago, and when that was captured the city surrendered and the war was virtually over.

The show was playing for the Fair at St. Louis; Cody had talked to me about having another World's horsemanship contest. The Fair would not start for a few months and by that time I would be alright again. I received a letter from an old friend who lived in Idaho Falls and he told of a race that was in the making and would I come and take part in it? I was still quite lame, but sent him word that I would go out there and look things over. I did. This race was one of the old time races such as [has] been since the coming of the horse into this country. The plains Indians were the first to indulge in the sport – then the white man joined in.

This race was run over trails – some of them very rough – no place for fancy, nervous horses. Many of the riders had the wrong kind of mounts for that rough country, and many of them found out their horses were no good after they trained for a short time. Seeing how my horses stood the steady grind for training, many of the riders asked me where they might get horses of the same breeding. I had a good supply of them at that time, but none for sale, so I made a deal with those

---

their home in Oklahoma Territory to take part in Teddy's Victory Parade. Once again, Hopkins has awarded himself someone else's achievement.

On June 18th, 1910, the New York Times reported - *"Million Join in Welcome to Roosevelt"* - "Behind the Roosevelt Carriage came the thirteen carriages of the Reception Committee.... and after them were the Spanish War Veterans, with the two little Abernathys, sons of Jack Abernathy, riding at their head. The two youngsters were cheered lustily along the line... flags were waved by thousands... along Fifth Avenue."

riders; this was it. They could ride my ponies – all it would cost them would be the feed, care and shipping bill.

Now, I was putting myself in a tight spot, for there were eighteen horses in this race who were of the Whitey strain. Some of them might fool me. At the same time, I wanted to see them race against each other – the winning of the stake did not mean anything to me for at that time I had plenty to lose. Now, that was the hottest race of one hundred miles I've seen yet. I rode a six-year old stallion which I named Blaze on account of the white mark in the face which run down over one eye.

I won that race only by eight minutes and three seconds with that bunch of ponies hammering the trail behind me. That was the closest ride I had been in. All of those ponies covered that hundred miles in less than fourteen hours of actual traveling. Some of them could beat Blaze as I found out later when I rode them myself. Three weeks later I rode one of those ponies over the same route against two large horses. My pony, Colonel, covered that one hundred miles in eleven hours of traveling with one night's rest between the mileage.

The contest at St. Louis was not what it should be for many of the riders did not come across the sea. When it ended I was called winner. It was the third time I heard the judges say I was the world's expert rider, but I did not feel proud of this for I had rode with men who were far better riders and better horsemen than I. After the Fair there were two years of showing all over the States. I got many calls to ride in army races, but I could not see why I should train a horse to race and then be told I must walk him with the bunch until the last mile, then have some sprinting horse leg it out and be called the winner.

The show crossed the ocean in 1903 covering England, Ireland,[52] Scotland. The people had not forgotten us for there was a full house every performance.

In 1904 we visited France again, camping by government permission on the famed Champs de Mars. After covering most of the French provinces we went on to Italy.

In France I was forced to take part in many private horse affairs – one a relay race, twenty miles to every horse. This was run in a circle of two miles. I used my own horses and finished the one hundred miles fifty-eight minutes ahead of the groups of riders. It seemed to me at the time that every person in France turned out to see that race.

The last week of our stay in France, Cody had me at the entrance of the show on horseback. They built a stand up off the ground. This was roped around like a fighting ring, and while I spent the time there I shook hands with the people coming in until my hand was swollen and sore. Cody knew how to draw the

---

[52] **Dr. Juti Winchester,** *Curator of the Buffalo Bill Museum at the Buffalo Bill Historical Center*: "According to our database of dates and places, Buffalo Bill's Wild West never went to Ireland."

crowd and the crowd meant money to him and that was the sole reason for my being at the entrance.

At La Perche, I rode in a hundred fifty mile race against nine other riders, winning over six hours at the finish. Those bobbed tail horses and the bobbing riders did their best and they were a sorry looking lot when they came in; my horse did not show any strain at all. Each horse traveled only twenty miles. The next day I bade farewell to many horsemen friends in France.

Our next stop was Italy, showing for the second time in Naples, Genoa, Rome, Venice. Cody said there were a number of cavalry officers who wished me to perform for them on their military grounds. Seeing I was not much interested, he then said those officers thought my trick riding was a fake and I would not be able to do those stunts outside of that fixed ring Of course, then, I agreed to perform for the Officers. Cody was in the crowd at the time; I think I did the best trick riding of my whole career that day;[53] Cody said he had never seen me do as well, and then confessed, saying he had lied to me as the officers had not doubted my riding, but they wished to have me in their company on that special day.

Then again I rode one hundred and fifty miles against the cavalry of Italy, against the same men who had ridden against on my first visit to that country. Austria, was the next country, then Germany. Here on our previous visit, I had gained many friends. The officers of the mounted troops came often to see me when I was off duty. I must ride with them through the fine parks and drives before bidding them farewell for the last time.

I rode one fifty mile race and one of one hundred and twenty five miles. I was to ride in another of two hundred and fifty miles but the show was scheduled to go into Belgium. This race was too late so I had to let it go. The people of Belgium are heavy horse raisers – mostly draft horses. In that country I was at rest – just one of the riders in the show, no one to bother me when off duty. But there was a man who had sent me a note saying he would like to talk with me about horsemanship, so I arranged to meet him.

This man spoke very good English. He commented on my riding and said, "You are from America, so you must know much about trotting horses."

Then he went on to tell me about horses bought in America – Hambletonions; I told him I did know a little about trotters and he asked me if I would go to his stables and drive one of his horses – there was something wrong with the horse – he did not go right.

---

[53] **Dale Yeager**, *Criminal Psychologist:* "Frank Hopkins profiles as a narcissist with sociopathic tendencies. Narcissists generally see themselves as special, uniquely talented individuals compared to other people in society. They also have a well developed skill for deception.

I drove the horse over a half mile track; he would break and run if I tried to get any speed out of him; when I came off the track, the owner asked me why did his horse break and run and was there any cure for that. I said, "Mister, your horse is not balanced." The man looked surprised, then told me that trotting horses were something new in his part of the country. Could I balance his horse? If there was a shoe-ing shop handy I could. There was: the horse was taken at once to the shop.

I swept the ground for about a hundred feet and trotted the horse over it, then measured his tracks and found the horse traveled too slow forward; he did not get his forward feet out of the way of the hind ones. So I shod him a little heavier forward, then drove him over the half mile track. That hoss could trot, and he did, but there was no running. Soon the news got round and I don't think there was a man who owned a trotter in that part of the country who didn't call to see me. Later, I will say more about the trotters in Belgium.

Then the show went to Bohemia and later to Russia.[54] There were three Cossacks who rode in the show and when they were in their own country I met through them many of those great Cossack riders. They asked me to ride in a relay race – I don't recall the mileage – I think it must have been about 200 miles and there were stations where every man must change horses – I should say the change was 15 miles apart. Those Cossacks had no mercy on their mounts.[55] The worry to those horses was worse than the race. My ponies were not afraid of me or of the road. They won the a race very easy. I also won three endurance races on the Russian border. Those people held many endurance races every year.

While riding one of those races I met a trader. He traded in wool and he was going to Mongolia where he had a large business. This man told me of races in that country, also of the small horses there; he said many of those ponies travel one hundred miles in a single day. He also told of the fine-blooded horses that were raised in Mongolia. This trader was anxious to have me go into that land with him and I promised that I would join him later on.

We were to show in other small countries. When Cody sailed for the States, I joined my German friend, the wool trader. He met me in Hamburg. Shortly after, both of us were to journey together into Mongolia. I talked about my horses – there were five with me. The trader, whose name was George Freimhoff, told me he would arrange for the shipping of my horses, but it would be

---

[54]**Dr. Juti Winchester,** *Curator of the Buffalo Bill Museum at the Buffalo Bill Historical Center*: "According to our database of dates and places, Buffalo Bill's Wild West did not go to Russia at all, in any of their tours."

[55] **Editors' note:** When Cossack officer Mikhail Asseyev arrived in Paris in 1889, having ridden 1,646 miles from Kiev in 33 days, his horses were in such fantastic condition that the President of the French humane society awarded the young Russian officer a superb gold medal.

about two months before he was ready to go. So I left my horses in the care of my man and I boarded a boat for home.

I learned that "pink eye" was raging among the horses in the northwest and when I got home I found out that many of my ponies had it. Old Josy had gone blind in both eyes. I felt very bad about this mare, for she had raised a large family of good tough colts for me, among them Hidalgo. This mare was a dark chestnut color, with a small white spot on her neck. She was in such a bad way I had her killed.

Her daughter, Josy the second, a fine albino mare, was also stricken with the "pink eye". This mare had a colt running at her side; the colt was dark chestnut with a silvery mane and tail and of all the colors of a horse I like that color the best. I soon cured Josey but I got a motherly old cow to nurse the colt. The "pink eye" had robbed me of some fine colts – especially those that were shedding their teeth. Then, I received a letter from my friend who said he would be ready for the trip into Mongolia and that I should come to Germany as soon as possible.

Now, of all the spots on earth, I believe Mongolia has the poorest way of transporting man or horse; in fact there is no way of getting from one place to another. After we left Russia, we had to wait days at a time till we could be driven by horse and wagon and then only a few miles at a time, so I asked my friend if he could ride in the saddle and he then told me he always rode those small ponies when in the livestock country, but we were miles from the sheep lands then. I asked him to ride one of my horses so we might be traveling instead of waiting for the route men and he agreed to ride.

Both of us shifted horses often, leading the other horses; in a few days[56] we saw funny little men herding stock, and they all had a band of wooly ponies not much bigger than Shetland ponies. These little horses were very block-y – I had not seen any horse of their build before. Those horses got all their food from the ground. Their owners did not feed them grain, nor did they stable them.

I thought it was a pity, but I soon learned these people were too poor – they scarcely had shelter for themselves,[57] yet they raise the finest stock in the world. Sheep, cattle and the best horses in the world are raised there, although you will not see the larger horse in the stock grazing lands. Those people don't get much for their wool or cattle; it is the merchants who reap the harvest. Some parts of

---

[56] **Editors' note:** In true Hopkinesque form, Frank seems to have overlooked the fact that the distance between Germany and Mongolia is approximately eight thousand miles. Moreover winter temperatures in Mongolia have been known to sink to –36 degrees Fahrenheit (-58 Celsius). Yet Hopkins claims to have made this epic, albeit unrecorded, equestrian journey in "a few days."

[57] **Editors' note:** The nomadic Mongolian people take their homes –*yurts* or *gers* – with them wherever they go, so it is absurd to state that they 'scarcely had shelter for themselves.'

that country are surely wild and the people are far from being civilized. In the southwest, there are many wild ponies – a different horse from those that are used by the herdsmen.

The wild pony has a stub mane, much like the zebra, that grows about three inches long. The ponies are all of one color – a dark buckskin, or a blend of buckskin, and they are built all alike. Of all the species of the horse family, those wild ponies are the most vicious – there is no way to gain their friendship and you can not subdue them under any conditions. I think I have as much patience as any man, but I gave up the job of trying to gentle those animals, although I surely gave it a long trial. The natives, afraid of these horses, will have nothing to do with them.

I heard many stories about how these horses could hold their own against wolves and other animals; that they would gang together and kill large wolves and also men if the men bothered them. I came to believe some of these stories after I tried to catch a pony from a small band. I got the pony, but if my horse was not faster than the bunch I surely would have been killed for those ponies tried to gang me as soon as I rode after them. They swung in a circle and charged, striking with their forward feet.

After many attempts, I got a colt of about three years. I had learned if I stopped my horse and stood still, those ponies would stop their charging, so I roped this pony and set my horse at the end of the rope; they circled to charge, but when my horse stood, holding the pony, the band of ponies came to a stand. Some of them pawed and squealed, others whistled their defiance, but they would not come closer. I had to drag that pony for he would not lead – choking made no difference to him, and that little lad would try to knock me out of the saddle. How I did admire his courage though. He was the gamest of all horses I met and I've handled some very game ones in my day. I roped nine of those ponies – every one was the same. The stories were true – they can't be handled.

I rode in twelve races against the stock riders – I don't know the mileage. They would say a certain ride was 100 miles; another 150 miles, but I could not get proof of it. I will say these herders' horses are the toughest species of horseflesh I know.

In the south, I found a more businesslike people. Some of them had been educated in our colleges in the States and they had the finest of horses – mostly of the racehorse type and here I raced in five rides against large horses. Those people were willing to bet heavy sums on their mounts – they were great gamblers. I wandered over many miles of waste barren land in that country. Once I was asked to journey to Tibet, but my time was up – and more. It was necessary for me to hurry back to the United States. The five horses I would not sell; it cost a lot of money to ship them home.[58]

When I again joined the show, I noticed that Cody was not the happy man I had known so many years. He had aged a lot in the short time I was absent; there was something wrong. The Wild West show had had its swing; now it was getting old and Cody's spirit appeared broken. He spoke to me one day after the performance asking if I would stick with him to the end and it struck me rather queer to have him ask such a question. I soon learned the reason, for that season the show was sold at sheriff's sale in Denver.

However, Cody managed to straighten things out and the next year the show was on the road. But the Colonel never became the same man again; he was sick and broken in spirit. I have no idea how Cody lost the large fortune he made with the show, but evidently it was gone. This was none of my business, of course, but I wanted to see that show go on, and I did my part by doing extra work to help out. He noticed this and appreciated it.

In two years, his hair grew snow white and the old plainsman had to be helped into the saddle, in fact he was only the outside shell of the great "Buffalo Bill" I had known since my childhood. Then, Major Gordon Lilly joined the show with his elephants. This was a funny thing in a wild west show and I guess everybody thought the same about it, for the Bill show started down grade from the time Lilly joined partnership with Cody.

I had met a man in Baltimore who was a horse shipper; he shipped horses all over the world and all classes of horses. In the fall of 1908 this shipper (Fred Bushing) asked me if I would take charge of a shipment for him to be shipped to Singapore, up the Bering Straits.[59] Most of the horses were of the large saddle-horse type; after making arrangements with the insurance company, I signed the agreement, and there was work aplenty – for many of those horses were sick. However, I did not lose a single horse.

When the horses were unloaded, I met George Eastwood, an Englishman whom I had met in England some years before. He was a first-class race horse trainer who had charge of a string of runners. He knew of my long rides in Europe. At once he told me of long rides there and also of those in India, across the straits, but I had none of my endurance horses with me. I could buy a horse, yes, but what would I get? – nothing except one of thoroughbred blood and what could I do with a tender horse of that breeding?

But I saw a horse – they told me it was a native scrub, not worth much. I bought him, a stallion weighing 875 lbs when I had him on the scales. Horses were very high in price, but native ponies were cheap and for this one I paid

---

[58] **Editors' note:** It would be interesting to learn how Hopkins "shipped his horses home" to the USA from land-locked Mongolia – a country with neither railroads nor ports!

[59] **Editors' note:** The Bering Straits are located between Russia and Alaska.

about twenty-five dollars in our money. I daresay he had never been fed grain and I had to break him all over to my style of handling.

I rode him in four races there from 50 to 60 miles each I should judge. Then went into India and rode him in three more. All of these rides were against thoroughbred horses or horses crossed with that blood. In my travels I have learned that endurance racing is as old as the horse. I surely would like to have brought that one-eyed pony home with me, even though he was only a scrub. I sold him in India for about, say, $600: not a bad price for a scrub. He had the real stuff in him and I saw it the minute I laid eyes on him. I sailed for England with my friend, Eastwood. That trip paid me well.

In June of that summer, I joined the Bill show. With the show was a gray horse – a bad bucker who had been hurting many of the boys for the past two years. They called him Hightower and he sure was a devil under leather. I itched to slip up in his middle, but every time I spoke to Cody about riding him, I got the same answer – "Stay off that horse, you." "When I want you to ride him I'll call on you – then maybe the horse'll kill you, like as not." I had watched that horse unload for two years and none of the riders stayed with him more than for one jump. I sort of gave up the hope that I would ever be permitted to try him.

But one night, while I sat eating with Cody, a number of his friends in the Guernsey Hotel at Keene, N.H. came to visit him and then Cody said, "Buff, it's your turn to ride Hightower tonight".

I was surprised and thanked him for the favor. His guests seemed surprised when I asked him, "You don't think he will hurt me, do you, Colonel?" He smiled, but I noticed he turned his head and winked when he spoke to his friends, saying, "You will see something in that ring tonight – its a good show when two bad actors meet." The horse was turned into the ring; I roped and throwed him, then I saddled the man-killer, put my boots into the stirrups and let him get to his feet. That horse sure was surprised, for I had that seat as if I was glued into it. It may have been only luck, but I had that seat and there I stayed. Hightower done everything that a true outlaw could do, still I stayed there.

It made him so mad he broke a blood vessel in his head and was bleeding to death. Cody rode alongside and told me to slide off. I thought the hoss was only sulking and would soon take off the brakes, maybe when I made a move to slide off, then turn and strike me. I was blind from the shaking I got. Then one of the riders picked me off the saddle.

At the hospital, I was told that the horse died before they could get him out of the ring. I have heard of other horses since then who were named Hightower, but to me there was only one. I can honestly say that he was the greatest bucker that ever threw a rider, and I have rode my share of that kind and have seen other riders take buckers, but there never was a second Hightower.[60]

When the show went into winter quarters that fall, I was left behind with a broken leg.[61] Father wrote often. He wrote that the horse dealers who had bought horses from us for years did not call to even look at the colts – most of those dealers were from the East and they had always been eager to get horses from our breeding, for I had raised a fine horse – a cross between the Morgan and Hambletonian. They were the best of gentleman's driving horses.

But the automobile at that time began to tell on the horse trade, especially the driving horse. I wrote to some of the dealers and they wrote back that no one raised a better driving horse than I did, but they could not give them away, let alone sell them. Now, it don't take long to have a lot of horses on your hands if you have a large number of brood mares that foal every Spring, that is, if you don't sell off the four years crop. At that time there were over sixty colts that were four years old, besides the breeding stock. Then there was the sucking colts, the yearlings, the two year olds and those that were three years old, all of them different ages. There was a large herd. These horses were bred from the best sires and dams that money could buy or that the best horseman could choose. Still, I could not sell them. Then, there were fifty more that I did not care to sell – they were colts and the brood stock of the Whitey strain.

It was late in January before I could travel on account of that broken leg. When I got home those horses were round and fat; Father would not allow them to be neglected although the horses were not worth feeding; he tried his best to cheer me up and said that I surely would find someone who would be glad to buy a fine lot of colts as those were. I had been hopping round on the sticks about two weeks, when Ed Tobel came to see me. I had always called him "Bud." This man had rode a number of seasons in the show and had contested against me throughout Europe and in this country. I believe Bud Tobel was as good a horseman as ever looked down over a horse's ears, but he had one bad habit – drink. He would go on a spree that would last a month and then he would stop, not to take a single drink even with his best friends, until he broke out again.

At the time he called to see me he was broke. He had been training polo ponies for George Minnick down in Texas, went on a spree and lost the job. Bud could train a polo pony with the most expert riders, but the drink rooted him. Bud was at home with my people; he knew he could not drink when he was there.

At the table that evening, he spoke of my horses and told me that the polo teams were using larger horses and that those horses of mine were about the right

---

[60] **Editors' note:** This brutal approach is in marked contrast to Hopkins' later writings for the *Vermont Horse & Bridle Trail Bulletin,* where he advocates being kind to horses.
[61] **Editors' note:** How did he break his leg?

type for the game. He had been into the Argentine with shipments of polo ponies. He said if those horses of mine were trained to play the game he could sell all of them in the Argentine. I made a deal with Bud that if he would let the drink alone he would get top wages. I must say he obeyed the rules and he surely worked hard on that bunch of horses. I often stopped him from working late into the night.

By the first of May, Bud had many of those colts as handy as a pocket in a shirt. He knew most of the buyers from the Argentine and he was well liked by those dealers. One day Bud rode out to Town and on his return he told me he had a letter from a dealer who would soon come to the States to buy a shipment of horses and that there was a large demand for large polo ponies, and if my horses were handy the dealer would buy all of them.

Now I could not help handling those colts but I told Bud to get four good men and get those horses in shape. It was the middle of June before the dealer came to look the horses over and my men played a regular game of polo twice a day as the dealer looked on. When one game was over, the dealer looked the horses over and bought that set of horses without rejecting a single horse. In this manner every horse was sold that was handy. The dealer said that they were the best lot he had ever bought and that he would buy every horse that was fit to play polo on his next trip in the Fall.

I made Bud boss of the ranch as it was too much for Father who was in his nineties, but Father could keep an eye on Bud in case Bud dropped his quirt. Cody was sending word often, asking me to come and help him out even if I did not ride in the ring, so I divided fifty dollars out of the sale of every horse sold to the polo pony dealer and this money was split between the trainers and Bud. Every man had a good pocket full.

Then I told them to break the horses the same as they would if the horses were their own stock; and the better the job they done, the more money they would get, and Father was to pay them every week. I believe those boys were the best polo pony trainers that could be found and they were paid more than any of the other raisers paid, besides giving them free board and lodging. They were worth it.

I bid them goodbye and rode with a stiff leg in the Bill show. In the Spring, Dan Monet the dealer from the Argentine wrote me asking that I send him every horse that could be used to play polo and to send Tobel along with them. The dealer wrote that he would pay me an honest price for the horses. I knew Bud was honest and the horses were of the best, so I wrote Father telling him to have Bud ship with the horses but to take only those who were well trained, and to have the horses insured. That shipment of horses landed safely with the loss of only one horse and there were thirty four in the shipment.

Tobel told them over there that I was a long-distance rider and soon I got letters from all parts of the Argentine inviting me to ride over there. I wrote

Tobel to arrange a number of rides and when he wrote back he said there were at least twenty rides waiting for me – none, of them over sixty miles, and most of them with the cattle raisers.

That winter, I shipped twelve of my little nags and had Bud go along. Now, you will be surprised when I say I rode sixty-eight rides from the 14th day of October to the 4th of March. After that I could not get anyone in that country to ride against me if I paid them to ride in a race, but I could get most any price for one of my stallions that I might ask. But all of the stallions came home with me.

Although I sold all the horses that were old enough to train, I knew the trade would not last for long. I would not breed my mares any more for I would have a lot of dooryard pets on my hands. I figured right, for the rush of polo ponies to the Argentine slacked after the third year. However, my herd was well cleaned up; in the end, the dealer bought most of my brood stock.

Many of the young mares that had been shipped for polo playing had been used as brood mares after these mares had played the game for a season. From time to time I see pictures of polo ponies from the Argentine – most of them have a wide white blaze running down their faces and that mark is surely the stamp of that sturdy Morgan stallion (Whitey[62]) who I had at the head of my herd for over 20 years. Every one of his colts bore that mark, even his grandsires had that wide blaze in their faces. On the ranch there were still the two year old colts, about 30 in all, and about 20 of the Whitey strain, old horses and all. I would not raise any more horses, but the Whitey family were not for sale. I did raise four colts of that strain after the drop in the market.

I rode my own horses in the show, so the few that were left were used up in a few years. Tobel rode with us in the show the Summer of 1911. I had bought some mean buckers for Cody and among this string was a mare called Topsy; she could unload the best of our riders – in fact she sent me to the hospital twice that season. The time came for Bud to ride that mare. Now, Bud liked to kid me about being throwed; he walked over to me as soon as he got the word to ride Topsy.

"See here, Buff, he said, "I'll show you how to ride that mare. Just watch me in the ring the next time you get her you will know how to ride a bucker." Bud went across the street into a liquor store and bought himself some false courage and when he came back I noticed he was well lit up.

I pleaded with him a long while to give me his ticket and take mine in exchange. He could ride any horse that ever wore hair, but I said, "Bud, if you step up on that mare, she is the last horse you will ever throw a leg over." When the buckers came out, Budd flipped the rope on Topsy; he done a good job of saddling her. I sat there on my horse and saw him tuck his boots into the stirrups.

---

[62] **Editors' note:** Earlier in this chapter Hopkins introduces the reader to "… my little albino mare 'Whitey.' This mare I bought from the army…"

No sooner had that mare gotten to her feet than Bud was turning over endways in the air. The mare sent him high; when Bud struck the ground he lay very still. Bud Tobel had mounted his last horse.

I had word from a man down in Tennessee that there was a hundred mile race and would I ride in it. This man was a cavalryman who I had rode against many times. The ride was three months away so there was time to train. Now, I had a horse in the show with me who was from the Whitey strain; this stallion was the color of slate, so I called him Blueskin. He sure was a game little horse. After the show went in for the winter, I began training Blue, Gypsy Boy and Chenango and after a few days I decided Blue was the horse. When I got to Tennessee I was told that the route would have to be changed for there was a heavy watch on the riders. I was asked too many questions when I took my horse off the train, but my answers came quick and clear.

There is a page missing from the original document, but it is clear that Frank Hopkins won the race.

"Is that pony from the Whitey strain?"

That started something. What blood was the Whitey strain? Where could those horses be bought? etc. etc. Then the Professor told them that I had the only horses of that strain; I answered questions until late into the night, still those men would have it that a horse bred for cavalry work had the most endurance. Some of them were a trifle peeved over me collecting so much money on that ride and the next morning some of them came to me and asked if I would place any money on a relay race. I told them that if they would cover the money that I had collected on the 100 mile race I would put it up, but the change of horses must be every twenty miles. They wanted to change horses every five miles but I stuck to the 20 mile limit.

They talked it over for a few days and then we came to an agreement to ride the same 100 miles over the same road, changing horses every twenty miles. The race to take place in 30 days. Then I sent word to father to ship four more of my stallions. One was that seal brown horse with a silver mane and tail; this horse was out of albino Josey. Then, there were two more of her colts that had cut cattle for a few seasons, called slickers by their riders. There was also old Major who had carried me over the road in many rides but not in races. He was now 16 years old. Father wrote saying I would make a big mistake if I did not take Major, so they sent him along.

Now, these riders figures that their sprinting horses could win that money back for them and I figured that I would surely lose the money if the relays were limited to five miles to each horse, but the money was put up and the agreement signed for a 20-mile relay. I used Blue for the first horse, Gypsy Boy for the second, Chenango was the third, Silver the fourth and old Major done his 20 miles in one hour and 41 minutes.

The first race was a stunning blow to those riders and their backers. But the relay race surely was a headache to the whole outfit. I had cleaned up over $6,000 on those two races and Gleason made aplenty. If I would have sold those ponies I'd have had all my pockets filled with money for I was offered fancy prices for all of them, even for the two that did not take part in the race. I had held them in reserve in case something were to happen to one of the others when training.

Gypsy Boy had the best set of legs of any horse I ever raised, but for some reason he had the body of a running horse – a little too long in the back to suit me. Gypsy Boy's mother died when he was born so he was hand raised and ran about the place. Now there was a band of horse-trading gypsies known as the Coopers who camped near our place, and there in Sundance those gypsies would buy up a large drove of horses each Spring, then drive them east, trading and selling until all were disposed of.

This colt whom I called Gypsy Boy wandered down to the gypsy camp; for three days I searched the country looking for him, knowing that the colt needed milk and that without it [he] would soon die. At sundown the third day, I saw that little white-headed rascal; he was with a small gypsy boy who was watching over the horses as they grazed near the camp. I led the colt home and my mother named him Gypsy Boy and she always spoke of that colt as her horse for she raised him by hand. Of course the colt got a lot of petting and this I did not like so well, but I could not say anything about it for mother was always very kind and thoughtful to me and she loved all living things.

Once I had Gypsy Boy in the show where I rode him every day: I soon got him to do what I wanted him to. But I know he longed to feel the gentle touch of my mother's hand and the following season while the show played at Cheyenne mother called to see the horse. Gypsy Boy made such a fuss when she stepped out of his sight I did not have the heart to ship him away from his old home and the only mother he knew who had fed and cared for him when he was a baby. Gypsy Boy was then 12 years old, he spent the rest of his life out there in Sundance. Although he was one of the best horses to do trick riding on, I could not take him away from home again.

The winter of 1913 I had my stable at Bridgeport, Connecticut. There I had 48 horses in all; 36 of them were those colts that were weaned when I sold their mothers to go to South America. The colts were now four years old – an extra fine lot of horses. The other 12 were the last of the Whitey family. I was training the colts to play polo. Some of them I had broke to harness.

There was a Japanese army officer who had written me that he would like to get some nice saddle horses for breeding stock. This officer, whose name was Sang Wo, I had met across the sea – in fact I had contested against him three different times, and learned to like him. He wrote that he was to come to this country to get a few American bison and at the same time he would buy horses to improve the saddle horses in his own country. I sent him word that I had the type of horse I believed would please his people.

A few days later, I was putting on a sleigh-riding party. There were a large number of people going on this ride. There was a gay lot of folks and among them was Bill Hart[63] and his sister Mary. This was a ride of fifteen miles. All of us had a great day of it, but on the return trip, as I drove the eight-horse team down the street where my stable was, we saw a large fire. At once, I knew the fire was at my place and I sent that team into a dead run with its human cargo screaming with fright.

I jumped from the sleigh and ran to the burning stable. The firemen grabbed me, but I left my clothes in their hands and ran into the burning stable; there were horses in there that I would save or perish with them. The burning timber was falling all about me and the smoke and heat almost blinded me, but when I called to the horses they answered me. I called first to Chenango and he answered; then I heard Blue.

As I cried out the names of most of the horses they whinnied out their answer – that was the only way I had of finding them. Finally, one after the other, they followed me over the falling timbers. I kept saying, "Come on, boys, come here." I could not see them but I knew they were trailing on after me as best they could as fast as I could cut their ropes. How we got out of that stable with the falling timbers I can not explain, nor do I know how those horses managed to follow me, but when I reached the street, all of the Indian ponies were huddled about me. I noticed that Silver was in bad shape – he coughed and held his nose to the ground. Doctor Shelby came to me and told me to put the horses on his lawn.

---

[63] **Janis Ashley, Administrator, William S. Hart Museum:** "The William S. Hart Museum has no information regarding Mr. Hopkins, and Hopkins is not mentioned in Hart's autobiography." William Hart was actually in California in the winter of 1913, preparing to begin work on a Western in which he rode "Midnight, a superb, coal-black animal."

WILLIAM S. HART

Before Roy Rogers and Trigger galloped across the silver screen, William S. Hart and his horse Fritz were enthralling 1920s movie audiences all over America.

In his best-selling autobiography, "My Life - East and West," famed silent movie star William S. Hart carefully documented his own life. Hart was a prolific actor, a crafty business man, a connoisseur of fine art and beautiful horses. In order to make his own roles more authentic, Hart had become friends with real-life Old West legends like Charlie Siringo and Bat Masterson. Hart was so revered that during a war-bond drive in the First World War he was greeted with a roar of welcome by sixty-five thousand Americans, who gathered on Wall Street in New York City to hear him address the crowd.

On June 25, 1926, it was Hart who was invited to be the guest of the State of Montana at the semi-centennial of the Battle of Little Bighorn. He addressed the audience in the Lakota language, to their surprise and delight. This true man of the west was honoured by a bronze statue that was unveiled at Billings, Montana, on July 4, 1927. Hart's autobiography contains many episodes which bear an uncanny resemblance to tales Frank Hopkins told at a later date.

Hart became so attached to Fritz, the horse he rode in his first film roles, that he bought him! In his autobiography Hart described Fritz thus: "I used a pinto horse named Fritz. He weighed only one thousand pounds, but his power and endurance were remarkable."

As I started for his lawn, I noticed my left arm was helpless where the shoulder was broken; there were bruises and burns on my body, for I was nearly naked. Silver walked around me; I laid the good hand on his head to calm him for I knew that little silver-tailed horse was dying on his feet, and finally he did lay down beside me and he went out like a light. I looked at the house – it was burned flat to the ground and the big stable had fallen. In that house was a collection of many things I had made during my life, including hundreds of photographs, some of them where I had been photographed with the royalty of Europe, others pictures of me taken in contests all over the world; some of my childhood, and with the troops, and some when I carried messages for our army.[64]

They did not matter much compared with my horses. When I saw that little silver-tailed horse lying at my feet, it was too much. Although I was badly hurt, I had to be carried away from his body stretched out there on the snow-covered lawn. I lost in all eighteen horses in that fire. Two of the Whitey family were burned so badly that I had to order them destroyed. I lay in the hospital until the following June.

When I joined the show again, the horse doctor told me that Blueskin was so cross that he was too dangerous to be in the horse-top. I went to see him – the horse did not seem to know me; his eyes took on a cruel look when I spoke. I knew at once then what was wrong – he had what is known as "stallion's mad-

---

[64] **Editors' note:** There had in fact been three fires in Bridgeport, which was where the famous American showman P. T. Barnum had his home. In 1857 Barnum's home, "Iranistan," went up in flames. In 1887 Barnum's stable burned down. And in 1889 Barnum lost another home, and many of his personal possessions, in yet another fire.

ness.[65]" I turned away and told the doctor to have the horse destroyed as soon as possible for it seemed the only cure. I did not ride much in the show that season, but I appeared in the ring.

The army officer from Japan called to see me that fall and bought all the horses that I had except those of the Whitey family. He also bought six bison. This little man said if I would take two of my ponies he would see that I got a few long rides or races. In his joking way he said I would get beaten in his country.

When the time came to ship the stock, I went with him, but I took four of my ponies. In that country I won 38 rides, none of them less than 60 miles. The longest ride was about 110 miles. I will say that the Japanese people are good sports and friendly; they did not want me to pay my own way and they even wanted to pay my expenses on the voyage home. They are up to the minute in every way. Of course their customs seemed a bit queer to me, but then I've found that in other countries too.

When I returned home things began to happen. I got a telegram from California that I should come at once: Buffalo Jones was very ill and he wished to see me. I got there just in time for that great plainsman passed on in a few hours after my arrival.

Two months later, I faced what I thought was the worst thing that could happen to any human being – my father, who would have been ninety-eight years old if he had lived three days longer, "passed on." He was a true plainsman. He was a doctor in his early days but he loved to do scout duty. He was often called in on bad cases in the army, such as taking off an arm or a leg, which was not such an easy experience in those days for the patient as it is now. But he preferred to scout. He served as a scout for over fifty years. Although he was always pleasant, I cannot recall ever seeing him smile, and he talked very little. Maybe there was something in his early life that saddened him, or else it was his living alone with his horse so much on the plains.

After his death, my mother was broken in spirit. She was only seventeen years older than I, a large woman who stood six feet two inches tall, who always seemed, before father went on, so happy and care free. Now, she seemed to take no interest in anything that went on around her. Although I was her only child, she scarcely noticed even me. Of course I realized she was no longer herself for she was always so very kind and thoughtful of me.

Five months after Father passed on, she followed him. Now I have been shot seven times, had bones broken, have been smashed up a lot, and always the background of my ancestors brought me through. But this blow of losing both parents surely brought me to earth. For a while I was so dazed that I was in a

---

[65] **Editors' note**: We have been unable to find a veterinarian who is familiar with the term "stallion's madness."

stupid state until I realized that there was still much in the world to be thankful for instead of brooding over what I thought my loss. I pictured myself as selfish when the Great Spirit had called my people to dwell with Him, the Maker of all things. It was the will of the Great Father and I was being selfish to resent it.

In the summer of 1916, many of the old riders visited the show; among them was "Death Valley Scotty." He had ridden with us a few seasons and he was a good bronc rider. Scotty was pleased to see me – he asked me to let him take one of my horses as he wished to take a ride around St. Louis, so I let him take my gray pony Purko. When the performance started in the afternoon, neither Scotty nor the horse had returned. I was not worried, thinking Scotty had met some friends.

That evening, Finlay, one of the boys, told me that there was a man looking for me on the lot, and that he was a police officer, and so I'd better take a sneak. Knowing there was nothing to fear on my part I took a look around and located the officer. He told me that both my friend and my horse were under arrest; Scotty was locked in a cell and the horse held in a stable. The charge was drunk and disorderly. It cost me $15 to get Scotty out of the Jug and $5 to get Purko out of the pound. Scotty had stopped at a few rum shops, got himself all liquored up and then he began putting on a one man wild west show by riding Purko into hotels and bar-rooms. Evidently the managers objected to the performance and had Scotty arrested. He was a good friend of mine, but when he went on a spree he sure was a wild man.

He told me at that time, there was to be a round-up at Fort Russell that fall. I promised I would show up in time to take part in it. When the show went into winter quarters, I took with me Purko and his full brother who I named Spot. Spot had been used in that mountain lion hunt with Buffalo Jones and Zane Grey[66] – that was back in 1906. Spot and Purko were now old horses, still I had chosen them for the round-up at Fort Russell; there I done some trick riding as well as riding buckers – in fact, I took part in all kinds of horsemanship.

One morning, as I was looking over the stock in the corrals, a young man asked me if my name was Hopkins. I said it was. He then told me that he had been asked to look me up for Teddy Roosevelt wished to see me. I went at once and found Roosevelt waiting with a number of his friends.

---

[66] **Dr. Joe Wheeler, Ph.D.,** *Founder and Executive Director, Zane Grey's West Society:* "In my Zane Grey Master Character Index (includes both fictional and real life characters referred to in Zane Grey's writings), there is no mention of Frank Hopkins. That does not mean that Grey never met or interacted with him, but it does strongly imply that he never played a major role in Grey's life...It is truly amazing to discover how many people down through the years have attempted to gain a modicum of fame by claiming some sort of association with Grey."

ZANE GREY

Zane Grey, the greatest storyteller of the American West, was born in Zanesville, Ohio, on January 31, 1872. His Zane ancestors had been vigorous, illustrious pioneers in America's "First West", the historic Ohio Valley, and his boyhood thrill at their adventures would eventually motivate Grey to novelize both his family's own story and the stories of many another pioneer homesteader, farm wife, rancher, cowhand, naive Eastern belle, camp follower, miner, Indian youth, trail driver, railroad man, desperado, buffalo hunter, soldier, gambler, wanderer and poor wayfaring stranger, as the great migration Westward coursed in waves across the continent.

In his youth Zane Grey was a semi-professional baseball player and a half-hearted dentist, having studied dentistry to appease his father while on a baseball scholarship to the University of Pennsylvania. But he wanted above all to write, and taught himself to write with much stern discipline so as to free his innate and immense storytelling capacity. Many a lean year came and went as he waited for a publisher to finally recognize a best-seller when it saw one. For Zane Grey became the best-selling Western author of all time, and for most of the teens, 20s, and 30s, had a least one novel in the top ten every year.

(By Marian Kester Coombs)

Teddy greeted me with that hearty buck-tooth smile he had and told me he had made a bet that I could ride 20 miles with a quarter of a dollar under both boots or the twenty-five cent pieces placed under the soles of my boots – that is, between the boot soles and the stirrups, and a third twenty-five cent piece was to be placed in the seat of the saddle and I was to sit on that quarter and ride 20 miles, and if the money was still there at the end of the ride, Teddy would win – if not, he was of course the loser. The men with whom Teddy had been arguing, said it was not possible; I listened till they calmed down and then told Roosevelt to be sure to have the agreement in writing and I would make that ride for him the following morning. I rode Purko with all the men in one car close behind me and I done the 20 miles.

At the end of the ride, they lifted my boots, one by one, and the quarter was there; also, when I raised, the other quarter slid down from the saddle seat. Teddy cracked wide open:[67] he told of many things that I had long forgotten and some things I could not even recall. I had been acquainted with him for many years and I remember when he first came to the CH Ranch;[68] he was then a pale

---

[67] **John A. Gable,** *Executive Director of the Theodore Roosevelt Association*: "Roosevelt was not a man who bet or gambled, and thus the tale about the bet and the ride seems bogus. Roosevelt was decidedly not buck-toothed, as Hopkins describes him. Roosevelt had very even teeth (remarkably so), and his smile was famous but did not reveal a buck-toothed mouth. There is no listing of a F. T. Hopkins in the index of the Theodore Roosevelt Papers in the Library of Congress - Roosevelt's correspondence files - and virtually everyone who knew Roosevelt is represented by letters in this collection. Sounds like this Hopkins told tall tales."

[68] **Editors' note:** Famous American biographer, Robert Easton, tried to confirm the existence of the CH Ranch in the late 1960s, when he was corresponding with Frank Hopkins' widow, Gertrude. When asked by Easton to provide a exact geographic location for the CH Ranch, Gertrude evaded the question by telling the author she had

faced young man, broken in health. I recall the first time he got into a stock saddle and he bounced around on that old pony's back for a week or more before he got on to the trick of keeping in motion with the horse – no one cared, for Teddy was there for his health – not to work.

I went away with the show and had forgotten about young Roosevelt. Two years later I came home to get some saddle horses and Father told me that my mustangs were running on buffalo grass along with a bunch of two year olds over in Nebraska and that the herd boss was young Roosevelt. I was surprised when I got over there, for Teddy was the hardiest looking man in the outfit – in fact I did not at once recognize him. Some while later, Teddy run cattle for himself over there in Nebraska; I can't recall how well he made out, but it was those few years out there that made the perfect man he remained to the day of his death. After that ride at Russell I regret to say that was the last time I saw him. I came to be a fair judge of real men and Teddy was surely one of them.

I rode in one 50 mile race over in Idaho that fall. I had not raised any colts for a few years; now my horses had been reduced in number for there were only five of the Whitey strain left – and they were getting along in years. There was no one interested in long rides as the roads were hard and even then there were cars to annoy a horse on the road. I noticed that I was not the man in the saddle I had been for I was getting hurt more often. It was a sure thing that many injuries were telling on me now.

As I looked back over my long trail I remembered I had lived quite a few years, but it was easy for me to compete against the younger riders who joined the show, although I was not the same as I had been a few years before. Although many told me I was as good as ever – some said I was better; but I knew better than any one else that the work in the saddle was getting to be real hard work for me now. Where the same work a few years before had been real pleasure to me, even the playing of the band made me shudder – it got on my nerves, and even now, I can't stand the blare of a band.

---

never visited the ranch. Her only clue to its existence was the vague comment that it was located near the town of Sundance, Wyoming. Easton immediately wrote to City officials at Sundance, Wyoming to try and verify Gertrude's claim. Surely the town's older residents would remember such a famous local celebrity as Frank Hopkins? Or perhaps they could help Easton pinpoint the exact location of the CH Ranch? *"I am trying to find out about Charles Hopkins, a frontiersman and scout, and his son, Frank Hopkins, an Army dispatch rider, who are said to have lived on a ranch in the Sundance area in the 1870s and 1880s. Anything you can tell me about them would be greatly appreciated,"* Easton wrote. Sorry, wrote back Phyllis McLaughlin from City Hall. None of the old people she had contacted in and around Sundance, Wyoming, had ever heard of the fabled Frank, nor could they recall a Hopkins family ever having lived in the area at all.

www.horsetravelbooks.com

The following spring (1917) the show was a sorry looking sight – the show bills had these words printed on them – "Buffalo Bill now is visiting you for the last time." The words were true – for Cody died that winter. Jess Willard, who was champion heavy weight boxer of the world at the time, took the show out on the road the following spring; they agreed to pay me $1,000 a month, but still there was no contract.

On the 1st of June the government took me from the show to do some secret work for our country which was at war with Germany.

The Bill show went high on the rocks in the month of August that year of 1918. If I had rode the season through with Willard, it would have been 32 seasons of riding for me in the show. That was a long time to ride in circles before the public.

I had many offers after that to sign contracts with shows, but when Cody died I decided I had had enough of the big top and wanted to spend the remaining days of my life otherwise. After the war, I met a Belgian friend at the Old Glory Hambletonian sale in the armory, New York City. He had come to the sale to buy colts for the horsemen of his country. He wanted me to return with him and assured me there would be a great demand for me on their race tracks.

I had been in that country when they first took interest in trotting horses and I was sure there were friends I had left behind there. I bought a number of two year olds at that sale for my friend as he turned the buying over to me. When the colts were loaded, I sailed with them. As soon as they were on shore, I got the job of breaking and training them. I also drove in races.

It was not long before I was in great demand and most of the horse owners remembered me from my first visit to their country for I had taught them several things about balancing and showing off their horses. Now these men saw that I was able to get speed out of many of their horses through my method of training. Of course, this is not horsemanship in the saddle; still, it is skilled horsemanship.

Some of these owners got to be very good drivers, most of them laid their methods aside after they saw me drive their horses and lower their marks. One horse that could not turn a mile better than 3 minutes, after I had handled him for a month could pace a full mile in 2 5-1/4 Many of these horses could trot in the 2/10 class where before a horse that could trot in 2/10 was called fast in that country.

Most of those horses were bought in America and were of the best Hambletonian blood. The next year, trotting races was the greatest sport in all Belgium. I turned out a number of good drivers. The second season they built more tracks and there were races all over the country. I drove in many of them. Some days, I drove in 10 classes. I was making money and a lot of it, but the heavy strain was wearing me out. The trotting association wanted me to sign a 10 year contract. I simply told them I was going home when the season was ended, and referred to the many good drivers that became experts in a short while.

I left that country a tired, worn out man as I had put in two years of the most tedious long hours every day, spending this time with both horses and drivers and owners without any recreation of any kind. I left behind many warm friends and I was happy to think how hard those good people had worked to give the trotting horse a place in their land. I had not done much myself, but there is a class of horse who will long remain in Belgium. I have been sent for since, and have visited that country twice in recent years and I must say that those people have some of the finest trotting and pacing races – even our horses and drivers would have to do their best to compare with them.

In the winter of 1922, I returned from Belgium for a much needed rest; I had planned to take things easy for two months as I was worn out from the two years of strenuous work of training and driving; the long hours devoted to the race horses in that country had tired me to the point that I was suffering from the nervous strain.

Now that I was home again, most of my time was spent with my five horses that were left from the Whitey family. The horses had run in a large corral for over two years, with a shed where they could go in time of storms or to avoid the hot sun. They were well fed during my absence – all of them were round and fat. They had not been used or taken out of the enclosure, neither had they been groomed: They were just as wooly as so many sheep, their manes and tails were snarled and twisted into rope-like strands. Although their shoes were gone, their feet were in good shape. Slowly, I worked on them every day until they were clean and their hides were glossy once more.

Caring for those little horses was more pleasure for me than it was work, for I had so longed to be with them The five ponies were all old now – none of them less than 18 years; still I treasured them and as I worked cleaning and shoeing them the memories of other days appeared often before me. One morning while I was shoeing Chenango, my old friend Dr. Petersen drove into the shed. After a welcome handshake, he asked if I could come over to his place and handle some colts which were not broke.

Now, the doctor was one of the best veterinaries I have known, and he was also a lover of good trotting horses and he owned a few Hambletonians that were hard to beat. The doctor liked to put on freak acts at country fairs and places where there were horse meets. When I had the shoeing done, the doctor asked me if I could train a horse to trot fast without a driver, as he thought that would make a big hit on the fair grounds tracks. He was pleased when I said that was one of the easiest things that I knew of to teach a horse.

I then explained how it must be done. First of all, we must chose a green colt that had not been broken for the act. Then the colt must be schooled on the track with a loose rein and the breaker must not speak to the colt at any time while driving the mile and use a tight pull on the line only when the colt needs straightening and to get the speed stride from him. Touch at the start with the whip; if the colt slows down, sting him with the whip but not hard enough to make him break and run.

The colt must be driven five or six miles in this manner every day for at least two months, before being on exhibition – at no time should the colt be driven in any other way. There should be a man who leads the colt on to the track although the driver is in the seat also, the same man should step out to stop the colt at the end of the mile. The driver should not speak to the lead man at any time while the driver is in the seat. With blinders on the colt, so that he can't see back, the colt will never know there is a man in the seat. But you can not fool any of those old horses who have been broken in the usual way.

After listening to my idea on breaking the colt for the job, the doctor said, "Buff, you're the only man I know of that has the patience to break a horse that will do a job of that kind." He said my plan was clear to him but that it would take a lot of patience.

Three days later, I was hitching that colt to my breaking cart. The colt took kindly to his first lesson and was led on to the track; the leader spoke to him to go on as I tapped him with the whip. I pulled slightly on one rein or the other to keep the colt straight, tapping him now and then to keep him going, easy at first, gradually increasing his speed. Of course, this colt had no company on the track – he trotted his mile alone. In two months' time, that colt was doing his mile without me in the seat and making better time. The lines were fastened to the seat. What a showing that colt made at those Fairs. He trotted his exhibition mile in true form and the colt's time varied little away from 2.8 ¼

He had been named Little Wanderer and was in great demand at trot meets; he started his second season only to be poisoned by a low-life cur who was jealous. He could not bear to see that colt turn the track alone at such speed. But I've met many of those miserable rats in my day who glorify in destroying a good horse or dog.

In 1924 I took a crack at rodeo riding.[69] I rode for Tex Austin at Fort Worth, Texas where I covered all the real buckers in the outfit and never hit the ground. After touring with the rodeo for three months I learned a thing or two – no matter how well I did, I was "gyped" out of the money – so I bid them goodbye and good luck to the broncs who were sure to break a few more bones before the end of the season – I knew there would not be any of mine broken unless I got paid for the pains I might suffer.

In the spring of 1925 I was engaged to drive and train trotters for a local association which Dr. P. was president of. The doctor spoke of some of my long

---

[69] **Editors' note:** According to the marriage certificate, signed by Frank Hopkins when he married Gertrude Nehler in 1929, he was born in 1885. But in order to be able to claim he was a dispatch rider and buffalo hunter, Hopkins had to pretend that he was born in 1865. If that were true, Frank would have been 59 years old when he 'took a crack at rodeo riding' in 1924.

rides. At the time there was a well known New York horseman in the group of listeners. This man disagreed with the doctor saying there never was a horse living that could carry a man on his back 60 miles in 10 hours – he said 60 miles was a long ways when measured and that maybe it was all right to guess or say that the horse had covered 60 miles but if the road was to be surveyed you would find the distance to be nearer 40 miles and it would be a mighty good horse that could carry a rider that far in 10 hours. The two men came to a heated argument and began to bet – one betting that it could be done and the other would give big odds that it could not be done on surveyed ground.

Finally, I stepped away from that horse I was shoeing and said, "Gentlemen, allow me to settle this for you. I will ride that 60 miles on any mile race track and place one thousand dollars that I will cover 60 miles in less than seven hours." I added that the horse I would chose for the ride was over twenty years old. Then I asked them to allow me one month before the ride. The following day the agreement was written up and I was to get $1400.00 if I covered the 60 miles in less than 7 hours. If I took ten hours on the ride I would receive only $500.00.

Before sunset, each man had laid down his money and we were all well pleased. I began to train Perko,[70] a silver grey stallion who was at that time 23 years old. When in good flesh, that hoss weighed 900 pounds. After one week of light training, I was sure that little mustang could still do his stuff. I had ridden him in long rides in his younger days and knew him to be as tough as they come. The word passed from one horseman to another. Many of my old friends called to learn the facts of the ride. I assured them the ride would be made in less than 7 hours and that the old Gutenberg track was the place chosen for the ride to take place. This track had been abandoned for many years; although the fences were still there the track bed was covered with a short, sour, grass.

The morning I was supposed to ride, I got to the track at 6 o'clock and jogged Perko around until the ride was to start. At 8 o'clock sharp, there were over a hundred people who had come to watch the ride and three times as many had gathered there who knew nothing about the affair. At 8 o'clock I rode out to the old starting post and got the word to go.

There was no rearing and battling for first place. I headed Perko out into the center of the track bed and set him into a swinging lope – not a fast gait; I looked at my watch to gauge the horse's speed. After he had turned the mile a few times, he knew what I wanted him to do for he settled down to a steady gait. I watched him very careful until twelve o'clock, then spoke to him, urging him along to a faster gait; when the horse settled down to his new pace there he stayed until the ride was ended at 25 minutes of 2 o'clock in the after noon. That

---

[70] **Editors' note:** Possibly the same horse as Purko.

ride settled a big argument for all times and also fattened the purse of a number of my friends as well as my own.

In the fall of 1926, I got into an argument of the same kind myself with cavalry men. This was a relay race of 120 miles – 20 miles to the horse. I asked if I could sign on to ride in that race. They were eager for me to pay the entrance fee and sign to ride. The ride was only three weeks away when I signed on and not much time to train myself and horses in, but I got them into shape. This ride was from Willimantic to Manchester Conn.[71] The ride led a roundabout way; on account of the hard roadbeds, we headed for Westmoreland then tacked back riding through Hop River and around the Bolton mountains into Manchester which is not far from Hartford. I had only five endurance horses of my own so I trained a five year old Hambletonian for the first 20 miles – the other five old campaigners were placed at their posts along the line; none of these five horses was less than 20 years old and the one on the last twenty miles was 24 years of age.

The rest of the riders held their own with me for the first 20 miles and the trotter I rode was real tired when I got to my first relay. Then things began to change, for that mustang soon took the lead and gained ground every mile. So did all of them as I changed horses. Still, I did not try to make extra time only to stay out there in the lead.

When I came to the last horse it was different for I know those boys intended to shove on with those sprinting, long-legged horses the last 20 miles was their only chance. But I had placed the right horse at the end of the ride – old Chenango. I started him off easy until he got his second wind, then gradually he increased his pace and I was out of the saddle a full half hour before any of the other riders came in sight. The correct time for my being in the saddle was 7 hrs. 48 min. 9 seconds.

In 1927 I again enlisted in Fred Beebe's rodeo for a short time and found the same "gyp" with him. That winter four of my ponies died of "old age." All of them were lying dead in their stalls looking as natural as though they were sleeping.

In the Spring of 1928 Chenango dropped dead while playing in the corral. The brave old stallion was racing around the corral showing me how good he was and suddenly he came to a stand and stumbled, then throwed his ears forward in my direction and sank slowly to the ground. He was dead before I could get to him.

---

[71] **Editors' note:** The distance between Willimantic and Manchester, Connecticut, is approximately twelve miles, not the 120 Hopkins claimed. Even a "roundabout way" could hardly have added 108 miles to the journey.

With the death of Chenango the last of a family of endurance horses was gone and my years in the saddle became a closed chapter although my memory is still clear as I look back at that mound of my youth. The picture is still clear with all the beautiful coloring of a western sunset.

The editors believe this manuscript was written in the late 1930s.

Chapter 3

1800-Mile Trail Ride – Texas to Vermont

INTRODUCTION

I wish all of the members of the Green Mountain Horse Association could have been with me when I spent an evening with Mr. and Mrs. Frank Hopkins, of Long Island City and Laramie, Wyoming, who has written this story of one of the greatest rides ever held in the United States. This ride started at Galveston, Texas, and finished at Rutland, Vermont, and was, undoubtedly, one of the longest endurance rides on record in this country. Mr. Hopkins is now over seventy-five years of age, and during his life has competed in 402 endurance rides, most of them being races. He lost only one of this number, and that proved, afterwards, to have been crooked.

He has performed trick riding stunts before all of the crowned heads of Europe and gave a command performance, with only one Indian companion before Queen Victoria. This exhibition was given on a new lawn at Windsor Castle and you can imagine what two wild ponies did to that lawn in two hours of rough riding. However, the Queen told him to forget the lawn as it could be replaced.

Frank Hopkins is the only white man to ever compete in the "Thanksgiving Day" 3,000 mile ride in which only Arabs were supposed to participate and he also won that ride.

I wonder how many of us could ride in a Wild West show for two hours every day for two years. That is what Mr. Hopkins did for two World's Fairs in Europe.

While a dispatch rider, he was shot seven times, and bitten three times by rattlesnakes. He has shot several outlaws for the Government, including the very bad Tracy for whose killing he refused a check for $3,000 given him by the Governor of the State of Washington.[72]. He speaks the various Indian dialects fluently and was a friend of Sitting Bull, Big Foot and many other famous Indian chiefs.

---

[72] **Jim Dullenty,** *Author of Harry Tracy, The Last Desperado (1989), A Place called Earp: the town named for Wyatt Earp (2001) and The Butch Cassidy Collection (1987):* "Harry Tracy… was arrested in Portland with a cohort in 1898 and put in the Oregon prison from which he and the cohort escaped in 1902 and after a long chase, was surrounded by two posses in August 1902 about 50 miles west of Spokane and killed himself. No one named Frank Hopkins had any role in any of these events.

His patience and native ability have enabled him to train horses other people could do nothing with and even today he can train them very well. He loves horses and good horsemanship, and has had many a fight with men who used cruelty, in place of training, to make a horse do the proper things. Some day Mr. Hopkins will write us an article on the training of horses – he has promised me that he will. I wish to thank Mr. and Mrs. Hopkins for a grand evening and for this story. – Harvey P. Wingate[73]

To one who loves the great outdoors, there is nothing quite so interesting as a Trail Ride. It makes little difference whether you ride the sage-covered plains and foothills of the far West or the rugged hillsides of the Eastern States. There is something fascinating about such a ride – the falling leaves moving about your horse's feet, the squeaking of the saddle leather beneath you. The busy horse seems to enjoy covering the trail fully as much as his rider. There is new scenery for every mile you cover, but in the distance will be a beautiful hill covered with green spruce or sugar maples, with their autumn leaves of red and yellow, you will be anxious to get to. And when you do get to this spot, there will be another that looks more beautiful, beyond. As the day draws near its end, maybe you will see a glorious sunset dropping behind the far away hills. So you have come to the close of the pleasantest day of your experience.

Caring for your mount is part of the day's pleasure. As a dispatch rider for the army during the Indian troubles on the Western Plains for nine years, I have known the thrill of many long rides. Some of these rides covered 200 to 300 miles. My mounts were fed on buffalo grass. They got the best care I could give them, although the best could not be much. There was one class of horse I liked best and would ride no other but this, even though there were many fine looking mounts offered me – I refused all but the Indian pony, a hardly little animal, no trail too long or too rough – a horse that could get along without grain and go without water for two or three days at a time. Still the Indian pony has a weakness – the sound of the human voice will worry him off his feet. I never spoke to my ponies while up there in the saddle.

There was one pony I shall always remember in particular and this horse will be remembered long after I have crossed the last canyon. I called him "Joe." He was given to me by a man who believed him a hopeless outlaw. This horse was still in the horsetrap where he had been caught as a wild Indian pony. I broke him in the trap; four months later I rode him on the buffalo runs. When "Joe" became used to the crack of the gun he was the best buffalo horse I ever expect to

[73] **James Davidson,** *Vermont Historical Society:* "Harvey Wingate was a trustee of the Green Mountain Horse Association. I judge that he was the one who introduced Frank Hopkins' stories to the President and editor of the Vermont Horse magazine, who was Dr. Earle Johnson of Rutland. Later issues of the magazine suggest that Harvey was also a horse breeder from New York."

hear of. He could stay with a run of buffalo till they were shot down and then race off after another run; he could lope off all day without dropping back into a walk. "Joe" was not fast, but he could wear other horses off their feet in a few days. I rode "Joe" from Galveston, Tex., to Rutland, Vt., the year 1886. I had been carrying messages for General George Crook during the Geronimo campaign down in Arizona. "Joe" was used in my string and when I was relieved from duty I rode him from Fort Apache, Ariz., to Fort Laramie, Wyo. On reaching there, I was told of a ride from Texas to Vermont. Buffalo Jones agreed to finance me if I would sign to ride in that race. Three days later I was booked at Fort Russell and started training "Joe" for the long Trail Ride. In three months, "Joe" was in the best of shape – fifty miles a day, three days each week, without a bandage on his legs or artificial courage (such as stimulants) of any kind. I allowed him to travel as he wished, not trying to force him to any particular gait; he preferred to lope or a flat-footed walk. Trotting was out of the program with this little stallion. Most of those wild ponies can lope along without much action – that is, they clear the ground and put their feet down very lightly. "Joe" had carried me on many long rides. I was sure he would reach Vermont ahead of the other mounts. Some of them were of the thoroughbred blood. I watched them exercise for a week while we waited down there in Texas. Fine looking horses they were, but too snappy and nervous to start out on a long ride of that kind.

On the sixth day of September, 1886, we started from the Old Point Ferry Slip, Galveston, Tex.[74] There were fifty-six riders in all – some were cowboys, others cavalrymen and six were bridle path riders (I was amused to see them bobbing up and down on their small flat saddles for I had never before seen the English type of saddle). All of the riders left me at the very start. "Joe" never cared about racing away with the bunch; he would just put one foot ahead of the other all day and never seemed to tire. The first day of that ride "Joe" was a little sluggish, which I thought might be due to change of drinking water. I did not urge him on, but after riding twenty-three miles, I called it a day. Under the rules of that ride you could ride ten hours or less if you wished. Each rider carried small cards that were to be signed and the exact time the rider stopped was marked on his card. This was done where the rider stopped and then checked by the judges. It was September 13 before I came up to the other riders. Four of those riding English saddles were in bad shape and their mounts were a sorry sight to look at – over in the knees and spread behind, their muscles trembled and twitched; those were out of the ride for good. The next day I passed twelve

---

[74] **Casey Greene, Head of Special Collections, Rosenberg Library, Galveston, Texas:** "We've referenced every newspaper between 1880 and 1890 but there is absolutely no mention of Frank Hopkins or a race from Galveston to Vermont. I think we'd better start a new file called 'Galveston Bogus Claims'."

more tired horses. "Joe" was feeling fine. When I took his saddle off at the end of the day he would swing his head and let his heels drive at me. I always let him roll after taking off the saddle. This may not be any good to a horse, but they all like to roll. On the 17th, "Joe" and I had passed the last horse and rider. We were in Mississippi where there had been a heavy rain and the yellow mud stuck to "Joe's" feet like soft snow, but he would shake his head, jump and play at the close of every day.

Our route was marked with red paint daubed on trees, fences and stones, so it was easy to follow. On this ride I weighed 152 pounds, my saddle blanket and slicker weighed 34 pounds; "Joe" weighed 800 pounds when we started the ride. I used a six-strand rawhide Hackamore without a bit. "Joe" did not like iron in his mouth – it seemed to worry him.

I got word from the judges when they caught up with me in the towns, that I was putting a lot of hills and valleys between me and the other riders, but I could not believe I had gained so much mileage. I had stopped to feed at mid-day in the town of Gallatin, Tenn. One of the judges stepped out in front of "Joe" as I was riding away and said, "You're riding against time now for there's not another rider within many miles."

I do not think it is good to rest too long in the middle of the day. Some riders do rest their mounts two or three hours but I have learned that a long rest is not good for horse and rider will both get tired. One hour is plenty. And keeping your horse on his feet fussing over him and rubbing him after the day's work is done is not good. I always taught my horse to lay down and rest after I had rubbed his back with a damp cloth, and let him rest for two hours before feeding. I gave him a good bed where it was quiet and let him alone for the night. A good rubbing in the morning will make him feel fresh on the start of a new day. I might say that a horse that has plenty of endurance in him is not without a background – even "Joe's" ancestors were of the Arabian blood. The pedigree of a horse does not stand for much if there is no bottom or stemming in such an animal, although they get along in their own class and are thought quite a lot of. The real Morgan horse that I knew years ago was a very hardy animal, but those horses have been crossed with the thoroughbred from time to time; this crossing did that breed more harm than good for they neither look nor act like the old-time Morgan. Each breed of horse should be kept in its own class. If I tried to run any of my endurance horses on the race track they would be out of their class and if a running horse was entered in one of those long rides he surely would come to grief as it was proven on that Galveston-Rutland ride. "Joe" and I were in Rutland[75] thirteen days before the second horse and rider arrived. That horse was broken down in spirit and body. The third horse came a few days later, a broken-

---

[75] **James Davidson**, *Vermont Historical Society:* "There is nothing in the local news-papers around that time about a race ending here in Rutland."

down wreck. I weighed "Joe" the following day after arriving in Rutland and he had gained eight pounds on the ride; he was seven years old at that time and I claim that it is the best year of a horse's life – at least I have found it to be so with endurance horses.

A large, heavy bodied horse with too much daylight under him will not make an endurance horse for he will pound himself to pieces on the long run. I would not train a horse, for a long hard ride, that weighed over 1,000 pounds. He must be close to the ground and well muscled with a short back and neck – the horse with a long slim neck will tire quickly. Today most riders want mounts that stand 15 hands or more – that is the first thing they will ask – "how high does your horse stand?" There are many other things to look at besides the height of a good mount. Some horsemen will speak of a horse's color which, in fact, only goes the length of the hair.

"Joe" was buckskin in color. When I rode him into Louis Butler's small stable at Rutland[76] that October evening many men of the town gathered to look him over – more on account of his color than anything else for many of them had never seen a horse of that color. Although "Joe" had covered 1,799 miles in thirty-one days,[77] without a day's rest on the trip, many of those horsemen

---

[76] **James Davidson,** *Vermont Historical Society:* "I can find no evidence of any stables on Elm Street at that time, no evidence of a Louis Butler - nor even any evidence of anybody called Butler owning or running any stables. The first evidence of stables being located in Elm Street comes in 1911, when a stable moved to that street. The bookkeeper was called Townsend Butler. These stables were very close to The Globe Hotel, which was used by theatre and circus people."

Editors' note: Despite his claim to having been the star of Buffalo Bill Cody's Wild West show for more than twenty years, according to employment records discovered at the Circus World Museum, Frank Hopkins worked for the Ringling Brothers Circus as a horse-handler in 1914 and 1915. That circus visited Rutland many times. It is highly likely, therefore, that when the circus was in Rutland, Hopkins would have lodged at The Globe Hotel and seen the nearby stables.

Editors' note: In an article entitled *Stamina of the Horse Past and Present*, a Hopkins co-conspirator named E. M. Dickey attempted to validate Hopkins' Galveston to Rutland race fantasy. In January 1948 Dickey, a cowboy-tailor living in Clifton, New Jersey, wrote, "The end of the ride was at the stable conducted by Lewis Butler, near the railroad station, in Rutland, on Elm Street. This old barn is still standing today, and two years ago [1946] was visited by the winner of the contest [Hopkins]. The old iron ring to which he tethered his pony ["Joe"] is still attached to the wall and on one of the beams, still discernible, are the letters F.T.H. [Frank Tezolph Hopkins] which he had carved with his knife almost sixty years before." James Davidson has pointed out that nobody who had been to Rutland would call Elm Street "near the railroad station."

[77] **Editors' note**: Hopkins' version of the Galveston-Rutland race was slightly different every time he told it. In *The Last of the Buffalo Hunters*, he arrived in Rutland 14 days and 4 hours before the nearest competitor; in this article he claims to have won by 13

criticized his color. "Joe's" average per day was 57.7 miles. I received $3,000 from Elias Jackson for that ride. Three weeks later I shipped "Joe" to Wyoming and bade farewell to those good people of Vermont. To me it was just one more long ride for my daily work had always been in the saddle. When I reached Fort Laramie, Colonel W.F. Cody was waiting for me. He wanted me to ride in his show, which was known as the "Buffalo Bill Wild West show." I played in the first Madison Square Garden, New York, that winter and then went to Earl's Court, London, England, the following spring. In fact, I stayed with Cody until his death, 1917. I rode in many endurance rides through Europe. After the World's Fair in Paris, France, I visited Arabia and rode in a 3,000-mile race, using one of my Indian ponies who also won that race. That pony was spotted cream color and white. He was a stallion whom I named "Hidalgo." I left him in that country of fine horses, for it was there he belonged.[78]

This article was first published in April 1940.

---

days. In *My Years in the Saddle* the journey lasted 30 days, rather than the 31 days mentioned above.

[78] **Elly Foote**, *Equestrian Explorer and author of "Riding into the Wind:"* "Hopkins' claim that one could run a horse into the noonday sun of Arabia for a couple of months straight, while feeding him weeds and only watering him every couple of days, should make the blood of any true horseman boil. The notion of a 3,000 mile race across the Arabian desert could only have been conceived by someone like Hopkins who had never been there."

Chapter 4

Gentling

The breaking of colts has always been a great study among horsemen; some trainers tell me that the well-bred colt will respond to training more quickly than one of unknown breeding – in fact there are scarcely two horsemen who will agree on the method of breaking or training. How many times have I seen fine, high-bred mounts rear and shy and even try to run away when a small, harmless piece of paper blew in front of them. Yet these horses were trained by expert horsemen! Right here I wish to say that I consider such training poor horsemanship. It makes no difference whether your colt is highly bred, scrub, fuzztail, wild mustang or anything that is horseflesh, he will respond to proper training.

After more than sixty years of handling all kinds of horses I do not find any difference in their breeding: horses are much like humans – some are nervous, others quiet, and there is also the mean-tempered horse – all must be treated accordingly. The highly intelligent horse is the one who is hardest to train. He will try to put it over on you if you don't watch him!

In training colts, there are a few things that should be kept in mind – rules that should be followed at all times. If you cannot control your own temper, let someone else train your colt; you must always have patience. Do not take the advice of anyone or permit friends to stand around looking on while you are giving lessons to your colt and do not have anything around that will attract the colt's attention from where you want it. Remember, your colt cannot reason as you can, although he can remember for a long time. I recall one horse that remembered his stall over twenty years. I had taken this horse away from the C.H. Ranch, Wyoming, when he was two years old, twenty-one years later I brought him back to the Ranch and when I loosed him, he walked past thirty-four empty stalls to get to the one he had been kept in as a colt – so I must admit they remember.

Patting your colt only makes a fool out of him – don't fondle colts if you expect them to obey you. It is well to place a well-fitting halter on the colt when he is a few days old, do not fasten a lead or rope to the halter. Allow the colt to wear the halter at all times. If the mare does not object, you can take hold of the halter, but do not stand in front of the colt and pull on it, for he will sit back and most likely rear at the same time.

When your colt is about six weeks old, you should teach him to lead and stand tied. This must be done in the presence of the mare. Get a four-foot lead with a snap fastened at one end and snap this into the colt's halter; now, have a piece of sash cord about twelve feet long, tie a Bowline knot in the sash cord so it won't slip; the loop should be about three feet across. Take hold of the halter, lead with your left hand, facing the colt. Now, flip the loop tied in the sash cord over the colt's hips, allowing it to drop down nearly to the hocks, then jerk on the sash cord at the same time putting a little pressure on the lead rope. Your colt may kick – don't notice that – but jerk the cord again, keeping both ropes tight. Remember, do not have the rope any longer than I have told you for you as well as the mare and colt might get tangled in the rope. If you halter break your colt in this way he will never be a trailer; that is, he will never hang back. Anything I dislike in horsemanship is to see a man trying to drag a horse along behind him by the halter or bridle. Yet we see this every day with horse handlers. Train your colt to walk with you – not to be a trailer. You do not want the sash cord after the second lesson. Each of these lessons should not take more than fifteen minutes. Lead the colt a little each day.

Now, teach your colt to stand tied. Stand in front of him and hold the rope. Be sure you do not look straight into his eyes or stare at him. The colt may try to walk away, but you just hold the rope firmly in your hands and do this over many times. When he stands fairly well by holding the rope, put it around a fence post but do not tie it, stand back at the end of the rope and hold the end of it in your hand so you can give and take on it to avoid hurting the colt. As the colt moves about watch how he takes to it. After a few short lessons you will find that you can hold him without slacking the rope. Repeat this a number of times and your colt will be halter broke for life. The lessons take only fifteen to twenty minutes each for about a week.

After your colt stands tied, it is well to pick up his feet, first on the left, then on the right side, for you do not want your colt half broken. You must break both sides alike – if not, your colt will not be properly broken. Now you have a halter-broke colt and have raised his feet a number of times. The colt is about two months old and it is likely you want to turn the mare and colt out on pasture. That is the best for them. Let the colt have all the play and freedom he wishes. When the colt is eighteen months old, start giving him the real gentling. Do not be in a hurry to get on his back for there are many things he must learn before putting on the harness or saddle.

1. Build a training pen eighteen feet square – no larger. This must be high enough so the colt cannot put his nose or head over it. Have the bars close together so the colt can't poke his head through the fence. Now lead the colt into the pen, take off his halter. You get in there with a straight whip. Crack the whip a few times, but not loud. This will start the colt to milling around the pen. As he passes you, lower the whip close to the ground and snap him on the heels as he is going away from you. Make as little motion with the whip as possible and do not strike him hard – just sting him a little. After the colt has circled

around you a few times he will turn his head to watch you as he passes. But do not look straight into his eyes or he will think there is something wrong. This is just the reverse from what some trainers advise, but after handling and breaking for many years I have found it best not to stare into the colt's eyes. When the colt walks to one corner of the pen and faces you, reverse the whip, with the tip end behind you and walk right up to the colt and lay the flat of your hand on his shoulder. Do not pat him. The mere touch of your hand is caressing enough. The colt might try to get away. If he does, crack him low down on the heels; this time he may rush right back to you. If so, lay your hand on his shoulder again, then bring the whip down gently in front of his nose. He will reach out to smell the whip and he will see that it is harmless. Now rub the whip down his neck and shoulder, then step to the other side and repeat the lesson, but do not go to his rear. Step in front of him, lower the whip gently and tap him lightly on the heel at the same time say "come here" and move back slowly. If the colt does not follow you, tap him again – a little harder this time. Step back as he follows you. Speak clearly when y ou give the command "come here," but not sharp or rough. When he follows you around the pen two or three times put the halter on and lead him out to his stable or runway, for that is training enough for one day. Although it may seem to the reader that it has taken hours, this lesson has taken not over twenty-five minutes.

It is well to remember that the first lesson taught to the colt is the one he never forgets so be sure it is done right. Repeat this lesson for three days until the colt follows you at a trot round the pen, and be sure he follows you as freely from the left as from the right.

2. Now, you must break his hind quarters. Your colt not only has gained your confidence but has gained a lot himself. Without this, you won't get anywhere. When you take the colt into the pen for the second lesson he will look for the next act, and he will take to it kindly. Get him to follow you, then lay your hand on his shoulder. He will stand. Rub the whip over his hips and down his legs. Slip behind him and reach forward with the whip and rub it along the sides – on both sides. Now, move slowly around the colt, leaning against him going under his neck and on both sides. Repeat these lessons for a day or two.

3. Who wants a horse that shies and bolts at the least thing that looks strange, or a horse that gets frightened at strange noises? Before you ever harness or saddle him is the time to break him of these faults. If he has confidence, he will trust you – that helps when breaking the colt from being scared of noises. Turn the colt into the training pen. Get a large can or pan and let the colt nose this before you start beating on it. Stand a few feet from the colt and tap the can or pan lightly at first, walking in a circle around the colt. Increase the beating as the colt gets used to it, then come closer and walk around still beating on the pan. Then give the command, "come here." He will follow you as you beat the can, caring not a hoot about it. Now, throw the pan on the ground – kick it around.

Soon you can kick it around his feet or behind him without frightening him. Then, get an armful of newspapers. Walk up to the colt, let him nose them. Then rattle a sheet of the paper and watch how he takes it. Do not scare him at first and soon you can rattle the paper, throw it on the ground and he will follow you, walking on the paper. Throw sheets of paper above your head letting them fall around the colt, some of them falling on him or blowing in his face.

4. Put a light open bridle on the colt; use a straight rubber-covered bit, with three-inch leather washers against the bit rings. Allow the colt to wear this bridle one hour the first day then use it when going over the lessons, but do not attach lead or reins – just let the colt gets used to the bit. Watch him, see how he takes to the bit. The leather washers will keep those iron bit rings from chafing his lips. When the colt gets used to the bit, place a three-inch leather band or surcingle around the body, back of the shoulders; have three rings sewed into the band – one at the center of the band to snap in the overhead check – one ring on either side about sixteen inches down from the center for the side lines. I use a piece of heavy elastic about eight inches long on the side lines that run from the bit to the belt. I bought this elastic from the makers of trusses for ruptures – there is just enough give in the side lines so the average colt won't fight the bit. The overhead check should not be tight, but it stops the colt from reaching down and pulling on the bit and rubbing the bit rings against his forward legs. You can turn your colt out in the pen without worrying about his getting his feet over the side lines – colts will bit themselves better than the trainer can do it. With the elastic sewed on the reins he will not fight the bit because the reins give. I had about sixty colts wearing these rigs in a large corral at one time and every one of them turned out in fine shape. The colt should wear this rig one hour a day for a week. All lessons should be given in the training pen. Now, nail a two by four on two sides of the pen. They should be about ten feet high. Tie a line on these two by fours above the pen stretched across the center. Hang old clothes of different colors on this line. Then, lead the colt into the pen. He may appear nervous at first – stay with him until he quiets, then lower the line gradually each day until the clothes touch the colt as he moves around. Soon he will not pay any attention as he learns there is nothing to harm him.

5. Your colt should have a few driving lessons, no matter whether you intend to make a saddle horse out of him or not. Take the short lines off that run from the bit to the body band; replace them with long driving lines running them through the rings on the band, but be sure not to buckle or tie the lines at the ends, for you might get them caught around your foot. Tap the colt with the whip at the same time saying "get up." He may try to turn toward you. If so, drop the line down near the hock and pull. That will straighten him out. Be on the lookout for this. Soon, he will learn to go straight. Give a quick but light jerk on the lines and give the command "whoa" and slack the lines at once. If he does not respond, do it all over again. When the colt has started and stopped a few

times at your command do not tax him further for that day, but slip up to his head and lay your hand on his shoulder as a reward. Repeat this lesson a few times. I have found it very important to have a horse stop when asked. Train him to stop the very instant you speak – it may save your life – it has often saved mine.

6. Now, if you should slip when mounting your horse, or something else goes wrong, you surely would not want to get a flying hoof side of the head or anywhere about your body. Here is a way to prevent getting hurt. Your colt has worn the body band and knows it is harmless. Place a saddle on his back – it is best to use a stock saddle and a breast plate; do not cinch the saddle too tight. Allow the colt to wear the saddle for thirty minutes the first day. After four of these lessons in the pen, take a burlap bag about half full of fine hay packed lightly in the bag, rub it lightly around the colt's shoulders working it lower and lower as he gets used to it. Be sure you do this on both sides as in all lessons. Then, work back to his rear with the sack of hay and rub gently round his hips and legs. This is enough for the first time. Repeat the next day and carefully work the sack between his forward legs, then do the same things on the hind legs. Repeat this for four days. Then, tie one bag of hay on either side of the breastplate so the bag will hang down in front of the forward leg clearing the ground about six inches. Tie two more bags to the horn or pummel of the saddle letting them hang just back of the forward legs. It is well to lead the colt around the pen a few times in case he gets scared at first, but stand away from him as soon as he quiets down. Do not tax him too long with this lesson – twenty minutes is plenty. Continue this for three days – 20 to 30 minutes a day, then attach the back strap with crupper to the saddle, hand one bag of fine hay on each side so the bags hang just a little in front of the hind legs and about eight inches from the ground. Lead the colt until you are sure it no longer frets him, then step a few paces in front of the colt, give the command, "come here" and make him follow you around the training pen. If you colt takes to this kindly, you should hang two more bags of hay from the back strap about ten inches from the roots of the tail, letting these bags hang around the hocks. Now you have eight bags filled with loose hay hanging around the colt's legs forward and behind – that is four forward and four behind. Repeat the lesson with all the bags hanging around the colt's legs for a number of times. You will be well paid for your time used in this lesson for your colt has no fear now when anything touches his sides or legs and if the riders slips or falls off the colt will stop and look around at his rider. I have broken many horses for trick riding and I rode them twice a day in Colonel Cody's Wild West Show and in all those years I was never hurt by my horse – although I have had hanger straps break and saddles turned when I was hanging low on the side of the horse or going under his belly, and the horses always stopped stiff legged when I commanded them to by saying "whoa." I once had twenty-four horses follow me out of a burning stable by just saying "come here" and in spite of burning timbers falling all around them, they obeyed.

Although some of them were badly hurt and had to be destroyed, still they remembered their early training.

How often do we hear of someone speak of the horse's mouth. Horsemen will ask, "has your horse got a good mouth"? Some will speak of a horse having a "cold" or "dead" mouth. There are still some strange things about horsemanship indeed. If a man trains his colt to obey the word of mouth instead of putting pressure on the bit, he will never know whether his horse has a good mouth or a bad one.

This article was first published in October 1940.

Chapter 5

Mustangs

With the coming of the automobile, some thirty odd years ago, it looked like the horse was nearing the end of his long trail. Many ranchers and small horse-raisers were stuck with a lot of horseflesh on their hands they didn't know what to do with; they turned their breeding stock loose in the foothills where the horses shifted for themselves until the war started in Europe, then there was a great demand for war horses – every stockyard near a seaport as filled with range horses – most of them were not broke even to lead. In three years' time our country was really short of horseflesh for farm work and pleasure stock.

Now the tide has turned and with many horse organizations springing up in all parts of the country, the horse still has a bright spot in the sun. Within a single year there have been a number of trail-ride clubs showing up in different states. All of this means more horse raising. It seems to me that if these breeders would stick to one class of horse, instead of crossing on different breeds, our saddle horses would be worth raising. There are good qualities in all breeds – some for one use, such as the running horse who has been bred for racing one mile or two at great speed, yet that horse has not the bone and cords required for endurance racing. There are many breeds of horses for different uses and each of those breeds should be kept in its separate class. If our breeders keep on as they are now, crossing on all breeds, the horses of this country in a few years will be nothing but a lot of scrubs.

Let us look at this breeding right; what is a scrub? Is it not a horse that has the blood mixture of different strains? Most of my life has been devoted to the practical study, training and riding of the endurance horse and I have not lived years enough to complete that interesting study, but there is one thing that I have surely learned after spending much money for horseflesh, and that is – the hot-blooded horse has no endurance. He may do very well in his own class – there are bound to be some better than others of course, but put the real hard work to him with a little hardship mixed in and you will find out that those horses are just "not there."

As a dispatch rider for nine years during the Indian troubles on the Western Plains, I tried out many different strains of horse. That kind of riding was hard on the horse and if he didn't have the stuff in him you'd soon find it out. Two or three hundred miles on a single trip was not unusual. The horse had to get his feed from the ground – all the care he got was to have his back rubbed off with a handful of buffalo grass. There were times when I had to race my horse for hours in order to save my life. Again, I would have a running fight with Indian scouts who were always lurking in the hills; the luckiest rider and best horse went on – the other generally stayed on the spot. Sometimes, there were rivers, good and bad, you had to swim your horse across. The winters back in those days were a good deal colder than they are now and the storms more severe – driving blizzards, cutting winds, deep snow and only a trail to travel – no shelter of any sort to put into. In the winter, I broke the limbs from cottonwood to feed my mounts and dug down into the snow where I slept in the blankets. Plenty of that kind of work and hardship will surely test out a horse. During those nine years – 1877 to 1886 – I had lots of time to find that comfortable spot on the old pigskin-covered McClelland saddle and to learn which type of horse could best stand up under real hardship. I rode the best of Kentucky Whips owned by the army; the more life and style they had at the start the more miles I had to carry my message on foot!

I remember one fine looking horse, weighing over eleven hundred pounds; he was bred in Kentucky but he died out there in Nebraska. I rode him out of Fort Robinson (Chief Red Cloud's old agency). After riding him about a hundred miles, all four of his legs were swollen, his ears lopped down the side of his head like a pack mule's and that horse actually started to die under the saddle. I could not leave a played-out horse for the wolves to tear to pieces, so I hung the saddle up in a tree and told that horse he was discharged from the army with my "forty-five." I trotted along until I got tired, then lay down on the trail to rest and got up to run again and in that was I delivered that particular message. It was the last Kentucky horse I would ride. The Forts I rode out of carried a string of ten or more Mustangs for my own use and none of those horses failed to make their trips. One, a little blueskin stallion of eight hundred and fifty pounds, carried me one hundred and twenty-four miles in twelve hours. I had to shove him on, for I was being followed by Indian scouts. When I reached Fort Lincoln, that pony was pensioned off and sent to Fort Robinson to spend the rest of his years which were thirty-six – a ripe old age for a horse, but not unusual for a Mustang caught wild.

At the time of Chief Crazy Horse's campaign, I rode out of Fort Robinson covering the other Forts. On the first day of December, 1880, I was sent with a message to Fort Bridger, a ride of about a hundred and eighty miles. When I started, the sun was shining, the sky was clear and there was about three inches of light snow that had fallen during the night. As I rode along, mule deer scampered among the scrub cedars. Farther along, I saw the fresh hoofprints made by a band of wild ponies who had probably fled before a prowling cougar. Coming from the high ridge about me, I heard the bugle call of an elk. As I rode along I noticed the dark moving forms of the bison as they browsed in the valley below. A spotted eagle screamed as he soared in graceful circles above me. It seemed a fine winter's day and even the hills belonged to the man who rode them. When I stopped to graze, the long, streaming shadow of my pony was no longer visible for the sun was directly overhead (it was mid-day). I loosened the saddle girths and my pony shoved the snow aside with his nose searching for buffalo peas, while I nibbled away at the dried beef I'd taken from my saddle bag. I could easily see Harney Peak in the Black Hills, and off to the west, the Laramie Mountains, the day was so clear. That afternoon, I rode into higher country and at sundown I made camp against the ledge of yellow craig. After breaking cottonwood branches for my pony, I built a bush lean-to; with a small case axe, I cut wood for fire. While I rested, a friendly coyote sang his evening notes from a pinnacle of rock above me. I dropped off to sleep with memories of the day and thoughts of the morrow before me. Throughout the night my pony would call and half awake. I'd say, "all right, boy," knowing that the mountain lion the pony smelled would not come close to human scent, but circle at a safe distance.

Morning broke clear with a high wind, the sun throwing long, red streamers across the sky. The pony was nervous. He knew as well as I did, that there was something coming on that gale of wind, and red in the morning is a warning to the plainsman. I was young in years but old in plains experience. As the pony climbed the ridges, large black clouds were gathering in the southwest. At mid-day, it began to snow and the wind howled through the ledges. I turned off my course and made for a pine and cottonwood grove in a large gulch. There I worked with my axe in a blinding storm until I had finished the shelter for the pony and myself. I cut light poles and wove cedar boughs through them. With a pile of cottonwood at one end of the lean-to, we were out of the worst storm I can recall. It snowed three days and nights. Every night, after the storm, the large grey wolves came. I kept a fire burning at the entrance of the lean-to and sat there all night with my rifle across my knee – now and then I shot one of those prowlers and then there was a fight. In the morning I could see where they had torn the wounded wolves apart, leaving only the bones and tufts of hair. During the day, I could sleep safely, but at night I guarded my horse. On the fourth day the food ran out and I dared not eat wolf because of the rabies germs they carry. There was not even a rabbit to shoot – the snow was so deep. About the eighth day, I was feeling mighty weak and my lips were parched. The following morning, I was forced to shoot my pony, skin his hip and slice off a piece of meat and eat it – warm and raw – I was really hungry. I stayed there for five long weeks – the horse meat froze solid and kept, and I ate it again, but roasted on a stick. Right there I learned that money isn't everything in a man's life, for I had four hundred dollars of good American money in my pocket – and would have starved to death but for the horse!

The weather suddenly got warmer and then came a drizzling rain which froze, making a heavy crust on the snow. I made a pair of snowshoes out of the horse's hide, and with a number of extra rawhide strings and a chunk of horsemeat lashed to my back, I started out for Fort Bridger. I made holes in the snow at night to sleep in (if one digs down aways in the snow and has good blankets there is no danger of suffering from cold). In six days I delivered my message.

I stayed in the Fort until April, then brought back the answer to that message. My Mustang shared with me these hardships which no other horse could. This is only one experience out of many in those nine years.

I could tell of Mustangs that carried me out when I had been badly wounded, even to swimming streams with me when I was too weak to sit up in the leather. Those little fellows have no "Style" but for me there is not another horse on earth for intelligence and endurance and I have been in many countries to find it so.

I have often been asked why the Mustangs should be hardier than other horses.[79] For many years they have run wild on the Western Plains, having been brought there by the Spaniards. History reads that these horses were of the best Arab blood lines; on the Plains, they had to fight the mountain lions, wolves and other enemies; man also was their greatest foe. Due to droughts, they were often without water and feed was scarce. In winter they dug through snow and frost for feed. Often they were forced to eat brush, or starve. Only the hardiest of them survived. There were no weaklings for breeding-stock in the spring. Year after year those horses were bred from the hardiest stock known to horseflesh. In-breeding made them small, but of great endurance. Our great West was conquered by the Mustang for it was not a "foot" man's country and other horses could not stand the hardships. I once heard Gen. George Crook say that if the cavalry could not overtake a band of Indians in two hours, it was best to give up the chase, for those wiry ponies would wear out all the horses on our frontier. Don't get the cow pony confused with the Mustang – they are different types.

After the Geronimo Campaign in Arizona, I was relieved from duty, and rode my buckskin stallion from Fort Apache, Ariz., to Fort Laramie, Wyo. Three months later, I rode the same horse from Galveston, Texas, to Rutland, Vermont.[80] This horse had been caught from a wild herd and like most of his

---

[79] **Editors' note**: Despite his repeated remarks about the durability of the American Mustang, Hopkins claimed that the toughest horses in the world were actually in Mongolia. In *My Years in the Saddle* Hopkins wrote, "I will say these [Mongolian] herders' horses are the toughest species of horseflesh I know."

[80] **Editors' note**: The most famous literary victim of the non-existent Galveston to Rutland race was Jack Schaefer, author of *Shane* and *Monte Walsh*. During the course of research for his own book about the 1908 endurance race from Wyoming to Denver, Schaefer began corresponding with Gertrude Hopkins. Schaefer wanted to confirm Hopkins' story about winning an endurance race from Galveston to Rutland as background for his own book. In a letter dated June 4th, 1962, the widow Hopkins told Schaefer, "Because of the SPCA of that day, the ride had to be kept secret until the very last minute. But they started on September 6th, 1886, at the Old Point Ferry Slip (Galveston)… and the winner received $3,000." Schaefer repeated the Hopkins mythology in his book, *The Great Endurance Horse Race*, published in 1963.

kind he was tough. Although I owned him until he died, I never knew the limit of his endurance.

When I returned from Vermont I joined Col. W.F. Cody's Wild West show. In the spring of 1887 I went with the show to Earle's Court Exhibition, London, Eng. Two months later, I entered one of my ponies in a long race from Earle's Court to Land's End, Cornwall, Eng. That pony weighed 850 pounds and he covered that ride of some 158 miles in twenty-eight hours of actual travel and finished nine hours ahead of the next best horse.[81] I rode a number of endurance rides throughout Europe.

Our next trip was to the World's Fair, Paris, France (1890). There I learned of a World's Horsemanship Contest to take place on the military grounds at Marseilles, this contest to be held from 9.00 a.m. to 11.00 a.m. every day, for one year. I signed up and rode with picked cavalrymen of all nations of the world besides riding in two performances daily with the Cody show. At the end of the contest my Mustangs were judged the most active for footwork and all round supreme for endurance and courage. A month later I was informed that the Congress of Rough Riders of the World intended to pay my expenses to Arabia where I would take part in the 3,000-mile race.[82]

The following spring, I shipped out of Genoa, Italy, for Aden, Arabia, taking three of my Mustangs, ponies that I had bred, and got them up to 950 pounds. They were strong and wiry, with the best of bone and muscle. I was worried about the strange country that my horses were to travel, but soon learned there was nothing to worry about – they took to the sand like ducks to water. They were sheltered under canopies like Arabian horses and fed vetches and barley which they also took to kindly. I soon learned that they were the best lot of horse thieves in Arabia that could be found anywhere and why shouldn't they steal a good horse from a despised Christian? I reported my loss to Ras Rasmussen[83] who told me not to worry, he would see to it that my horse was returned shortly – and in less than an hour my horse and the two thieves were brought before me. Ras handed me a whip with three lashes branching out from the handle and told me to use it on the culprits, but I refused, preferring to remain on friendly terms with these strange people. When the thieves fell to their knees in the sand

---

[81] **Editors' note**: Compare with this episode as described in "My Years in the Saddle" when Hopkins declared the distance to have been 200 miles, and that he came in 12 hours ahead of the nearest competitor.

[82] **Gordon Naysmith**, *Fellow of the Royal Geographical Society and Long Rider:*. "On my 20,000 kilometre long equestrian journey from South Africa to Austria, I rode through the same area that Hopkins claims to have crossed on horseback. I never discovered a single oral tradition which would suggest such an endurance race had been run at any time in Arabian history."

[83] **Editors' note:** Note this man was named Ras Yankin in "My Years in the Saddle," not Ras Rasmussen.

praising Allah, I did likewise and told them it was Allah who saved them from the lash and brought my horse back to me.

This 3,000 mile race is held every year since the domestication of the horse which dates to B.C. and I was the only rider other than an Arab to take part in it.[84] The long ride started from Aden; a hundred of the finest desert horses and many from the limestone sections entered the race, the most perfect group of horses I ever expect to see – those from the desert were gray or white, those from the high land chestnut, some sorrel and a few black. The route led along the Gulf of Aden where the air was not too dry for our mounts; then our trail went along the seashore to Syria. We then turned from the sea and rode up the border between Syria and Arabia; part of the way was limestone and the rest flaming fine desert sand. Water was scarce, the air dry and hot. The Arabian horses could get along without water pretty well, but my Mustang began to gain ground once he got into the desert although he got water only once a day. At times there was no water for almost two days, still my "Hidalgo" went on and at no time did he appear weakening although he grew gaunt and lost flesh. There were days of sand storms and then it was impossible to go on. Horse and rider rested between the camels that carried our feed. When a rider got out in the lead, two camels were sent ahead with him and these camels were changed three times on the ride. Many horses dropped out; when we entered the desert only five finished and I was in Aden thirty-six hours before the next horse came in and that it where the ride ended. Every rider had to cover the same route – the time lost through sand storms did not count for all riders fared alike. It was the horse that came in first who won the race, and any horse that got back to Aden surely deserved his title of winner.[85]

I also won a 500-mile ride in the limestone country with a half-brother of "Hidalgo," and a 150-mile ride in the sand desert with the third pony; they were

---

[84] **Dr. Mohammed Talal Al-Rasheed,** *scholar in Arabic and English literature and history:* "The idea of such a race in Arabia is a non-starter and can be debunked simply from an intellectual point of view without even getting into the ludicrous logistics of it. It is a shabby fantasy. The notion of marathon races is Greek. It has never been part of Semitic culture. The tribes of Arabia are used to hardship and conservation. They are practical and would consider such an endeavor as plain and simple madness. A Bedouin would move his family and animals hundreds of miles in search of pasture. But ride across Arabia to cross a finishing line? Inconceivable!"

[85] **Magdy Abdul Aziz,** *Vice President of the Egyptian Endurance Riders Association:* "It is against all tribal Arab tradition to hold long distance races. Historically the Arabs raced their horses for short distances, and when they were on the war path they rode their camels with the horses in tow until they were near the site of battle then mounted them for a quick attack. At around the time of the alleged race the horse breeding tribes were suffering from severely diminishing numbers of horses due to the transfer of many of their best mounts to Egypt 30 years earlier, and a drought that affected the area for years."

all from one stud but from different mares. I left my three stallions with the great horseman Ras Rasmussen who was an Arab by birth but of Libyan extraction. He was a fine man and remained a true friend of mine until he passed on in 1918. "Hidalgo" died the following year, a fine little horse with an iron heart. I have been lucky to raise and ride those hardy ponies, and have given special performances with them before crowned heads of Europe, contested in three World Horsemen contests, and also spent thirty-two seasons with the great showman, Col. W.F. Cody, but all the credit of those performances I give to those little Mustangs of our Western Plains.

This article was first published in January 1941.

Chapter 6

Endurance Horses As I Know Them

Of all the questions asked me during my years of horsemanship, the most frequent has been, "What breed or strain of horse do you consider best for endurance riding?" Although this is a hard question to answer, my reply has inevitably been, "the horse that can stand up under the hard training that is necessary to prepare him for such work."

In training my own horses for endurance rides, I soon learned that if the horse showed the least sign of weakness at the start, it was best to stop training that particular horse and begin with another; you cannot patch up a horse who hasn't legs strong enough to carry his body – all the rubbing and bandaging will not strengthen them – it may weaken them. If I noticed one of my ponies bracing when I stopped him, that horse also was out of the training string. What I mean by bracing is this: if he stretched out, as many high-class saddle horses are trained to do when standing. Experience has taught me if a horse braces all four feet out from under him *naturally*, it's a sure thing his back is weak – then, to me, he is not worth feeding.

It does not take long to detect the courage in your horse when you start to train him; most horses with 'style' and over-action are lacking in heart and courage when given real, hard training. For instance, when I expected to take part in a race of say a thousand miles, I did not intend to come in third or fourth at the end of that ride – it was my ambition always, to finish first. So I trained for it. I knew that a horse who could not stand up under fifty miles a day for the last two weeks of his training would never carry me on a long ride. There are many riders however who believe if they ride a horse a mile or two each day and feed him well they have given him all the care and training they consider necessary; surely, the horse is in good flesh and spirit. Here let me say the endurance horse needs far more careful training than the one mile race horse. Of course, his training is different from that of the speed horse.

I never believed in being in a hurry at the start in training, rather preferred to go slow and watch how the horse hardened. Some horses harden quickly, others do not. I always taught my horses to lie down and rest after their work. It is well known that most horses will stand on their feet no matter how tired they are, but I've always thought it best to get my horses off their feet as soon as the saddle was taken off. If they are taught to lie down they will stay down and rest for hours.

When a horse gets hardened, he should be dried out gradually until he is satisfied with three twelve-quart pails of water daily. Most riders feed too much hay and overfeeding of grain does the horse more harm than good. Fussing over and rubbing a tired horse after a hard day's work is one of the biggest mistakes made by long distance riders. I always brought my horse in cooled out at the end of the day, brushed the dust from his hide, washed out his mouth, nostrils, eyes and his sheath and up between his hind legs, then gave him a slap on the breast and said "lie down" and he would drop to the straw while the words were in my mouth. I let him rest two hours before feeding. As it is naturally for all horses to roll, I usually let him roll before brushing him. Many riders do not like the extra work of brushing. Personally, I prefer to see my horse happy, so at the end of the day I let him roll all he wants to and shake himself; I always loosen the saddle girts when stopping, if only for a short time.

In sixty years of long distance riding I never used a bit in my horse's mouth, believing the bit will worry any horse a little – many of them will pull on the bit and fret, some will hold their heads higher than is comfortable for them. All these little things help to wear the horse out on a long trail. Talking friendly with your mount while up there is not a good practice either for he is paying attention to you instead of the trail ahead.

Ofttimes I have been asked "What is the best weight and size for the endurance horse?" In my opinion, the horse is no larger than his ability, and not a bit smaller. The best endurance horse I ever knew weighted eight hundred pounds and stood less than fourteen hands high and I was his proud owner. He never won blue ribbons, neither did he take a silver cup, for pedigrees were unknown to my "little yaller plug," but I want to say that little stallion earned his feed and a few thousand dollars to boot. He was one of those mutton-withered fuzztails that no one would care much about owning – a wild mustang, given to me because he wasn't considered worth halter breaking; besides, he was wild and spooky and there was a bullet waiting for him just about when I happened along by the horse trap. I watched him race in the horse trap and even before laying a hand on him knew he was of the endurance type. He had the heavy, strong bone, cords, muscles, required for hardship, although I admit he did lack style and action. This pony seldom carried his head above the level of his back; his joints were short in the ankles; all four feet were placed well under his body. I never saw him rest a foot – he stood on all four. Often, I gave him three months of the hardest training a horse could stand, yet there was no sign of filling in of the tendons or bone trouble of any kind, neither do I recall a single day that he did not shake his head and let his heels fly when the saddle was taken off, but I do remember my many narrow escapes from being hit by those flying hoofs! On a long ride, that little horse could not be beaten.

I do not wish to give my readers the impression that I dislike those fine blooded horses – on the contrary, I have owned many of them in my day and admire them as much as any horseman, and often go quite a distance just to lay a hand on their slick hides. We should be fair-minded about our horsemanship;

each breed of horse can be used for what it is bred for and no one breed can be used for ALL purposes. My sincere opinion is that mixing the blood of different strains is fast destroying the real good horseflesh throughout the world. The English Thoroughbred has been bred for speed for over four hundred years and there is not a horse living that can take his place on the running track; it is well to leave him on his job on the race track course. Why waste that blood that has been carefully built up for so long on heavy work stock and raising scrubs which are neither running horses or draft animals? The Arabian horse has been crossed so often that there are truly few of the straight Arab horses in existence today; they have been crossed for the purpose of getting a larger horse; still, the quality of the true Arab is not there. Our Arabian Horse Club of America has some of the finest straight blooded Arab horses in the world and there are still some in Egypt.

To return to the endurance horse: In endurance riding, I have noticed it is the small horse close to the ground who wins on the long, hard rides. Size in the saddle horse does not mean much to me – some large horses do very well for three or four hundred miles and I've seen them miles ahead of the bunch at the start, then go to pieces in the next hundred miles. I noted that those horses who got out in front the first day or two and made a lot of mileage were the ones that were out of the ride first. Always keep an eye on that lazy hoss who hangs back there in the tail drag, for he may pass you some day and you won't see him again until that ride is over. That's how I started out on my long distance rides – never in a hurry, for there were miles before me. A mistake most riders make is to shove the horse a certain number of miles in one day; some plan to cover a stated number of miles every hour. A horse is not a machine. How does he feel about this? Although your mount cannot tell you in words, he will surely tell you by his condition at the end of every day. Many a real endurance horse has been ruled out of a ride because he was overtired from being shoved too hard for a few hours at the beginning of the ride. If the horse acts a little sluggish when starting out in the morning, let him loaf for that day. I've often stopped riding after a few hours when my horse was dull (probably due to change of country, feed and water). When the rules did not permit such layoffs, I would not sign to ride in that race. I always allowed my horse to travel as he wished with a loose line. Some prefer to hold their horses' heads up on a tight rein because it looks "stylish" but that foolishness only worries the horse and tires him. I rode all day without taking the rein in my hand, but when I wished to turn my mount on the trail I twisted slightly in the saddle.

It is well when training for a long ride to teach the horse to walk fast – that is the best gait for a long ride; too much trotting is out of the question. If you can get hold of a true loping horse, he is best for a long distance. However, such a horse is scarce amongst highly bred stock. The Mustangs are the true lopers and travel to that gait altogether in the herds. I once rode one of these twenty miles at a lope without slacking back into a walk or trot. This was done to win a bet for our late President Theodore Roosevelt. The ride took place at Fort Russell, Wyo. The judges followed on bicycles, so there was no chance of changing gaits. Roosevelt won his bet. One thing about that ride may sound queer to some readers – at the start, there was a twenty-five cent piece placed under each of my feet on the wooden ox-bow stirrups, and one under me in the seat of the saddle. If they were not there at the end of those twenty miles Roosevelt would lose the bet. However, he "collected" when I raised in the saddle and the last of three quarters slid down the side of the saddle seat. I had rubbed knees with "Teddy" many times on narrow trails and he had seen me do the same trick often although not at a lope the whole distance.[86] A rider must have years of practice in "sitting tight" to accomplish this trick, but as it had been my business to perform all kinds of tricks in the saddle as a showman before the public of the world, that little trick was only a matter of sitting close to the leather, and sitting close is a mighty good thing to learn if one intends to ride for a long distance. The style of riding might change from time to time but horses are the same as they were years ago, only they are more tender and cannot stand the hard knocks that those cold-blooded nags had to stand or die trying to.

My Mustangs lost a lot of their hardiness if I stabled and blanketed them in the winter, so I gave them good dry sheds with large runways, and they were free to run in and outdoors as they pleased. They surely were as tough as pine knots.

Next to the Mustang for hardiness, I believe are those old-time Morgans, so hard to find today. I well remember those short-legged chunks – much like the small horse of Holland. My father probably was the first man to bring those horses into the Northwest. I can recall when he went East and bought a number of mares and stallions although I was only a small shaver at the time and recall it only as one waking from a pleasant dream. Father had been wounded at the wagon-box fight and was laid up for a long time but when he got well enough he went to New England and brought those horses back with him. They came by rail to North Platte, then were driven overland to Laramie. The first winter, all of them lived on the range without housing which is unusual for stable raised stock. In a few years he had a large herd and every cowboy in that part of the country was proud to ride one of those C.H. horses and would say, "this yere one is a Morgan and the best cow hoss in these parts." And they were top stock horses; many of them had a great burst of speed from a standing start; they could handle those old moss-horned cattle that weighed twice as much as they did. It was a

---

[86] **John A. Gable,** *Executive Director of the Theodore Roosevelt Association*: "Roosevelt was not a man who bet or gambled, and thus the tale about the bet and the ride seems bogus. There is no listing of a F. T. Hopkins in the index of the Theodore Roosevelt Papers in the Library of Congress - Roosevelt's correspondence files - and virtually everyone who knew Roosevelt is represented by letters in this collection. Sounds like this Hopkins told tall tales."

pretty sight to see one of those horses come to a square stop with sixteen hundred pounds of beef at the other end of the rope. Those horses weighed between nine and ten hundred pounds and they could bust any bull or steer on the range all right. Father liked the straight blood in stock so the Morgan blood remained clean as long as he lived. In thirty years' time though they were spread all over the North and South-west. That blood at the present time can be seen in every Western state today, although the horses have changed, for they have been crossed with other blood and are much larger.

Although I did not pet or fondle my horses, nor allow anyone else to, it is likely I showed my appreciation by careful handling, kindness, and care.

Recently I saw a great horsewoman of the country riding one of the finest saddle bred horses that could be found anywhere. The horse had the best of manners. I also saw this fair equestrian giving the horse lump sugar from her pockets, and talking to her. Yet, when this woman mounted, she worried that horse every minute she was up in the saddle by the slightest movements of her arms, thus making tension on the reins. I merely mention this, to show how unknowingly some riders can worry a horse. To a man who has had a horse between his knees most of his life, these little things are quite noticeable.

This article was first published in July 1941

Chapter 7

A Judge's Impression of the Ride

The Green Mountain Horse Association's Sixth Annual One Hundred-Mile Trail Ride was a colorful event this year. It would be hard to find a group of horses in better condition, so few of them showed signs of tiring. All actually finished in good spirit. The weather was cool and without rain during the whole period of the Ride. Taking part in this Ride were a splendid group of horsemen and horsewomen who would class as excellent riders in any horse event.

Some of the trails are quite severe, with many long, steep grades; nevertheless, the footing was good and not a single horse injured the entire one hundred miles.

On the second day, three very good horses and riders lost the trail losing two hours or more before they finally straightened out, thus putting them out of the contest.

I observed a spotted gelding on the Ride loping beside fast-walking horses, but he stuck to his gait which is the true gait of the Indian War Pony. This horse showed other signs of having such blood in his veins; for instance, he loped all the way, except when walking. Some horsemen not acquainted with that gait, expected to see this spotted horse out of the Ride the fist day and remarked that it was poor horsemanship to ride the horse at that gait. Personally, I feel that it is better horsemanship to ride your horse at his *natural* gait than to try to force him to a gait that will wear him out in a few hours. It would be well nigh impossible to make that spotted horse trot under the saddle or any other place without actually abusing him. However, that spotted horse came in as fresh every day as he was going out – not even gaunted at the end of the 100 miles and he only lacked three points toward winning first place as the best endurance horse on the Ride! It is well for us to forget about show horses and the bridle path, for the 100-mile ride does not blend with that little trot in the park before breakfast. On a real long, hard ride, the true loping horse will wear out six good horses who trot under the saddle. I realize this is a very broad statement, but I have seen it proven many times and history repeats itself in that famous long, hard rides have always been won by the loping horse. So, trail riders, don't condemn the true loping horse nor doubt the horsemanship of his rider, for the rider is using good sense when he allows his horse to travel his natural gait.

There were so many fine horses and good riders on all breeds and classes that the judges found it extremely difficult to arrive at their decisions. However, I can assure the riders that every horse and rider had the most careful attention of the judges. The riders were probably not aware that their judges and the recorder were up most of the night discussing and arguing the points of every individual rider and his or her mount, nor that these same judges even deprived themselves of viewing and enjoying the fine Morgan Horse Show in order that they might come to the final decision. Even then, the judges were an hour and a half late with their lists, the competition was so close.

There were many large horses, also small ones, who did very well. Noticeable in the small horse group was Number 25 on the program on her little Indian "squaw" pony "Midnight." Although this pony is more than twenty years old and weighed but 790 pounds, she went all the way with the bunch and probably was in as good condition at the end of the Ride as the others.

The Johnson twins made an attractive picture on the Trail. They rode all the way on their spirited mounts and showed remarkable horsemanship in carrying their horses along at an even, open gait.

The stable in Woodstock, with its high posts, is well equipped to care for a large number of horses. The excellent hotels, inns and lodging homes are close by to accommodate the riders and there is not a more convenient nor lovelier spot in our country to hold one of these rides. I really believe that any one who rides on these trails will gain more knowledge of riding than in any other way. Some of the riders were overheard to admit that they would be better acquainted with trail riding next year.

I have been asked to give our readers a few "pointers" such as I have gained through experience during my years in the "leather." Right here, let me say that you can not tell how good your horse is by just looking at him – only covering the trail and lots of it, will condition your horse for a long hard ride. Another thing – do not jump or nerve up your horse in any way while training for a long ride. Be careful about balancing your mount while in the saddle; be sure to have your horse balanced as nearly as possible in his shoes. Often, a rider is unaware that his horse may not be naturally balanced; one horse might step with one forward foot an inch or more farther than the other, or it might be in one hind foot. Some horses travel too fast behind for their forr'd feet; it makes an awful lot of difference in his riding if a horse is balanced. If you wish to find out if your horse is properly balanced, take your horse by the halter and trot him over a stretch of soft ground – about fifty feet – then measure the horse's tracks, from the toe of the hind foot to the toe of the forward foot – be sure to measure five or six tracks on each side; if the horse steps a half inch or one inch or more shorter with one forward foot than he does with the other, that foot should carry a little more weight in the shoe. If it is a hind foot, the same method should be followed, *i.e.* a little more weight in the shoe. If your horse travels a little faster behind than he does forward, there should be a little more weight put on both forward feet so he will throw them out. Of course, I can not tell you the amount of weight for an individual horse – you will learn that by having a little heavier shoe put on the foot. Keep trying it out until you have him stepping exactly the same length with one foot as he does the other. An unbalanced horse is quite noticeable, for he will have a little more knee action in one leg than in the other. There are some owners who will have a horse for years and not notice this. It will however make a vast difference in the riding if your horse is perfectly balanced. To keep your horse balanced, it is wise to make a chart showing the weight of the individual shoe for every foot and the size of the nails used, so your horse will be properly shod the next time and save you the trouble of balancing him again. If your horse is balanced when shod, wearing down his shoes will not unbalance him as he will probably wear down his four shoes alike.

Look at the feet often, if there are any signs of thrush, treat at once, for thrush will lead to many foot ailments, even to low heels and dropped soles and pinched hoofs.

Remember, if the tree of the saddle does not fit your horse, he will not go right, no matter how the saddle is padded. Your saddle may fit many horses, but it may pinch the only horse that you choose to ride, or your weight may cause the saddle to bring pressure on the cantle end of the pads. These things are not easily detected on short rides, but you will soon notice them if you ride your horse over rough, hilly trails.

Some saddle-trees are not open enough at the withers for one horse, even though the saddle may fit another horse well. If the rider should come to a long, hard climb for his horse it is likely that the rider will let his mount take the hill slowly, while at the same time he (the rider) flops back in the saddle to rest himself, thus putting all his weight in one spot, digging the cantle into his horse's back – and there you have a sore back for the horse – even though you cannot understand how it came there. It is a sure thing, though, that the soreness came from the rider taking things a little too easy going up hill.

Padding your saddle too light will cause small skin corns. They don't appear sore when you feel of them, but when there are enough of them together, your horse will fret and worry.

Going down hill will sore the horse if the saddle does not fit properly. The English style or flat saddle, is rather hard on the horse's back regardless of how carefully you watch. It is not for long, hard riding. Many riders who have taken up long riding have changed to the moderate stock saddle, even though they could not be persuaded to use one until they learned of the comfort for both rider and horse.

Girth galls or pinches may be avoided by stretching your horse after saddling. This is done by taking the horse's toe in the right hand and placing the left hand against his shoulder, then pulling forward on the toe, thus pulling the skin wrinkles from under the girth.

Two or three small buckles on the girth will also dig into the horse and cause lumps on either side. It is far better to use cinch straps and do away with buckles entirely. Oh yes, they don't look stylish, but they are comfortable for any horse.

The head gear for your horse may suit you, but does it suit your horse? If not, he will have spells of fighting it. You have seen pulling horses and horses who seemed incurable. Riders, let me tell you there never was a horse who would get behind the bit and pull if that bit was hanging in the stable instead of being in the horse's mouth. I have broken some of the most vicious pullers that ever grabbed a bit and the cure was always effected by taking the bit out of the animal's mouth and gentling him with a choke cord, thereafter riding him with the old time hackamore bridle. No horse will pull without a good reason and in this instance it is the pain caused by the bit that does it, although there is no soreness visible. On the other hand, it may be shallow nerves or flattened bars on the under jaws; broken bars may lie under the skin in a horse's mouth all his life without giving him any trouble, but when coming in contact with the bit, your horse will pull and rave; some horses go stark mad from the sense of pain. Take this tip from an old timer, riders – put a little LePage's glue on the seat of your pants and stay close to the leather and keep your feet in the stirrups – don't ride on the bit. A fairly loose line makes a happy horse and contented rider. It makes no difference whether your horse is three years old or thirty, hot blood or cold – they all respond to proper gentling if rightly done. I have gentled wild horses twenty years old or more who never had come into contact with a man before, and they took to their training kindly; in fact, I would rather gentle and break a horse who had never been handled than one raised in the stable, fondled and patted from birth. During my years of handling all kinds in different parts of the world there is only one horse I recall that I could not gentle and there was a good reason for my failure to do so – the horse's brain was diseased.

While in Woodstock, some of the riders asked me for a few "tips" on long riding and I hope they understood me right. I was not talking merely to hear my own voice, but was passing on to those younger riders the benefits of my years of hard-earned experience. I have nothing to lose or gain by it and am always glad to give this experience to those who feel they may derive some profit from it, for my days of polishing saddle seats have about come to a close; but the lump in the throat and flush to the cheek when approaching a group of horsemen in the saddle is always there.

Good Fortune favored me for nine years in getting dispatches through for the Generals on the Western Frontier, likewise throughout the thirty-two seasons of my active horsemanship with that super showman, Col. W. F. Cody, and in successfully contesting against picked cavalrymen of all the nations of the world.[87] Meeting those riders in Vermont put a little more color in the dye. I

---

[87] **Dr. Juti Winchester,** *Curator of the Buffalo Bill Museum at the Buffalo Bill Historical Center:* "The public and the press were excruciatingly fascinated with Buffalo Bill and followed his every move in print, and noted everyone associated with him. Study of contemporary newspaper accounts reveals not one single article linking Hopkins to

enjoyed to the utmost being with them if only for a short while, and I hope to meet many new riders in addition to this friendly group in such a splendid Association. I know of no better way of spending a vacation than on the bridle trails in the Green hills of Vermont.[88]

This article was first published in October 1941.

Cody. The European tour, especially, was documented in minute detail both by the Wild West show administrators and by the foreign press, and nowhere in all of this material do we find Frank T. Hopkins mentioned in the least way.

[88] **Editors' note**: The following interview took place on 5th April 2003, with Martha Parks, an eye witness to the 100-Mile Trail Ride which Frank Hopkins judged, and later wrote about in the above article. Mrs. Parks and her husband were active competitors at the 100-Mile rides in Vermont during the 1940s. When contacted by the editors of this book, Mrs. Parks immediately recalled Frank Hopkins and was happy to share her memories. She was both amazed, and amused, to learn that Hopkins was not what he claimed to have been.
"I have not thought about them [Frank and Gertrude Hopkins] for years.
Hopkins only judged the one trail ride in 1941, I think.
In the picture of him with the cowboy hat and boots, he looks like a pretty big man. But I was surprised when I met him in Vermont to find that Hopkins was not very tall.
Hopkins didn't ride when he came to judge that trail ride.
His story was his hips had been injured during bucking horse competitions. He wore a tight restraint to keep his hips from popping out, had a rolling kind of a walk and used a cane. I guess that came because his hips weren't stable. Hopkins was going downhill and I remember thinking he was past his prime.
The Association [Green Mountain Horse Association] paid for the Hopkins' accommodations at the Old Woodstock Inn. It was a ritzy hotel, which was off-base for us! But the judges got paid even then.
My husband and I had lunch with Hopkins and his wife in one of the little stores around that time in Woodstock [Vermont].
I don't remember much about Gertrude. She was a chubby little woman, and I think she was younger than he was. I was rather young myself at the time so I wasn't a very good judge of people's ages. They never made any reference to children.
My husband was hungry for horse experience and there were hardly any books available on horsemanship in those days. So he was enthralled with Hopkins, who told us about his Galveston to Rutland ride and spoke about his many years working with Buffalo Bill.
We had nothing to measure Frank Hopkins' stories against, so of course we believed it all!
Hopkins certainly had a good imagination!"

Chapter 8

Hunting Buffalo

When, in remembrance, I live over my years in the saddle, it seems to me that buffalo running was about the hardest test on horse and rider. Some buffalo hunters rode out in the early morning, hid their horses in the brush, set up their crotch-sticks on which they rested their rifles, then waited for the bison to pass. A single hunter might get three, possibly four, buffalo – sometimes these men failed to see one in a week. Of course, they were not professional hunters.[89] There was another class of hunters who would run buffalo over cliffs or into deep gulches – such men got very little for their hard work, for the hides were torn and therefore worthless.

The most prosperous hunter of my day was Buffalo Jones. It has been said he became wealthy from hunting the old "bowbacks." It was my privilege to shoot for him up on the Yellowstone during the winter of 1878 when there was a large herd on both sides of that river as far up as old Fort Kehoe. Jones kept a string of ten ponies for my personal use; they were wild, spooky, most of them as wooly as sheep for they lived in the open in all kinds of weather. They were plenty tough and liked to race with the buffalo herds. When I first started with Jones, he gave me six men who skinned the buffalo I dropped; one of these men was an old hand at the game, and one morning as I started out to turn the herd into the wind, this man called to me. He said, "Now, Laramie, let me tell you a thing or two about dropping these 'buffs.' Look for the spikehorns two years old – maybe three. Shoot them in the neck, close to the head – that will drop them, and they will stay warm till the skinners come along for they will only be paralyzed. Hides bring good money and skinning a frozen buffalo means a slashed hide that won't fetch much money." After listening carefully to the old-timer, I went in for the neck shot. In less than a month I had sixteen skinners following me on the runs and I seldom gave them the task of skinning an old bull or cow. As we were moving camp one morning, Jones threw his mittens at my pony just to see him buck, remarking "that Laramie kid is as wild and wiry as the bunch of cayuse he rides."

---

[89] **Editors' note:** Frank H. Mayer, a nineteenth century buffalo hunter and author of the book *The Buffalo Harvest*, contradicted Hopkins emphatically. "Billy Dixon once took 120 hides without moving his rest sticks. A colonel I knew on the range told me of counting 112 carcasses within a space of 200 yards. Bob McRae once took 54 hides with 54 cartridges."

GEORGE SHANTON - The real "Laramie Kid"

George Shanton was carried off by Indians when he was six years old, and by the time his parents rescued him he had acquired an intimate knowledge of the Indian way of life. After procuring his first pony, he learned the art of horsemanship and lassoing.

In 1881 at the age of 13, he and his parents ended up in Fort Laramie, Wyoming. He learned to rope and ride two-year old broncos, to hunt coyotes, and reach from his saddle and yank badgers from their burrows.

George and his brother Harry (also sometimes called the 'Laramie Kid') both became equestrian luminaries in William Cody's Wild West show.

The famous author Mark Twain lived with the Shanton family and he wrote about his time there in *Roughing It*. Then novelist Owen Wister spent some time with Shanton, and eventually wrote the novel *The Virginian* based on Shanton's adventures.

When the Spanish American War came in 1898, Shanton was chosen Captain of Torrey's Rough Riders.

President Roosevelt sent him to the Canal Zone which, as Commissioner of Police, Shanton made a law-abiding community. George Shanton was awarded the Congressional Medal of Honor and is buried at Arlington National Cemetery.

Now, there was a rule among the buffalo runners, that if the "dropper" shot an off-colored buffalo, the skin went to the dropper. One morning, I sighted something white moving among the bunch just as I started them into the wind. As the sun came up I could plainly see it was a cream-colored spikehorn – too far ahead for me to shoot. That afternoon, I took the back track – past the skinners – for there were buffalo enough down to keep them working until dark. When I came up to Bob Rice, I told him about the spikehorn and he said, "I'll go out in the morning and rope that calf for you, but keep still about it in camp, you little cuss, and I'll be with you before it gets light in the morning." Bob took great pride in being slick with his rope and he sure twisted a mean loop! He and I rode out before daybreak. There, on the level plains were our buffalo standing, chewing their cuds. Beyond, were two huge buttes not more than thirty feet apart at the base. As we encircled the herd at a safe distance, waiting for daylight, Bob saw the light-colored buffalo moving at the upper end of the draw, between the buttes. I rode out to the far end of the draw, while Bob stayed at the other end. We waited there until we could see clearer. Bob shouted, "Run them down this way." The sound of his voice started the "buffs" on a stampede; I turned the few that were in the draw and ran them Bob's way and as I drew nearer to them I could plainly see that the cream-colored one was not a calf but a large spikehorn – maybe in his third year. They were under full speed when Bob threw his rope, which fell true, catching our "buff" around the neck, close to the shoulders. When the horse tried to hold, both cinches parted. Bob sailed over the horse's head and landed in a sitting position on the ground while he watched his rope and saddle go bounding down the valley.

I began to drop buffalo, for the skinners were riding out from camp. Late that afternoon, I came to my prize all tangled up with the rope and greasewood brush. To make sure, I made a few more hitches and left my riding jacket tied to him so the wolves would be sure to smell human scent which they fear, knowing they would not dare to close in on my prize. It was after dark when I rode into camp with Bob's saddle. Jones inquired why I stayed out so late, warned me not to make a practice of it. When I told about tying my prize however, he ordered the driver of our hide wagon to hitch up the mules and all hands went along. If anyone thinks it's easy to load a buffalo into a wagon, he is surely mistaken. We finally dragged this one into it with the aid of the lead mules. This "buff" sold for $300. I sold him to Dick Rock over in Idaho. I was doing fine for my first season on the buffalo runs. Although it was very cold, we got lots of hides that winter. No one was paid a regular wage, but when the hides were shipped in the spring, every man received his percentage from the hides, Jones taking a third of what the hides fetched.

Early in March, General Terry sent for me to carry messages, so my buffalo-running days were over – for that season. The following winter I was at it again. Jones went after the large herd in the Southwest and wanted me, but the General said he might need me at any time and I had better stay nearer where he could locate me, so I shot for Dick Rock and Zeth Smith on the Yellowstone River. The Crows and Blackfeet Indians were making trouble for the buffalo hunters on both sides of the River, to the extent of shooting a number of men belonging to another outfit. Rock wanted to change our hunting grounds. One evening I talked with him about this and told him I would ride out and talk with an old chief, "Dark Moon" who I knew was friendly toward my father. I found the old chief sitting by the fire in his tepee, told him I craved his permission to run buffalo on his side of the River. He at once lit the long pipe which was filled with red willow bark, and handed it across the fire to me with a "Weeachin." "Buffalo there are many in my country – more than my people need – but many white men run them away and when the snow is deep my people must go far for meat, so my scouts run the hunters away from the herds." I told him if he would permit me to hunt in the valley he could have all the meat.

With a burning stick from the fire, he wrote me out a picture permit on deerskin, giving me the right to shoot buffalo.[90] It read: "So far as a horse can

---

[90] **Professor Ione Quigley, Chair of Lakota Studies, Sinte Gleska University:** "There are numerous discrepancies in Hopkins' accounts, such as the fact that a chief would give a permit to hunt. I find this questionable. Natives will tell you anywhere that all are entitled to hunt and feed their own, wherever and whatever it might take."

Editors' note: Despite, Professor Quigley's remarks, a drawing of a so-called "buffalo hunting license" has been discovered in a book by Charles B. Roth, the man who is credited with widely publicising Hopkins' mythological tales in the 1930s. Four years after the death of buffalo hunter, Frank H. Mayer, Roth published a book entitled, *The Buffalo Harvest*. One of the illustrations Roth used is that of "Mayer's hunting license for the buffalo ranges." This suspicious document was supposedly issued to Mayer by a Comanche chief and designates where he shall hunt and give him "full permission to kill

run from the River in four days." Then, I must turn the herd back. He was to have the meat at any time he cared to take it and none of our men should molest his men, woman and children; I could hunt for four moons and since I was doing the shooting, I should carry that permit or hunting license with me at all times to show his men who rode the range. All other hunters were run out of that country. When I rode into our camp, Rock and the skinners were pleased to see that piece of deerskin and know that only our outfits could run buffalo in the Crow country.

It took six 8-mule teams to haul our hides that winter and the herd was growing larger as many new ones were coming into the valley from the higher ridges. I had a large string of ponies; most of them were top buffalo horses before the season was over. You could get a pretty good price for a horse trained on the "runs," no matter what he looked like. From three to five hundred dollars was the running price for a well-trained buffalo horse. Rock sold all of those ponies in the spring, intending to have me break a new lot the next winter, but when I learned he sold that string I refused to drop buffalo for him another season. You could buy any amount of wild mustangs for three dollars a head at the trap, but when broke to run "buffs," they brought real money; and why not? There wasn't another horse in the country that could stay with them for a single day. If you thought they got tired, just try to catch one of them the next morning!

I have read articles by well-known authors about "those thundering herds which were lead by an old shaggy-headed bull." I have never seen one of those herds; I always saw an old, wise, *cow* leading the buffalo and of all buffalo I have hunted, it was always that old cow who would scent and see us. First, she would mill around the bunch and grunt until she worked them into a stampede, then she would take her place in front. You would find her out there in the lead when they had run themselves out. The bulls always travelled on the outside of the herds and fought most of the time when they were not browsing or running. It was easy to locate them by the sound of their horns cracking. They would fight for no apparent reason – just plunge at one another. Buffalo look to be sluggish and lazy when viewed in a zoo, but don't be deceived – they are as quick as a toad lapping lightning – they can turn in a flash. You can sidestep a charging steer or range bull – if you have the nerve to do it – but you will be hurt if you take such chances with an old bowback; you might as well approach a grizzly bear as get near a cow buffalo with a young calf at her side. It is true that buffalo will run at the sight of man; they will stampede for no apparent reason. I have seen them grazing peacefully without anything to disturb them, then one may start at full speed with the herd close behind. They will run for miles. When tired, they'll swing into a rocking gait, much like the pacing horse. When the first snows come, the buffalo travel into large valleys and you can see them

---

as many buffalo as he can." Mayer himself made no mention of this imaginary Indian hunting permit in the text.

coming in small groups. Their dark forms against the snow-covered hills are quite noticeable. They stay in large herds until the calves are born and strong enough to travel (about the middle of June) then wander away in small groups for the summer months. At calving time, which takes place on the winter pasture, one can see many circles which most plainsmen call "fairy rings." These circles were made by the bulls as they walked around the cows and their young, all night, in order to keep the wolves away. The path of those circles was not over a foot wide where the bull had walked; the circle was about ten feet across. Some of these circles were worn down to a depth of four to six inches in a single night. There were wallows which the buffalo dug with their feet – many are visible on the plains to this day. Water stood in these pits. Buffalo rolled in the mud and water. Mud baths were one of the buffalo's daily habits. There was always a pack of lobo wolves running alongside the buffalo. This kind of wolves are not real killers for they got plenty to eat without killing. When the buffalo were wiped out those buffalo or lobo wolves dispersed – probably they could not survive. None have been seen these many years.

Then, there was the buffalo bird, who lives with the herds and could be seen perched on buffalo backs and buffalo heads. These birds made their nests in the buffalo skulls that were scattered over the plains. Buffalo always run with their heads to the wind. If a herd had been run all day by hunters, you would find them next morning not far from where you had stopped running them. When starting them in the morning, you had to be sure which way the wind was blowing or they would stampede your way. It is impossible to change their course once they start – and they start in high gear.

I once took the ride of my life on a big "bull" buffalo. Some of my rides on bad bucking horses have grown dim in my memory, but that ride on an old bowback will always remain fresh. I had been running that herd for two months, so they were getting cross. Every morning the herd was larger as many new buffalo were coming down from the North. One morning, I turned them into a heavy wind which burned my face like fire. Water was streaming from my eyes – it was so cold. Above the valley, near Fort Kehoe, were a number of large buttes. The herd split when it came to one of those buttes. At that time I was watching the "buffs" which were rubbing against my pony on one side; I could see a number of spikehorns and was waiting for them to raise their heads so I might get a shot at them. Soon, I felt my pony zig-zagging under me.

There I was – surrounded by hundreds of buffalo. Many had come in on the other side of the butte, catching my pony in the middle of the herd. Now he was getting badly squeezed for they were bumping that little horse from both sides. I dropped the rifle and grabbed both hands full of buffalo wool and pulled myself up onto that old bull's hump. It was always considered a disgrace in my part of the country to pull leather and I can honestly say I have never grabbed the saddle horn when riding broncs. But I will admit pulling wool out of that old bull's shoulders and I got my spurs so tangled it was hard to get them loose.

I was fourteen years old at the time; the only way I can describe that ride is like a man on a log going through a rough rapids.[91] There were buffalo ahead of me and on both sides of me and behind me, running close together, their horns cracking as they ran. I must have been up there three or four hours for they had tired and were pacing, their tongues hanging out. I noticed there were not many buffalo on the River side of me and the old bull was bogging down. His feet made a "popping" sound when he pulled them out of the mud. He was heavy and broke through the frozen ground. Soon he came to a standstill, not paying any attention to me up there on his hump. I watched a few tired buffs pass, then slid down from my wooly seat and made my way into the alders beside the River. There I stayed till the buffs had passed and then I started back afoot. There were dead and crippled bison lying along the valley. I walked till I was tired, then built a fire and dropped off to sleep. The following morning, I climbed to the top of a large hill; there, in the distance, I saw buffalo browsing. To the east were dark moving spots on the snow. These spots were our skinners, out looking for their dropper. I broke sage, made a fire on the butte and in less than an hour, Jones and his men rode up on wet horses. They led one of my ponies – but not the one I left, to ride on that bull, for he (the pony) was trampled so badly I could only distinguish what was left by the hoofs, mane and tail hair. I've been on some mighty tough rides and have ridden some tough horses in various parts of the world, but that buffalo gave me the biggest thrill of them all.

I shot my last buffalo on the Cannonball and Morrow (?) River, South Dakota, the winter of 1885 – that was the last herd. There were a few in the Yellowstone park and some scattered on the plains – those were cleaned up that spring, for the hides jumped in price to $60 for prime hides. Old cow and bull hides were bringing from $20 to $40 apiece where heretofore they had brought only $2 to $3. In past years, you could not sell calf hides at any price, but now they were bringing $40 a bale, ten hides to the bale. Hides had been rising in price for the last four years. The Indian troubles were over so many outfits went in for buffalo running. Men left their business in the East, brought their outfits out and began running buffalo. The government did not say "clean the buffalo off the plains," but it encouraged hunters to do so. If a buffalo hunter rode into an army garrison, he could get all the cartridge he wanted, free of charge. The word was passed along – "kill the buffalo and you will subdue the Indians." The rifles used by the buffalo runners were made by the Sharpe people and called the Buffalo Sharpe.

---

[91] **Editors' note:** Compare this account with Hopkins' previous version of buffalo riding to be found in "Last of the Buffalo Hunters. Though the details differ, Hopkins apparently lifted the buffalo-riding story from Major John Burke, who told *The New York Journal* in 1897, "The ride on those buffalo was just about the same as riding down a rapid Canadian river aboard a saw-log."

This rifle was not made after the buffalo were wiped out. It carried the army cartridge. There have been many stories written about hunting the bison on our Western Plains, but I doubt if the writers ever ran the herds. Col. W.F. Cody was supposed to be one of the greatest, if not *the* greatest, of buffalo hunters of all times. Bill Cody was too heavy to run buffalo, so how could he drop many on one run, for a top buffalo horse wouldn't be able to carry a man of his weight more than two miles at the speed he would have to go to keep up with the herd. The droppers were always boys, light for their horses to carry who could stay with the herds all day.[92] In my last years of dropping I was getting too heavy for the job although I weighed only about 140 pounds. Cody and I were good friends up to his death and he once told me exactly how many buffalo he had shot during his lifetime. He died in 1917 and his hunting is not intended for this article.

To horse-minded folks, this article may seem somewhat off key, but the buffalo running was done with the toughest horses known – the American Mustangs. There is no use in talking, if you've been there, then you know. It's the only life worth living, your towns to me are but a jail, and I'll gladly trade their comforts for the saddle and the trail!

This article was first published in January 1942.

---

[92] **Editors' note**: Leo Remiger, one of the co-authors of the *Encyclopedia of Buffalo Hunters and Skinners,* dismissed Hopkins' claims to have been a famous nineteenth century mounted buffalo hunter. Remiger, and his fellow authors Sharon Cunningham and Miles Gilbert, have spent years compiling what is believed to be the largest private collection of buffalo-hunting knowledge in history. Their four-volume collection about the American buffalo-hunting industry will be the most in-depth study ever made. When author Remiger read Hopkins buffalo-hunting accounts, he was quick to denounce him as a fraud. "Hopkins is a phony! He got it all backwards. You hunt buffalo from a stand so you can keep the carcasses in a central position. Hopkins was obviously just repeating stories he had read. We don't know of any contemporary sources that even mention him."

Chapter 9

Riders and Their Records
By Colonel Parker

To whom it may concern:

I recently ran across an article, written by a Doctor Johnson, in the Remount Association's magazine, *The Horse*, concerning the 100-Mile Trail Ride held at Woodstock, Vt., last August. In this article he mentions, as the judges of this event, the names of a Doctor Neal, John Williams and Frank T. Hopkins, speaking of the latter as a veteran long-distance rider. It would indeed be interesting to know if this is the same Frank T. Hopkins who was a dispatch rider during the 70's and 80's in this great West of ours. He was, in those days, known in every camp, fort and army post throughout the West as the "Laramie Kid" and carried dispatches for the various generals on the frontier, including Gen. Alfred Terry, Gen. George Crook, Gen. Hugh Scott and Gen. Nelson A. Miles.

If this is the same man, you will, no doubt, be interested to know more of his activities as a rider of the plains. If so I am enclosing a brief outline covering some of the history relating to him and others who made daring rides through the Indian infested country of those early days. If you wish to use this data, you have my permission to do so.

Sincerely yours,

COL. R. PARKER[93]

---

[93] **Editors' note**: Evidence strongly suggests that the author of this article, the so-called "Colonel R. Parker," was none other than Gertrude Hopkins, the wife of Frank Hopkins. The Long Riders' Guild discovered a treasure-trove of Hopkins-related material at the University of Wyoming. Ensconced within the Robert Easton papers was the original handwritten copy of this article – in Gertrude's handwriting!

Born in Rutherford, New Jersey, in 1891, Gertrude played a starring role in her husband's campaign to promote his mythological past. According to a letter from a publisher addressed to famed Buffalo Bill Cody biographer, Don Russell, Gertrude Hopkins was intimately involved with the creation and promotion of the Hopkins myth.

"Back in 1934 one of our authors [Charles B. Roth] got in contact with an old-timer named Hopkins; my author was primarily interested in Hopkins as a long-distance horse rider. Hopkins wrote up a manuscript; this is what I'm sending you. On the basis of this, my author queried Hopkins for details on certain things, and Hopkins would dictate the answers to his wife, who wrote them in letters to my author," wrote the publisher.

Some people have recently tried to lay all the blame for the Hopkins mythology at Gertrude's door. This is not the case. Frank Hopkins himself first went public with his Old West lies when he spoke to a Philadelphia reporter in 1926. At that time, Hopkins was still married to his Canadian wife, Marian. Although Frank created the "Laramie Kid's" imaginary exploits, Gertrude was his willing assistant. After Frank died in 1951,

Most of the long, hard rides which were ridden by western plainsmen have proven inaccurate. In many cases they were over- and in others under-estimated, as the trails over which they rode were not surveyed until long years after those rides were made.

Countless tales have been told regarding those early cattlemen, who with their cowboys drove vast herds of cattle to the Kansas markets and northern ranges, and many of these men are credited with wonderful rides over the long trails, but seldom were they called upon to exert either themselves or their mounts, unless the cattle were forced into a stampede by storm or by raiding Indians bent upon running off the stock. It was on these occasions that these men did most of their hardest riding. Often faced with death, either from Indian raiders or to avoid being run down and crushed to death beneath the hooves of the frenzied cattle, they rode for their lives. Stirring stories have been told of the cavalry, which during those early days literally lived in the saddle. Forts were few and far between which forced the men to frequently camp in the open, without shelter. The life endured by both men and horses was a hard lot. These troopers rode with full equipment, and it took a horse of great stamina to carry both rider and his equipment, when forced to race for miles in giving battle with the Indian raiders, but traveling as they did in large groups, they at least had a fighting chance for their lives.

Another group of men who deserve great praise, and about whom we read innumerable stories, deal with the scouts who piloted the caravans across the unchartered plains on their migrations westward. These intrepid souls were a hardy and reliable body of men and well deserve all the credit attributed to them in helping to settle the West.

Of that daring and resourceful body of men known as "Dispatch Riders," who hourly, day after day, faced almost certain death in carrying dispatches between forts and army posts, we seldom see records, yet these riders, many of whom were mere boys, rode the unmarked trails, covering great distances and at a speed that is almost unbelievable. Like many other riders, they were often credited with more or less mileage than they actually rode. Their lives were in constant danger and many met a sudden and tragic death while carrying their first

---

the widow Hopkins continued to promote this cottage industry of lies until her own death at their home in Long Island City, New York, in 1971.

While Frank can be credited with having fooled the readers of the *Vermont Horse & Bridle Trail Bulletin*, in Rutland, Vermont, Gertrude's claim to fame is that she personally misled famous American author, Jack Schaefer, and well-known magazine writer, Anthony Amaral, into publishing her husband's equestrian fantasies.

There is, however, no evidence to indicate that either Frank or Gertrude Hopkins financially profited from these tales. It would appear that theirs was a psychological motivation.

message. Others, more fortunate, got through for months before encountering any serious setback...... A good reliable dispatch rider was always in great demand and held in high esteem by army officer and civilian alike. Some made a spectacular entrance into the service, but when faced with a crucial test, lacked what in western parlance is known as "guts" enough to meet the crisis.

I recall one such rider by name, Johnny Breen, who made quite a name for himself as a dispatch rider in Nebraska during his three years in the service, chalking up to his credit many long, fast rides. During this period, however, there was little or no trouble with the Indians. Then came the uprising of the Sioux during the spring of 1882. Leaving Fort Custer in a jubilant mood, Johnny headed for an outlying post, and had covered some eight miles of his journey when he encountered his first band of Indians. Discovered by the Indian scouts, Johnny was soon burning the breeze back to the fort, closely pursued by the whooping Redskins. More by good luck than his management the rider succeeded in reaching the fort, where, in an hysterical condition, he related his experience and, throwing the message upon the general's desk, declared he was through and had carried his last message.

Of another caliber was King Stanley, credited with being one of the best dispatch riders in the service, one who never failed to deliver a message entrusted to his charge. Often when telegraph wires were down and stations destroyed, King made rides of from three to four hundred miles and in many cases was forced to shoot his way through the Indian-infested country when attacked by the Indian scouts bent upon lifting his scalp.

Another "Paul Revere" of the plains, and a staunch friend of Stanley's, was a youth known at the army posts as the "Laramie Kid," although his real name was Frank Tezolph Hopkins. He was a true son of the West, born in Fort Laramie and brought up in army life, where he early in life learned the ways of the frontiersmen. It has been said that he celebrated his thirteenth birthday while carrying his first message for Gen. Alfred Terry. It was just ten o'clock in the forenoon of August 9, 1877, that the "Kid" rode out of Fort Laramie, headed for Twin Buttes, in the Shoshone Valley, a distance of 168 miles away...... and it was at sundown on the thirteenth that he again reached Fort Laramie and made his report,, covering the round trip of 336 miles in less than FOUR DAYS.... and this through the rough and unsettled wilderness.... A correct record of that ride was made and hung on the walls of the general's office at Fort Laramie for many years, until it was removed by Gen. Nelson A. Miles when the old fort was abandoned about 1889[94]... In later years, after the roadbed had been laid over

---

[94] **Louise Samson,** *Curator of the Fort Laramie National Historic Site:* "Although General Nelson A. Miles was a well known Indian Wars' figure, he did not command Fort Laramie, and the Twin Buttes in the Shoshone Valley that Hopkins references, on any logical historic route would have been closer to 600 miles round trip than 336."

the same route or trail, it was discovered by clocking a number of cars that the distance could not have been over 146 miles, one way. Hopkins always claimed he had ridden 140 odd miles, one way, when questioned about this ride.

Two years later saw King Stanley and young Hopkins facing death side by side, as the pair were trapped by Crow Indian scouts, at Grantrice Pillars, Mont. For three days the valiant pair of dispatch riders fought against great odds, without food or water; both were wounded during the fight, but refused to admit defeat, displaying the heart and courage to fight on until rescued from their precarious position by a troop of cavalry, brought to their rescue by a friendly Indian scout.[95]

King Stanley was at this time only twenty-four years old, while the "Kid" was about fifteen years of age. Both were experienced frontiersmen, experts with either rifle or hand gun, which they never hesitated to use when forced to defend their life or property..... Both Stanley and Hopkins were outstanding examples and in no way comparable with the host of ruffians and rowdies which frequented the army posts. Stanley and the "Kid" always attended to the duties allotted to them and were entrusted with carrying messages by the commandants in Nebraska and the Dakotas.

Life around the army post was a "nightmare" to both men and their officers, however, when Stanley and the "Kid" were off duty, and it was this display of over-exuberance in "pestering" the garrison that finally ended in the separation of the pair by orders of General Crook, following their mischievous act of stampeding a pack train of mules, which resulted in scattering army supplies all over the adjacent territory. Harassed by their misdeeds, and knowing there would be no peace while they remained together, General Crook ended the confusion by ordering Hopkins to Fort Lincoln, where he would work alone, and likewise assigning Stanley to Fort Robinson. The general remarked, "Plenty of work and separation is the only cure for that pair of rogues."

---

[95] **Editors' note**: Compare this episode at the non-existent Grantrice Pillars, Montana, with another incident in *My Years in the Saddle*: "I carried many messages, all the time getting farther away; soon I found myself in Montana. I had spent the night at Grantrice Pillars. My horse was an army charger who appeared to be very tired from the day before, so I led him, thinking he might limber up after a mile or so, but in less than that mile the horse was riddled with bullets and his carcass served as a barricade to save me from that hot lead. However, I did not miss all of those shots and I do not think any man ever used a Springfield rifle any faster than I used that one. I will never know how many Ree Indians shot at me that morning for they were in heavy brush and I was passing on a beaten trail. For over four hours I lay there and returned shot for shot. Finally, some Blackfoot Indians heard the shooting; they rode a long time before they got to me and I know for sure that they did not get there any too soon. Now, the Ree was enemy to the Blackfoot. The Blackfeet cared for me as well as did the Sioux and they also sent out a runner to make known my whereabouts and my condition."

At this time trouble with the Indians reached its height, the raiders killing and laying waste all along the frontier from Nebraska to Montana. It was during this trying period that King Stanley demonstrated his remarkable endurance as a "saddle slapper" and the epic performance of a little mustang stallion, called "Uney," which carried him a distance then estimated to be 700 miles in the remarkable time of SEVEN DAYS.

Here I would like to make a correction, for the sake of posterity, in the matter of keeping the history of this ride correct. Twenty years later that country over which King Stanley made his record ride was surveyed by the railway engineers from Fort Custer, his starting point, to the Great Basin, Montana. The actual distance covered was 537 MILES …. instead of 700 miles. Regardless of the facts established and considering the number of times this little pony raised and put down its feet, while traversing that number of miles in seven days' time, it was, and still remains, one of the most stupendous and strenuous rides ever recorded in the annals of the West…. In citing this ride of Stanley's, I am not attempting in any way to detract from any of the glory to which he is entitled, but simply to prove that often riders were credited with covering a greater distance then the actual mileage measured. As often also proved the case, many others COVERED A GREATER DISTANCE THAN THEY WERE EVER GIVEN CREDIT FOR.

For instance, let us consider the ride made by Frank T. Hopkins from War Bonnet Creek to Fort Lincoln, as a sample of those which were greatly UNDERESTIMATED. Hopkins had been attacked by Sioux Scouts, while carrying a message to an outpost camp, about eight miles east of the creek. On his return journey the scouts surprised him while crossing a creek. To escape, Hopkins was forced to race his pony in the direction of Fort Lincoln, which lay many miles away… It was his only choice. Many scouts were scattered over the country at the time and these acted as relays, for his original pursuers, in an attempt to run down the valiant dispatch rider; but Hopkins' pony proved equal to the task of maintaining the lead and carried its ride to safety. When Hopkins reached Fort Lincoln, the date of his message showed he had been on the trail ONLY 12 HOURS….. At the time officers at the fort made light of his accomplishment, "Not a bad ride, Kid,"… "Pretty good work, boy," were the remarks passed. At this time they claimed the "Kid" had ridden 80 MILES in the 12 hours.

Years later, when the automobile road was put through from Lincoln, out into South Dakota, it crossed War Bonnet Creek, at White Clay Banks, the very spot where the "Kid" had shot his way clear from his enemies. FOUR DIFFERENT CARS CLOCKED THE DISTANCE for the sole reason of ascertaining just how many miles Hopkins actually rode. EVERY CAR ALIKE REGISTERED 124 MILES. The road runs as straight as the crow flies, so even had the "Kid" "cut trail" at any point on his ride, he could have in no manner reduced the distance;

in fact, he would have ONLY INCREASED THE DISTANCE which was registered by the cars. As Hopkins was well acquainted with the country he was riding in, it is likely he stuck to the straight trail.

The "Laramie Kid" made many rides during about ten years of his dispatch-riding career... for which he never received the credit due him, either in time or the mileage he covered, and he rode many....both in the north and in the southwest. One of these "stiff" rides made by Hopkins is well worthy of mention, one which he made while carrying messages out of the Red Cloud Agency (Fort Robinson, Neb.). Hopkins had been sent with a message to Fort Phil Kearney. Riding one horse and leading another, to which he changed often on the ride, he made good time to Kearney. At the fort he secured two fresh horses and continued on to Fort Russell, Wyo. Stopping only long enough to secure the return message, he took the back trail to Fort Kearney, picked up the two horses he had left there and rode on to Fort Robinson. Hopkins was nine days on that ride, during which period he never saw a bed, for he slept on the ground as his ponies rested and grazed. It takes a tough man indeed to endure such treatment, but Hopkins proved that kind and despite the exposure and punishment he underwent during this trying ordeal, he suffered no ill effects. According to the general's notes, Hopkins was credited with having ridden 700 miles in nine days. The route he covered and which was put down at 700 miles, proved later to be OVER 800 MILES... Hopkins used four horses in making this trip, and he could have hardly gotten there and back without riding the latter number of miles.

Both King Stanley and Frank T. Hopkins carried messages through the hardest and most hazardous campaigns known in the history of the West, during which they no doubt experienced hardships that will never be known, and while many succumbed, they both lived to recall them.

In 1884 King Stanley was wounded and that injury put him out of the saddle for the remainder of his days. Hopkins, although records show he was shot seven different times, refused to give up and rode on, carrying messages until the end and did not leave the service until after the Geronimo campaign, down in Arizona, and the capture of the wily Apache chief during the spring of 1886.[96]

---

[96] **Editors' note**: Hopkins' connections with the Apache chief, Geronimo, are indeed curious. On the one hand, he expressed disdain for the Apaches, writing that they, "seemed tricky and a filthy lot and of a very cruel nature... they resembled Eskimos more than Plains Indians." Yet according to Gertrude Hopkins, Frank's Indian grandfather was Geronimo! She claimed Geronimo was not an Apache but a secret Sioux Indian living in exile with the Apaches. In a letter to Robert Easton, Gertrude asserted that Frank was a member of an Indian Royal Family, which included Chief Joseph of the Nez Percé, Crazy Horse and Black Elk of the Lakota, and Geronimo, all of whom she said were related. When a disbelieving Easton queried Gertrude's claims, she replied defensively. "I only have Frank's word for it that Geronimo was his grandfather. But it seems to me he ought

Hopkins always claimed that King Stanley was the best rider and greatest horseman he ever knew. This statement he made many years after he had left the trails and had become famous as a horseman, among the best cavalrymen of the world.... Talking with King Stanley, a short time prior to his death (which occurred in 1927, at the age of seventy-three years), Stanley remarked that he never was a match for Hopkins in the saddle at any time the two rode the western plains or since.... In all likelihood this matter will ever remain a mystery, as to which of these two renowned and outstanding horsemen was the better rider, but the records which they hung up would indeed be hard and, perhaps, well nigh unbeatable.

Hopkins, who now must be nearly eighty years of age, I am told, is still active, although he no longer rides. Long may he live, this veteran of the Old West, who rode and fought, both as boy and man, giving the best years of his life that meant the settlement of this great West of ours.

This article was first published in July 1942

---

to know his own grandfather. I once saw a picture in a book of Geronimo, and when Frank got hopping mad, he certainly looked like him! Frank did tell me he knew Chief Joseph was Geronimo's brother. As to what you say of the history books, I know they don't always tell the truth."

Dale Yeager, *Criminal Psychologist:* "It is clear to me that Hopkins had a co-dependent relationship with his wife, Gertrude. Her willingness to continue his lies after his death and to create new lies shows his manipulation of her."

Chapter 10

Buffalo Bill as I knew him

[Note from the editor of the Vermont Horse & Trail Bulletin – *No one now living knew Col. W.F. Cody, "Buffalo Bill," as well as Frank Hopkins. This fascinating story from our old friend whom we have all learned to love, is reminiscent of another period in our American life that makes interesting reading.*]

Colonel W.F. Cody, as most Americans know, was that great showman called "Buffalo Bill." I can remember him from my early childhood; he often came to Fort Laramie and at such times he stayed with our family. He was then running a wagon freight business. A few years later, he started a small wild west show which was hauled from place to place by horses, covering towns in two or three states in one season.

In 1886, a man by the name of Nathan Salisbury joined Cody, or rather, Salisbury hired him as a drawing card. This Salisbury was one of the largest theatre promoters of those days and he knew how to suit the public – he turned out the finest show of horses and horsemen the world has ever seen. Every individual rider was subjected to a real test before being hired to ride in this show. Many who thought themselves first-class horsemen were turned down.

When the Indian troubles were ended, I was no longer needed as a dispatch rider. The West was getting tame; the large herds of buffalo were gone and the Indians were living on reservations. There was none of the excitement I had known since I was a boy. I took on a few long rides and also broke colts for ranchmen.

On my return home to Wyoming from the Ellis Jackson (Lucky Baldwin) ride to Vermont, I found Big Bill Cody and Nathan Salisbury eating dinner with my folks. Cody rose to his full six feet seven inches,[97] stretched out his hand and said, "Howdy, Laramie, been waitin' for you the past few days." He and Salisbury wanted me to ride in circles for their new show. They offered what seemed to me at that time a big price to do it, but I learned soon afterwards that their price was a mere nothing to what I actually earned for them. However, I

---

[97] **Dr. Juti Winchester,** *Curator of the Buffalo Bill Museum at the Buffalo Bill Historical Center:* "Buffalo Bill was six feet one-half inch tall. He might have seemed really tall to somebody who was not very tall at all. And, for most of his life Cody was a string bean, so he might have seemed taller. However, six-seven is huge and especially for the nineteenth century. Had he been that tall he would have been an exhibit in a sideshow."

joined their show on the twelfth day of November, 1886. This was held in the old Madison Square Gardens. This Garden was an old wooden building located on the exact site where Stanford White, the famous architect, built the second "Garden" in about 1890. When I rode into the ring where rehearsal was going on, some of the Indians charged at me with their ponies to count "coop" as they would to an enemy, but this was now only in fun, although we had really been enemies on the Plains not many years before. I spoke their language fluently, so it was easy to get along with them. Among these Indians were many warriors. Occasionally, one would tell me how near he had come to "getting me" at some spot where I had passed with a message in my dispatch-carrying days. It was told good-naturedly, sometimes in truth, other times jokingly. I know there was a lot of lead thrown my way in those years of carrying messages and I surely know how a travelling bullet sounds and just how it feels when it hits!

After a few days' practice, the "Bill show" started with a parade up Fifth Avenue, New York, Cody riding at the head of it, waving his "sombrero" to the onlookers. Coming straight from the western plains as I did, this many people crowding so around our horses worried and confused me, and I didn't like it.

When the show started – it was the afternoon performance – the Garden was packed; the aisles were filled with standees. First, all riders entered the ring on their horses, then Salisbury spoke to the audience about Cody's career and continued telling about me as a dispatch rider. My act was on first[98] – it was to change horses five times around the ring at full speed, changing to a different style every time, the horses going as fast as they could. I made it without a miss. The cheering of the crowd upset me so badly I was too upset to take part in the rest of the show. Salisbury tried to comfort me by saying if the crowd didn't like the act they wouldn't cheer and that they did not cheer so much when Cody did his shooting act. But talk didn't help much – I wanted to leave at once and get back to the wide-open spaces of the West away from the crowds. I refused point blank to bear dispatch in the evening performance of the show if Salisbury announced my act. He promised he would wait until I had done my riding and gone out of the ring. He kept his word and it helped, for in a few days, I was over the panic, although I never did like to hear the crowd cheer – it gave me the chills even to the last days as a show rider.

---

[98] **Editors' note**: Despite Hopkins' "modest" claim to have been the first act in the Wild West show, authorities agree that the first act was always the "Grand Review," which introduced the Rough Riders of the World (including Cowboys, Indians, Mexicans, Cossacks, Gauchos and Arabs.) Following this mounted exhibition of the world's greatest horsemen, the second act was reserved for Annie Oakley, the greatest personality developed by the Wild West show. Her first few shots often brought forth a few screams of fright from women in the crowd. But Oakley, known as "Little Sure Shot," soon put them at ease and prepared them for the continuous crack of firearms which was to come.

Cody had me ride with him in the Buffalo Hunt which was only chasing a dozen buffalo out of the ring with blank shots. Later on, I learned that this was done to get me used to a crowded house. For the first month, they would not let me do any trick riding; when I'd gotten more used to the crowds making fools of themselves, Salisbury asked me to do a little trick riding, warning me about keeping calm as the audience would probably whoop it up after a while. He'd say, "Now, go out there and show them something they never saw before." Nothing bothered me much after the first trick riding except maybe the band and I still can't stand the noise of a big band.

When hired to ride in the show I agreed to furnish my own ponies. Some of these had been schooled for trick riding, more for my own pleasure than anything else; they came in handy now. One evening, Black Elk (a Sioux) and I gave the crowd a big surprise by racing our ponies at their best speed, the whole length of the ring, changing horses when they passed each other in the center of the ring without slacking the pace. This is the hardest thing to do on horseback and I had never seen anyone perform that feat other than Black Elk and myself, so it seemed to me a pretty good trick. One rider throws his body back on his horses' side to allow the other rider to grab the horn of the saddle and swing into the saddle while the rider leaning backwards must grasp the saddle horn of the other horse as the horse races past. One little slip-up and it's just too bad – the rider gets pretty badly smashed up. I missed a time or two learning this trick and the result is still noticeable in my walk. Black Elk and I learned this trick along with many others when we were small boys and now we were in our twenties playing our tricks on pony back the same as we did then, but amusing throngs of people every day.

We played all that winter in the Garden. It was a surprise to me where all the people came from – the house was always packed.

That spring, Cody told me we were going to England. I didn't relish the idea of an ocean between me and the Western plains. Nevertheless, on the 18th of April, 1887, the show shipped on the S.S. *Colorado*[99] which had been chartered for that trip. We had a tough crossing, encountered many storms, most of the bison died and had to be dropped overboard, horses sickened – some died – we had about eight of the bison left for the show out of about fifty-four. We set up at Earl's Court, London, England. It was the year of Queen Victoria's Jubilee. Our posters were displayed in prominent places and there were special ones showing Black Elk and me changing horses in the air, one of us facing one way

---

[99] **Editors' note:** In Chapter 3, *My Years in the* Saddle, Hopkins states they traveled to Europe aboard the SS *Nebraska*. In reality, the Wild West show sailed aboard the SS *State of Nebraska*.

the other the opposite; the trick itself was a whole lot harder to do than it looked on that poster![100]

The first evening performance, Black Elk and I performed many of our tricks, the last one changing horses riding towards each other from opposite ends of the ring. Then something happened – the crowd cut loose and swarmed into the ring. In a few seconds our ponies were completely surrounded by people and it was a good half hour before we got the people all back into their seats. Salisbury ordered Black Elk and me out of the ring and told us not to come out in the other acts that night. Cody liked to tease me and often played friendly tricks. This time he said, "Your trick riding out there with Black Elk was so bad the crowd almost mobbed both of you and if you go out there again tonight they'll finish the job."

Early in June, Nate put on a long race from Earle's Court to Land's End, Cornwall (England) (about 212 miles one way). The rider and horse who got there and back first was to get one thousand dollars in gold. This race was widely advertised; for a week many riders signed up to take part in it. Most of them used "hunters." I asked Salisbury's permission to enter that race. At first he thought it might be foolish to attempt to ride on one of my small ponies against those fine-looking hunters. Cody said to him, "You might get the surprise of your life, Nate, if Frank takes one of his own ponies over the road with those hunters eating his dust." Cody was willing to bet my pony would return to Earle's Court hours ahead of the bunch; Salisbury took Cody's bet, told me to train my pony and ride in the race. I chose a pony which had been ridden seven hundred miles in as many days by a famous rider – King Stanley. I raised this little stallion – his sire and dam were caught wild from the Red Desert Herd – these ponies were well named for their toughness and "Uney" was just as tough as his forebears – he loped away out to Land's End and back in forty-six hours of actual traveling and when I rode him into the stable Cody remarked, "This talk about lopin' hosses tiring is the damdest lot of rot I've heard and how many horsemen here ever saw a true loping horse?" Cody knew what he was talking about; that same pony sired some of the best endurance horses the world has ever known, including my "Hidalgo," the stallion who beat some of the best Arabs in their own country and he was a true loping horse; all his family before him were true to that gait. Well, old "Uney" won the Earle's Court race; he finished fourteen hours forty-five minutes ahead of the next best horse.[101]

---

[100] **Editors' note:** Despite an intensive search by the historians at the Buffalo Bill Historical Center, no poster of Frank Hopkins, with or without Black Elk, has ever been found.

[101] **Editors' note**: Compare with "My Years in the Saddle," where Hopkins claims the race was more than 200 miles and that he finished twelve hours ahead of the next-best horse; compare also with the article, "Mustangs," in which he writes that his pony

Cody was kind to man and horse. He liked to think of the riders as one large, happy family. He'd walk through the stable, calling every horse by name and often patted and fondled the animals. The evening of my return from that long ride, I went to the stable to care for "Uney" and found Cody talking to the pony. He asked me if I could teach "Uney" to go out into the ring alone. He thought it would be nice to have Salisbury announce the winning horse of the race. I promised to have the pony ready for that act in three days. I placed a small stand at the far end of the ring, underneath the big light, put some carrots on the stand, then walked across the ring with "Uney." This was repeated many times when the show was not going on. Every time the pony got the carrots I stayed a little farther back from him. After days of training "Uney" walked across the ring alone. Then came the evening performance when all the riders who had taken part in the race rode into the ring circled about and rode back through the curtain. The small stand was then placed at the far end of the ring with a small piece of carrot on it. "Uney," wearing his best saddle and a hackamore, loped across the ring, got his bit of carrot and posed; then he pawed the tan bark and whinnied, much to the delight of Cody (and the audience). When Cody spoke, "Uney" started for the curtain at a fast lope. Even hard-shelled Salisbury rubbed "Uney's" nose after that performance.

Queen Victoria attended often. Once, she rode around the ring in the old Overland stage coach. One evening in August, Nate asked me to come to his office. Thinking he was about to lay down the law for something he thought I'd done – (I was usually cutting pranks in those days with the other riders) I walked into his office ready to face whatever he had waiting for me, but was greeted with "Frank, I have something very special for you to do. I'm confident you'll do it right. Queen Victoria requests that you and Black Elk give a special performance on the Buckingham Palace lawn before her guests. This," he continued, "is quite an honor and you must not whoop it up or use any rough stuff outside of your trick riding, and both of you must dress in your best parade clothes. Cody and I'll be there and if you don't act right we'll square with you later." Then he poked me in the ribs with his thumb and said, "I know damn well you fellows will do things right out there and we're going to be mighty proud of both of you."

The following afternoon, about two, Black Elk and I were ready to perform. Each took along three well-trained horses. That side of the Palace facing the tennis grounds was packed with people who cheered as we rode onto the lawn. Men in bright uniforms rushed up to take charge of our extra ponies – some carried blankets for the ponies when we changed. No signs of Cody or Salisbury – they kept in back out of our sight fearing we might get nervous. The lawn was soft; our ponies threw large pieces of sod high into the air and I rode over and

---

"covered that ride of some 158 miles in twenty-eight hours of actual travel and finished nine hours ahead of the next best horse."

apologized to Her Majesty, fearing that the lawn would be destroyed entirely if we continued. She just laughed and said it could be replaced and to go right ahead. So I went back to Black Elk told him we'd go on and do it right and we did; after about two hours of trick riding, changing ponies often, that lawn looked like a lot of hogs had been rooting in it all summer! The crowed shouted continuously while we were performing and we gave them all we and the ponies had. Her Majesty gave us tea on the second balcony – Black Elk could not speak English nor understand it so I acted as interpreter. The Queen talked freely with us and asked a lot of questions. She was just the grandest, motherly little lady.[102] Cody and Salisbury were not so far in the background, taking everything in but we could not see them. That evening, while getting ready for the evening performance, Cody came into the stable looking very serious; he said, "You fellows made one awful mess out of things over there this afternoon and if any one asks if you know anything about trick ridin' tell them the truth – say NO." I stared at him – finally, when he could hold out no longer he broke into a hearty laugh. "You two can have the evening off – you surely earned it; you gave 'em all you had and I'm tickled."

Along about this time the show was getting bigger. Major Burke joined us with many others – Annie Oakley, Buck Taylor, Death Valley Scotty among others, some army officers; there were some two hundred riders in all and as many or more saddle horses. We played there for nine months before we toured Scotland and Wales, giving two performances a day and training horses for new acts. Riders had to keep themselves well trained and physically fit for their acts – no pleasure in show business then for a rider, we had to put in sixteen to eighteen hours every day. I have actually dropped to sleep while in the saddle. The parades were worst of all – I'd cut out sometimes and go back to the horse-top for a snooze. Cody soon stopped that, however, by having me ride beside him at the head of the parade.

There was always something to take up our time in Europe. When not in the ring, people wanted to talk with us about the West and the horses. They'd wait around until they got your ear and when they did it was hard to get away from them. Sometimes, I hid in the stall with my favorite horse guarding me to get a

---

[102] **Editors' note**: In *Black Elk Speaks*, published in 1932, Black Elk shares his memories with John Neihardt, including recollections of his trip to England with the Wild West show. "One day we were told that Majesty was coming. It was Grandmother England (Queen Victoria)… We danced and sang, and I was one of the dancers chosen to do this for the Grandmother… She was little but fat and we liked her, because she was good to us. After we had danced, she spoke to us…. 'If you belonged to me, I would not let them take you around in a show like this.' She said other good things too. She shook hands with all of us. Her hand was very little and soft. We gave a big cheer for her…" There is no mention of Frank Hopkins anywhere in *Black Elk Speaks*.

little rest from them and woe to anyone who tried to get by that horse and disturb me!

Two boats were charted for our return to the U.S.A. It was a happy moment for me when I saw the lines cast off the dock and I knew I was on the way home. I had made up my mind I was a poor showman who always longed to go back where there were no crowds.

A large dock had been built for our ships at Staten Island (part of it was still standing a few years ago) and there was more building at our winter quarters. The "Bill" show was a huge success but all I wanted was to square up and go home. Salisbury tried to persuade me to sign a five-year contract explaining that the show would soon go to the Jubilee in Rome and that I could not leave when they needed me more now. I learned a lot about Salisbury by being around him and I was not in any hurry to sign his contract, knowing full well it was drawn up for his own benefit, not mine. The day that Cody and I left for the West, Salisbury asked me to promise that I'd return ready for work in two months. I said I might consider it if my wages were doubled, but I would not sign his contract; this was the first of many breaks I had with Salisbury.

Well, the show went to Rome in the spring; I was with it. We played in the ancient Coliseum for a whole year without moving anywhere else. We had with us trained cavalry men from every country in the world in their different uniforms. It was a beautiful sight to see them on parade. At this time, the Congress of Rough Riders of the World was organized and there they had their first world contest. It was given two hours every day for the whole year. The contest took place in the arena from nine until eleven in the forenoon and the show itself had two performances every day. I rode in all three without missing a single performance. After the fair was over, there was a race of 250 miles on the Austrian Border. Italian, German, Austrian cavalrymen took part in it. I was asked to ride in it and used one of my small loping stallions. He finished some hours ahead of the next horse, a German hunter.

The show toured many countries including Russia,[103] Germany and the small countries surrounding them.

In Paris, France, our show played for a year at the World's Fair there. The Congress of Rough Riders of the World held its contest on the military grounds of Marseilles. Again, I contested, riding also twice a day in the "Bill" show besides. When the fair ended, the Congress of Rough Riders of the World paid all my expenses and sent me to contest in a three thousand-mile ride on the deserts of Arabia.[104] I took part in three different rides there and returned to the

---

[103] **Dr. Juti Winchester,** *Curator of the Buffalo Bill Museum at the Buffalo Bill Historical Center:* "According to our database of dates and places, Buffalo Bill's Wild West did not go to Russia at all."

[104] **Editors' note:** Hopkins told three different versions of the journey to Aden, Arabia story. In this article he implies that he went to Arabia from France. In "My Years in the

United States to take part in the Buffalo Bill Wild West show at the Chicago Fair. Before the fair started, I took on four pretty stiff rides – one of them the toughest race of my experience; this race took place in the Canadian northwest. There had just been a race of two hundred miles – most of the riders in it were mounted police – after the race I was challenged to ride against the winning horse. To make it more interesting I agreed to give the other horse and rider four hours' start. The second day, there was a snowfall that froze during the night, forming a stiff crust; this made it hard going, still, my pony loped along. I left Canada with full pockets and a tired pony, but not licked.

After the Chicago Fair was over, the "Bill" show began to get ancient. Cody was in bad health from which he never recovered. We toured the States and Canada each year, the show growing smaller as each season came around. In the spring of 1907, Major Gordon Lillie's small show joined up with us.[105] That was the beginning of the end for the "Bill" show. Lilly was a little too much of a business man; our old riders lost their old spirit and many of them quit; the show was on the downward slide. Every winter the Congress of Rough Riders of the World sent me to contest in different parts of the world – in fact in every country excepting Turkey.[106]

I've often been asked what I considered the best horse; I guess there are good and bad ones in every county. The Arab horses in Arabia seem to me poor specimens of that fine breed, yet I've seen good ones there too. The Arab horses in Egypt are a fine lot – the same strain in our own country here are better than in other countries. Most of the horses are cross breeds which can be traced back to the Arab or Barb. Summing them all up, I really think our horses are as good as any in the world. They won't stay that way though if our breeders keep on crossing all breeds as they have been doing lately. Giving these crosses a pedigree does not help – there's a correct name for a horse as well as anything else that has the mixture of many strains of blood.

This article was first published in October 1942.

Saddle" he states that he shipped his horses to Arabia from the United States. And finally, in "Mustangs," Hopkins writes "I shipped out of Genoa, Italy, for Aden, Arabia, taking three of my Mustangs."

[105] **Dr. Juti Winchester,** *Curator of the Buffalo Bill Museum at the Buffalo Bill* Historical *Center:* "Cody and Major Gordon Lillie, a.k.a. "Pawnee Bill," became partners in 1909."

[106] **Editors' note:** Although Hopkins wrote that he never went to Turkey, he did claim to have won a race in Arabia in 1890. At that time, Arabia was part of the Turkish (Ottoman) Empire, which stretched from the Balkans to the port of Aden, where the nonexistent 3,000 mile horse race supposedly started. The country known today as Turkey did not exist until 1924.

Chapter 11

Horses and Horsemen

Horsemanship should begin with the raising of horses, and successful raiser selecting only the best breeding stock, for even the best ofttimes proves not good enough.

The care of brood mares should not be neglected; keeping them in dark stalls should be avoided. My own experience has taught me that the mares who run outdoors the year 'round produce fine, husky colts. It is important that both mares and colts be sheltered from storms and bad weather, in a place where they can run in and out, at will. During cold weather, brood mares need more feed. Blankets are not necessary – in fact, the mares do better without covering, since Nature provides them with heavy coats of hair in Winter. Naturally enough, scientific horsemen will not agree with me on this, for the simple reason that they have never tried it.

After weaning, the colts should run outdoors the year 'round, if the desire is to raise hardy horses. When the colts are a month old, they should be halter broke, and this is the time to pick up their feet (on both sides) often. Personally, I do not sanction the practice of patting and fondling them as this encourages the colt to become unruly.

At eighteen months of age, the colt is ready for gentling, part of which consists in teaching him not to fear strange noises or unfamiliar objects. I prefer schooling colts in a training pen not over eighteen feet square; thus the colt can not get away and is also forced to obey his trainer. When giving the lessons in the pen, it is best to take off the halter; this gives the youngster more confidence than he would have if you pulled him around by the head. Most horsemen are in too much of a hurry to put on the harness or saddle, whereas it is wiser to have the colt perfectly gentled first. The bucking colt is not confined to the range type alone. I have seen stable-raised colts that would buck for all points of the compass, but none of them will buck, kick, or get excited if properly gentled before saddling.

The colt should not have the bit in his mouth for the first year of working under the saddle; using a well rigged up hackamore will teach him not to go against the reins and it is far better to pull him around and give him lessons in reining with the hackamore than it is to spoil his mouth with an iron bit.

No horse can be considered "handy" if it requires two hands to handle him under the saddle. Training colts at the end of a long line running them around in circles seems to me a foolish bit of horseplay though I am aware that this is practiced frequently by some of our most up-to-date horsemen. There is not a colt handled in this manner that obeys rightly, for he can do about everything he has a mind to, at the end of that line. Too often, we see "jaw crazed" horses – that means they were never gentled nor taught anything except to be pulled around by the bit. Such horses are also termed "high spirited"; most of that "spirit" lies in that bruised jaw caused from too much tugging at the bit. Then too, such horses are called "mean" and condemned as "outlaws," when the fault really lies with the trainer. I recall a little stallion, the meanest bunch of muscles and bone ever wrapped up in horse hide, who had been caught as a wild mustang and sold from the Trading Post at Fort Laramie, Wyo. The horse breakers tried to take the rough edge off him by choking him down and throwing him every day. This game little horse fought without giving an inch of ground. He was finally classed as a "killer" and outlaw. He was run into a small corral and left alone. I watched this little feller fight the burning ropes that choked him, but every time, the horse "won the round." Admiring his courage, I could not forebear telling those breakers they might learn something from that mustang if they hung 'round long enough. They said he was mine if I wanted to feed him in the corral, so every day I cut grass and fed the horse, by holding the feed in my hands. At first, he would not come near the bars. After a few days, he was hungry enough to make a grab at the grass and jump away. Later, learning there was nothing to harm him, he would poke his muzzle through the bars. Finally, I got him to eat grain from a wooden measure held in my hand. As I was only a boy then, it seemed to me I'd accomplished something and I ran over to Chief Sadheart's tepee to tell him about a wild horse eating out of my hand. "Hi-w-in" he said, and started out for the corral with me in tow. There the old Chief told me of many wild horses he had tamed. He said to me, "this horse is not bad – just afraid of man" and added that I should look through the skin and see the real horse who was all good, not mean. He then called my attention to the stallion's markings – a black roan, the white of his face spreading down the sides of the jaws. Both front legs were white nearly up to the chest. There was a white spot on the hips that reminded me of a bootjack and from this mark the pony got his name of "Bootjack." Within a few months, under Sadheart's tuition, I trained the first wild horse which I owned and which was my true friend until he died – full of arrows – five years later. The remains of this brave little animal rest not far from where he fought those burning ropes of the horse breakers. I always recall old Sadheart's words – "when you can see through the skin, you will find the real horse."

Since the early days of horsemanship, there has been more or less superstition among horse handlers all over the world. The Indians thought of their buffalo horses as something sacred given them by the Great Spirit that they might run down the bison to feed their people. Those ponies, always faster than other horses, were not used in battle, nor did the Indians ride them to the hunting grounds. It was a custom of these people to have the mother of a great warrior place a bison robe over the buffalo pony when he was being led to the hunting grounds – this was supposed to bring much meat. Such beliefs do not end with these simple people – they are prevalent among highly educated folks in other places. I recall an instance while riding with the "Bill" Show in Lexington, Ky., where I met a horse raiser who invited me to his farm and showed me some of the finest horse flesh I ever saw. He spoke of the mares and colts on pasture a mile or two down the road. The darky hitched a fine-looking mare to a light buggy and as we rode along I commented on the graceful action of the mare. The road was rough, with deep wheel ruts. Suddenly, the mare stumbled. Immediately my Kentucky friend laid the whip on to that mare, raising ugly welts on her slick hide. He sawed and jerked on the reins, finally getting the mare under control. He explained, "if I did not put the whip to her she would stumble again the next time she came to that spot." He may have been right – she did not stumble when we returned – but disfiguring the horse seemed to me a cruel fancy.

Over in France, some years ago, all horses were docked; roaching their manes and pulling the hair out of their docks leaves them the appearance of a mule. Aside from being a part of their beauty, Nature has given horses manes to fan themselves with while traveling fast, and has also given them tails to protect themselves from flies and other insects, but man is never satisfied – he thinks he can do a better job.

Show horsemen are in a class by themselves. They show horses with many gaits. One of the features of the Show ring is jumping over bars. I cannot see the slightest reason for doing this – for jumping is the best way I know of to destroy a good horse. Any horse that has been used in the Show ring for any length of time is usually a nervous broken-up wreck.

There is no horse living who naturally has more than three gaits – walking, trotting – (or if left-handed – pacing) and running. All other gaits are artificial and if such horses are not steadily schooled in these gaits, they will soon forget them; in fact, if turned loose, they will never use them. Show horses sometimes tire of this ill treatment and become real man haters.

Then there is another type of horseman – what I call the "paper and pencil" horseman, who can tell you to the ounce just how much feed a horse should have according to his weight. He gives fine talks on his research work and advises us how to sit in the saddle for perfect balance; he does not, however, consider that all horses are not built alike – some are heavier forward than others – so this sort of "balance" applied more to machinery than to the horse. If your horse is perfectly balanced in the shoeing, then step up to his middle and ride him – you'll have no further trouble.

As to the feeding – one horse may gain flesh on his rations, while another of the same weight might not only lose flesh but knock the stable down at night, looking for more feed. Such horsemen can tell you all these things – yet they lack the simple art of picking up a horse's feet or tying a halter rope correctly. I've seen them drum on a horse's tendons and pull on the fetlocks, when a thumb and forefinger pressed on the right spot will cause any horse to raise his foot readily.

With some horsemen, the quality of a horse is overlooked, so long as he stands over fifteen hands and is a good color. The best horse I ever saw was less than fourteen hands high and many good horses died trying to follow him after that sack of gold at the end of the rainbow.

You all know that fellow who shows up around auction sales and horse affairs, wearing a clumsy pair of riding boots, his heels decorated with plug spurs. He's looking for the super horse – one that will never exist. This horseman reads all the horse books and is well enlightened on horsemanship, so far as the *books* go. He can tell a breeding expert who has probably spent a lifetime on a certain breed, just how to improve it, and raise horses that can be used for any purpose – from a draft horse down to a Shetland pony! His ideas are all right, but some of us get awful drowsy when he had the floor.

Then, there are horsemen who spend all their spare time riding on the bridle paths in our large cities. They usually are very kind to their mounts, carry cube sugar in their pockets, and believe in having the most up-to-date tack, with an entire disregard of how the horse feels about it. Their riding master has taught them all about horsemanship (except what they really should know). Some of these riders pet and fondle their mounts when someone is looking on – often, though, these horses come into the stable with bleeding mouths from too much riding on the bit or having them "in hand." After a few summers the horse steps out a little proud forward. Yes, he is getting old. His owner thinks about getting a new horse, full of fire and life, to take his place. Any dealer is willing to take the old horse, providing he also gets a good amount of money in the trade for the new horse. The ole horse finds a new home in some riding academy where he is jerked around by Tom, Josie and Kate, for the remainder of his days, his former owner not caring a trooper's damn what becomes of his faithful old friend. But these horsemen are always in the latest "style."

Some of us recall the horse days before the coming of automobiles, when we often heard someone say his horse could *road* along ten miles an hour. Such a horse was worth owning then and now, if he could keep it up for any length of time. These horses were not plentiful – I've owned a few – some could travel ten miles an hour and stay out all day, and be ready to do it all over again the next day. You won't find them in pedigreed stock though. This sounds bad, but it's true enough. I've spent many years learning it and paid the price to know. There seems to be no record of a long, hard race being won in our country by a pedigreed horse. I am not condemning our fine-blooded horses – far from it – and it isn't because they have not had the opportunity, for many have been entered in such races and have been the first to drop out. However, we are not all long distance racers and do not require such horses.   Once you ride a real mustang, however, you will probably agree with me as to his endurance.

It has been my privilege to visit most of the cavalry schools, including Vienna. All have their own ideas of schooling horses and most of them are good. I've long heard of the horsemanship of the Russian Cossacks and they are considered great. After spending four months with them, I did not approve of their methods of training.

History dates the Arab on horseback for hundreds of years. I have found some Arabs hard on their mounts, not taking the care that is usually attributed to them of their horses and racing them until they drop from exhaustion (when raiding other desert tribes). Arabs ride only mares – the stallions are used for breeding and spend most of their lives standing tied by the hind leg to a stake driven in the sand. When a horse colt is foaled, he is killed at birth (unless they want to raise him for breeding), the mare's milk being used for human consumption. There is better horseflesh and as good horsemen right here in our own country as can be found anywhere. If one starts early in life, grows up where there are a number of colts foaled each year to handle, there is no reason why he should not make a first-class horseman, but it is well to overlook some of the nonsense that goes with horsemanship today.

I once heard a great horseman, O.R. Gleason, say, "take your horse's head away from him and you take his feet away from him also." This is quite true, for more horses will fall on a tight rein than those allowed to have their head and see where they're putting their feet, especially in rough country. If you think I am mistaken, watch the sports sheets of your daily papers and take a look at the pictures of horses thrown with the riders on the ground about twenty feet ahead of their mounts. All of these riders had their horses "in hand" as they say, riding with a tight rein.

Now, let's switch to a large cattle range in the far West and watch the horses cutting cattle. They can turn on a nickel and hand you some change while at full speed, and come to a square stop with a heavy steer at the end of the piece of "twine." And remember, they are not working on a lawn mowed field – yet they very seldom fall. You will notice, every horse has his head free (with a loose rein) to balance himself and see where he's placing his feet. We should not scoff at this kind of horsemanship – it's a beautiful sight to watch a well-trained "cow hoss" work, and it takes a real horseman to train him. You will note also, they never use a martingale on a horse.

Our plains Indians are some of the best horsemen in the world. I have yet to see their equal anywhere. I've watched them gentle wild horses and their method of doing this varied according to the horse they handled. The wildest horses were herded into the river – where some of the breakers would swim with one arm over the horse's neck close to the shoulder. Others rode along the river bank on both sides, keeping the horse in the stream. After a time the wildest horse became gentle and seldom tried to buck when mounted. We can credit to these same plains Indians our oddly marked horses which our westerners are so proud of today, like the Overos, Tobianos and Appaloosa. The Palomino was also bred by these people, although there is nothing left now but the color. Such horses were bred for war mounts, every tribe having its own color or marking. They bred them true to this particular marking.

The best individual horseman I knew was a Gypsy – of the Stanley-Cooper band who have long been known to us as horse traders.[107] "King Stanley" was happy when he was training colts and he spent a lot of time milling amongst them in the corral – sometimes he carried a saddle blanket on his arm – otherwise a bridle. He was never in a hurry to saddle a colt, but when he rode out of that pen it was surely gentle and broke! He could ride one horse more miles per day without playing out the horse than any other man I knew and as an all around horseman I'd like to see his equal. Although "King" spent thirty years of his life mostly in a wheel chair, he was a horseman to the end.[108]

Professor O.R. Gleason was another expert. I met him through Mr. Dickerson (whose son now has Travelers' Rest Arabian Horse Farms) before the coming of the automobile. At the time, I was riding with the Buffalo Bill Show and our setup was in Memphis, Tenn. I put on an act which called for much horse training. When Cody, with his cowboys, freed the Deadwood stage coach from a band of raiding Indians, I was shot off my horse in the ring and lay there until the sham battle was over and the ring cleared of all riders. My horse then lay down

---

[107] **Brian Shovers, Research Librarian, Montana Historical Society:** "We do have a single article about King Stanley from a Montana newspaper of June 7th, 1929, which describes the major events of his life. According to this article, his father was an English gentleman adventurer, and his mother was a member of the Chase family of Rhode Island. They married and headed to California during the '49 Gold Rush. King was actually born in Dayton, Ohio, on a wagon train journey back to Rhode Island from California in January, 1853. I find no mention of gypsies anywhere."

[108] **Editors' note:** In placing famous frontiersman, King Stanley, in a wheel chair for 30 years, Frank Hopkins is following his usual practice of pretending to be an intimate friend of a famous historical figure, latching onto that person's legend, and then maligning that person after his death. Hopkins did this to several genuine American heroes, including Buffalo Bill Cody, Sitting Bull and Zane Grey. Hopkins' claim that King Stanley spent 30 years in a wheel chair, however, is one of his more improbable literary inventions. According to the *New York Times*, King Stanley led an action-filled life. At the beginning of the 20th century the old frontiersman "changed his pony for an automobile. He traveled back and forth the United States in all sorts of weather and over roads that were often no roads at all. Only two weeks before Stanley's death [in June 1929] he and his wife reached New York by motor from the Pacific Coast."
The *New York Times* concludes the article with the remark that Stanley's "body bore the scars of sixty-two knife and bullet wounds received in 'the old days'."
Clearly, Stanley was not crippled and in a wheel chair.

beside me, pushed himself over till his saddle touched me, then, pretending I was badly wounded I grasped the saddle with one hand and my pony rolled up on his haunches bringing me to a reclining position on the saddle, when he got to his feet, took a step ahead, turned back, picked up my hat and then started to carry me out of the ring, to the thunder of applause. This was all done without my seeming to give the pony a signal of any kind and that is what interested Gleason. He wanted most to find out how I directed my horse through this act without a single motion or signal. He was interested most in this – not in me – but when our season ended I joined him in his horse training exhibitions and traveled with him for three winters.[109] I must say he was a real trainer. His books probably are still on the market and they are worth reading.

In mentioning the plains Indians, I neglected to say that Chief Gaal[110] did more in the line of breeding for color and endurance in war ponies than anyone. He was not only a horse raiser but a great warrior who led the Cheyennes against Custer. I saw him riding with his band on to Standing Rock Reservation; he dismounted, took off his war bonnet and untied the knot in his horse's tail (to show his people they should not go on the war path again). Gaal died two years later, a spirit-broken man and I shall not forget his giving me his most prized possession – a spotted stallion. Following the Indian ceremony of surrender, Gaal placed the reins of his horse in my hand and said "H-is-teen" (for you). When I hesitated to accept what I knew to be his most prize possession, he added in his own language, "he is yours – to show my good friendship to you – keep him and his good blood, and may the evil spirit never be your friend." I am not ashamed to admit the lump in my throat and the thought that maybe the white man should stop trying to teach the Indian and let the "Redman" teach him a few things worth while.[111]

This article was first published in July 1943

---

[109] **Editors' note:** Famous equine professor, Oscar Gleason, did in fact employ a well-known assistant. His name, however, was not Frank Hopkins but Norton B. Smith, of New Brunswick, Canada. Gleason thought so highly of Smith that he dedicated his famous book, *The Breaking and Taming Wild and Vicious Horses,* to his apprentice.

[110] **Editors' note:** The correct spelling for this Chief's name is Gall, not Gaal.

[111] **Dr. Vine Deloria Jr.**, *leading Native American scholar, retired professor emeritus of history at the University of Colorado and author of many acclaimed books:* "Hopkins claims an intimate knowledge of Chief Gall of the Standing Rock Reservation who, he asserts, gave Hopkins his horse when he agreed to live on the reservation and died two years later. The problem here is that Chief Gall was a member of my grandfather's congregation at Wakpala and lived long after he came to the reservation; his relatives are well represented at Standing Rock today and will be astounded that Hopkins knew more about their ancestor then they did."

Chapter 12

The Mustang

A friend of mine, amateur historian of the West, asked me one day if I could name the most significant animal on the American continent.

"Think carefully before you speak," said he, "because there are many important animals – cattle, sheep, buffalo."

I replied: "I don't have to think before I reply to this question. I already know the answer."

"All right. Let me have it."

"The Mustang is the most important, most significant animal in America."

He replied, "I agree with you absolutely. I just wanted to see whether you agreed with me."

This statement of mine is absolutely true, as any one who will study Western history will discover. It sounds extravagant to say it, but I honestly believe that without the Mustang there would be no Western civilization. It was the sturdy legs of this game little native horse which carried our star of empire into the West.

As has been pointed out before, the country west of the Missouri River was not a footman's country. East of the Missouri the footman could make his way. He did. The early pioneers of the Mississippi Valley, the Ohio Valley, the Mohawk Valley, were footmen. They could travel through the woods, carrying their equipage on their backs. But when they set out across the desert plains, when they reached the towering fastnesses of the Rocky Mountains and beyond, they needed help. They needed some form of transportation beyond what they themselves provided.

The West was a horse country.

The Indians knew that. They had large herds of Mustangs. The first mountain men, Sublette, Ashley, Fitzpatrick, Birdger, knew it. The first gold-seekers knew it. The first wave of farming pioneers knew it. The empire builders knew it.

And the horse which they used was the game little Mustang. He was not native to the country, for he was introduced by the Spanish conquistadores, but he had lived long enough in it to be thoroughly acclimated. He was small, but hardy. He was tough. He could subsist on scanty fare. He was plentiful, in a wild state. But the white settlers, taking what they thought was theirs by right, trapped him, trained him, and he became their principal help.

The Mustang served mankind well until a few years ago. Now, from the articles I have read in *The Horse*, he is facing his last stand. To let him go would, in my opinion, be a major American tragedy. In my day I have watched the destruction of the buffalo, the antelope, the passenger pigeon. But we lay their destruction to a benighted, profligate generation. If we permit the Mustang to disappear we may be accused of these same qualities. And we will deserve the accusation.

But I don't want you to think that when I make a plea for the Mustang I am being sentimental. It isn't that. There's some sentiment attached to it, of course, and I don't like to see the bond between the old and the new destroyed. But the Mustang has a very practical value which it is good business not to throw away.

He has qualities which horsemen need. He has indeed, all the qualities that go to make up an ideal saddle horse. What are they?

First, his endurance. I have spent sixty years in the saddle, taking part in more endurance races than any other man in history.[112] I never rode another animal but a Mustang. Others were offered me. I rejected them. The reason is that I knew what the Mustang strain means: it means a horse that can keep going day in and day out, that doesn't need bandaging, fussing with and that can win endurance races where the "rules" are made to its order or not.

Once when I was riding as a messenger for General George Crook he told me;

"Frank, if troops can't overtake a band of Indians in two hours, it's better to give up the chase."

"Why, General?"

"Because they'll never in this green world catch them. Those wiry ponies of theirs can go ninety miles without food or water. They can wear out all the cavalry horses we have on the frontier."

He knew.

The second Mustang quality it would pay us to have in our saddle animals is intelligence. You can't beat Mustang intelligence in the entire equine race. That's natural enough, too. These animals have had to shift for themselves for generations. They didn't have grooms keeping them out of trouble or trainers showing them what to do. They had to work out their own destiny or be destroyed. Some were destroyed in the working out of nature's survival law. Those that survived were animals of superior intelligence. It doesn't hurt any horse to have intelligence. The Mustang knows what intelligence means.

Third, he's an economical little horse. He can live where a stall-fed animal would starve. A friend of mine was telling me about accompanying a border patrolman in Texas. He was mounted on a fine big modern horse, this friend of mine was. The Texan, a grizzled old fellow, was riding a flea-bitten little dun

---

[112] **Kathleen Henkel,** Executive Director of American Endurance Ride Conference, "We have never heard of Frank T. Hopkins."

Ann Hyland, Expert on the history of endurance racing and the author of many books including, *The Endurance Horse, a World Survey*, said "I have never heard of Frank Hopkins."

Mustang. They set out. They were riding through mesquite-covered hills. My friend, looking down on the little horse of his companion, thought, "I'll walk his legs off by nightfall. This will be good."

But when mid-afternoon came, so hard was the pace, it was the big horse that faltered. And by night-time my friend was afoot. But the little Texas Mustang was going as strong as ever. Next morning he was ready for another day of it. The bigger horse was so badly "stove up" he couldn't be used for five days.

Now, that little Mustang ridden by the Texas hadn't ever tasted grain. He was grass-fed all his life. He picked his own food from the country, could live where even a cow would starve and knew how to take such good care of himself that he was always ready to go.

You have probably inferred from what I have had to say on this subject that I'm heartily in favor of the Mustang Refuge in Arizona, that was once advocated by *The Horse*.

That project strikes a responsive chord in the heart of an old frontiersman like myself, and I know that there are thousands of other old timers who will feel as thrilled as I do about it. It seems to me that it is the opportunity to build up a typically American horse, something we do not at the present time have.

We have horses which we hail as typically American – the Morgan and the Standardbred. But they're merely replants of horses either from Arabia or from English Thoroughbred stock. But the Mustang is as American as George Washington, and America is a vast enough land, an important enough nation to have a horse of its very own. That means the Mustang.

In South America, in the Argentine, they had a native horse corresponding to the Mustang of the United States, the Criollo horse, you know. But they have always been more far-sighted than we. They took the Criollo, built up the breed, and now have a stud registry for the native horse, have important horse shows in the capitals every year, and in other ways have given their natural asset importance.

It is pretty late in the game for us to do the same thing here, for only a remnant of the Mustang herds remain. But it isn't too late. That is the point – it isn't too late for us to jump in now and save what we have of Mustangs and, if we choose, to build up the breed until we have a horse of which we can be proud – a staunch-legged, enduring, intelligent, easy-keeping, useful, all-around American saddle horse.

I know that the Mustang can be built up, because in past years I have many times experimented and bred endurance horses from Mustang strains. I do want to make it clear, however, that I do not mean we should cross the Mustang on larger breeds and produce a hybrid which is neither one nor the other. I mean we should take the Mustang, in this refuge, and weed out the inferior specimens, breed the superior ones and gradually evolve a top breed of genuine Mustangs. – *The Horse.*

I well remember some of the great rides made on Mustangs. Fitzgerald, one of my friends of the old days, who, like the rest, left me standing guard alone (he passed on two years ago) was the last of dispatch riders, excepting myself. One of his rides was on a small Mustang called "Fan Tan" not over 14 hands high. "Fitch," himself, stood six feet three inches and weighed over 180 pounds. During the Moddox War, he rode that Mustang about 300 miles in thirty-seven hours, with no rest for either horse or rider. Where would some of these large weight-carrying horses of today call a halt on such a ride as that? My rough guess is about forty miles from the starting line!

One article is not big enough for me to write of some of the real hard rides I remember even if I had the time to tell of them.

One of our members owns a Mustang who is known to most riders who have taken part in our 100-Mile Trail Ride. Although this mare, "Midnight," is thirty odd years old, she always holds her own on the trails and comes back in good spirit at the close of the day. This mare was caught wild from the Skull Creek band of Mustangs and shipped to a dealer here along with a number of other unhalter-broke ponies. This horse dealer still handles a few carloads of these horses occasionally. "Midnight" was shipped here twenty-eight years ago and was sold on the halter to Mr. Charles Rankin, who took her to Connecticut after training her to the saddle. He sold her to play polo in Dedham, Mass. A few years later, her owner died, and the mare was purchased and returned to Connecticut. There she shifted hands three times before being bought by her present owner. The mare was now along in years but not broken in spirit or endurance. "Midnight" must be about thirty-three years old now. They tell me that as a polo pony she was fast, very quick to turn and never seemed to tire.

Many people do not like Mustangs because these horses will not take abuse – such as having their mounts full of iron bits, or riders constantly tugging at the reins. Mustangs will just tell anyone who rides them to "do it right, or get off and walk" – and most of them are capable of making you walk if they are not treated right! I have found them to be gentle, very friendly, and perfectly willing to share all kinds of hardships with me, and have never known one to quit or fail me in any way.

This article was first published in January 1944.

Editors' note: Few people would dispute Hopkins' assertion that the Mustang is a strong, intelligent, hardy and historically important breed of horse. Although Hopkins is on the record as promoting the Mustang, it is only as a result of this international research project into Hopkins' mythology that disturbing evidence has been discovered which suggests that the Indian impostor known as Grey Owl may have been the role model for Hopkins' Old West and Indian fantasies, as well as having provided Hopkins with the idea of "championing" an endangered animal from the American frontier.

Dr. Donald Smith of Calgary University is a published expert on Indian imposters. According to Smith, Grey Owl was in fact an Englishman named Archie Belaney, who was abandoned by his parents at the beginning of the twentieth century. Belaney immigrated to Canada after the First World War, and reinvented himself as "Grey Owl."

In his book *From the Land of Shadows – the Making of Grey Owl,* Dr. Smith reveals that, exactly like Frank Hopkins' fantasy father, Belaney's imaginary new parent had served as a scout for the US government, was stationed at Fort Laramie, was a personal friend of Buffalo Bill Cody and was married to an Indian woman! Grey Owl and Hopkins also shared a similar, albeit non-existent, childhood which consisted of living and hunting with the Plains Indians. Upon reaching young adulthood, both men falsely claimed to have been employed in Buffalo Bill's Wild West show.

Grey Owl shot to fame when he authored a book in 1931 which called for the preservation of the endangered Canadian beaver. Though the motive was indeed a worthy one, the English Indian imposter quickly realized that his fortune was made. At his first public speaking appearance, Grey Owl collected seven hundred dollars from an enthusiastic audience.

In his book *Grey Owl, The Mystery of Archie Belanie,* author Armand Garnet Ruffo quotes Canada's most famous fake as saying, "As soon as I got on stage, I saw all those silver-dollar heads beaming up at me, their expectations cracked open like a full bottle of gin."

According to Ruffo, Belaney understood that he was giving the public what it wanted. Ruffo quotes Grey Owl as saying, "If they want romance, give it to them. Butter the facts, spread it thick. The point is to get the message across, isn't it?"

This early day "beaver whisperer" went on to fool the British Royal family and hundreds of thousands of trusting Canadians. Even when Belaney was finally unmasked, there were many sympathizers who excused his actions because he advocated saving the beaver.

Frank Hopkins apparently used the Englishman's blueprint of deception when he began championing the Mustang a few years after the Grey Owl phenomenon had swept the literary market. By the mid-1930s Hopkins had already stolen the identity of the real Laramie Kid, and lifted passages from the 1932 edition of "Black Elk Speaks." It would seem that his efforts to save the Mustang was the final piece of the imposter puzzle which, like Grey Owl, Hopkins created for himself.

There is however a remarkable difference between Grey Owl and Hopkins.

A mountain of evidence exists, including photographs, which show Grey Owl working with beavers in the Canadian wilderness.

However, there is no documented photograph of Hopkins, the man who claimed to have won more than 400 races on Mustangs in countries all over the world, actually riding one of these legendary horses!

Chapter 13

Carrying Notes for Uncle Samuel
By Gertrude A. Hopkins

One recent snowy afternoon, a few horselovers who had been to see a shipment just in from The Remount sales, called on their old friend, Frank T. Hopkins, to talk "horse." Later that evening the conversation turned to the usefulness of the horse in war, and Frank, a dispatch rider of the Old West, told of the value of a good horse to the riders of the western plains.

During the Indian troubles on the western frontier, dispatch riding – carrying messages on horseback for army officers – was indispensable. The dispatches were carried between forts and outpost army camps, often to far distant stations where messages were telegraphed on to the War Office at Washington. Most of these dispatches were carried through rough country, sometimes at night as day riding through hostile country was too hazardous. Night riding was a ticklish business, though, the rider had to be familiar with the cunning of the redskin, together with the ways of Indian warfare, and he needed a thorough knowledge of the country to be covered.

The worst enemies of the dispatch riders were outlaws who traded guns and ammunition to the Indian warriors; these "traders" were lawless whites who made a living defying our Government and killing anyone who might come across their pack-trains or their trail. Many a young and inexperienced dispatch rider gave his precious life by innocently crossing the trail of such outfits. Usually, seeing white men, he would ride right up to have a word with them (so he thought), but he never lived to tell it; they knew a dead rider could not report having even seen them. These outlaws invariably left evidence pointing to Indians, not to themselves as the killers of such riders. For instance, Frank heard in forts and army camps of bodies of dispatch riders being found stuck full of arrows; these arrows, viewed by an experienced observer, proved they were never shot from a bow! On the contrary, the gashes were cut in the bodies with a knife and the arrows then inserted!

A danger that always confronted a night rider was the Indian scouts hidden in the foothills; these scouts were sure to hear the beat of your pony's hoofs. Whereupon the alert rider might hear the sharp cry of a coyote – not quite perfect – for it was purposely imitated that way by the Indian scout. If the dispatch rider knew his Indians right, he would answer with the short, choppy, yelp of the female coyote; then the Indians, thinking the answer came from one of their own traveling scouts, would not move from where they lay bedded down – and once again the dispatch rider was safely (?) on his way.[113]

Another time, the message carrier might hear the call of a horned owl, or the bawl of a bull elk – never perfect of course – the dispatch rider who knew his business was able to answer these calls correctly. If not, he was just in for a horse race and a shooting match. Any man who had not the courage or will to protect his mother's darlin' son and put up a scrap, had better stay out of a dispatch rider's saddle!

In those days the army had many kinds of horses and they were all used by "green" dispatch riders. However, after they "learnt from experience" they decided that only the mustang was the dispatch rider's standby – the horse that would stay under the saddle and take everything as it came – night or day, come storm or cold, blinding sleet. Rider and horse had to swim the icy rivers and they faced the blizzards together. Often, rider and horse fought hard, running battles. Some of these horses were known to carry their wounded riders to safety, crossing rivers and through passes where it was hard even for a man alone to travel. They say a dog is man's best friend – F.T. has his own thoughts about that.

Sometimes, those ponies gave their riders warning of danger ahead. Frank had some that acted "nervous" when going along the trail, now and then swinging their heads from side to side to pick up the scent in the air. This generally meant Indians were in hiding close by. Personally, I've had ponies turn right around and head back down the trail, getting under speed.

Occasionally a rider might be called upon to act as interpreter. Indian chiefs would sit in council with army officers and the rider who was known to carry a "straight tongue" was chosen by these chiefs to speak for their people.

To quote Frank, "I well recall one message I carried from Laramie (1877) to the old Summer camping ground of the Ogallalas. The ground was tramped hard by many years of Indian moccasins treading it: above the camps was the dying scaffold where they laid their great peace chief, 'Conquering Bear,' with the bull neck shield and bow beside him; tho' he had lain there some years, the remains were still intact – wrapped in rawhide – I rode to the white tents of the soldiers and delivered my message to Colonel Bradley. Nearby, stood many chiefs around a large council tent, among them the Bad Face, 'Red Cloud.' When I turned from the council tent, Chief 'He Dog' touched my arm in a friendly

---

[113] **Dr. Vine Deloria, Jr.** *leading Native American scholar, retired professor emeritus of history at the University of Colorado and author of many acclaimed books:* "Frank Hopkins …knew nothing about Indians except what he was able to pirate from existing literature and cultural trivia."

greeting, asking, 'Will you speak for the Lakotas as they sit in council with the soldier chief?'[114]

RED CLOUD

Red Cloud (Makhpiya Luta) was one of the most important Lakota leaders of the 19th century.

Much of his early life was spent at war, first and foremost against the neighboring Pawnee and Crow.

From 1866 onwards Red Cloud organized the most successful war against the US ever fought by an Indian nation. The army had started to build forts along the Bozeman Trail, which ran through the heart of Lakota territory in present-day Wyoming to the Montana gold fields. Red Cloud launched a series of attacks on the forts, and his strategies were so successful that by 1868 the US government had agreed to the Fort Laramie Treaty.

The peace did not last. Custer's 1874 Black Hills expedition again brought war to the northern Plains, a war that would mean the end of independent Indian nations. Red Cloud cultivated contacts with sympathetic Eastern reformers, especially Thomas A. Bland, and indeed he occasionally pretended to be more sympathetic than he really was to the white man's ways.

Red Cloud did not endorse the Ghost Dance movement and so, unlike Sitting Bull and Big Foot, he escaped the Army's occupation unscathed. Thereafter he continued to fight to preserve the authority of chiefs such as himself, opposed leasing Lakota lands to whites, and vainly fought allotment of Indian reservations into individual tracts under the 1887 Dawes Act.

Red Cloud died in 1909.

"I agreed and shortly thereafter was seated beside General Bradley with the Indian chiefs in council about us. 'He Dog' was first to speak, his strong voice booming across the village and echoing back from the cliffs. He said, 'There are a few things I want to say here – the Indians will not have the traders' sons as interpreters; they speak with crooked tongues with the result that we have been in many wars with the whites. And the messenger who brings the crooked words in his mouth will fall on the prairie like a gut-wounded buffalo, his bones to whiten in the sun.' Then he laid his hand on my shoulder – the sign that I should repeat his words. When I interpreted to Bradley, he seemed surprised, looked around over the Indians. Then all the Bad Faces and their chief, 'Red Cloud,' left the council. I had made friends on one side and enemies on the other. These few words started a government investigation eventually settling all the Indian troubles in the Northwest.

"Now, 'Red Cloud' was for peace with his own people but always craving power and making trouble with the other bands. He went to Washington asking to be made chief over all the Sioux. The Government knew that 'Red Cloud' did

---

[114] **Dr. Vine Deloria Jr.** *leading Native American scholar* "What hogwash that is! It doesn't take a brain surgeon to show it is absurd."

not even carry the power of a shirt-wearer, tho' he continued to make trouble, having 'Crazy Horse' killed at Fort Robeson. 'Crazy Horse' was lighter in the skin than most white men, and had light brown hair. His word could always be depended on. He lost his life through the 'crooked tongues' of the traders' sons who were urged on by 'Red Cloud' and his band of Bad Faces.[115] It was not so with me. I was not taught hatred at my mother's breast and had played with white boys at Laramie and Indians up on the 'Holy Road,' and they were all my friends and I needed them many times when I got in tough spots.

"The traders and the men who ran the wagon freight wanted the Indian troubles to continue and would do most anything to stir things up as it kept them going in a profitable business. There was big money in horse trading; the Sioux had large herds of horses – they sometimes darkened the hills, there were so many. Now, if the traders could get a scrap going between the soldiers and a band of Indians, it was easy for the traders to run off a large band of horses and make a good money turnover. Many were American horses and there were some good mules. If these traders got horses down on the Missouri (River) out of the Indian country, there was no trouble selling them. General Crook stopped their 'racket' by seizing all horses when a band of Indians came to the Reservation and would not issue rations to them until they rounded up their herds and brought them in. The money the herd brought in was set aside for the Indians – so they say. However, I have never actually known of an Indian receiving any of that money. They surely lost their horses though – and their freedom. In the spring of 1882 all bands were on reservations in the northwest, stripped of their only wealth which consisted of these herds of horses."

There was still trouble with the Apaches in the Southwest. General Crook was in charge down there and wanted a few dispatch riders – not because he loved them – so Frank went along!

This article was first published in April 1944.

---

[115] **Dr. Vine Deloria, Jr.,** *Native American historian:* "Hopkins should have been awarded the 'World's Greatest Liar' award. The problem is that these distortions of Indian history, the slandering of famous chiefs and leaders, and the presentation of these lies as history cannot be easily erased once they are promulgated as fact."

Chapter 14

The Truth about Buffalo Bill

Colonel William F. Cody, was an outstanding showman who played the part of "Buffalo Bill" on the Theatre Stage and who was for many years, the star in the greatest horse show on earth known as – Buffalo Bill's Wild West.

I have read much that has been written about his career, heard some great stories told concerning his life's history, and often wondered how well acquainted the authors of those stories were with Bill Cody.

Cody bounced me on his knee when I was a small boy[116] and I was in close contact with him until his death in 1917.

Ned Buntline and Major Burke were responsible for the ballyhoo about Cody; they wrote it for Nathan Salisbury who promoted both the stage play and the Wild West show.

They say Cody was the greatest buffalo hunter of all times. Buntline, in his bally-hoo claimed that Cody rode out on his famous horse "Brigham Young," rounded up a run of buffalo and drove them right into Fort Macpherson and shot them there. Old "Brigham" must have been an unusual hoss, I've never seen a pony who could steer buffalo off their course, but evidently old "Brigham" could handle them like range cattle!

It is true, though, that Cody drove the hide wagon for Col. William Matterson who supplied the meat for men building the U.P. (Union Pacific) Railroad. Matterson was the real, original Buffalo Bill who had hunted buffalo years before Cody was old enough to hold a gun, but Cody shot most of his buffalo under the big top with blank shots. Cody never claimed to be a great buffalo hunter in his life and those he shot from stands, not from horse-back.[117]

It is the general belief that Cody was a frontier scout for many years – actually, he was a Scout for nine months at Fort MacPherson, his duties were to ride out and meet the wagon trains and bring in the mail bags. The remainder of his time was taken up by playing cards with army officers in the Fort.[118]

---

[116] **Editors' note:** Compare with "The Last of the Buffalo Hunters," where Hopkins writes that, "It was while shooting for Madison and Hitner that I met William F. Cody…"

[117] **Editors' note:** From an article on the Buffalo Bill Historical Center website entitled "William Frederick Cody," by **Paul Fees**, former *Curator, Buffalo Bill Museum:* "Supplying 4,280 buffalo to feed railway construction workers during eight months in 1867-1868 earned him his nickname, 'Buffalo Bill.'"

[118] **Captain George Price** in his *History of the Sixth Cavalry:* "Wm. F. Cody is one of the best scouts and guides that ever rode at the head of a column of cavalry." **General**

Cody was believed to be a great shot with the rifle; the audience in the Bill show saw him shoot clay balls which he never missed. How could he miss when he used mustard-seed shot in the shells? Every shot covered a radius of about six feet. Cody was not an extra good shot – just fair.

When I was a very young boy, Cody operated a wagon-freight business out of Laramie. It was in those years he was supposed to be doing all this Indian fighting that we hear about.

I once read of Cody being one of the Scouts with General Terry at the time of the Custer-fight but I happen to know on that date he was playing in Salisbury's Stage play at the old Howard Theatre in Boston, Mass.

In 1878, Cody had a small show which was hauled over the road with horses; this "Wild West" he ran a few years; after that, Salisbury put on the Buffalo Bill Wild West show, with Cody at the head of it. So long as Salisbury was owner and manager, this show made millions and went to all the World Fairs in Europe. In it were only the finest of riders, including picked cavalry men from every nation in the world. When Salisbury died, Cody carried on alone. He was a life-long friend of mine, yet I must say he was a very poor business man, spending his spare time drinking with his so-called "friends." As he grew older, the old Barley-corn burnt him out, though he looked the picture of health when riding in the ring, he was only the outside shell of the man I know in my boyhood; he had to be helped into the saddle and out, his hair got so thin it was necessary for him to wear a toupee. But for all of this he never lost his pose as a showman. He was always kind to his riders and horses and often spoke of them as one big family. I was rider and ringmaster in the Bill show for thirty-two seasons.[119] As a former dispatch rider for nine years during the Indian Troubles I have also taken a hand at buffalo running. In those days, Cody was not in the army or on the buffalo runs. When did he do his stuff that Buntline wrote about? I have seen eighty snows and as many grasses – Cody could not have done much before my time which was known as "the bloody years on the plains" and he surely never claimed any of that bally-hoo.

Was Cody a great plainsman? Yes – as a showman he could not be beat.

Where did Cody get the title of Colonel? When the Spanish American war broke out, Cody organized a group of riders, mostly cowboys, under the name of

---

Eugene Carr "His eyesight is better than a good field glass... he never seemed to tire and was always ready to go, in the darkest night or the worst weather, and usually volunteered, knowing what the emergency required".

[119] **Dr. Juti Winchester**, *Curator of the Buffalo Bill Museum at the Buffalo Bill Historical Center*: "If Hopkins was the "ringmaster" for the Wild West, why do we not find his name listed as such, when even the pile drivers and the dish washers got their names in the programs? Hopkins' accomplishments certainly would have been used to bolster the Wild West's publicity - had any of the claimed events occurred. Cody had a canny press agent and he never missed a trick."

the old 7th Cavalry, and General Miles made Cody a colonel. When these riders went into camp for training, word came from the War Office that Cody's services were not required.[120]   Then Woods (later Lieutenant Colonel Woods) and Theodore Roosevelt (later President) took over the troops which were known as the T.R. Rough Riders. Cody got more riders from the plains and went ahead with the show business which was run by Salisbury at that time.

In 1908, Maj. Gordon Lillie joined up with Cody and from the first day Lillie started in to run things to suit himself, for his own benefit; nine years later Cody was without a dollar, the Bill show was something of the past and the great star who had played the part of Buffalo Bill was laid to rest atop of Lookout Mountain (Colorado).

This article was first published in October 1944.

---

[120] **Editors' note:** In an article entitled "Col. Cody, the Rough Riders, and the Spanish American War" on the Buffalo Bill Historical Center's website, *University of New Mexico history professor*, **Paul Hutton**, wrote: "On April 25 the U.S. declared war, and on that same day Burke declared that Gen. Nelson A. Miles, commanding general of the U.S. Army, had asked Cody to join him as a scout. "Buffalo Bill will come back again," Burke declared, "but he will leave a record behind him that neither Cuba nor America will be apt to forget, while Spain will remember him with a groan.".... Cody would "serve on the staff of Major General Miles as chief of scouts" with the rank of colonel. Ironically, despite all of Burke's press agency, Cody thought the war a mistake. On April 29 he wrote his friend George Everhart: "I will have a hard time to get away from the show – but if I don't go – I will be forever damned by all – I must go – or lose my reputation. And General Miles offers me the position I want. George, America is in for it, and although my heart is not in this war - I must stand by America." Cody, who held the Congressional Medal of Honor, did not need to prove either his courage or his patriotism in 1898. As a 52-year-old veteran of the Civil War and Indian Wars, he was a bit long in the tooth for campaigning in tropical climes. Even more pressing was his responsibility to the 467 employees in his Wild West. He delayed joining Miles while the show moved on to Philadelphia, Washington, and Hartford. Still, he made preparations to depart, sending two horses – Lancer and Knickerbocker – to the general in anticipation of joining the campaign. Cody waited too long for, as he had predicted, the war was over quickly." Reprinted here by kind permission of the Buffalo Bill Historical Center.

Chapter 15

Horsemen and Horsemanship

Every year many good tempers and horses are ruined by men who, new to it, take horseback trips. A man from the city goes on a Western hunting trip, say. Horsemanship is new to him, and his kind of horsemanship is certainly new to the horse. Both suffer. The tempers sometimes recover, but spoiling a horse is a more serious matter. Yet all any man needs to know about horsemanship, in order to get the most out of the horse and his trips, is a few simple rules and practices.

Ever since I was seven years old I have been a horseman; not an amateur with a couple of saddlers in a boarding-stable somewhere on the outskirts, but a professional horseman earning my living by the saddle. When I was 13, I was a full-fledged dispatch rider out West. Later I went into endurance racing, and never was beaten. Three times I won international contests to determine the world's most expert horseman. So what I am going to tell you is the result of living with horses for more than sixty years.

The most important single thing in horsemanship is to adjust yourself to the horse. Here is where many men who profess expertness fall down. They try to make the horse over to their ideas, instead of adjusting themselves to the horse. I refer particularly to the matter of gaits. A man must handle a horse to his gait, not try to change the horse from one gait to another. So find out the gait best adapted to your horse. With some horses this will be the trot; with others it will be the gallop, or lope. The gait that the horse favors is the one he can follow with least fatigue. In all my years of horse handling I never tried to reform a horse's gaits. I changed horses if the gait of one did not suit me. It was the easier and more satisfactory way.

The kind of riding I am going to discuss in this article is not bridle path or show riding. In their places, I have no doubt, these forms of riding are estimable. But their place is not afield, where you ride day after day over mountain trails or pathless wide spaces. That is the kind of riding I want to discuss; the riding of the outdoor man. And it is as different from the other kinds I mentioned as day is from night.

The first requisite of a good outdoor rider is a tight seat. Now a tight seat depends on two things: a long stirrup and perfect balance. The long stirrup is necessary for balance, so we can say that the long stirrup is the first essential to correct riding. This form of riding is generally referred to now as the plains style, because we men of the Western plains, who rode hard, who rode far, who lived in the saddle, found it to be best for our use, mastered it, used it altogether.

I realize that trying to teach the plains style to any one in so short an article is difficult, if not impossible. In fact, I doubt if any one, no matter how diligently he practices, can learn it after he has grown to maturity. It takes a lifetime to master. But there is no harm in learning it as well as you can, for it is by far the most effective way there is to ride. Also the safest.

Lengthen your stirrups until the ball of your foot rests snugly in the stirrup and the leg is practically straight. You are now "sitting down in the leather," as we used to say. Stay right there. Don't go bobbing up and down; don't rise to the trot; don't stand in the stirrups. Sit tight, no matter what the gait. The position of the upper body, indeed, should not change one particle as long as you are in the saddle.

It's a pretty sight to see a man ride this style, if he can really ride. But few can. The old timers who learned to ride it are mostly gone; and the younger generations don't get enough riding practice to master the position. And that seat is the snuggest of all. Old time riders, cowboys and cavalrymen, who rode this way could be separated from their mounts only by an end-over-end tumble. An ordinary fall or trip didn't dislodge them; when the horse got to his feet they were still on his back. Why, even a bullet didn't budge some of them from their saddles. I myself was shot seven times while on horseback – but I never lost my seat.

This way of riding is not only pretty to see, not only the tightest and snuggest of all ways, but it is also the only practical way on long rides.

When a man can ride for an hour, then put himself in the hands of a masseur and have the kinds and stiffness rubbed out, it doesn't matter much how comfortable he is while on the horse. But if he has to get into the saddle at sunup, ride all day over hot, rough, hard country, then get off the horse at sundown – and do it all over again for three months hand-running, he seeks the way that is easiest on himself and on his horse. And the way I just described is it.

Young riders often ask me what ability in a horseman I consider to be the most important. I always reply that it is the ability to keep the horse happy. I mean it. If a horseman can keep his horse from worrying, keep him in a happy, even mood all the time, he will get more out of the horse than he can in any other way. It's commonsense that he should. Yet how little it is heeded! You've watched cowboys "haze" their horses, beat them with quirts, spur them up, then jerk them to their haunches, and in every other conceivable way persecute them. Pretty poor horsemanship this. But the indictment doesn't stop with cowboys. I've seen polo players and fancy riders fret their horses even more. And then they wonder why the horse doesn't do more for them or why he doesn't stand up as well as some other fellow's on a long day's ride. Treating the horse is like treating any other servitor. You can drive your help in home, office or factory and get some work out of them, of course. You can encourage your help, keep them happy, get twice as much. So with the horse. Take your choice.

I like to see my mount throw his ears forward, look at the road ahead and take in everything that goes on, not paying the slightest attention to me up there on his back. That means a happy, carefree horse; a horse that I know will be under me at the end of a long day, because he has not a thing in the world to worry about.

You will notice that I say I don't want the horse to pay any attention to me. Does this mean that I don't speak to him? It does. Talking to a horse, diverting his attention from the job, wearies him more than any other single thing. I never speak to a horse when on his back except, of course, to give an order. Don't talk to your horse. And never pat him or make over him. Fondling a horse spoils him.

If you ride on some outfits in the West, one thing that will strike you is the way they neglect the grooming of their horses; if you frequent polo stables or riding academies of the East, one thing that will strike you is the great care they give their horses. Cowboys look with disdain on curry comb and horsebrush; stable grooms look on the cowboys as savages and on their horses as cow. Which are right?

Neither and both. By that I mean, they are both wrong and both right. To neglect a horse, as cowboys do, does the horse no good, while to over-coddle and over-care for him, as hired grooms do, is often more harmful than beneficial. I really believe that many fine horses, polo ponies and the like, are spoiled by too much care, too much bandaging of their tendons, too much fussing over.

My own practice, which always worked out 100 per cent, is to brush the horse thoroughly to keep his hide clean, but never to rub nor to fuss with him when he should have rest. If my horse has worked hard, I clean his hide of dust, wash out his mouth and sponge off his back with a medium-wet sponge or rag. Then I give him a good bed and let him rest. Once I heard a horseman say that an hour's cleaning was as good as two quarts of oats. I told that horseman that it was better to give a tired horse that one hour of rest; then he wouldn't need the extra feed. In Arabia, I observed the great Arab horsemen caring for their horses in almost the same way I cared for mine. There are no better horse handlers anywhere than those desert Arabs.

Now comes feeding. It is important, of course. Yet it is really a simple subject. Experience has taught me that there are only two foods for the horse – oats and timothy hay. Buy the best. Cheap food is dear food in the long run. Occasionally I have met men who do not feed their horses, but let them pick grass for a living. The only trouble with such men is that they are too stingy to buy feed. They may delude themselves that their horses will do as well unfed as when properly fed. But they don't delude the horses. If anyone feeds a horse right, the horse tells the story. If not, the story is there. In all my years, I never saw a horse that told a lie. I suppose that if you go on a trip, you will have to take the horse that is offered you, but if you can make a choice and want my honest advice, it is this: Pick out a lazy horse every time. This may sound strange. But the lazy horse, or the level-headed horse as I prefer to call him, is one that will work without worry. I always selected them for my long rides, never one of those highstrung devils so much praised by horsemen as having so much fire and life. I want a horse that will walk all day unless I call on him to shake it up. I never had a horse on any of my long rides that I didn't have to make pound the road.

When you start out on a long ride there is one cardinal rule: Take it easy in the beginning. That animal under you is the most remarkable thing of flesh and bones ever put together, capable of unbelievable endurance. But it can't be abused or pushed too hard at first. My own practice in my long rides was always to take it very easy the first day. Others passed me in the beginning; I passed them in the end, when passing was something important.

There's been a good deal of bunk passed out about what the horse is really capable of doing. You've heard tales of riding 150 miles a day, 200 miles, even farther. Horses vary in their ability to endure. So do humans. Some horses can carry you 50 miles in a day, others 100. And you can't tell from looking at a horse whether he's a 50-mile animal or a 100-mile. The farthest I ever rode a horse in a day was 124 miles; had to that time. I always thought too much of a horse to ride him till he dropped of exhaustion.

It's common among horse men now to praise big horses and look down on small ones. But I've never found any specifications, linear or avoirdupois, that could tell me what a horse could do under the saddle. A horse to me is no smaller than his ability and no longer. I have seen 700- and 800-pound horses carry 180-pound men in 40-pound saddles all day, day in and day out. In the same outfits I've seen other horses, larger, weighing 1,000 pounds and over, that couldn't stand the gaff of every day use but had to be rested and used only on alternate days. There's no rule of size or appearance that will enable you to judge how good a horse you have. Only the road will do that. Sometimes the most likely looker turns out to be the most useless performer – while one of those horses that doesn't look like ten cents will win honors.

I never put a measuring-stick on a horse or put a horse on the scales. If he has the right bone and muscle and is put together right, he's what I'm looking for. My ideal horse is short in the back, well ribbed out to hips, with long muscles covering the kidneys. He has a fairly long hip, fairly straight hind legs closely linked between joints. His shoulder is deep, is fore or upper arm well muscled. His color doesn't make a bit of difference to me. But the quality of his bone does. Beware of clean, thin limbs and long slim ankle joints. Pick a horse with strong bones and close-linked joints.

Now I want to give you a few words about mounting. That is important, especially if you have to ride a strange horse. About the worst thing that can happen to a horseman is to be dragged. Even expert riders dread it. If you learn how to mount properly, and dismount properly, you can avoid most of that danger.

The way to get on a horse that is strange to you or on a horse that you know will bolt or buck every time you mount is to "cheek" him when you get on. Cheeking is easy. This is the way of it: Take hold of the left rein in your left hand and also take the cheek of the bridle in the same hand just above the bit. Put your other hand on the horn. Now pull the horse's head around toward you, at the same time springing into the saddle. He can't do anything until you get up on him, and then you don't care what he does. If he is inclined to jump around and be restive, your cheeking him around to you keeps him from getting out of control until you are seated in the leather and prevents your being dragged by a horse that bolts when you get only one foot in the stirrup and are helpless. When you dismount, use the same system: pull his head around, hold it there, and step off.

Chances are you're not going to ride many bucking horses, not if you can help it. But if you get on one that does buck you want to know what to do. Here is what: if you're entirely green and don't care about the embarrassment of jumping off, the best thing is to leave the horse as gracefully as you can. Take hold the horn with your right hand, swing your feet clear of both stirrups and slide off the left side. But with a little experience you can ride the ordinary straight bucker easily enough. The main thing to remember is to sit down in the leather and stay there. And keep your balance. I add one more rule: keep your chin pressed hard against the chest. There's a reason for that. If your chin is there you are in no danger of getting your neck snapped when your horse bucks viciously.

Give your horse a fair deal; treat him as considerately as you would treat a human assistant; see that he gets proper feed and a decent place every night to rest; do not demand impossible things of him – and he will carry you with satisfaction wherever you choose to go.

This article was first published in January 1945

Chapter 16

Only a War Horse

"Comanche," the only survivor of the Custer massacre, was a light bay lineback mustang, purchased by the army Quartermaster from a trading post in St. Louis, sent with a number of other horses to Fort Laramie, Wyoming, for use as a troop horse in the new Seventh Cavalry. This horse had been trained with a one-rein Indian chin-strap to be guided by the sway of the body and touch of the knee. He acted awkward on the parade field when put into bridle. Being under-sized for a troop horse, he was at once condemned by General Custer after which Captain Miles Keogh, a veteran of many wars and a judge of good "hoss" flesh and bad whiskey, bought "Comanche", for his cost price of ninety dollars. Following a few days of training, "Comanche" appeared on the parade field again – this time at the head of Company I, ridden by Captain Keogh. Since it was the custom in those days for cavalry officers to own their own mounts, there was not much Custer could do about it. "Comanche" soon learned the bugle calls and went through all of the drills with the best of the experienced mounts. This training was only play to "Comanche" for he had formerly been a buffalo horse and raced many hours carrying his Indian master on the buffalo runs. This play on the parade field was cut short due to the fact that the Seventh Cavalry marched away to campaign against the raiding Crow and Cheyenne Indians, Custer's rangy thoroughbred prancing and tossing his head. As the band played the old Civil War song, "Marching Through Georgia," "Comanche" merely walked briskly along at the head of his company. Soon he would be racing against horses of his own blood and feeding on wild buffalo grass.

That summer campaign was a hard one. Indians fired the plains and valleys behind them as they fled into Canada, leaving nothing for the cavalry horses to eat. Even the returning pack mules were a sorrowful sight as they came back, their packs high with empty saddles. All along the trails, many of the horses lay dead and stinking and wolves were so filled up with horse meat they lay down to eat. Sore-footed soldiers led their starved horses. Custer's spirited Kentucky thoroughbred hanging back at the end of the bridle rein as they came along the Upper Platte. "Comanche," although gaunt and hungry, still carried his master. Custer glanced sharply at "Comanche" who was some distance in the lead. It's likely he recognized him as the horse he had condemned. The General was weary from that long march and dragging his spirit-broken mount behind him did not help matters much. Three days later at Fort Laramie, this Kentucky bred horse was buried beside the Platte River.

Shortly after its return from that hard campaign the Seventh was mounted on new horses, with the exception of "Comanche." It was a cool, September morning, white frost still lingered on the grass, as the Seventh Cavalry stood at horse on the old historical parade field at Laramie. General Sheridan had left his office in Washington to command the armies in the West. There would be winter campaigns now – he ordered the Seventh transferred to Fort Lincoln. Custer, dressed in Indian buckskins instead of the regulation blue, stood beside his horse, some distance from the troops, his long yellow hair falling in ringlets about his shoulders. Behind him was the square-jawed Captain Benteen who stared at Custer, a glint of hatred in his eye. In fact none of the other officers looked any too pleased. "Custer's" commanding voice rang out "mount up" then he turned his horse facing the band and gave orders to play "Garry Owen" – which was the South's own song.

A long line of blue uniformed troops on fresh horses stretched out along the Bozeman Trail – the full cavalry of six hundred, loaded pack mules hefting and shifting their packs as they fell in line at the rear, facing a long, tiresome march to Fort Abraham Lincoln. Many of the horses pranced nervously: to "Comanche" it evidently was just one more long trail – he did not waste any energy nor seem to worry – in his veins flowed the blood of the true Arabian horse – famous war horses for thousands of years.

At Lincoln the "Seventh's" rest was short: it was sent on another long march to camp supply, Indian Territory – where the Seventh was in constant warfare.

Custer got himself into a tight spot when he shot up Chief Black Kettle's camp. This chief had always been peaceful and had papers sent him from the war office to show. Now, the "Seventh" had been on the march all day, looking for Indian camps; at sundown, the scouts returned, telling Custer they had smelled smoke from an Indian camp. The General called a halt with a few men and the Tonto scouts, they found Black Kettle's camp without any signs of a guard – even the pony herd was unguarded and the scouts drove it away.

Custer held his troops away until midnight then charged on the sleeping village, not taking the pains to find out whose camp it was. Indians fought in the bitter cold with nothing on their bodies but their gun belts, holding off the charging horsemen while the Indian woman and children made their escape. Chief Black Kettle was shot, his peace papers still grasped in his hand, whereupon his nine-year-old son grabbed his father's pistol and fired until he himself was shot to death.

In the darkness, many Indians rode out from two camps farther down the valley. The cavalry was not aware of these two camps; these Indians trapped Major Elliot and his men, killing all to the last man. The horses and men were in bad shape – the Seventh rode back to headquarters at Fort Lincoln, many of them mounted on Indian ponies from the captured herd but "Comanche" carried his bearded master.

Custer had been court-martialed just the year before and after this episode was called to Washington again. General Sheridan pleaded that Custer be restored to his command. There was more trouble in store for Custer – now he was a marked man – even his troops turned against him on account of his overbearing attitude.

The part Custer played in the Black Hills gold rush really put him on the spot. The Sioux and Cheyenne warriors were planning to kill Custer, for they considered him their enemy since their friendly peace-chief "Black Kettle" had been killed. Indian women, as they bent over their beadwork or rubbed a stubborn piece of deerskin talked in low voices – "surely there will be trouble if 'Pahuska' (long hair) leaves Lincoln to fight again." Even "White Antelope" woman whose father was always for peace, murmured – "now there will be blood in every track, horses and scalps for all." When Custer kills the "friendlies" what chance have the other bands? This woman "carried much power" amongst the Sioux. Her voice was heard in council with the chiefs. Indian scouts would be on every hilltop, watching the slightest movement of the Seventh Cavalry.

Young Rain-in-the-Face, an athlete, outstanding runner and the pride of the Sioux Nation, had been locked up by Captain Tom Custer, brother of the General; he escaped however and left this note – "If you bother my people any more, I shall one day eat your heart." This was only one of the many other things that pointed to General Custer's nearing the end of his career.

The morning of March 17, 1876, the Seventh Cavalry began its ride into history. General Grant was President; he had forbidden Custer to enter this campaign against the Sioux and had placed General Alfred Terry at the head of the Expedition. Somehow, things were patched up so Custer rode at the head of the Seventh. His usually long flowing yellow hair had been cropped close at Fort Lincoln, which gave him a somewhat different appearance. The regiment again paraded the circuit of the Fort in columns of platoons, marching away with the band playing "Garry Owen." Beside the General rode Mrs. Calhoun and the General's wife, Mrs. Elizabeth Custer. The ladies were permitted to go along so far as the first halt, then they were to return with the paymaster who thought it best to hand out the troops' pay far from the dives and bar-rooms of Lincoln. After the noon halt the ladies bid farewell to the troops and returned with the paymaster and a guard, to the Fort. That's the last Mrs. Custer saw of the General, except that three days later the people of Lincoln saw a mirage. They saw for a fleeting moment the Seventh racing across the sky. This was not unusual as mirages in that part of the country are common.

"Comanche" had survived eight years of hard campaigns and performed his duties as any good soldier would; he was still in the pink of condition and would be loyal to his master till death and hereafter.

The Seventh marched for eight days. General Terry sent Reno and his company southward on a scout. They came across a wide Indian trail, leading towards the Big Horn Mountains. Reno, being a good soldier, did not follow this trail – he obeyed his orders and returned to report his findings.

On June 21, 1876, Colonel Gibbon with the 17th Infantry and Custer with the 7th Cavalry met General Terry at the Yellowstone and Rosebud rivers. In the cabin of the supply ship "The Far West" General Terry arranged their campaign. Custer's orders were to march to the Powder River on a scouting expedition. He was told not to hurry, but to take forty-eight hours on the march – for it would take Gibbon and Terry until the 26th of June to get there. When Custer found the broad trail left by Reno, orders did not mean a thing to him – he shoved along on a forced march. His scouts turned back and told Custer there were many Sioux, far too many for him to attack. Meanwhile, the General split his troops, sending Reno off to the East while he rode up the valley. He was twenty hours ahead of the time planned for Generals Terry and Gibbon. Custer would certainly need their help. Reno rode straight into ambushed Cheyennes. However, when these Indians saw the troops were not led by Custer, they rode away, up the valley after the General, leaving only a few braves to hold Reno from helping Custer. "Crazy Horse" and his mighty warriors rubbed out Custer and left without scalping him for they considered his scalp not worth taking[121]. General Terry came up, as he had planned, on the 27th June; there he found Reno and his men huddled against a small butte. Scouts reported the bad news. On the battlefield, General Terry found "Comanche" bleeding from bullet and arrow wounds, his saddle swung under his belly – "Comanche" stood there, over his master. They removed the arrows and treated his wounds. With men leaning against his sides, they led "Comanche" to the boat, when the boat reached the landing he was loaded onto a wagon and taken to Fort Lincoln where he was in a sling for over a year until he recovered from his wounds. General orders were that "Comanche" was never to be ridden again. He was often saddled though and led in parades by a member of Company 1. Once, when he was turned out to graze, at the sound of the bugle call, "Comanche" raced to the parade field, taking his place at the head of his old Company 1; there he went through all the drills without a miss. I was stationed at Lincoln at the time and was an eye witness to that act – although "Comanche" served eight strenuous years in warfare and was badly shot up in the battle of the Big Horn, he lived until 1891.

If there was another war horse of "Comanche's" courage, handed down to us through the mists of time, I have failed to hear of it. From early childhood, I clearly remember "Comanche," also when I was a young man at Fort Lincoln.

Upon his death, they removed "Comanche's" hide, mounted and placed it in a glass case in the museum of the University at Kansas where it probably is today.

---

[121] **Editors' note:** It is indeed curious that in this article Hopkins forgot to mention that, according to *My Years in the Saddle,* his father, Charles Hopkins, was General Custer's scout and the only white survivor of the Battle of the Little Big Horn!

"Comanche" also stands in bronze on the battlefield in the Little Big Horn Valley.[122]

This article was first published in January 1946.

---

[122] **Gregory Michno**, *Author of Lakota Noon: the Indian narrative of Custer's Defeat (1997) and The Mystery of E Troop: Custer's Gray Horse Company at the Little Bighorn (1994) and Encyclopedia of Indian wars : western battles and skirmishes, 1850-1890:* "I sat down in my den with all my western books, armed with pen and paper, and was prepared to hunt up what I assumed would be many fine points that bordered on the truth. It only took a minute to see that I had no need of my books. These items are so atrociously phony that they are actually amusing. I will touch on a few points. Comanche was probably 1/4 mustang and 3/4 European breed. He was purchased in 1868, not in 1866 when the 7th Cavalry was first formed. The horse, with 40 others, was taken to Ft. Leavenworth by Tom Custer, the general's brother. From there he went to Ft. Hays in central Kansas. Maj. Joel Elliott examined them and found them all "a choice lot." George Custer never saw Comanche when the horse joined the regiment. He had been court-martialed and was in Michigan when Keogh got Comanche as a replacement horse after his was injured while on campaign with Alfred Sully in September 1868. Keogh and Comanche were never at the Battle of the Washita, for he escorted Sully out of the area when Custer returned to take over.

Hopkins's sense of geography and time are horrid. The sequences are so befuddled and anachronistic as to be nearly impossible to sort out into the real historical order. Custer never chased the Indians to Canada; he never lost his own horse to starvation and exhaustion; he and the 7th were never based out of Ft. Laramie; he never took his regiment along the Bozeman Trail (and the Bozeman goes to Montana, not to Ft. Lincoln in North Dakota). The 7th didn't go from Ft. Lincoln down to the Indian Territory; Custer never used Tonto scouts; he didn't attack Black Kettle's camp at midnight; Black Kettle had no "peace papers" in his hands. The 7th did not then march back to "headquarters" at Ft. Lincoln after its 1868 fight on the Washita--Ft. Lincoln was about 1,000 miles north, and it was not even built until 1872.

Rain in the Face left no note for Tom Custer, obviously, for he could not read or write. Custer did not start on his final campaign on March 17, 1876 (it was May); Libbie Custer was the one who saw the mirage; Reno disobeyed orders and did follow the Indian trail; Gibbon was with the 7th Infantry, not 17th; Custer was not to march to the Powder River; Terry gave him no specific orders to meet anywhere on 27th June; Custer's scouts actually told him he needed to attack on 25 June, before the Indians could escape.

There is no bronze statue of Comanche in the Little Big Horn Valley."

www.horsetravelbooks.com

Chapter 17

Understanding Horses

How well do you understand your horse? This noble animal has always been a friend to man – kind, helping him till the soil, carrying him into battle, fighting bravely, and sharing his pleasures. Unfortunately, to many the horse is only a beast of burden to be used for work or pleasure and when no longer useful, is given no thought as to what becomes of him. To me, this powerful animal is also the most beautiful of all creatures that walk the earth.

Horses, though highly intelligent, are like children in that they must be taught. Science tells us that horses and dogs cannot tell colors, nor can they remember. I recall a statement once made to me by Professor Gleason that horses cannot tell color. I begged to differ with him and he asked me for proof. We were on a ranch in Wyoming where there were at that time a large number of suckling colts; the brood mares varied in color – some were spotted. I cut out of the bunch six mares – a dark buckskin, a black, a white, a golden sorrel, a spotted mare, a dark mare with a white rump (an Appaloosa). Their colts were placed in a corral, out of sight of the mares. Then I called the Professor. Here were the mares – with their colts all marked so there could be no mistake.

There was a man to lead every mare off to a distance of nearly a quarter of a mile and the mares held about two hundred feet apart. The men made sure the mares didn't whinny to call their colts. The first colt led out belonged to the spotted mare. It ran in a straight line to its mother and every colt when let loose went straight to its dam. Not one made a mistake or varied from the straight line to its mother!

I recall one horse in particular, who after twenty-two years, remembered the stall where he had been kept as a colt, also the watering trough on the opposite side of the large barn. When this horse was turned loose, he walked past thirty-eight straight stalls to get to the one where he had been kept as a colt – and he walked around the tier of stalls to get to the water trough.

In schooling the colt, be sure you give him his first lessons correctly – for it is the first few that he will always remember; those that follow won't mean so much. You can have a gentle, easily-handled colt if the first lessons are given properly, or you can have a head-tossing, rein-pulling, nervous mount. It depends altogether how your colt has been handled at the very start. Teach him then what you want him to do and you will have no more trouble.

If you are the nervous type, you have no business training colts; neither should mean-tempered, overbearing individuals train colts; the colts will be much like their handlers.

Don't get the idea into your head that you must show the colt you are his master and teach him to fear you – he will see right through this very quickly. Speaking sharply, jabbing with the bit, are sure signs that the handler is a mean-tempered individual with no feeling for the hurt to his horse's mouth.

The secret of handling horses is to get them to really like YOU not to merely like what you feed them from your hand. In my years of training I do not recall giving a horse anything from my hand in payment for what I got him to do – nor do I believe in fondling and pampering him and if anyone can get his horse to obey more correctly or quickly I'll be glad to meet him. I know there are many horse folks ready with that old salt shaker when they hear or read anything different from the usual method they have been taught in handling horses.

In the East, most handlers use the English way of training. They seem to think a horse is not much good unless he can jump. They run the horse around in a circle with a long lead line, cracking a whip. The horses are taught to jump on this lead line. Very few horses care about jumping and it surely is not good for them. Many a fine horse is spoiled in his first season of jumping. To those who are not acquainted with other kinds of horsemanship, this appears all right. It is, however, far from pleasant for the horse and it is quite noticeable to the experienced onlooker.

I have ridden quite a bit in rough country where there was much fallen timber and have never seen a downed tree across my trail that I could not ride around and bring my horse back without his being lame. Any horse who has been jumped much will show the effects of such jumping, especially in the shoulders; after a few seasons he will go to pieces. Here on Long Island where there are fox hunts every year, the country is fenced with split rail fencing for that purpose. Many good "jumping" horses are destroyed and their riders get pretty well smashed up. Horses resent being treated thus and become unruly.

I recall one horse owned by a friend of mine, Austin Spoffard. He bought this horse in Kentucky as a finished Hunter. After two seasons of hunting, this horse would start to run away when mounted, no matter what rig was on his head or who rode him. Finally, Spoffard called me by telephone and asked me to come down, although he doubted that anything could be done for the horse. I went down to look him over and when they led the horse out of the stall I noticed his ears were laid back and the look in his eyes anything but pleasant. There was nobody about this place that the horse liked. On looking him over I asked; "How much do you want for this horse?" Spoffard said, "How much will you give? He is real bad and might hurt you." The deal was closed when I offered $100 and said I would take my chances. I took my bill of sale and led the horse away. I did not try to ride him but got into the training pen with him for just fifteen minutes every day for a week. He soon was a changed horse, no longer laid his ears back and the look in his eyes was pleasant. With a well-fitting hackamore on his head, I walked him around a large corral, turning him into the fence when he tried to bolt, at the same time calmly giving the command "stop." First to the right, then to the left, he was turned into the fence. He soon learned to obey and would not go against the rein. The rein was always slack; this was new to him as he had always been handled on a tight rein with a jaw-breaking curb. In less than a month that horse grew so quiet that it was necessary to call on him if I wanted to get him into a trot; he was really lazy. Well, I gentled the horse and lost a good friend; Spoffard was the maddest man on Long Island when he saw one of his neighbors riding that horse two months later on a fox hunt! I had made a neat-looking hackamore that looked much like a bridle and this rig went with the horse when I sold him, also the story that good horsemen do not hang onto their horse's head but ride in their saddles and not all over the horse, bobbing up and down and wearing out their mount. The man who bought this horse from me spent a few days with me before buying him and gave me what is considered a very good price for a first-class hunter. He also thought my training was well worth the price. This horse "Alex" has been used on many hunts since and came to be known as one of the best horses at that game and still wears that "bridle on a loose rein."

Don't think for a moment that I don't make some mistakes – I often do, even though they are corrected at once. Recently I made one while training a three-year-old Arabian in a training pen. He took to his training kindly and then I took him out into a larger enclosure where he ran and played. I watched him a while then walked to the far end of the corral and called "come here." At once the colt came running – he did not stop until his nose rested on my shoulder. That was all very fine. I then slipped his halter on and led him to his stall where he was used to being kept. Now here was the mistake I made: this colt was eating; I stepped into the stall, unsnapped the rope from the halter, then walked back about twenty feet from the colt and gave the command "come here." At once the colt got all excited, threw his ears forward while his eyes took on a wild, scared look as he started at me through the iron grating on top of the partition of his stall. His grain didn't mean a thing to him but my command did. He probably thought, "How can I come to you when I am tied?" Although the rope was unsnapped, he did not know it. There were some people talking nearby and I doubt if they noticed my mistake. I stepped back, got a long lead rope, fastened it to the colt's halter, took my stand in the same place and gave the command "come here," at the same time giving a slight pull on the line, then slackened it. The colt at once rushed out and put his nose on my shoulder; he was still a bit nervous but quieted when I talked to him in a low voice and returned him to his stall. A small mistake like that, if not corrected immediately, will make a horse lose confidence in you. The owner standing by, did not notice this; I hope the colt overlooked it.

I have often been asked what "gentling" a horse means. Although there are many things connected with "gentling," the first is to show your horse you are his friend in such a manner that he will have the confidence to come to you when in trouble and if he is frightened will look to you for protection instead of trying to run away. My article on "Gentling" appeared previously. Gentling in a training pen is not to put fear into your horse but take the fear out of him and teach him that you are his friend. If the colt becomes real scared, he will crowd against you and it is hard to get him to move away while he is frightened. Horses that have not been gentled will rear and bolt and try to get away – so "gentling" is really important.

Some years ago I gentled a range colt and trained him to being "ground tied" by giving him a few lessons on the stake rope. This colt had been run off the range only three weeks and still needed training under the saddle though he was doing very well. A friend came riding along while I as giving the colt a mile or so on the road, calling "You're just the man I want to look at a horse I want to buy." We rode along slowly to the Lazy D Ranch, dismounted, leaving our horses ground tied – which means the reins are thrown on the ground. As we went over to the corral, a covered wagon came along the road with two mustangs running as if they smelled a panther; the canvas curtain was flapping out behind the wagon and this frightened my horse he took off in high gear and my friend said: "There goes your colt." I got up on the fence and called: "Come here, Britt, come here." Although that colt was leaving that part of the country, he turned at once and came to me at full speed, still frightened and trembling. The "gentling I had given him was remembered and he came to me for protection. I remember this horse for many years – that was the only time he ever tried to run away; I could hardly blame him for being frightened with all that noise and the curtain flapping out over him as the wagon passed him.

There is one more horse I'd like to mention – one that I understood. I was carrying an important message during a heavy thunderstorm. When the lightning stopped, it was so dark I could not see my horse's head. Suddenly my horse stopped on the old dirt road, turned around and got into his loping stride again. A few minutes later I heard water lapping against the horse's legs and then reaching my own feet; the Grand River had overflown its banks and was rising fast. I then felt my horse going up hill where there was no water. To a man who could not see, this was something long to remember; had it not been for that horse's "sense" I would have been drowned with him. Had I tried to rein him, we would have been drifting down the trail to God-knows-where. I dismounted and stood there in the darkness soaked to the skin, waiting for daylight, muttering a prayer of thankfulness for a horse and rider safe out there in the bad lands of South Dakota.

The question has been asked, "Does the cold-blooded horse respond to training as readily as the well-bred horse?" to which I reply: "Yes, they learn things more easily than those hot-headed horses." For many years I have had to have patience with horses as well as humans; I've noticed often a man will take advantage of your good nature and put you down as a simple fool when you are merely having patience with him, whereas the horse seems to have sense enough to appreciate your friendliness towards him. I have trained many wild horses that never came in contact with a man before; these horses were the easiest to train; at first, they might come at me striking out with their front feet because they were cornered in the training pen, but when they learned there was nothing to harm them, they became friendly and obeyed my command more readily than horses of highly-bred stock. You can't expect to have a wild horse friendly if you rope him and choke him down, then have a man get into the saddle and spur him until the horse is busted or winded. That kind of horsemanship is nearly as bad as the horse-show method of training, and about as cruel.[123]

Now think about the hackamore horse; it is a big mistake to think anyone can take his horse out on the road or trail and ride him with a hackamore. The colt or old horse should be trained in the corral and taught to stop and turn at your command – not to be pulled around by the reins. The hackamore horse should obey at all times on a loose line – in fact any horse should obey on a slack rein, whether in the bridle or hackamore; if not, it's plain to see that horse was never gentled or taught anything except to be pulled around by the head. Many horses will pull on the reins and fret when under the saddle. If you take the pains to trace back to that horse's early training, you will find that the pulling habit started with a scratch of the spur or a sharp clip from the crop when the trainer got out of patience while giving the first lessons. If your horse has some sort of

---

[123] **Editors' note**: Hopkins' writings reveal a Jekyll and Hyde relationship with horses. In an article such as this one, he is advocating being gentle and kind. At other times, he boasts about riding a horse to death! Compare the "compassionate Hopkins" above with "bronco-busting Hopkins" from *My Years in the Saddle*, set in June 1909.

Hopkins wrote, *"Cody said, "Buff, it's your turn to ride Hightower tonight". I was surprised and thanked him for the favor. His guests seemed surprised when I asked him, "You don't think he will hurt me, do you, Colonel? He smiled, but I noticed he turned his head and winked when he spoke to his friends, saying, "You will see something in that ring tonight – its a good show when two bad actors meet." The horse was turned into the ring; I roped and throwed him, then I saddled the man-killer, put my boots into the stirrups and let him get to his feet. That horse sure was surprised, for I had that seat as if I was glued into it. It may have been only luck, but I had that seat and there I stayed. Hightower done everything that a true outlaw could do, still I stayed there.*

It made him so mad he broke a blood vessel in his head and was bleeding to death. Cody rode alongside and told me to slide off. I thought the hoss was only sulking and would soon take off the brakes, maybe when I made a move to slide off, then turn and strike me. I was blind from the shaking I got. Then one of the riders picked me off the saddle. At the hospital, I was told that the horse died before they could get him out of the ring."

Like many of Hopkins' fantasies, this one actually has a different outcome. The editors have located a photograph, taken in 1910, which shows a very healthy Hightower bucking his heart out in a Wild West show – the year after Hopkins supposedly rode the famous horse to death!

fear when you are on his back, it will always remain with him through life unless corrected – and very few horsemen know how to correct bad habits in the horse. Many try with the spur and jerking on the bit which makes matters worse. Horsemen, you can not correct a fault in your horse while riding or driving him – the only place to correct these bad habits is in the gentling pen (which should be 18 feet square and high enough so your horse can't put his head over the fence). Treat him kindly, make him mind you; above all, don't give him anything to eat from your hand as a reward for minding you.

If our readers think this kind of horsemanship is just "talk," call round some day and watch old man Hopkins in the training pen!

This article first appeared in July 1946.

Chapter 18

Trail Horses

One hundred miles of trail in the beautiful green hills of Vermont are still marked with hoof-prints made by the horses who covered the recent Annual Trail Ride of the Green Mountain Horse Association; wind and rain may soon blot out those hoof-prints but the trails will be there for another year and the winter storms cannot erase the memory of the horses and riders who took part in it.

Many of them have been over the trails on former rides, some were newcomers who had never been on a long ride before, all of them, including the children, seemed to enjoy this experience. Some riders wondered if their mounts were bred right for trail horses – there is no such thing; it is the condition of the horse that counts for trail or endurance, and the trail or road is the place to give the horse the work. A few miles every day for two months, before the ride, will put your horse in condition. It is bad to let the horse graze on grass for this will soften up his muscles. I have been on a few endurance rides and noticed there is not any special breed of horse for the trail; some horses are a little tougher than others because they have had more training; a good horse can be classed as "good" whether he has a pedigree or not. Some half-breeds, as they are called, do good work, they do not appear to tire or go bad in the legs. I saw one of them two years ago who had won four outlaw races, one after another, during a period of two months. The owner told me the sire of this particular horse was Standard-bred and the dam just "horse." I said it was the horse blood in his mount that counted on those hard rides. A few days later, I saw the mother of this horse; she bore the Pitchfork brand on her left shoulder. This indicated to me that she came from the Crow Indian Agency in Montana. Now, if we had a little more of that "horse" blood in our mounts today, they would have better bone and endurance. Showing how good a horse is – on paper – does not make him good on his feet or on the trail.

There is a horse used for cattle work in the far West and Southwest known as the Quarter-horse. This is not a new breed – I remember them many years ago, but here in the East, most horsemen think these horses are bred for racing with a burst of speed for a quarter of a mile or so and therefore these horses are often entered in races. As a matter of fact, they are bred mainly for handling cattle; they have powerful hind quarters which enables them to throw their weight on their hind legs when coming to a square stop. They are also very cool headed and well-mannered; most of them have the best of bones and do not require a great deal of care for they are a horse of all out doors and not the hot-house type;

you will find them all "horse" and that horse-blood in your mount is what counts in the end – it is what is needed in trail horses.

Although there were horses of many breeds in this year's Ride I noticed no Arabians. They were a fine looking lot, most of them in good condition and not tired at the finish of the Ride. The cool weather, without rain, was in their favor. The judges must have had a hard time judging that lot of horses since so many of them looked good at the finish. The little seven-year-old girl on her spirited blue roan surely made a picture on the trails. Undoubtedly that Ride will always be bright in her memory no matter how many rides she takes part in through the years to come. We should encourage these children for they are to carry on in the future. Most of our great horsemen throughout the country started handling horses as small children, some on ranches, others on farms and still others on the bridle paths of our cities. They usually grow up to be good citizens as their time is taken up with a favorite horse and they are not influenced by bad company.

There will be other rides over those beautiful green hills and trails of Vermont and it's likely everyone who attends will enjoy being there; to me this year's Ride was a little more interesting than the year before. I was out on the trails every day as well as up at 4:30 every morning milling around among the riders in the stable; everybody seemed to have a good time at the campfire supper out at "Fergie's" Farm singing around the burning logs and as the evening grew old many wandered away into the darkness bidding us good-byes and hoping to meet again.

There is something about a horse that appeals to most folks even if they have never handled one; they have amusing reasons sometimes for buying one. Right here I am reminded of the old hoss-trader trying to get rid of a horse with a bad trick. The trader, catching a certain look in your eye, thinks you like that particular horse. He might say, "Now, I don't know if I can let you have this horse – my wife thinks a lot of this mare – I had better talk to her first – you know how it is, I want to keep peace in the family." As a matter of fact, the trader's wife is perhaps nowhere near the neighborhood at that time, has probably never seen this horse and doesn't care a hoot about the transaction anyway. Finally, after a lot of talk, the deal is closed, the trader gets his money and is rid of the horse and the buyer gets a runaway or balky horse on his hands – all because the trader's wife loved that hoss.

I've loved horses as long as I can remember, but I do not fondle them or let them get too friendly with me; I do see to it that they get whatever is coming to them in the way of good care and kind treatment and I always get their utmost confidence in return. As a child, my mother encouraged me in caring for motherless colts that I brought in off the range. Every spring I had many to care for – some were chilled to the point of stiffness. Mother let me bring them right in to the kitchen beside the old big cook stove and helped me rub them till they were able to get on their feet. Many times I stayed up all night caring for them –

seldom one died. I'd rob the milk from cows that had calves to feed these colts, and I'd milk gentle mares with colts by their sides. I got bowled over often by the old mares – some of them would chase me out of the feed corral. I did not always escape without a few blood blisters where they nipped me in the seat of my pants as I crawled through the rails of the corral. One new milk cow would give milk enough to feed four new-born colts; but they soon needed more milk than the cow gave so I had to figure close. Those baby horses learned to eat ground grain when a month old – that helped some, although the younger ones needed milk. I was so busy there was no time to get into idle mischief. I do believe that any boy who grows up with horses is bound to make a good horse-man – a horse is good company. A horse will not get you into trouble unless you teach him to jump – then he may jump into your neighbor's vegetable garden and leave you to foot the bill. It's all your own fault – don't teach your horse any foolish tricks!

This article was first published in October 1946

Bibliography

Abernathy, Alta: *Bud and Me – the True Adventures of the Abernathy Boys*, Texas: Dove Creek Press, 1998

Al-Khalbi, Hisam Ibn: *Les Livres des Chevaux,* 1928 French translation of the mediaeval Arabic manuscript: E.J. Brill, Leyde.

Amaral, Anthony A.: *Hidalgo and Frank Hopkins*, "Horse Lovers," July 1963, pp. 28-29

Amaral, Anthony A.: *Frank Hopkins – Best of Endurance Riders?* "Western Horseman," December 1969, pp. 110-111 and 191-194

Amaral, Anthony A.: *Quest for Arabian Horses became a Desert Odyssey*, "Smithsonian," September 1975, pp. 42-49

Amaral, Anthony A.: *Mustang – Life and Legends of Nevada's Wild Horses*, Reno: University of Nevada Press, 1977

Black Elk and Neihardt, John: *Black Elk Speaks, Being the Life Story of a Holy Man of the Ogalala Sioux*, New York: W. Morrow & Company, 1932

Blackstone, Sarah J.: *Buckskins, Bullets and Business – a History of Buffalo Bill's Wild West*, West Port: Greenwood Press, 1986

Buckingham, Roy: *Off Go the Halos from Western Bad Men*, "The New York American," circa 1920s, pp. 1-5

Burke, John M.: *Buffalo Bill from Prairie to Palace*, Chicago: Rand McNally & Company, 1893

Burke, John M.: *Buffalo Bill Bids you Goodbye*, "Wild West Show Program," 1910.

Collins, Dabney Otis: *Great Western Rides*, Denver: Sage Books, 1961

Cornillon, Florence, *Le Cheval et l'Islam,* Toulouse: Ecole National Veterinaire de Toulouse, 1993.

Davenport, Homer: *My Quest of the Arab Horse*, New York, B.W. Dodge & Company, 1909

Deadwood Pioneer Times: *Characters Famous in the Days of the Pioneers*, "The Deadwood Pioneer Times," July 8th, 1929, pp. 8-9

Dickey, E.M.: *The Spanish Horse or Mustang of the West*, "The Vermont Horse & Bridle Trail Bulletin," October, 1941, pp. 145-148, 157

Dickey, E.M.: *Stamina of the Horse, Past and Present,* "The Vermont Horse & Bridle Trail Bulletin," January 1948, pp. 11-14

Dobie, J. Frank: *The Mustangs*, New Jersey: Curtis Publishing Company, 1952

Dodge, Theodore A.: *Long Distance Riding*, Boston: Henry S. Dunn, 1898

Easton, Robert Olney: *Lord of Beasts – the Saga of Buffalo Jones*, Tucson: University of Arizona Press, 1961

Erskine, Gladys Shaw: *Broncho Charlie – a Saga of the Saddle*, New York: Thomas Crowell Company, 1934

Fee, Art: *I Rode Steamboat – King of the Bucking Broncs*, "Westerner," February, 1971, pp. 48 and 49

Gleason, Oscar R.: *Gleason's Treatise on the Taming of Wild and Vicious Horses*, Baltimore: J. Cox & Sons, 1889.

Grey Owl: *The Men of the Last Frontier*, New York: Scribner, 1932

Grey, Zane: *Roping Lions in the Grand Canyon*, New York: Grosset & Dunlap, 1924

Hammer-Purgstall, Joseph: *Das Pferd bei den Arabern*, Vienna: Kaiserlich-Königlichen Hof- und Staatsdruckerei, 1854

Harris, Albert W.: *The Blood of the Arab – the World's Greatest War Horse*, Chicago: Arabian Horse Club of America, 1941

Haynes, Glynn W.: *The American Paint Horse*, Oklahoma: University of Oklahoma Press, 1976

Horning, Nonie F.: *The Great Horse Race*, "Western Horseman," November 1968, pp. 52-56

Howard, Robert West: *The Horse in America*, Chicago: Follett Publishing, 1965

Hunt, Frazier: *Horses and Heroes – the story of the horse in America for 450 years*, New York: Scribner & Sons, 1949

Hyland, Ann: *The Endurance Horse – a World Survey of Endurance Riding from Ancient Civilization to Modern Competition*, London: J.A. Allen, 1988

Kimble, Fred: *My Shooting Days – Part 1*, "American Rifleman," November 1936, pp. 11-13.

Kimble, Fred: *My Shooting Days – Part 2*, "American Rifleman," December 1936, pp. 14-16.

Kimble, Fred: *Master Duck Shot of the World*, Chicago: W.C. Hazleton, 1923

Long Lance, Chief Buffalo Child: *Long Lance – the Autobiography of a Blackfoot Indian Chief*, London: Faber and Faber, 1928

Mahoney, Lois Elaine: *California's Forgotten Triumvirate – James Ben Ali Haggin, Lloyd Tevis and George Hurst*, San Francisco: San Francisco State University, 1977

Meyer, Frank H.: *The Buffalo Harvest*, Denver: Sage Books, 1958

Meyer, Frank H.: *The Rifles of Buffalo Days – Part 1*, "American Rifleman," September 1934, pp. 5-9

Meyer, Frank H.: *The Rifles of Buffalo Days – Part 2*, "American Rifleman," October 1934, pp. 12-14 and 26-27

Montana News Association: *Colonel Stanley, Last of the Indian Scouts; Life Spent En Route from Here to There*, "Montana News Association," June 9[th]1929.

Moses, L. G.: *Wild West Shows and the Images of American Indians*, Albuquerque: University of New Mexico Press, 1996

New York Times: *Buffalo Bill at the Polo Grounds*, "New York Times," June 17th 1884, page 2

New York Times: *One of Barnum's Arabs Shot*, "New York Times," August 2nd 1886, page 1

New York Times: *Things at Hand*, "New York Times," November 14th 1887, page 2

New York Times: *Barnum's New Wonders*, "New York Times," December 31st 1887, page 1

New York Times: *Barnum's Latest Additions – A Squad of Genuine Bedouins who will perform at the Circus*, "New York Times," March 29th 1888, page 8

New York Times: *Hippodrome and Bedouins*, "New York Times," April 3rd 1888, page 7

New York Times: *A Real Buffalo Hunt – Buffalo Bill's Herd Stampede on Staten Island*, "New York Times," August 13th 1888, page 8

New York Times: *Arabs for the World's Fair*, "New York Times," March 28th 1892, page 8

New York Times: *World's Riders with Buffalo Bill*, "New York Times," May 2nd 1894, page 8

New York Times: *"Buffalo Bill's" Great Wild West Show and Congress of Rough Riders*, "New York Times," May 13th 1894, p. 2

New York Times: *The Laramie Kid's Career*, "New York Times," July 8th 1894.

New York Times: *Wild West Show Opening*, "New York Times," March 26th 1899, page 16

New York Times: *Indians See the Fish – "Heap Great Sight" exclaims Old Iron Tail*, "New York Times," April 29th 1900, page 7

New York Times: *A Buffalo Bill Indian Dead*, "New York Times," June 29th 1900, page 3

New York Times: *Wild West Train Wrecked*, "New York Times," July 30th 1900, page 1

New York Times: *Buffalo Bill's Wild West Show*, "New York Times," April 3rd 1901, page 9

New York Times: *How the Wild West Show has Developed*, "New York Times," April 7th 1901, page 26

New York Times: *Buffalo Bill Show Sails*, "New York Times," December 4th 1902, page 16

New York Times: *Nathan Salsbury's Funeral*, "New York Times," December 29th 1902, page 7

New York Times: *The Red-Indian Hunt in Rome*, "New York Times," December 6th 1903, page 16

New York Times: *Bucking Bronchos on Ship – Cowboys have trouble with a herd consigned to Buffalo Bill*, "New York Times," March 19th 1904, page 5

New York Times: *Million Join in Welcome to Roosevelt*, "New York Times," June 19th 1910

New York Times: *Colonel King Stanley, Indian Fighter, Dies*, "New York Times," June 1929

Peck, Leigh: *They were made of Rawhide*, Boston: Houghton Miffin, 1954

Peterson, Nancy M.: *Buffalo Bill's Lost Legacy*, "American History" October 2003, pp. 50-56

Philadelphia Public Ledger: *Call of the Wild Subway Lures Hero of Novels Here*, "Philadelphia Public Ledger," March 28, 1926, pp 1 and 4.

Remiger, Leo; *Encyclopedia of Buffalo Hunters & Skinners, Volume I*, Union City, Dixie Gun Works, 2003

Roth, Charles B.: *Brains Plus Endurance*, "The Horse," March-April, 1935, pp. 18-20

Roth, Charles B.: *Great Riders*, "The Horse," March-April, 1936, pp. 16-17

Roth, Charles B.: *The Toughest Race*, "Horse and Horseman," January 1937, pp. 31-33

Roth, Charles B.: *The Mustang and the West*, "The Brand Book," May 1945, pp. 1-9

Roth, Charles B.: *The Biggest Blow since Galveston*, "The Denver Westerners Monthly Roundup," January 1956, pp. 5-15.

Ruffo, Armand Garnet: *Grey Owl – The Mystery of Archie Belaney*, Regina: Coteau Books, 2003.

Russell, Don: *The Lives and Legends of Buffalo Bill*, Norman: University of Oklahoma Press, 1960

Russell, Don: *The Wild West – A History of the Wild West Shows*, Fort Worth: Amon Carter Museum of Western Art, 1970

Rzewuski, Count Waclav Seweryn: *Impressions d'Orient et d'Arabie,* French translation of the 1830 Polish text, Muséum National de'Histoire Naturelle, Paris, 2002.

Saxon, Arthur H.: *Enter Foot and Horse – a History of Hippodrama in England and France*, New Haven: Yale University Press, 1968

Schaefer, Jack: *The Great Endurance Horse Race – 600 miles on a single mount, 1908, from Evanston. Wyoming, to Denver*, Santa Fe: Stage Coach Press, 1963

Shoebotham, H. M.: *Forts and Trails of Old Montana*, "The Billings Gazette," circa 1960s, pp. 1-5

Simmon, Scott: *The Invention of the Western Film – A Cultural History of the Genre's First Half-Century*, Cambridge: University of Cambridge, 2003

Smith, Bradley: *The Horse in the West*, New York: World Publishing Company, 1969

Smith, Donald B.: *From the Land of Shadows – the Making of Grey Owl,* Saskatchewan: Western Producer Prairie Book, 1990

Smith, Donald B.: *Chief Buffalo Child Long Lance – the Glorious Imposter*, Alberta: Red Deer Press, 1999

Spring, Agnes Wright: *Buffalo Bill and His Horses*, Denver: Spring Printers, 1953

Thorp, N. Howard: *Pardner of the Wind – the story of the South-Western Cowboy*, Caldwell: Caxton Printers, 1945

Thorp, Raymond W.: *Spirit Gun of the West – the Story of Doc W.F. Carver*, Glendale: Arthur Clark Company, 1957

Vernam, Glenn R.: *Man on Horseback – the Story of the Mounted Man from the Scythians to the American Cowboy*, New York: Harper & Row, 1964

Wade, Carlson: *Great Hoaxes and Famous Imposters*, New York: Jonathan David Publishers, 1976

Winstone, H.V.F.: *Lady Anne Blunt*, London: Barzan Publishing, 2003

Worcester, Donald E.: *The Spanish Mustang – from the Plains of Andalusia to the Prairies of Texas*, El Paso: Texas Western Press, 1986

Young, John Richard: *The Schooling of the Horse*, Norman: University of Oklahoma Press, 1982

Index

The Long Riders' Guild Press

(www.horsetravelbooks.com)

The mission of The Long Riders' Guild Press is to preserve and publish knowledge about equestrian travel.

Hidalgo by Frank T. Hopkins is an exception in that it is a book about one man's equestrian travel fantasies. Because Hopkins' tales have gone unchallenged for nearly one hundred years, they have created an untold amount of mischief. That is why, in order to set the record straight, The Long Riders' Guild Press decided to publish all the known writings of Frank T. Hopkins.

The books we normally publish reflect what we ourselves passionately believe in – fewer physical possessions, individual freedom, the ancient bond between human and equine, and the mutual search with our horses for personal growth and boundless geographic horizons.

Having ridden in various countries and on four continents, publishers Basha and CuChullaine O'Reilly can attest to the fact that before the formation of The Long Riders' Guild and **horsetravelbooks.com** there was a global-wide lack of knowledge regarding equestrian travel. For 6,000 years brave men and women have been climbing onto horses and setting off in search of adventure and freedom.

Yet despite being mankind's oldest link with the horse, this timeless equestrian legacy, and its attendant books full of accumulated knowledge, had nearly disappeared, not just from the marketplace, but from all human memory. So **horsetravelbooks.com** was created to put all the great equestrian travel tales into print, in their original languages, for the first time in human history.

Frank T. Hopkins has thus earned the dubious honor of being the only equestrian travel imposter published by The Long Riders' Guild Press.

Our list of titles is constantly changing, so please check our website, **www.horsetravelbooks.com**, for the latest information regarding authentic equestrian explorers. To learn more about equestrian travel, please visit The Long Riders' Guild website, **www.thelongridersguild.com**.

DATE DUE

JAN 0 5 2005			
ILL 3/25/06			
ILL 9-19-06			
GAYLORD			PRINTED IN U.S.A.